CW01629333

The Crooked Medium's Guide to Murder

Stephen Cox

Copyright © Stephen Cox 2025

All rights reserved. The moral right of Stephen Cox to be identified as the author of this work has been asserted in accordance with the Copyright, Designs and Patents Act 1988. Full legals at back of book.

Cover by Matt Bright, Inkspiral Design

ISBN: 978-1-0681644-0-8

This book is dedicated to the bookish friends I met on the way. Other booky people are largely colleagues, not rivals.

And of course, to my nearest and dearest who put up with me.

Advance Praise

Seances! Murders! Fraud!

The Crooked Medium's Guide to Murder has it all. This is true historical fiction, where the Victorian setting is more than just set-dressing; it permeates the very fabric of the story and the wry, understated character voice. With the perfect mix of meticulous research, emotional depth and a rollicking good story besides, Stephen Cox delivers surprises to the very end. If you, like me, love a crook with a heart of gold, then these queer old birds are sure to capture your heart.

A genuine pleasure from start to finish

Eris Young, fiction editor Shoreline of Infinity

I loved this book! Victorian murder mystery meets "ghost" story, with delicious sprinklings of compassion and mischief...

Caroline Day, Sunday Times bestselling author of Hope Nicely's Lessons for Life

Chapter 1
The Mysterious Coachman

The church hall of St Martin the Ragged, Scamperdour Street, Thameswake, London

A Sunday afternoon in March, 188-

> *We would be failing in our duty to our readers if we did not report that the notorious spirit-monger Mrs Ashton has returned to London. Whether in a slum church in the docks, or in the parlours of the prosperous, this sham is up to her old games. We do not deny that some who profess Spiritualism are wholly sincere, nor could we ever criticise those who seek solace for their deepest grief. What we can say is that Honoria Ashton carries with her a malodorous history – of midnight flits and unpaid bills, of greasepaint and mummery, of disappointment and dishonesty. Does this music-hall trickster truly raise the dead? We*

say only that if you invite her to dinner, count your spoons.

The Orb

A church hall of dark wood and brass, gaslight struggling to cheer it. Mrs Ashton jabbed the smoking coals of the stove with the poker, coughing, trying to goad it to warmth. Soon her poor flock would come to hear the voices of the dead and as their shepherd, she ought to prepare.

Damn that editor – that jackal, Philistine, scourge. Damn the trouble he would make for her. Damn his innuendo and lies. When had she last stolen a spoon?

Oh, the mayor of Calais's silver ladle. That didn't count, that was retribution not theft.

Twenty-five minutes to the hour, a drab London sky through high windows.

'Tha bacon's shoddy stuff,' Mrs Bradshaw said. A foot taller than her hinny, and scowling, Braddie set the table with plates of sandwiches under rough cloth, simple fare for the people of the docks. 'If you don't pay a man, don't expect his best.'

Rain drummed on the roof and Braddie's foul mood filled the room like a storm off a northern hill.

They had quarrelled at breakfast, when Braddie had hunted and found the hidden bills: a delightful new Japanese table, and a tasteful landscape Mrs Ashton had picked up for a song. Braddie spun a nightmare prophesy of bailiffs and moneylenders and Queer Street. The Scottish creditors finding her. Mrs Ashton believed that if you ignored the accounts, they lost their power over you. Something usually turned up.

She was six months returned to London and still her weekday respectable meeting – her income – struggled to grow. These Sunday meetings were for common folk. Men and women, dockers and sailors and workers in factories and laundries, some without honest work at all – she gave them hope. So many struggled even to cling to their own rung of the Great Ladder of Society.

Braddie winced; her back must be bad. Two vast teapots waited for the kettle.

Oh, dear one. Dear Braddie, stern disapproval the natural set of her well-worn face. Once, Braddie had taken her walking in her birthlands – the North Country– and Mrs Ashton had seen on that bleak moor a lone crag of grey rock, standing fiercely alone. Just like Braddie, true, solid, and uncompromising. She even dressed like a moor side, in dour greens and browns and greys.

Braddie was her right hand, the floor beneath her feet, the glowing stove in her home, the only one to whom all her secrets were open. Eight years her 'dear heart'.

Mrs Ashton walked over, looked to check they were alone, and craned up to kiss her – as a lonely lass greets her returning sailor, or the sailor the lass.

A flicker of a shy, warm smile and 'Well, Honeybee,' Braddie said. 'Tha tea won't mash itsel'.'

Mrs Ashton checked herself in a hand mirror. Dressing well was part of the magic. She flouted convention here by wearing no hat, no gloves. Artifice hid the march of time, the grey hairs and wrinkles. Her dress was the latest style. She did not mourn the passing of the crinoline, although the tight front and the extravagant skirting and bustle behind was almost as impractical.

A thump at the door. Mrs Ashton called, 'Come, come, all are welcome.'

Anyone might come to hear Mrs Ashton bring the voices of the dead. The grieving, the curious, the spectacle-seekers. Mockers, roughs, a swell slumming it or a journalist. Some objected to her message, some that a woman dared to preach anything. But Mrs Ashton had lived on her wits for a long time and, in any case, men of sturdy build and fierce expression drank nearby, at her expense and alert to her metal whistle. Braddie had strong arms, a mighty stick with a metal core, and the courage to use them.

A tall stranger in a dripping cap and cloak entered. The fastenings gleamed with silver, an embroidery she could not make out. A coachman, perhaps, from a wealthy house or an extravagant one. Servants of the wealthy were always warmly welcome at her gatherings for what they knew: the words they could drop and the doors they could open.

'Welcome, friend,' she said, and he touched his cap.

'Mrs Ashton? I have a message from her ladyship, ma'am, and I am to wait for your answer.' A country burr, and silver whiskers.

How exciting.

'Do sit by the stove, take tea. We would not want you to catch cold.'

'No, thank you, ma'am.'

To her annoyance, the man took a letter from under his cloak with one hand, stepped forward to give it to her, then stepped back – almost military in his precision. Now to lay a hand on his would be obvious and awkward.

Expensive paper, sealed, a faint delicious scent. Mrs Ashton took a little knife from her bag and slit it open. The same crest as the servant's livery.

> *Lady Barrington-Stewart presents her compliments to Mrs Ashton and asks her the favour of an appointment, hoping that Monday or Tuesday afternoon would be convenient as to time, and that Mrs Ashton's own residence would be acceptable as to place. Their mutual acquaintance, Lady Westfall speaks most highly of Mrs Ashton's gift. Willoughby, who bears this message, can bring your reply swiftly and can be relied on. Absolute discretion is required.*

Mrs Ashton spent a little too long reading it, hoping for more. She knew a person of quality would shudder to visit her modest rooms in a fading street. Clearly, the lady wanted to meet her unknown to a third party. Husband, father, mother, priest?

Lady Westfall? A patron lost through her own folly. Yet wonderful that the peeress still spoke highly of her powers. Barrington-Stewart rang faint bells. Wealth for certain – brewing and railways. Certainly, she knew a Liberal MP held that name, and a fine speech had been in the papers, urging peace and prosperity for Ireland. Braddie had scorned it. 'Telling the Irish to be good oxen and love their yoke.'

Mrs Ashton produced a diary, consulted it, and said Tuesday afternoon would suit her. She wanted to strike quickly, but how fatal to leave no time for research.

'My memory, I cannot quite recall. Some sad business or other?' How vague the nets she threw over the side, hoping for a fish. No one consulted Mrs Ashton when full of the joys of life.

Willoughby sighed. 'Oh, her ladyship's mother, God bless her. Her ladyship's a never been the same since she was taken.'

When, man, when? 'And I read about her husband...in *The Times* I think...?'

'I a-drive her ladyship anywhere she wants to go,' the coachman said.

Mrs Ashton gestured. 'Braddie, bring me my writing set. I must give Lady Barrington-Stewart the courtesy of a note.'

She needed to keep the coachman – ideally to come close, ideally to touch him and use her gift. Always a risk. The harder she had to work, the more likely the touched would feel something beyond the normal – a chill shiver, or an unbidden thought. Her enthusiastic note said little but elegantly.

The coachman came close, and she touched his hand. *Opened him*.

Some people she could open easily, and some required tiring exertion. Some minds were orderly and well lit; others hid their secrets in dark cellars and locked chests. Always, thoughts at the top of their minds came easiest.

Oh, a torrent of scorn about her. This shameless woman of twisted promises – the master's ferocity about table-tappers and spirit trumpets was more than justified.

This crooked music-hall show, robbing the grieving. It wasn't English, not Christian, not right on church property.

Mrs Ashton's probing had stirred him up. What if the master asked where the mistress had been? Stern but fair, a husband had every right.

But... her ladyship so blonde and pretty and so stricken with grief... reminded him of his wife Dolly as a girl. Willoughby had the uncomplicated loyalty of a family dog. He wanted to please both master and mistress.

The mistress's mother had died, and that death hung over the house like mourning cloth these two years. Something deeper too...

Too long connected, Mrs Ashton's migraine stabbed, and she stopped. The man somehow took his cue, nodded, put on his hat, and turned to go. She closed her eyes and massaged her temples. The cost of her gift, and just before her meeting...

The door shut, too firmly. They were alone.

'A bad one, hinny?' Braddie knew, held her hand in concern, and Mrs Ashton squeezed reassurance.

A wealthy and grieving lady and a hostile husband. What a gift this dreary day

No time to brief Braddie. Here were the children. Maisie – dark, smart, and determined was almost fourteen, approaching womanhood, and by necessity a stand-in mother to little George and Tildy. Tildy was always spooked by Braddie and her staring blind eye. The three were children of Empire, their dead mother half Irish, half Indian.

Mrs Ashton crooned, 'Dearest children, a long time since luncheon. Why not help yourselves?' They might not have eaten today, their cupboard emptied by the public house and the bookie, but even poor children have pride.

Smart and resourceful, Maisie was such a find. All sorts of curious work at which she excelled – watching and fetching and being a hidden witness. A lass who would not turn a hair if asked to steal a notebook to be read and then put it back unnoticed.

Maisie said, 'Show Mrs Ashton yer washed yer hands,' but Mrs Ashton had already spotted the wet sleeves. Clothes told you so much.

Mrs Ashton closed her eyes and prayed aloud and for as long as hungry stomachs might tolerate – a prayer to He that loved children and the poor, who fed the hungry.

The children muttered. Mrs Ashton opened her eyes and smiled, the sign for the children to fall on the food like the Assyrians, a wolf on the fold. Braddie, grumbling, cut the sturdy cake and ruffled the children's hair, said they were such trouble.

Aunthood was the lending library of motherhood; you could give the darlings back when they became tedious.

Mrs Ashton was ready. A little fortifying brandy in her tea, a lozenge to freshen her breath. She ate little beforehand, the same nerves in the stomach as the actress or tightrope walker.

Her people came.

A disappointing turnout, doubtless the rain, and not a single newcomer.

Mrs Ashton opened with the Lord's Prayer, then sat at the weather-beaten piano and led them in a well-known hymn. She played adequately, and the congregation... well, they sang.

Time for the main business. No dim rooms and conjuring tricks with cloth and smoke – as she often said, God's work must be done in the light.

Mrs Ashton stood and raised her hands.

'Dearest friends... for Jesus calls us to be His friends... hear the good news. All His promises are true.' She knew the power of the pause, where to put the weight in a sentence.

'Death is a brief journey to a blessed forever. Where we see clearly in the Lord's light and understand. Islands of summer with gentle winds and sunlight dancing on the waves... tables groaning with plenty... endless snowy hills with sledges and hot chocolate...' The children there loved sledging.

'Best of all, we meet those who have gone before, kinder and wiser. In the land of love, they have become its disciples. There, work does not weary us, and we can have rest. All can be forgiven and understood. There is no sadness there, except knowing the sadness of those still to come, who hurt and grieve and who have lost trust in promises given. Brave souls will make the hard journey back with the good news... They come across the river of mist to the land of the living.'

They wanted to hear the dead, and she summoned them in her own fashion. People told her what she needed to know or she wheedled it from them, putting out words as bait and seeing what they bit on. The gold was her gift – opening them to find their sorrows and desires. That and her voice, worthy of the finest stage, which could feign man or woman, child or adult, north or south, the drawing room or the roughest gaff with ease.

She brought her spirit guide – a Cavalier gallantly slain for his king – brave and witty, and one of her best creations. She thought herself in spirit a Cavalier, and Braddie surely demonstrated that curious creation of the age, a Godless Roundhead.

A few of her regulars were almost cheery. She told them they were loved and heard and wanted. She walked on the dark path with them. Where they had erred, she preached that a generous mending of the wrongs and a humble reconciliation with the wronged would free them from the guilt.

The work often wearied her, but she remembered the people helped by it.

Two portraits gazed down, the icons of the age. A cheap reproduction of the Queen-Empress in her perpetual mourning, and a blue-eyed milk-skinned Jesus carrying a sheep. Surely a Jesus that pale would have burned bright red under that blazing sun.

The last of her flock left. Soon the time would come when the couple would be in their rooms, and the door locked to the unkind world. Eyes closed, Mrs Ashton stroked her friend's great, worn hands, and memory conjured the scent of Braddie at bedtime. That hand oil fashioned by Braddie from herbs with country names – bishop's frock and lover's meeting and white crow-flower. This anointment renewed sacred vows.

Mrs Ashton loved this task, long and slow, the smooth skin of the mistress against the rough hands of toil. The slow, subtle, rhythm of the hands and the warmth of the oil worked their union. She would free Braddie's long hair from its severe knot, hair grown weary and frail now. Each night the ritual, then there would be bed and the inevitable quarrels of the day put aside. Hands smooth with oil served in other uses.

Mrs Ashton had used men, enjoyed them, even loved them, but Braddie disdained them. In bed the lovers chose who was the servant and who the mistress, who the leader and who the led, who the bold soldier and who his coy lass. Either might be, or both might, or neither. Either might use a few words to spin the story they would play, or hands and mouth alone would guide the other.

At Mrs Ashton's neck shone her jewel without price, a brooch of a golden bee – Braddie's gift of eight years past. In return, Braddie wore Mrs Ashton's mother's ring on a chain round her neck.

Mrs Ashton gave a fervent prayer. *Let young Lady Violet Barrington-Stewart bring us easier times. Lord, feed your sheep.*

Chapter 2

Preparing for an Esteemed Client

Mrs Ashton and Mrs Bradshaw's rooms in Middleton Street, Monday

Research your client. Mrs Ashton's unpredictable gift worked best when she knew the questions to ask. On Sunday night, the couple read the standard reference works and the last month's papers. Mrs Ashton had dispatched messages to her contacts, little birds who flew among the wealthy, picking at their leavings. Lady Westfall wouldn't respond, so she wracked her brains for mutual acquaintances. Eager Maisie had been briefed to harvest intelligence about the Barrington-Stewarts, foreman of a little gang of spies. The cunning urchin demanded payment in advance.

That morning, Braddie waved bills before Mrs Ashton had finished her coffee. 'Bailiffs! We should take tha table back, hinny.'

Not this again? 'Oh, what a fine piece it is, completely à la mode. Unlike this *hired* furniture' – her hands spat her distaste – 'it speaks of taste and distinction. With a lady visiting...'

Braddie snorted. 'You were gulled. It's no more Japanese than my mother's goat.'

'Well, dearest, let's take it back, strip the walls. Dress in an *onion sack* and serve Lady Barrington-Stewart tea from a *pickle barrel*. Seat her on a *pauper's coffin*.'

Braddie growled. 'I'm tired of flitting, and borrowing, and thieving, and never knowing if it's the police at the door, or worse.' This could be a long storm – Mrs Ashton enjoyed a good argument - but they had work to do.

'Dearest, our fortunes may be made this week. May we leave the table for now?'

Mrs Ashton's first port of call was the marvellous Grand Philosophical Society and its most admirable library, adorned with a handsome and efficient cadet-librarian. The secretary offered her lunch; he was a friend, a believer, and usually a mine of information.

Later she would take tea twice, with two cynical men with a nose for what lay behind political and social news. Braddie meanwhile sought out radical friends, among them two scurrilous journalists, for relevant gossip. She sent notes to friends in service who might know something.

The secretary had heard that the lady concerned had been indisposed, missing a great charity event of which she was patroness.

'They say this is more usual than not these days. Alas, she took her mother's death hard and she is prone to melancholy.'

'That can be all. But is there more?' Mrs Ashton kept her gift secret, fearing what men of power would want from her if they knew of it.

'My dear Mrs Ashton, she is married five years this summer and they have not been blessed with children. I am a bachelor and this is pure speculation, but is it not true, such a great lack means sadness for most women afflicted? A man like Sir Charles will surely want an heir.'

Information about the husband abounded. Sir Charles Barrington-Stewart MP was in his thirties, a baronet, and six years in the House. A handsome man, his tawny hair and confident manner were a boon to sketch writer and cartoonist alike. 'A lion of the back benches and a rising man,' proclaimed *The Times*. He boxed, rode, fenced, and shot: a Justice of the Peace, and a Master of the Hunt.

Lady Barrington-Stewart was a great beauty of ancient and wealthy family. They supported unremarkable charitable works – schools, hospitals for body and mind, lifesaving, seafarers, and lifeboats. Charles's beloved older brother had drowned in his youth.

Sir Charles had condemned Spiritualism on the floor of the House. 'These parlour preachers offend both reason and religion. Were our simple ancestors so very wicked to throw them in the river?'

So, to the crucial death of the lady's mother, as told by the inquest and the obituaries. Rose, Lady Herncastle, was a widow living with her daughter in the lavish Corwood Manor, Belldownshire. The jury had found that death was due to an accidental overdose of laudanum. The deceased had been a martyr to insomnia and her digestion but, as the coroner had been at pains to stress, all witnesses had confirmed her as resolute in faith and in reasonable spirits.

Mrs Ashton smelled a rat. Suicide was shameful, and the coroner had not wanted it spoken.

The obituaries were kindly to the point of dullness. Some rich women have little personality left; others keep it for their family and friends. Lady Herncastle had not been often in society columns and she had all but vanished during her husband's long illness and the mourning which followed his death.

The lady's brother, the count, rose in the service of the Empire, guarding some frontier of the Raj. Her two older sisters were grand ladies in the North, no fans of London society.

Not enough on Lady Herncastle, the mother! Yet such a wonderful trinity of blessings in a young prospect – severe grief, an unsympathetic husband, and a lady of considerable *personal* wealth. Well handled, Lady Barrington-Stewart might be a bird laying regular golden eggs.

Mrs Ashton, mindful of cost, took a crowded omnibus that smelt of sweat and smoke and damp. She had seen a proposal for a two-storey 'bus', with a staircase, so designed that even women in fashionable skirts could ride above in the fresh air. It was an age of earthly miracles. She shunned the underground, a claustrophobic Hades, like travelling in a smoking stove.

Their grey parrots Eleanor and Sarah greeted them with enthusiasm, jumping up and down on their perches. Eleanor announced, *'Poxy bawd! Poxy bawd! Heaven's knocking shop!'* Eleanor's vast and vulgar phrasebook meant they were rushed to the bedroom if visitors came. Their twin darling canaries just sang.

Sarah begged for a treat. *'Bring tea dear'* – her only phrase.

Braddie handed her hinny a restorative drink. Her dear heart needed few notes to recall what she'd learned of their client's husband.

'Tha man has a temper,' Braddie said. 'A thieving footman beaten, then paid off. A poacher half drowned. But they canna give names or dates. And he punched a heckler once.'

'Good to know. Do we have any friends of friends in service, or in neighbours' houses, by any chance?'

'Not a bite.'

They talked it through, and – as was their way in private – referred to their client with scandalous informality. 'Why doesn't Lady Violet find comfort from her sisters? Why did Lady Herncastle choose to live with her, bringing two old dowagers under one roof?'

'Violet's the baby, so the favourite mebbe? And you know, the Sir quarrelled with his brother, who fled to Paris.'

Braddie scowled. Paris was both fun-loving and French, and it was hard to know which she disliked more.

'Drink, gambling, women, debt?'

'Tha full pack.'

Mrs Ashton fell silent, trying to see her way forward.

Braddie sighed and began her well-worn lament. 'I wish we were awa', Honeybee. Some little cottage, with a garden. A strong lass to help my aching back.'

Her dear friend's dream might bore her to insanity.

'Sweetness, that will need a tidy sum... a good income to live on.' Did couples married in the usual way endlessly return to the same conversation?

'Chasing treasure always leads to trouble,' Braddie grumbled.

'What else can we do? My darling, I can hardly marry, can I?'

Some men were attractive and might understand their place. Yet any such practical arrangement would break Braddie's heart. Each was mistress of the other's heart, and they did not need powers to know each other. No, a man was out of the question.

How fleeting their current pleasures might be. Braddie was older and her life had been the harder. A precarious life, and beneath any enjoyment yawned the abyss of poverty, illness, and age.

As always, Mrs Ashton must have optimism for the two of them.

She kissed Braddie. 'Such a long face, my dear, like the vicar's donkey. I know what will cheer you up. Let me rub your poor back.' She knew each inch, each scar. It was a map of misfortunes – prison, workhouse, accidents. Yet in bed, Braddie could be as coltish as a girl.

'There's much to do...' But Braddie smiled, at least a little. Oh, her friend's ardour rekindled. They knew each other in the truths of the body as well as in the spirit. Afterwards, Mrs Ashton would send a boy to buy flowers for Braddie, but also to embellish the room for the grieving, wealthy daughter and wife. So much was riding on tomorrow's visit.

Chapter 3
A Lady Calls

Their humble rooms, Tuesday afternoon

The bell rang exactly on the hour. Mrs Ashton's pulse fluttered, as the matador's heart must flutter before the bull, or the boxer entering the ring. Eleanor had squawked a new atrocity at breakfast. *'Christ's thunderbox!'* The dear, affectionate birds were banished to the bedroom.

Braddie showed Lady Violet in. In life she outshone her portraits – young, beautiful, and sad made a potent combination. She was still in her twenties, and the purple and black of late mourning, so unflattering to most, emphasised her pale skin and hair. She seemed a blonde China doll, too delicate to take out and play with. Mrs Ashton had a keen eye for artifice. Grief had been hard – dark marks under her eyes adroitly hidden, the tiniest of facial lines covered up.

Mrs Ashton bowed. 'Lady Barrington-Stewart, welcome.' A ponderous name for a slip of a girl, but socially ignorant to address her as anything else.

'Mrs Ashton, how kind of you to see me.' She smelled like her note, delicious.

'Only my pleasure. Mrs Bradshaw, the tea please.'

Another woman came too, pretty in dove grey, dark where Lady Violet was fair, but a resemblance around the nose and jaw. Her clothing placed her well above a servant, but of lesser standing than the lady.

'My companion. My dear cousin, Miss Esme Shilling.'

Nothing about her in any of the research. *Damn.*

Mrs Ashton spoke warmly. 'All are welcome, my lady. I hope you do not mind if Mrs Bradshaw stays. She has the second sight, as had her maternal grandmother. It may help us.'

Braddie's teeth would grind at that lie she loathed. It countered the argument some snobs would make about Braddie being in the room. Braddie's piercing observations afterwards were invaluable – sometimes hilarious.

'Of course,' the lady said.

They sat, Lady Violet shifting to be comfortable, fussing with her reticule. Nerves were common, but the why mattered. Braddie served tea, took none, and sat a little away. Miss Shilling took her tea black and only sipped it. The time would come in the narrative of the lady's woes when the host might touch the client's hand.

Her visitors showed such keen hope. 'When did you learn about the spirit world?' Lady Violet asked.

'I was six. A girl had drowned in the millpond, forty years before. I had a vision, her dressed in grey, clothes from an old picture book but dripping wet...'

She had told the lie so often, embellished so well, that she almost believed it herself. It had been a simple nightmare, but something of that childish fear made the telling real.

'... but I came to see we have nothing to fear. For most of those who come over the river bring good news, consolation to those they left behind. Yes, malicious spirits are not unknown, but we have the love of Our Lord. Against His name, they have no power.'

Lady Violet shivered. 'My husband does not believe in spirits returning. Of course, he is a good Christian, a good man.'

'Some scoff. Yet so many see in Spiritualism the fulfilment of promise. Her Majesty herself has consulted with trusted persons to reach her poor dead Consort. Many respected clergy approve, and a true scientist must accept evidence.'

'Of course.'

Find the client's history. 'Have you attempted to reach the other side before, my lady?'

'Twice, but an utter failure. My sisters disapprove, even more than my husband. Yet truly I must try again. Lady Westfall's recommendation gave me confidence. Dishonesty is not unknown... I hope that does not offend you.'

'Yes, some seekers are not honest. How fallible mortals can be. Tell me why you need to reach the other world.' For all her work, Mrs Ashton had but the barest bones to understand the mother, Lady Herncastle. It was weak stuff to summon a convincing fake. She must guide Violet to tell her what she wanted.

'My mother died two years ago. I find no solace, no joy in anything. Not company or music or exercise, neither town nor country. Some twist of fate took her from me.

Whatever idle tongues say, she was stoic about her illness and in good spirits...'

'A good woman,' said Miss Shilling.

Miss Shilling did look wan, far from well.

'We cannot know every purpose of Providence,' Mrs Ashton said. 'Every woman misses her mother, who brought her into this world. Maybe, just maybe, I can find Lady Herncastle in the other realm... Tell me more of her.'

Listening helped, a word here, a word there. In her experience, people needed solace, or release from guilt. Mrs Ashton always told herself she could help the grieving and relieve their pain. Weary work if she did no good.

Frankly, the recital of the mother's virtues and interests proved unrewarding. A few things stuck.

'Lady Herncastle lived with you. Did your husband...?'

'Sir Charles insisted, my father being dead. He honoured my mother for my sake. My mother thought him an excellent match. His mother, the Dowager Lady Barrington-Stewart, has always been kind to me. She is so unwell, the poor woman, such a worry for us both.'

Mrs Ashton tried a jab. 'Some men can weary of their wife's mother.'

'No.' A hesitation there. 'There were discussions, sometimes. As there might be on any side in a family. She deferred to him, of course, as was only right.'

'Discussions about what?'

'Sir Charles's brother is a fool with money... given to drink and gambling and... undesirable companions.'

Miss Shilling's elegant face pouted disapproval.

Lady Violet's gloved hands clenched. 'Sir Charles quarrelled with Rupert about the debts. My mother wanted to try a reconciliation – as a route to Rupert's reformation, of course.'

'Whose side did you take?'

Lady Violet fidgeted, looking away. Why?

'A wife must support her husband,' she said eventually. 'In strictest confidence, Rupert had forged his brother's signature to borrow money. Sir Charles could have called the police. Instead, my husband was generous. He offered to set him up in the colonies, if he stayed there, but Rupert refused. It ended things between them.'

'And you have been married almost five years now?'

'Yes.' That quiet tone seemed underwhelming. 'I am lucky in many ways.'

Sometimes a doctor must draw blood. 'But not yet blessed with children...'

A hit, a palpable hit. Lady Violet gasped, produced a black-edged handkerchief, and touched it to her eyes. 'No, although it is my deepest wish. I have been a good wife to him, but in that duty, I have failed him. It is the most painful subject, Mrs Ashton. Please, let us leave it.'

'I am sorry, my lady. Mother Nature is sometimes slow. These things take time.'

'Mrs Ashton, I must be frank. My mother's death makes no sense. She took each dose of medication with her diary open, noting it as she did it. The medicines were checked, so was it some momentary folly? I need to know she did not choose to die.'

'You wish me to seek your mother on the spirit plane to find out how she died.' What a knotty problem. Her client was hungry for answers, but how to use this to best advantage? If in doubt, stall her. 'Not everyone recalls the moment of their passing.'

'People gossiped, the most malicious stuff. Will you try to reach her?'

Mrs Ashton considered the great risk of getting this wrong. Maybe the Cavalier or one of her other imaginings would get more out of her client. Maybe she must start and improvise... give enough crumbs to string her along.

'I will try, though there is something awry on the spirit plane.' Best to prepare her client for disappointment.

'Will you dim the lights?' Lady Violet said.

'God's work should be done in the light. Join us please, Mrs Bradshaw. If you do not mind, I find bare hands aid our circle. But no matter.'

Mrs Ashton took off her gloves, but her highborn guests watched her do it with surprise and gave no sign of following. Braddie brought a chair so each of them held a hand of each of their guests.

Mrs Ashton closed her eyes and led them in the 'Our Father', that old heathen Braddie barely moving her lips. Ashton urged silence, stillness, and waiting... The street was not noisy as London went, but she could hear horse-drawn vehicles rumbling over the cobbles, a street vendor, someone singing a cheery ditty. That gurgling pipe in the house.

Mrs Ashton had a few stock phrases about the gulf between the worlds, the river of mist that divided them. She poured them out like cream. She hoped her prompts would bring relevant detail to mind.

Mrs Ashton opened Lady Violet, cracking her open like a book so she could glimpse within. And what a gush of hidden emotion flowed into her – an agony of sorrow, with notes of guilt and shame. This woman lived in terror, ruled by her husband's anger. Endlessly placating his disappointment that she was barren, she did all he asked physically. He would rage if he knew she was here, forbidding her from any part of that *crew of liars*. Her heart fluttered every time she remembered him shouting. True, he never struck her; he took out his anger bellowing and without warning, smashing a jug, hurling a book, or thrashing a tree with his whip.

Miss Shilling held her hand tighter – she was anxious – but Mrs Ashton focused. Seeking to open two usually failed with both.

'A troubled spirit...' Mrs Ashton said. 'Very distant. Someone reaching for help...'

'Mama!' said Lady Violet.

'I don't know. Come nearer, strange spirit, and speak to us. What message do you bring?'

Banging in the street, how distracting.

'Let us keep our focus on the eternal,' said Mrs Ashton, holding her eyes shut through considerable effort. How draining to hold the connection through distraction. She needed a small perfect detail of Lady Herncastle or two, snared from Lady Violet's mind to convince her.

'Spirit, give us a sign you are she we seek. Some private sign only you would know.... some incident in the nursery... some private name.'

More banging. She was sure now it was the front door of the house.

'Tha housekeeper will get it, mistress,' Braddie said.

'You have travelled far,' Mrs Ashton said to her imagined spirit. 'Have courage, step forward!'

Lady Violet's mind wandered, distracted. The vague images of mist and shades that Mrs Ashton had spun in words disappeared from her mind, replaced by tetchiness and muddle. Then a gasp of pure terror. Lady Violet dropped both hands she was holding, ending the connection, and she stood.

'It must be Sir Charles,' she said, as if she spoke her doom.

A rap on their own door must be the housekeeper – who had all the backbone and resolve of a milk pudding. Mrs Ashton hung a red tasselled cord on the apartment's doorknob when she was communing with spirits and not to be disturbed.

Mrs Ashton had dealt with ample trouble in her time. She composed herself and stood. The housekeeper's reedy voice called out, 'You have a visitor.'

A man's voice of angry command. 'Let me in!'

'I am ready to receive him,' Mrs Ashton said, projecting confidence, walking to be closer to the door than Lady Violet. Braddie took her countrywoman's stick in her hand, as if she needed it to walk.

The door swung open, and the man strode in, brimming with an energy that cartoons and sketches had only hinted at. Sir Charles was a handsome clean-chinned brute with a piercing gaze, well over six foot, and he stood to command the room. His stick had a silver top. Everyone rose.

'I gave strict instructions we were not to be interrupted,' Mrs Ashton told the housekeeper. Admonished, the woman gulped and scurried away.

'Sir Charles, I believe. Good afternoon, and welcome.'

The baronet ignored Mrs Ashton and held out his hand to his wife.

'My dear, not the most fruitful use of a spring day. Let us go and discuss this elsewhere.' A measured voice but not expecting disagreement.

Lady Violet had her handkerchief out. 'You have spoiled everything. May I not seek advice?'

'My dear, you put old Willoughby in the most terrible position, the poor chap. Expecting an honest servant to lie for you. Quite unfair, if I may say so. Not like you at all. Miss Shilling, may I trouble you to go and wait with Willoughby and Prudence please.'

Miss Shilling rose at that order but did not move.

'Now,' Charles snapped.

Lady Violet stiffened her back. 'I didn't ask dear Willoughby to lie. You will not punish him for my actions.'

'The man is a treasure. I forgive him twice, once for his honesty and now because you plead his case. Let us talk where no grubby carnival barkers are listening.'

Sir Charles's smile to his wife left Mrs Ashton chilled. This man expected obedience. She summoned every ounce of authority she could. 'This is my parlour, where we do God's work.'

Sir Charles looked down at her with a sneer. 'No glowing rabbit from the hat yet, Mrs Ashton? No headless monks on parade?' His gaze returned to his wife. 'My darling, let us go. If you want spectacle, I will buy us a box at the Egyptian Hall. We'll find the same magical thrills but cheaper, and without the pretence and fraud.'

His wife looked at Mrs Ashton, pleading. 'I wish to talk to Mrs Ashton. I... I think she has a true gift.'

The golden fish had bitten. Praise be!

Charles growled. 'My dear, she is reckoned a notorious sham even among her crooked crew. She preys on the unfortunate, as a she-wolf does the lamb.'

'We have not finished, sir,' Mrs Ashton said.

'You will not see my wife again,' he glared at her. 'My dear, I have no wish to quarrel with you. What do you owe this phantom juggler?'

'We have not discussed money.' Lady Violet stood firmer than Mrs Ashton expected. Esme Shilling moved towards the door, looking back. Her expression was hard to parse, and she blushed and looked away when she was observed.

'Well, let us see if she can force herself to accept a coin or two. Full and final payment.' Cool now, arrogant, and fancying himself the humourist. 'Well, *Mrs* Ashton? If, indeed, a Mr Ashton ever existed.'

What a quandary. Lady Violet had taken to her, so far. Provoking the man might make future access to the wife impossible.

Mrs Ashton summoned her dignity. 'Sir Charles, I cannot accept a farthing – I have not completed what I was asked to do. You must know that my dear husband, the late *Major* Ashton, served his country with great courage and character. His name will not be maligned here.'

'Give this to the poor,' said Sir Charles, his voice close to snapping. He found some coins and flung them at the Japanese table. They bounced off. 'My dear, I will not give you an order. Come with me, and I await your correction.'

Lady Violet caught Mrs Ashton's eye and managed a wan smile.

'I am coming, dearest. Thank you, Mrs Ashton.'

'Au revoir.'

That man of power eyed up Mrs Ashton and Braddie as if he sat on the Bench and they were poachers.

Mrs Ashton hesitated. To open someone at a distance took more effort, failed more often, and was harder to maintain. Still, nothing ventured... Mrs Ashton opened him and she could not hold her gasp.

Pure hatred burned under that controlled mask, against everyone leeching from his wife's sorrow. As expected, such an opening gave her only the single dominant thought.

Sir Charles contemplated raising his stick, then with one brutal blow or two, striking Mrs Ashton in the face with the metal head... *Break her nose or jaw. Show her.* He imagined the scream, the blood. *Knock her to the floor then beat her while she whimpers.* Iron discipline held his rage back, not any minim of scruple.

Mrs Ashton shook, she couldn't hide it. Breaking the connection, she stepped back and thought for one instant she might topple. The brute turned and followed his wife. The door slammed and a vase trembled, and the couple were alone.

'Nasty piece of work,' said Braddie, kneeling to find the coins. 'She's the rabbit and he's the fox.'

Mrs Ashton breathed, trying to calm herself. Her hands shook. 'The monster wanted to smash my jaw.' Vicious thug. 'Such rage, such a house of sorrows ruled over by a bully. Did we finish the port?'

One of Braddie's raging storms brewed.

'Don't go all mushy over her, hinny.'

'Who?'

Their visitor was pretty, in that languid society way, and she'd shown surprising backbone. But Braddie's jealous nose was misleading her. Honestly!

Her dear heart glared. 'You know who. Honoria, she's trouble and that radgie de'il of hers... well.'

Oh, dear heart, don't be afraid. Mrs Ashton moved to the vase of flowers. She pulled out an early bluebell – forced indoors, no doubt. Mrs Ashton understood the couple's love as the perfect safe harbour to which she would always return. Why not the occasional pleasant excursion? Braddie saw the partnership as a fortress island, never to be left.

'Good heavens, angel, our client is far too milk and water for me. The man no longer needs to raise his voice or his hand. He has her trained like a dog. Yet, two years later, she is unreconciled to her mother's death. So much so, she will disobey him in the face of her fear. Intriguing, isn't it?'

'Don't play Lady Galahad, it will only mean trouble... Don't moon over her like some schoolgirl.'

How infuriating. Move things on.

She showed Braddie the flower. 'Dear heart! Remember that day long ago, the beautiful day you showed me the bluebell wood.' Sweet memory, making love in the open air. 'Bluebell for *constancy*. I promise, when we can, a little house with a garden, where we can plant our own. Let me fetch the port and the last of the sultana cake. I need your wise head on what to do next.'

Braddie shuddered. 'I hate dealing with Them.'

She lumped the rich, the law, the clergy, and the entire male sex together in that one contemptuous word. Mrs

Ashton took Braddie's free hand and touched it to her cheek, the golden honeybee brooch, and then her heart.

'Dearest, you deserve an easier life.'

Lady Violet held great possibilities, but her fearsome beast posed difficulty. Her mother's death might have been suicide or accident... but seeing into Sir Charles's fearsome soul, another dreadful possibility beckoned. Had the mother got in that ferocious man's way?

Great opportunity but significant risk – these were interesting times.

CHAPTER 4
The Ambitions of Miss Maisie Kendrick

Second floor back, 13 Jonah Court, Wretchmarket, Thameswake. Friday

The family's grimy rooms in Jonah Court were one room split by ragged curtains. Rats worked their scurrying mischief under the floors. Maisie had heard Pa go before first light, red-eyed and guilty, to look for work. He'd eaten the last food, for a docker cannot work empty to find the rent. Everything would be far worse on the street.

Maisie had work for Mrs Ashton today, a real adventure. A wicked sir puffed up with his money and importance, and a weeping childless lady in danger. Mrs Ashton might need her for weeks. The sexton had told her something odd last night, about people snooping on the two strange birds. Maisie must get the kids to school then investigate.

She got George and Tildy waked, wiped, and decent, and gave George the medicine she hid under her women's rags, so Pa wouldn't drink it. Thank goodness for Mrs Colquhoun downstairs – she was a mighty gap-toothed ogre, but she'd loved Ma and had a soft heart, which meant porridge for the three of them and bread to take for lunch. Payment was the stern lecture Maisie knew by heart, on the heathen failings of Mrs Ashton – the warning of the Holy Father against ghost-mongering – and the desirability of good, honest, reliable work.

Mrs Colquhoun had the whole downstairs floor of the building for her needle-girls, and Maisie sewed for her when nothing else paid. Such long dull work, and if her mind fled to far-off lands or solving mysteries, she made mistakes and the work had to be done again.

The jeering rhyme 'Tinker, heathen, darkie, thief,' followed everywhere the three Kendricks went. Yet, Mrs Colquhoun's carrot-headed brood, including two hulking apprentices, were gallant protectors. Friends with fists; no one dared risk more than jeers.

The streets were shiny-washed with rain, sparkling – dark islands of shit in a silver sea. Every day she saw those who lived in holes, or under a piece of stolen canvas. Barefoot in the dirt, your cuts festered. She remembered how she had raged when the kids' boots were stolen. Mrs Ashton had replaced them, bless her.

When she could, Maisie took the kids to school, trying to keep up their spirits with the hug at the gate. But Maisie had to earn a living... School had books and posh people's libraries had more books than any one person could read. She was no more allowed in those than she'd ever be invited to Buckingham Palace.

The steamship and the railway meant you could go most anywhere in the world, balloons could soar above mountains, and submarines even went under the sea. Only eighty days to go round the world. She'd *rescued* that book from a hawker...

Yet London was the centre of the world – almost a country – with palaces and flophouses, bright taverns and squalid drinking holes, churches and knocking shops, tall warehouses in sooty brick and squat lean-tos. Wood and iron and mud and stone – a cauldron of sweet and bitter, old and new, rich and poor, steam rising and sewers stinking and factories smoking.

Tildy asked questions about last night's chapter of Rani and the Tiger. Her mother had told them that tale and had showed how her *daadee ma* sat telling it, stiff-backed and with special gestures. Maisie performed it too, spinning the story out episode after episode until the kids were asleep, throwing in leprechauns and cowboys and Hanuman the Monkey God, and Cú Chulainn and a talking bull who walked on water and Saint Bridgit and railway trains out of control and the pawnbroker who lent silver against your heart as pledge and the three old washerwomen of the North who decided when you would die.

One more hug at the gates, and Maisie was free. She ran through shining streets to the Burning Bird, to see what Sal knew. Maisie ran, skirts flying, boots ringing out on the cobbles, herself again. All were about their business

Streets crowded with horse-drawn buses and drays, a wounded soldier with his barrel organ, and a rough dock prophet on a crate shouting, angry about the End of The World. Roofs dripped and the sparrows played in the puddles.

Everything about Sal was big. She ran the pub like a sergeant major and she could stop a fight with a whistle. 'Thought you'd come,' Sal said, dismissing the drayman.

'Some odd cove asking after your Mrs Ashton last night. Generous with his coin, beers all round, bit of a flirt.'

'Can you tell me who, and what he said, and what he looked like?' Maisie produced her notebook.

'Jabez Trephine, enquiry agent.' Sal fumbled in her apron pocket and handed over a card. An address in Rigger's Row. 'A fox in trousers. Straw hair, medium height. Porcelain teeth and a jacket a flash bookie would think too fast.'

'Who was he working for?'

'He dodged that. A big punisher with him in a sailor jacket, sips a glass and says nothing. Trephine full of himself. Who were the strange ladies and what did people think about raising ghosts and the like? The strange birds were drunks, and one step off Queer Street, and had the bailiffs round, most mornings. Jump in quick if they owe you. Had anyone ever seen Major Ashton or was he a mysterious phantom vapour that only Mrs Ashton could see? Mrs Bradshaw been in prison, did anyone know what for? Stolen goods or running a bawdy house?'

Hardly an Abbess! Braddie liked kids but her judging gaze would give any grown man the wilt.

Ask six drinkers in the Bird, you'd get twelve bits of gossip. 'And what did people say?'

'Some told him to go to hell, some took his money and spun him some nonsense or another. And some stuck the shiv in – your boss has heard it all before. So loud, he wanted the whole bar to hear.'

An enquiry agent should use charm and discretion. This brass neck was a cunning way to find Mrs Ashton's enemies and spread scandal along the way. Sir Charles was a cunning villain.

'Your employer crossed anyone recently?' Sal asked.

'Maybe.'

'She should be careful. I'll ask around, see if anyone knows more about this Trephine.'

'Thanks, Sal.'

For a preachy do-gooder, Mrs Ashton rubbed a barrel of people up the wrong way. Not least, she didn't pay her bills.

Maisie would head straight to Middleton Street to pass on the news.

She ran. She saw her cully, Dongmei Li, in trousers talking to a Chinaman she didn't recognise. No sign of Dongmei's boss, the strange churchy Makepeace lady from the Mission, who was determined to Save Maisie. Her family needed the free clothes and medicines, and there were books she could borrow, but the being Saved bit stank.

Dongmei raised a hand and gave a pretty smile – tougher and funnier than she looked. Maisie waved back.

Working for Mrs Ashton was better than sewing. She helped Maisie with disguises. The spirit-monger loved the theatre of Maisie being a boy, or a servant, getting the detail right and showing how she could her bind her chest if she wanted to pass better. Her employer was a brilliant teacher of voices and actions – how to play posh, or out of town, or afflicted in the head. 'Dear child, the right voice and manner will open doors.' No day working for the two old birds was ever boring.

But Mrs A was a false coin. Maisie liked her, liked her generosity, but no one raised any dead.

Maisie ran, passing the river of people. Sailors and thugs and pitiful barefooted beggars, this man almost naked, this one pretending to be the victim of a shipwreck. Swells going home after their frolics in the sinful pleasures of the poor – rat-fights and dog-fights in low dives, the villains buying girls younger than Maisie for their pleasure, and smoking opium. She saw two Lascar seamen with their strange-scented tobacco and a clutch of the new poor Jews from Russia, ring-locks showing – every type of common people working, skiving, sodden drunk at daybreak, or looking for their fortune.

London had its spoiled pedigree pooches, but it was a city of dockers' dogs too: tough, lean survivors with fight.

Mrs Ashton pulled her tricks so many times. She brought back people's loved ones, men and women and children, with different accents and all. She could stand like a man, or like an old, crippled woman. People wept and said, 'Oh, ma, ma, it is you!' or 'Bertie my boy... it has been so long' But outside her meetings, Mrs Ashton could mimic the vicar, the sexton, or Sal in the Bird, note perfect. Speaking right proved nothing.

That first time, when Mrs Ashton had summoned their dead Ma, who called Maisie *cushla macree*, her voice was so kind and encouraging. Maisie had cried, even in front of all those people. She so wanted to believe. Maybe Pa would not be ripped open and sad if Ma came back with messages, and the voice enough like Ma to fool the younger ones.

Ma not coughing up blood, Ma not dying by inches. Pa not drowning in tears and stout and chasing three-legged nags to make good.

'Sing our favourite song, Ma,' Maisie said, squeezing her brother's and sister's hands. 'Like every bedtime. "The Briar Rose".'

Ma could sing like an angel, but she'd never sung that. It was one of Mrs Colquhoun's songs. Mrs Ashton had a lovely singing voice, could sing in Ma's voice, and knew 'The Briar Rose', but she was a bold liar. And cardsharp clever because Maisie laid more cunning traps but never caught her out again.

But the meetings made George and Tildy happier, and Mrs Ashton's patter made others happier too. That pale, shaking clerk had looked like death, and Mrs Ashton preached on hope, not drowning yourself, never looking his way. It was aimed at him, she'd swear it on Ma's grave, and Mrs A gave him an hour private afterwards. He came for months, started smiling, then he got a girl and had far better uses for Sunday. Sometimes Mrs Ashton berated bad people to undo what wickedness they had done, precise in her condemnation, and they rose and confessed, which was better than a fire-eater with a dancing dog.

After a month, Maisie suggested Pa came, but he never would. 'God died when your Ma did. She's gone, Nubbin. She's gone.'

There were steadier jobs than Mrs Ashton, but nothing could be as interesting.

The two old birds explained the law, and new methods for nasty men. Maisie carried a shiv, and Mrs Bradshaw had showed her cunning fighting tricks, including one with two ripe plums that made her male cullies wince.

Maisie hid her three precious books in Mrs Colquhoun's rooms – the dictionary, the atlas, and the astonishing Memoir of Mrs Kate Warne. Her heroine had been a real lady detective for Pinkertons in America, perhaps the first in the world. She had saved the life of the great Yankee Lincoln.

Thameswake could not hold Maisie. She would settle for no less glory in her life. She would bring security for her family, banishing hunger and want to distant memory. The jeers she grew up with would become just the screeching of the gulls.

Chapter 5
An Important Correspondence

Mrs Ashton's rooms

If one believes the press, we face a plague of phantoms. Leave London, with its plague of dim-lit parlours and flying trumpets. We are told of the sound of two hosts clashing weapons on the slopes of Plynlimon where Owain Glendower once fought the English; or a great black dog terrifying a geologist near Cromer; those young lasses reporting impudent pixies in rural Dorset; and a faceless maiden in a Fife castle, bewailing not her cruel fate centuries past but the modern bathroom improvements. Some speak of a vast unknown spiritual realm shown to us in glimpses. Others speak of that vast and well explored kingdom, Folly, and its four great provinces: Intoxication, Insanity, Credulity, and Dishonesty.

The London Panjandrum

Mrs Ashton continued to research her client and that brute. Twice in speeches – on Ireland, and on giving a lifesaving award – Sir Charles had mentioned his older brother, drowned as a youth in a boating accident. 'My teacher, my hero, my example. A better man than I.' That death made him the heir. Having a flavour of the man, Mrs Ashton revisited the inquest reports with a searching eye. However, the witnesses were clear it was an accident and that Charles had fought with courage to save his brother in the water, at considerable risk to his own life.

A messenger brought a plain envelope in an unfamiliar hand. However, the letter inside had a familiar scent and handwriting. Lady Violet.

Dear Mrs Ashton,

I am truly sorry that our meeting was interrupted. I would ask you to forgive my husband his ways, and the discourtesy he showed you and Mrs Bradshaw. Please know that he is so keen to protect me from all harm, having lost others dear to him through misfortune and folly from his youth. I will work on him to have a more open mind. I am convinced that you have both the talent Lady Westfall says and a kind and understanding heart.

I am returning to our house in the country, as my mother-in-law has had another decline. I am one of those she remembers. She has grown dear to me these passing years and if she is taken from us, I do not think I could bear it. My husband will remain in London on business, anxious as he is about her health – I am to send word twice a day. You will have seen that there is talk of a reordering of the government, and he is needed in town. I have so many questions and I wonder if we may correspond?

There followed several intelligent questions for Mrs Ashton – arguments from scripture and the disapproval of the Rector, how a medium could reach one individual spirit from the millions of departed, what next steps were possible. All easy to answer in beguiling ways, using charm by the yard, beckoning the lady on...

I do hope we shall correspond to explore this rare gleam of hope for me in these dark times.

I am most grateful for your time and again my apologies for my husband's zeal in my protection.

Then under Lady Violet's elaborate signature:

Please write to me care of Madam Arditti, at the Dower House on the Corwood Manor estate. She is my old music teacher fallen on

> *hard times and our correspondence will not trouble my husband. V.*

Tremendous, if perilous, news. Her client had taken the bait and, with fashionable hypocrisy, intended to evade her brutal husband's orders.

Mrs Ashton took her time to craft a suitable reply. For some reason, her husband the Major came to mind. She turned her wedding ring to and fro – a shield, her symbol of honourable widowhood. Ten years ago, each out to con the other. What a fire between them, what flair. Two years, then a bitter betrayal – flight with every penny of her money, a furious Irish wife still living – then he'd drowned off the Italian coast. The Major could keep deep secrets from her, but Braddie was always open.

Mrs Ashton had chased any mutual connections about Lady Violet's mother, however tenuous, but truly she needed a source inside the household or to find former servants or companions.

Mrs Ashton could almost taste Lady Violet's grief. Accident, suicide, or foul play? Who might want her mother dead? The will offered no excitement – her 'widow's third' by law reverted to her son, Lady Violet's brother, and her own money was divided between all four children, each already wealthy.

Mrs Ashton might visit Lady Violet. Country houses posed great possibilities if the husband was tied up in London. Mrs Ashton could argue that spirits lingered near the place of untoward death. On the other hand, they were full of watching eyes; in Sir Charles's childhood home, most servants' first loyalty would be to him.

Throughout that day, the post brought notes and letters which were far from delightful. Worse than bills, Sir Charles showed his vigorous displeasure.

Braddie returned from an afternoon collecting debts and placating tradesmen. She deployed a particular frown as Mrs Ashton recited her woes.

'Dearest, this man Trephine has been to my bank, asking the most impertinent questions. How does he know I bank at Mallards of Elder Street?'

'You tell tha posh marks you use the same bank as the Queen. Bragging today brings bruising tomorra'.'

'And he told our landlord I am days from bankruptcy. And listen to this note, from a friend of mine. "An enquiry agent by the name of Jabez Trephine, most intrigued about you, and most unwilling to say on whose behalf he called. My dearest Mrs Ashton, I declined to be drawn, and he began a series of absurd slanders. I dare not write the vulgarities he used. I rang the bell for him to be shown out and, henceforth, never to be readmitted."

'The dear secretary at the Philosophical Society too. The last thing I need is someone stirring up my jealous enemies there. And the vicar of St Martin's called. Sir Charles himself complained to that Pilate in purple, the bishop, and the dear vicar faces an Inquisition for lending us the hall. We may need another venue.'

'Ald Nick, I said the man was trouble.' A silence fell, meaning, *I told you so*. 'Is she worth it?'

'Dearest,' Mrs Ashton pleaded, 'she is comfort and plenty in one fashionable gown. And cunning enough to engage with me wholly behind his back.' Lady Violet offered such an opportunity.

Braddie stood stern as an iron door. 'Our creditors are skittish. We must scatter a little siller to keep our credit.'

'Dear heart, even your hard work cannot spin silver from straw.'

'Milk tha little banker, then.'

Her middling meeting gathered at the home of a senior official at her bank, a man of unbending probity. Respectability was the air the dear man and his wife breathed, and any scandal would be a disaster. What if Trephine sent roughs to the house? What if her Scottish creditors connected the vanishing 'Mrs Leveret' with Mrs Ashton?

'I have written asking for a meeting. He must hear of the malice from me before someone else.' Fine phrases must march to order. *Were not the apostles slandered and persecuted?*

CHAPTER 6
A Truth Revealed

At home, a few days later

Let all bitterness and wrath and anger and clamour and slander be put away from you, along with all malice.

Ephesians 4:31

A fading light, and Mrs Ashton and Braddie were in their rooms, hoping for quiet domesticity.

A banging on the house door, its vigour no pretence of politeness. Three knocks, and then six.

Braddie looked up from her sewing. 'Not good.' She put the garment aside and looked around.

'Your stick is by the door,' Mrs Ashton said, putting down her book and standing. She marched to the room door and opened it. The housekeeper fluttered and flapped on the stairs – she had all the steel of a pickled jellyfish.

'Send your oldest for a constable, at once.' The Major always said Mrs Ashton could add a note of command to anything. 'No one that brash can be up to any good. And summon Mr Oliphant.' Their gentle neighbour was a mighty-fisted professor of the ring, once acclaimed as the Black Bull of Barbados. Retired now, he could still be most persuasive with a few lilting words.

'Let me in, you fraud, you witch!' A man's voice, angry, and familiar. Sir Charles.

The neighbours would see. They might intervene.

'Stay there, I need a witness if any wrongdoing occurs.'

'Oh Lord,' quivered the housekeeper. Heavens, the woman was useless. Her younger boy hid behind her. Braddie was behind Mrs Ashton, stick in hand.

'Who dares to make such a barbaric noise and in front of children?' Mrs Ashton called.

'Let me in, Ashton, you pestilence. Now.'

Mrs Ashton took off the chain and slid back the bolt, opening the door so she could see. She must make him use force to enter the house. In the street, people stopped to watch, and a front door opened. Witnesses were good.

Sir Charles burned red in the face and held that stick, that weapon, ready to hammer again at the door. Furious, a raging lion. Yet he did not step forward and he lowered the stick. A raging man who can keep control can be the most dangerous.

'Let me in, for God's sake, you thieving hag.'

Mrs Ashton smelt brandy.

'Do not take the holy name in vain. Sir Charles, you are drunk, and you will not enter this house of peace.'

'Damn you, you old bawd.'

'Don't be vulgar. There are children in the house, and people watching. We have sent for the constable.'

'I will lay a charge under the Vagrancy Act, you old fraud.'

Mrs Ashton addressed the street, a voice to carry. 'I have offered this man no insult, caused him no injury, and he threatens violence on my own doorstep.' She raised a dramatic finger. 'Will this man, a Member of Parliament no less, strike a defenceless widow?'

'Stay. Away. From. My. Wife.' His faint spittle on her cheek.

'On my mother's grave, I have not seen her since the meeting you rudely interrupted.'

'She wrote to you.' He held out his hand. 'Give me her letter. Everything she ever sent.'

'I will not. Mr Oliphant, how delightful to see you.' The noise alone must have summoned her friendly neighbour, who came along the street, both confident and measured in his pace. His great mastiff trotted cheerfully at his side.

'Why, Mrs Ashton, what is this fine fellow about? Dear sir, why all the noise and commotion this glorious day?'

Sir Charles looked sideways, unfazed at the size of both the man and the dog looking at him. Oliphant might be grey-haired, but he taught boxing to young gentry. Yet Charles was much the younger, and armed, and surely the faster...

Sir Charles tipped his hat to Mr Oliphant. No fool, to pick a fight in the street.

'A personal matter, sir, and a brief one. My apologies if I disturbed you.' He was cooling down, ready to talk his way out. 'The letters, Mrs Ashton. If you please.'

'They are at my bank,' she lied.

Through gritted teeth, 'You are a fiend, preying on my wife's good nature.'

'She knows her own mind. A private correspondence on spiritual matters, not touching on you at all.'

He smiled, ferocious. 'I will give you five pounds for the letters, now, in cash.'

An obvious trick, to show her as venal and untrustworthy. 'They have no value as the world knows it, but great worth to me.'

A quiver. 'Ten pounds!'

If Lady Violet became a disciple, far more beckoned.

'Not for all your worldly goods, Sir Charles.' She could do this all day.

He banged his stick on the step, raised his voice. 'I forbid you from seeing her or corresponding with her.'

'I will pray for you, Sir Charles. A man high in the councils of our country must bear a heavy burden. Yet wrath is a sin, and we must not bear false witness.'

Mrs Ashton almost wanted him to strike her, so publicly. That would prove expensive for him, and ruinous to his public character of progress and decency.

She took a pace, onto the top step. She heard Braddie cry, 'No, mistress,' and come closer behind her. Mr Oliphant took a step closer, raised a great hand, and the mastiff began a low growl. Now her retreat would be difficult. Sir Charles took a step back and down, out of instinct. Alas, he did not fall on his backside. The stick touched the steps, and his left hand was free. She seized it and opened him.

'She is a good woman...' Mr Oliphant said.

Whatever line she wanted to spin – showing her innocent and wronged, defending his wife – disappeared in a moment. Mrs Ashton gasped as fury poured out of Sir Charles, like fire raging across a dry heath – his titanic struggle not to seize her by the throat. In his mind, Sir Charles had eight fingers choking her… imagining the resistance of her larynx fighting his crushing thumbs, his strength and power… her face bulging, her cries stifled… her hands gripping his wrists but their meagre hold weakening.

The connection made her heart race; her pulse soared till she was dizzy. She could not breathe. She knew it was only in her mind, but her throat believed the crushing pain…

The world shrunk to his terrifying rage. Sir Charles's pleasure showed a lust for blood, watching the fox torn to pieces by the hounds. He imagined how Mrs Ashton might die… imagining how her face would contort and darken, the tongue lolling… the frantic fluttering of eyelids and her hands giving up and slipping from his wrists… and then the face was not Mrs Ashton's. This was a deep memory. He strangled another woman, a slip of a girl in her teens, past struggling… Sunlight and ancient trees.

Mrs Ashton stepped back, barging into Braddie… but for three breaths the link did not break. In those breaths, the woman dying with Sir Charles's hands at her throat became Lady Violet. How he resented his wife – barren, joyless, and disobedient.

Sir Charles stared at Mrs Ashton, both shocked and confused. She gasped, desperate to breathe properly. Sometimes those she opened felt a shadow pass, a moment of déjà vu, or a curious jolt. How long had it truly been? Time had slowed, but in practice it couldn't have been more than a few seconds.

True memories shine out in the mind – he had killed that girl. No wonder the fantasy of murder today felt so real.

Braddie, a fierce warrior, waving her stick. 'Awa' with you, you brute, you monster. Awa', awa', scaring my mistress half to death.'

Mr Oliphant put his hand to Sir Charles's shoulder. 'Begging your pardon, sir, I think it best you go.' The dog barked, a loud third voice.

Sir Charles could have been walking in the park. He touched his hat again and said to Oliphant, 'With pleasure. I will not be back. But may I shake the hand that felled the Glasgow Goliath?'

'I meet every man as a friend, but leave the lady alone,' said Oliphant, putting out his hand. Sir Charles swapped the stick to his left hand and shook the boxer's vast paw.

'By Jove, what a grip! An honour.'

Then Sir Charles stared Mrs Ashton in the face.

'Pray we do not meet again.'

He turned and walked down the street, whistling 'Hearts of Oak', and tipping his hat each time he passed a lady.

The door shut, and Mrs Ashton found herself weeping in Braddie's arms. The hidden depths of the man's soul showed a devastating horror. Sir Charles had killed a woman, and he would do it again. Yes, he hated her, but he also held a deep burning rage against Lady Violet. Her client faced a mortal danger.

CHAPTER 7
On The Trail

Their rooms, a week later

> *That great bulldog of science, Professor Huxley of the Royal Society, has been assaulted in his home before he was due to give a public lecture on Scientific Education. No intruder has been found and the great biologist is far from forthcoming on exactly what happened. The common gossip is that it was some spectral apparition, but of course, the professor is foremost among those who believe the cold light of reason evaporates any such vaporous absurdity.*
>
> *The Times*

Braddie stirred in the bedclothes. 'What's wrong, hinny?'

Dawn in their bedroom, and Mrs Ashton sat at the table, unable to sleep. That shocking image returned to her again and again, burning bright. Maybe that knowledge was the weapon to defeat him.

Lady Violet had written Mrs Ashton a letter cutting off all contact. She heard Sir Charles's voice in that handwriting and a little smudge suggested a tear. Mrs Ashton used her rich imagination to see Charles standing behind his wife, dictating. Mrs Ashton pored over the books and maps she had wheedled from the library with a ruler and a draftsman's compass.

'We will have to use all our brains, dear heart. We have one edge that brute does not. I know of his vile crime and now he must pay for it.'

Braddie swung herself up, a little grunt covering the pain of her stiff back, poor dear. 'The man should be hanged. Since we canna expect that, we should get out of his way. Leave London.'

'But dearest, perhaps we could get proof. Proof would bind his wicked power – or end it.'

Braddie snorted, pulling on a gown. 'The people who write the laws are above them. They look after their own.'

'It is an outrage. A Member of Parliament, a man with the ear of the Home Secretary, a Justice of the Peace. I lived him killing that poor dear girl, a child of God. I lived his joy in it.' Mrs Ashton shuddered at a memory so cruel and vivid.

'Who? Where? When? Was there a witness?'

Mrs Ashton pondered.

'No witness. A good many years back, a young man's crime.' She could not explain that instinct, but she could trust it.

'It's a wild goose chase.' Braddie came over and drew up a chair. 'You have nothing.'

'Let us be methodical. Location... a vision of country, oak trees. He noticed the foxgloves in bloom. I guess he was between fifteen and his early twenties. Most likely around his family estate, or when he was at school. Harrow, I recall. A day's ride from either gives us two circles to look in. A brown-haired country lass, poor, and shorter than him.'

Braddie snorted. 'Why on horseback? He might have gone by train. And these toffs go to stay at each other's houses all the time. Don't the family have a place in Grennard, and Dunnock House?'

'Well, then the whole of Belldownshire and Derbyshire, over ten years – and rather fewer around Harrow. Three locations. In an ordinary summer, we have foxgloves from July?'

'Until September,' Braddie said.

'I have set a friend or two on the newspaper archives, and I will write to a few enthusiastic historians of crime. We could widen the search if that fails.' Even as she said it, she could see it might come to nothing. Girls and women simply disappeared. Or maybe she'd find a dozen strangled women to waste her time and money.

If only she could open Sir Charles again. The right prompt would produce the details. Her body shuddered at the idea.

Braddie took her hand.

'If we go to ground, that radgie de'il will soon lose interest,' her dear heart said.

'My dear, have courage. Right will prevail. We won't take any silly risks.'

The world might come after us anyway.

The parrots picked up on the mood. Eleanor muttered, *'Papist, Papist, fool of a Papist,'* while Sarah plaintively called for tea.

Thugs had appeared to disrupt her poor meeting that week, and purported creditors had tried to gain entry to her middling meeting, embarrassing its hosts. Sly, knowing stories appeared in the newspapers that Mrs Ashton was about to do a flit. She had been in the middle of discussing a loan from the bank. Her dear banker friend trusted her powers and character, but the matter turned fraught.

'My dear lady, my hands are now tied.'

Nastiest of all, *The Orb* had offered a reward for anyone who could prove the Major, her husband, had truly existed. After all this time, she remembered his manly smell, his moustache tickling. But even she didn't know his true name.

The next day, at breakfast time, the housekeeper brought a large envelope with a business-like air. It came from a firm of City solicitors. Inside was a more familiar envelope and its scent. The covering note merely pronounced that 'The enclosed is forwarded in line with our client's wishes and be assured replies sent via this office will be forwarded promptly to her by confidential means.'

Mrs Ashton carefully examined it, as scholars might look at new Assyrian tablets, or astronomers inspect a provocative and unexpected star.

She handed Braddie the letter. Braddie wrinkled her nose.

'Lady Violet,' Mrs Ashton said. 'What do you make of it?'

'Bertie's strumpets!' squawked Eleanor. A new one, and Mrs Ashton wondered if Braddie encouraged the bird. The slander of royalty was new.

Braddie read it aloud. The canaries trilled in their cage and far away Mrs Ashton could hear the man with the hand-organ in the street.

My dear Mrs Ashton,

I must ask forgiveness for my earlier letter, written at my husband's direction. On reflection it went beyond anything he had a right to ask. Of course, you may not come to the house against his express wishes, but I hope that I have not offended you and that we can still correspond.

Thank you for your recommendations on Spiritualist literature, which are proving most illuminating.

I do wish that circumstances would allow us to meet. My words cannot express my deep need to speak with my mother and I am sure if anyone has the power to put my mind at rest, it is you. Sometimes Mama seems near me, but it brings no consolation. Perhaps visiting the scene of the tragedy would assist you in this search, although of course I cannot invite you to visit it.

The train stops at Bellingley, and we usually have guests met there. The Bellingley Hotel is a country place but clean and extremely respectable. Perhaps some other matter of business could bring you to the county?

My friends are in London, my brother in India, and my other family scattered, although scrupulous about correspondence. My sisters, admirable in their faith, are unbending that Spiritualism poses great moral danger. I am reluctant to travel while my dear mother-in-law is so stricken. In her grave illness, I can scarcely share a deep confidence with her that touches on her son, and which might divide her loyalties. I do wish I had my mother to confide in, and if you could reach her, that would be a tremendous kindness.

You are a woman of strong moral character and yet I trust you would listen to my dilemma with gentle insight. It is not something I can – something I dare – commit to paper. I know my duty to my husband although this has proved so hard, over you and other matters, and of course I know to follow my Christian duty in all things.

Do write back, my dear Mrs Ashton, and

be assured that my husband cannot discover this correspondence. This route, unlike the last, cannot be betrayed.

Braddie then handed it back. 'Huh.'

Curiosity can become as seductive a vice as drink. 'What deep matter touches on the woman's dreadful son?' Mrs Ashton said.

'Who cares? Your lass is waggling her skirts, hoping you'll come running.'

Mrs Ashton had not expected enthusiasm but that was vulgar.

'Dearest, not so coarse! There is more going on than the death of her mother. How intriguing. Oh, don't look like that.'

Braddie looked sterner than a sergeant major. 'Don't get snared by her nonsense.'

'He's a vile brute. But she is inviting us to conspire with her against her husband.' Lady Violet was beguiling, but not the way Braddie thought. Intriguing certainly, rather than romantically enticing.

'Wake up,' Braddie said, slapping her palm with the back of the other. 'We shouldna go near her. He'll have us shot as poachers, or some other mischief, mark my words.'

'Is the dilemma something to do with her mother-in-law, or not?'

'Violet's realised he's a bad 'un. So should we.' Braddie looked hurt, almost pleading. 'Hinny, don't.'

There were rich pickings in country houses. Yet the risks were obvious, and they grew as she mused on them. 'Well, there's little point in going. Even if he is in London, the country servants will not keep her secrets. He will soon learn, and the longer before he finds out, the more trouble he will raise.'

Braddie breathed out, and her relief touched Mrs Ashton's heart.

'I'll drop her a note,' Mrs Ashton said. 'I will press her to be clearer. Perhaps we could conduct some important psychic experiments and ask for her financial aid. If they fail, it would be because she isn't here.'

Even as she said this, she wondered if Lady Violet travelled to other houses, whether she might ride with a trusted servant. A meeting on neutral ground...

'If you must. I'd just drop her, the minx.'

Mrs Ashton took both of Braddie's familiar hands, her thumbs mapping their rough backs with knuckle hills. 'Sweetheart, every fee is a step towards our retirement.'

'Not if we spend it on fancy new hats and hansom cabs and wild goose chases.'

'No more clothes, my darling. A strict economy in everything.'

A hasty postscript on the letter confided that Lady Violet trusted three men absolutely: her solicitor in London; her godfather, dean of a western cathedral; and an old school friend of her brother, one Captain Cairngorm who lived in Belldownshire. To each was appended a different wording to prove their *bona fides.*

Chapter 8

Departures, Horses' Hooves, and a Knock in the Night

The Barrington-Stewart town house, some days later

> *As Sir Charles Barrington-Stewart moves closer to high office, an unfortunate phantom from the past enters the country without fanfare. His disinherited brother Rupert returns to London following years of sordid delight in Paris and Rome. Tidings of great joy for London's bookies, actresses, publicans, and shady promoters of exotic railway shares. Sir Charles has the art of putting money to profitable use, but Rupert is vigorous only in squandering it through vice.*
>
> *The London Panjandrum*

Maisie's team had failed to find anything useful about the old dead lady, or anything else. At first, Maisie had steered clear from watching the house, because Willoughby might have seen her outside the ghost meeting. But failure so far had made Mrs Ashton cranky. Playing a lad, Maisie had been chased off by a bad-tempered groom.

Lord Muck's house was a palace of cream stone in a grand square of such houses. How in a city of dark smoke did the rich keep their houses bright? She admired the pretty garden in the middle which only the spoiled posh kids could use, behind the railings with their nannies. Trees in the private gardens flowered white and pink, and the daffodils and crocuses were out. People came and went but you needed a reason to hang around there.

Maisie dressed as a maid, and she had a cover story about a notorious grouch called Lady Morgan who insisted she wait for her friend's replies. Well-armed, Maisie could moan about her mistress's meanness and her unpleasantness, and the care lavished on her eight Pekinese dogs, and make stuff up with impunity. She sewed, 'cos if you looked busy, people were less likely to make trouble.

This morning, there'd been two gentlemen in top hats, a string of delivery boys, a maid from another household. Two ladies collecting, and various hawkers sent packing.

Then, after lunch, Charles got into a carriage, and Willoughby drove him.

Maisie tried the mews. Another groom inspected a chestnut horse's hoof and tutted.

'What's wrong?' she asked. The groom looked up, frowning. About the horse, not her, she thought.

'She's lame. This stuff isn't working, I'm going to try something else.' He had a country sort of accent, like Willoughby. *Belldunshur*, which they wrote Bell-down-shire. Brown hair, patchy whiskers, nothing grand in looks. Many men wore beards like Pa, but Sir Charles chose to go clean-chinned – and most male servants followed his example.

'Can I watch? I've been told I havter wait for a reply. Last time took *hours*. Then she has me run back with another note.'

'Suit yourself.' He reached for a big dark bottle and a ball of brown cloth, and worked on the horse's hoof. It stank like Satan's privy and the horse shifted, keen not to put its weight on it.

'Is this a fair berth to work in? Lady Morgan drives me doolally.'

'The master's a fair man. Likes things right; he's fretting over old Fancy here. His father, rest his soul, had no patience with the sick ones.'

'The man likes horses more than the staff then?' Maisie tried cheek which flushed out the truth.

The man laughed. 'Well, that hits the target for some I could name... but not him. He has his ways, and slackers are sent packing, but he's fair. Her ladyship, poor woman, she's kindness herself when one of the staff is sick. Cook must whip up something delicate for the invalid and she must have updates twice a day... You're a nosey one.'

'Lady Morgan works through maids like gloves. I'm looking for a new place.'

'My sister Prudie would know. Steady on old girl, steady on.' The horse settled, he said, 'She's gone with her ladyship to the country. Her lady's maid.'

He said this like it was something superior.

'Can you ask her for me?'

'Don't know when I'll see her.'

The doctoring of the horse continued.

Maisie asked about children of the house. 'None yet.' He looked troubled. 'You know, we had one of they reporters round here the other day. Willoughby told us not to gossip about callers, or the family, or anything. You're not a reporter in disguise?' He laughed at the idea.

Maisie had often thought a girl reporter, like a girl detective, could get where men might not. Maybe there was gold in reportering.

'I only want to know if it's a good house.'

'Well, I've said that. They can pick and choose though. Don't get your hopes up.' He flashed a smile. He led the patient to her stall, then went to a sink and washed his hands. Maisie noticed a rash on them, and scratches.

'I'd better go and see if the message is ready,' Maisie said. 'I need to be there when it is. See you again.'

'I have an understanding with another lady.' He said it gentle.

'Cheek,' Maisie said, deciding to look cross, then deciding to laugh. Flirting sometimes got where mere snooping wouldn't. She didn't like soppy stuff herself.

She gave her pretend maid's name, and he said, 'I'm Wilkins, but they call me Forty.'

A good day's work. In Mrs Ashton's rooms, her employer listened with care to her report.

'I assume Miss Shilling returned to the country?'

'No one said. We tried all sorts of things.'

'Find out more please. Let me settle what we owe.' That odd Birmingham-Oriental table had gone, and two of the pictures. Mrs Ashton had a little safe somewhere for her money and her notebooks. However, she had a money bag out and carefully counted out coins.

Mrs Bradshaw was packing.

'I've been called to Portsmouth, dear child – a private meeting with an old naval gentleman. Recommended by a friend.'

Maisie knew private meetings could be lucrative, and Mrs Bradshaw would go as her guard.

Pa had work this week – you could not fault him for trying – and he brought them fried fish and potatoes. George's cough grew worse if anything. The free dispensary was a room full of people coughing, and inevitable lectures.

On the third day, the sky sat sulking, neither raining nor being sunny. The family in the house on the left had gone to the Continent, and the few staff were too bored to shoo you off. Maisie-the-maid sat on the step there sewing. Maisie got to talk to two delivery boys, one of whom got so fresh with her, she had to invent a madly jealous sweetheart, 'taller than you', who boxed. There were always people coming and going.

Forty and the grumpy groom in finery brought out the carriage and its two brown horses. Forty nodded at her and she smiled back. She had a plan to hide her face if Willoughby turned up. Forty looked twitchy and scratched his neck.

Here he was, out the door. Sir Charles! This was the closest she'd got.

The wicked lord, walking slowly, helping a young lady in grey down the three steps at the front, with his head bent to hers. The woman clung to Sir Charles's left arm – the wicked lord rather blocked Maisie's view – and she wore a big hat. An older lady fusspot followed with three small bags and an umbrella.

All the business of getting the lady and her companion into the carriage, and Sir Charles looked round and saw Maisie. He looked at her for a moment which stretched into two – did that frowning gaze rest on her a moment too long? She kept her face bored, though her heart was in her mouth, and she turned her face to the sewing. He'd never seen her. Maybe he had a description, maybe he recognised seeing her as a boy. She always told people she was 'black Irish' or that her Ma was Spanish if they were nosey.

She heard the coachman ask, 'Which end of Harley Street, sir?' and Sir Charles snapped, 'Just get us there.'

Forty came over to her and she knew she needed to be friendly and not rattled. She gave him a smile.

'Waiting for a reply. Is that Miss Shilling, so unwell?' Maisie said.

Forty's face turned cross. 'Don't be nosey.' That was a yes.

'Oh dear,' said Maisie. She started a long story about Lady Morgan and her hypochondria about her dogs. She liked to meet household dogs so they would see her as friends. But Forty said, 'I'm back to the country. I can't wait to breathe clean air again, not choke in this wicked Gomorrah.'

Maisie woke in the dark, someone banging at the door. Pa stirred, cussing. She rolled out of bed, threw on a sweater, and found the poker. The door would not stand a brutal charge.

'Open up, open up.'

'Who is it?' she said. Pa muttered something, drunk of course.

One of her gang, a docker's son and one of Mrs Ashton's runners. 'There's been a fire at Mrs Ashton's, while she's away.'

She opened the door in Ma's shawl. 'Tell me everything. Do they know?' Pa stood groaning and trying to light the lantern.

Frightened, and somehow excited, she went back in and threw on her clothes. The lad waited in the kitchen, with Pa crawling towards wakefulness. Pa dared not miss work. Mrs Colquhoun would need to look after her brother and sister. She told Pa, then scribbled a note in case his pickled brain forgot.

The lad said, 'Where are they staying? When are they back?'

'Give me a moment, I'll remember,' Maisie said, rubbing her eyes.

'We wanted to send a telegram when the office opens but no one had the address. Firemen and everything, their place wrecked top to bottom.'

'Anyone hurt?'

'No. Someone raised the alarm. The clamour could have woken the dead.'

Maisie and the lad ran, as if running fast enough would magic them back to before the fire. There was pink in the sky when they got there. The firemen had gone, but a dozen people stood around, not quite sure what to do. One of the blue terrors talked to a neighbour under the gaslight, licking his pencil each time he wrote something down. Coughing and crying, the housekeeper sat on a neighbour's step, wrapped in a blanket. Her little boy clutched his toy dog. A great scorch mark scarred the front of the house, like a dragon had breathed on it, the smoke and flames pouring up. The downstairs windows had shattered; a tired-looking woman was trying to sweep the glass into a pile, and a slick mere of dark water.

Heavens, the two old birds were there, in coats and travelling hats! Two wooden chairs in the street together. Mrs Ashton sat staring into nothing. Maisie once wondered what 'looking like death' looked like, and now she knew. Braddie, red-eyed, urged a tin cup of something on her dear friend. At their feet, the empty canary cage.

'What happened?' Maisie said.

'Ald Nick! That snake, that wolf that walks like a man,' Braddie said. 'They say the place is ruined. All done on purpose. All her fine clothes, everything thrown around... a robbery, then a fire. We don't know what's burned, what's stolen... Tha wicked scheming villain.'

'We think they killed our birds, our precious darlings.'

'Man is the worst beast of them all. All their frills and la-di-dah, they're just brutes and robbers. That de'il.'

'My files, my letters,' Mrs Ashton said, like she was in a dream. 'A book I had for you, Maisie dear...'

'I'm glad one of us kept some things at the bank,' Braddie said.

A neighbour said, 'Mr Oliphant can't be roused. His housekeeper found him dead drunk on the floor, not even with his shoes off. And his dog can't be found.'

Mrs Ashton looked all peculiar. Maisie had never seen her old and tired and sick like this. She began to recite.

'"Deliver me from mine enemies, O my God: defend me from them that rise up against me. Deliver me from the workers of iniquity and save me from bloody men. For, lo, they lie in wait for my soul: the mighty are gathered against me; not for my transgression, nor for my sin, O Lord."'

Mrs Ashton gulped at the cup Braddie offered. Even over the stench of burning, Maisie could smell spirits.

'Wicked cunning,' Braddie said. 'Tha naval gentleman was all crookedness. Aye, he's real, but he is awa' and it wasna him as wrote. Expenses sent in advance, then delaying us meeting till nightfall. Honey... My mistress realised it was a put-up job, and we got the Parliamentary train back. Worse than a cattle-truck. I've had better nights lost on the moors.'

'This took planning,' Mrs Ashton said into the air. 'What has he stolen from us? Assassin. Barbarian.'

And to Maisie's surprise, stern old Braddie began to cry, trying not to, but soon letting out big sobs. Maisie hugged her, the three of them together. Awful to lose their home and their things, but she wondered how soon before they could go in and look for clues. Would Kate Warne be defeated? Maisie thought Warne's fictional rivals were small beer, but even they wouldn't stand for this! Queen Boadicea had taken up arms to avenge her daughters' honour; the Rani of Jhansi went to war defending her kingdom.

A flutter of feathers, and down flew bold Eleanor the parrot, timid Sarah fluttering up high.

'By John Brown's manky trews!'

'Our precious darlings,' Mrs Ashton sobbed.

Ma said sometimes the world was strange as well as bad. A man could murder a woman and laugh, but shy at killing a pet.

Chapter 9
Sanctuary and Shameful Secrets

The house of Mrs Ashton's banker, two days later

We are pleased to note that the fire in Mrs Ashton's phantom-laden parlour hurt no one. Indeed, by some astounding providence her rooms were empty. It is widely reported that she is having difficulty paying her bills. But we are sure that the insurance will prove timely, and the involvement of Scotland Yard is merely a necessary precaution.

The Orb

The second day in their banker's house, a temple to middle-class Evangelical dullness. Braddie seethed, watching the banker's wife and her hinny fuss over an old wide-skirted chestnut dress the wife had found for the refugee. Disaster had struck and her Honeybee still wasted time on flummery. Braddie hated her foolish servant's dress, too short for her height, with a ridiculous frilly white collar. But that's what there was, and had she complained?

London was not safe. Surely, they should be after a boat or a train?

A hellish burden to stay under someone else's roof. It meant prayers before breakfast and readings at supper, and no privacy and playacting a humble drudge every minute.

Her hinny's flock had rallied round. The banker and his wife had taken them into their own home. Scotland Yard, dancing to some high-up's orders, had sent a rude detective looking for insurance fraud. That fool of a landlord had failed in his simple duty to pay the premiums. Not even the police could twist these facts.

The earnest banker's wife said, 'Those few stitches make an excellent fit, Mrs Ashton. Bradshaw, do you agree?'

'Lovely, ma'am,' Braddie said.

'Oh, I'm not sure,' said her Honoria. Captain Swing! You're not meeting the Ald Kraut Baggage, woman.

The powerful hand of that monster, that de'il Sir Charles. What a warning! A well-oiled plot had ruined them, using a big crew. Mr Oliphant plied with beer in the tavern and then drugged, his mastiff missing, probably shot. Literature denouncing Spiritualism scattered to imply religious cranks. A thorough search before setting the fire – and the little safe taken.

Braddie heard the message: *I could have killed you both.* Now every shadow held an assassin.

Stop fussing, hinny! Run, where Sir Charles could never find them. Their English friends in Deauville – a street almost English and devoid of tha de'il's spit, garlic – or go to ground in the North. Or America, where her hinny thought big money could be made. Everything there grew bigger and brasher, including the spirit-mongers and the credulity.

This defeat broke Braddie's heart. Each flit was a disappointment, with new friends slowly made left behind. Endless schemes ended in tears and ashes. And Scotland, they'd left so much trouble, she constantly worried it would find them. Oh, a cottage, a safe, steady life – simple comforts. Get a poor woman who needed work to help them raising fresh fruit and vegetables, and livestock. Maybe on the edge of a market town, with a library and one good hotel for visitors. Time to read before the fire.

'You have been so kind,' her hinny said to her hostess. 'I feel that I need a little rest.'

The worrit clasped her hinny's hands and said something about blessings, and then at last she left. Her hinny had raised the banker from a sorrow about his son so profound he could not walk. Honoria's power meant she could talk and understand and heal. Born that lesser species, a man, her hinny could have become a fancy mind-doctor rather than a ghost-mongering fraud – her hinny did more good than most quacks. As her hinny used it, the spirit game brought risk and enemies.

The second the door clicked shut, Braddie said, 'We need to run now, hinny. Tha man will stop at nothing. He's been made Great Laird of the Chamber Pot, or some such stupid title.'

'Dear heart, we discussed this. The higher his rise, my angel, the more brutal his fall. We shall find the evidence of the lass's murder, and then he will be powerless against us. I smell other dark deeds. Did Lady Violet's mother cross him and die? Even proof of the arson would destroy his career.'

Honeybee drove her crazy. Her wit, her determination, how she could see a ray of light in anything... Her hinny dazzled her with delight. But always, this reckless waltz with danger, along the edge of an abyss.

'You think the blue terrors and the judges and the high and mighty care about some long-dead common lass? We have no proof. The next time, he might kill us.'

'Method will be our saviour, my darling. I would love to open that villain, Jabez Trephine. I am sure that grinning head holds dozens of Sir Charles's worst secrets.'

Braddie began to boil. 'Next time, it will be a knife in the back.'

'But the important papers were at the bank, or in Mr Oliphant's safe. And, dear heart, I wish them joy with your clever accounts.' Braddie's code lived in her head. She'd begun to reconstruct them with her hinny's help.

Time for sense. 'We should call in every promise, everything we are owed, and go.'

'And let Sir Charles murder his wife? A patroness who is doubtless even now wiping her eye at our misfortune and opening her coffers?'

Did Honoria chase the lass or the gold? Hard to tell. Everything about this screamed danger.

Braddie tried to breathe, half strangled by her hinny's endlessly roving eye and the way she enjoyed the jealousy it stirred up. Their vows had been simple and Braddie kept them. Why hurt her with these dalliances?

'The lion tried to bite your head off, and you still want to poke him.'

'Dear heart, let us stop the beast having us for lunch. Nothing more. I am tired, let us talk later.'

'You would not do this for a commoner.'

Her hinny flushed. 'Dearest, you are unjust. I risked jail for the railwayman's widow, that ungrateful slattern. Do you not recall? Or Carlisle, facing down that dreadful man, so that poor woman could take her child?'

How much of this obsession chased money and rank, and how much romance? How much rode that giddy and stumbling horse, her hinny's conscience?

In someone else's house, Braddie could not slam the door or raise her voice. Honoria had danced into her life and showed her happiness. And not a day went past without her dear heart goading her to fury.

Braddie picked up *A Plea for Atheism*, its cover singed, then sat in the chair and held it so her hinny could see it. She would read the strongest parts aloud and threaten to discuss it in the servants' hall. Mocking Honoria's piety was the only goad which always drew blood.

A trusted man brought Mrs Ashton's mail, and she knew one envelope contained another. Mrs Ashton enjoyed Lady Violet's scent before opening the letter. Words were pleasant, but what better statement of regard than this substantial cheque from the lady's personal account. A monstrous cloud but what a silver lining! Mrs Ashton must dazzle with her reply – vague threats of danger, an air of scandal and hostile powers. Something that might flush out more money. Disguises and spies were not cheap.

Mrs Ashton must contrive to meet Trephine, safely and unguarded.

What was Miss Shilling doing in London, and which Harley Street address did they visit? Did she smell scandal, which could topple the most ambitious man?

Mrs Ashton looked at the directory of doctors and sighed. The Creator in His munificence gave logic to women as well as men. Why would Sir Charles take Miss Shilling unless she was the patient? Yet, for a man that wealthy and well connected, any Harley Street man would hurry to visit the house. Therefore, either this required immobile equipment – even the gentry were known to travel to the dentist – or Charles had some other reason.

Obvious! If a doctor visited, the house would know his name. From the name, it might be possible to learn his specialism. Did Sir Charles want to hide what ailed Miss Shilling from the household? Perhaps the visit to the street of doctors had to be under a pseudonym.

Time to spend silver to reap gold. She dressed Maisie and an associate in servants' clothes. Then they worked Harley Street, attending those specialists who fitted the criteria, the most likely first.

'Miss Shilling's compliments, so sorry for the inconvenience, did she drop her little prayer book when she was here? She came with Sir Charles Barrington-Stewart, Monday, and we have looked everywhere else...'

Miss Shilling was nobody, but surely that darling of the papers Sir Charles would be recognised under whatever name.

Meanwhile, Mrs Ashton schemed to reach either the young coachman or the dithering companion. Perhaps she should confront Trephine at his home, with Mr Oliphant or another. She had found an old friend of Lady Violet's mother, now living in reduced circumstances in a Midlands rectory, and begun a correspondence, but she would need to go in person to unlock crucial secrets. Letters to Lady Herncastle's friends and acquaintances – gleaned from charity work and social columns – had fallen on stony ground. This is where a patroness proved invaluable.

Mrs Ashton made slow progress on all these; her swift spies got to the answer from Harley Street before she did. Sir Charles had chosen to taken Miss Shilling to a glorious star in the diseases of women.

Oh, she smelt something ripe indeed.

Armed with a pseudonymous appointment, Mrs Ashton went to Harley Street. She did so object to a male doctor for these most personal of matters. She had chosen the trailblazing Dr Elizabeth Garrett Anderson for her own care – they said a hundred women were now studying medicine. How wonderful.

Her first wild intention was to fake a disorder and let the man examine her. Braddie slammed her great hand on the table in anger and disgust. No! The second plan was simpler and less intrusive.

Mrs Ashton had to pass an ordinary doorman and ascend to the first floor. A woman in a kind of refined nurse's uniform answered the door.

No doubt Sir Charles had also consulted the man about Lady Violet's inability to produce an heir. The doctor was a stretched, spindly, starved-looking kind of man with a jutting jaw.

'Sir, I do hope you can support the Committee to Abolish the Contagious Diseases Acts. It is an outrage to women of all classes, an outrage against Christian morality...'

The law allowed the authorities to seize any woman on whim, and subject her to an intimate examination, in case she suffered from a venereal disease. Women of every class backed the campaign against it.

The man looked solemn.

'Most certainly, I am with your cause. Indeed, I remarked on it to Sir Charles Barrington-Stewart recently. He asked the Commons if they would tolerate their own wives and daughters suffering such assault.'

Mrs Ashton blinked at the glorious opportunity and leaped.

'So inspiring. He is a great support to our cause. You must know Miss Esme Shilling.' And, her hand an inch from his, she opened him.

The man kept an iron face and sidestepped the question. She barely heard his smooth lie. The most obvious and the most profitable truth. Esme Shilling was pregnant and frightened by her state. Sir Charles was fiercely attentive to Miss Shilling, and worried for the baby's health. His wife could not know. Neither the specialist nor Mrs Ashton had the slightest doubt what that meant: Sir Charles believed himself the father.

Mrs Ashton tried to fit together a new picture.

'Are you all right?' Suspicion of her motives.

'A momentary pain. Some faintness.' She needed to divert him. In any case, lights before her eyes and a stabbing at her temples. Back to the wall, she had used her power too much these last days.

He helped her, then wrote a modest cheque to the campaign. She thanked him and left.

The public Sir Charles took many positions Mrs Ashton admired. An ardent supporter of universal education, he wanted the female age of consent raised to sixteen and he held advanced views on married women's property. His vigorous energy championed the latest laws to protect workers from injury.

We are angels raised from mud, she mused. Then the most obvious point hit her. Suppose Lady Violet died soon. Sir Charles could marry Esme – and he would have his heir.

CHAPTER 10
Betrayal and Revelation

Their rooms in the banker's house, close to suppertime

That vision of Sir Charles, his hands round Lady Violet's neck – it haunted her. The terror in the last gasping breath of that other girl. Why was Braddie so unreasonable?

'Is an innocent woman nothing to you? If she were to die, and Sir Charles to remarry... he has his heir.'

Braddie held a new letter from the lady in question away from her true love's hands. 'Twenty-eight miners died in Durham yesterday – an explosion. Two paragraphs in the paper, and the owner won't even pay for tha coffins. Where is your worry about their widows and bairns?'

How unjust! A miner's widow, a railwayman's orphan, would always touch her heart and open her purse. She could think about two things at once.

'Lady Violet came to us for help.'

'She'll be the death of us. I'm tired of hearing of her.'

There came a soft knock at the door. The banker's wife called, 'Are you all right? Is it bad news?'

'A difficult spirit,' Mrs Ashton called. 'Do not be alarmed.'

You could not reason with Braddie in such a state.

'Are you frightened she will send me her garter? Read the letter, I have no secrets from you.'

Braddie, stone-faced, began to read. In a few moments, her frown turned to surprise. On the second page, she whistled, and as soon as she had reached the end, she began to read aloud.

> *My dear Mrs Ashton,*
>
> *I feel that only you could offer spiritual guidance, as such good spirits do flock around you. The matter is one requiring the utmost discretion. I am betrayed by two people of whom I had a right to expect more, the bonds of fidelity and love and friendship broken, the laws of God and man defied. I dare not write what has occurred, but it leaves me desperate and alone.*

'Well, your fancy-piece knows what her husband has been up to.'

Mrs Ashton struggled to find another interpretation. 'Keep going.'

> Your letters are wise and prophetic. I can now see that the spirits told you of this trouble, and something of what it might bring. How

> I need your assistance!
>
> You asked about untimely deaths to see what troubled spirits haunt me. This house has been here long, and it has its share of unhappy stories. Of course, my dear mother, and before I ever knew of the house, my husband's older brother drowned in a boating accident. A century past, they say a servant girl hanged herself, perhaps from the shame that now falls close to me. How harshly men treat women, and how fierce is my husband's anger. I must confess for the first time how truly frightened I am.
>
> My dear Mrs Ashton, I need a wise woman to guide me.

Mrs Ashton's mind whirled. Look for advantage of course, but also, what might happen? For a divorce, a man need prove only one act of adultery, but a wife must prove other vicious crimes as well. Easier to destroy Sir Charles's hopes of higher office through scandal than for Lady Violet to leave the bonds of this awful marriage.

> *My husband is detained in London, he thinks two weeks or more. Please can you contrive to visit me, not in the house where too many eyes watch and to which the other party might return? We might seek truth from the restless*

> *spirits, and you could offer me your guidance. I have such need of it.*

'Then there's some Bible piffle, sin and all that. Might mean something to you, hinny.'

Braddie had an unreadable look. The endearment suggested her temper had cooled a little. An open invitation, funds, and a wronged woman to use against Sir Charles. Danger, but also opportunity.

'Then it finishes. She should write for the stage.'

> *I am a weak woman – betrayed, terrified, friendless, and alone. I feel surrounded by great danger. My dear Mrs Ashton, you and your power are my only hope.*

Mrs Ashton held out her hand and took the letter.

Braddie growled, 'Unsafe at any price, you fool. Tha bank balance means nothing when you are dead.'

'Dearest heart.'

'You're on your own,' Braddie said, stern as a northern crag. 'Go, get strangled by that man, or shot in the night. See if I care.'

Mrs Ashton never needed to open Braddie and never wanted to. Certain signs hinted that Braddie might be wooed to some sort of compromise. Not tonight, not with what they knew now. But it would come.

She read the letter herself now. The words so desperate, the hand a little faster but still controlled. Reared in the hothouse of wealth, her sweet little prospect suffered the cold winds of wickedness. Could Mrs Ashton's revenge and new fortune come from those pretty hands?

'Enough, my dearest.' Mrs Ashton took Braddie's hands. 'How you labour for my comfort and fear for my safety. I am blessed beyond any woman of high rank.'

She raised those hands to her mouth, kissed them, then a touch of her tongue between thumb and finger... a promise.

The bounty of pleasure never palled. An hour devoted to giving her dear heart joy always helped to sway her. It would be some endeavour to find where they could do it, perhaps safest at the house of their theatrical friends.

Mrs Ashton resolved to be bold. She would put a noose around Sir Charles's neck, in one fashion or another.

Oh, how great the joy of being right. Mrs Ashton grasped the letter from the Secretary of the Philosophical Society.

'Dear heart, I have found the murder.'

Braddie looked up from her sewing.

'A village lass strangled in eastern Belldownshire, the summer before Sir Charles went to Oxford. They say the police made the most dreadful mess of the investigation, and it was never solved.'

'Near his family home?'

'No, that lies to the west. But he might well have been staying in Grennard, between the two. My friend writes that the editor of the local paper covered the infamous case as a young reporter. Sweetness, he keeps an archive on it. A visit to this Mangold's Wood should satisfy me this is the crime. Be not afraid! Sir Charles has no reason to be out of London while he is performing the Parliamentary gavotte.'

'He owns the town,' Braddie snapped. Indeed, the family wealth started in its breweries and brickworks.

'I will take Maisie, and you may stay if you prefer. Penelope at the loom.' The couple needed someone younger and faster to watch, to run errands, to be a witness and shin a drainpipe if needed. Again, Mrs Ashton must invest for a greater reward.

'My life, you will not go, I won't let you. Listen, woman, I see raging trouble ahead.'

'They brought fire and death into our house. We have a potent weapon... Let him imagine the coarse hemp round his neck.'

'He's Ald Nick himself, but we should be awa'. He'll ne'er be tried for his crimes. Ne'er.'

'Nonsense. He could not be sure of that. Besides, he has enemies – in the press, and in all three parties in the House. You may despise the Prime Minister, but even his acrobatic conscience cannot swallow murder.' Mrs Ashton swung into the argument with Braddie with great enthusiasm. Victory was inevitable, since she would simply pack to go, and in time Braddie would have no choice but to capitulate. She always did.

The banker's house was watched night and day; she must assume by agents of Sir Charles. Mrs Ashton used quieter moments to concoct a story that would put his agents off their trail.

Chapter 11
A Journey and a Vision

London, after Easter

We spied Mrs Ashton at her Easter devotions in an ancient cathedral, gloriously attired for the Resurrection and as ever determined to take the Eucharist. It appears that life in London wearies her, and we learn from a most reliable source that she will soon depart for the Continent without settling her bills. We know it is true for she utterly denies it. Her creditors should move quickly, and as for the Continent, we think kindly enough of the honest people of Abroad that they must prepare for the invasion. Veni vidi fraudavi. I came, I saw, I picked your pocket.

The Orb

Two old theatre friends of Mrs Ashton – the sweetest couple she knew – were as David and Jonathon, as King James and his George. They had offered the blasphemous parrots sanctuary, and they were delighted to play a jolly charade in female dress. It was not Braddie and Mrs Ashton who took a hansom to the railway station at dawn, but a couple who could pass. On the Dover train, in a first-class carriage, two women would disappear and two men would surface.

Later, Mrs Ashton, Braddie and Maisie settled in another first-class railway carriage, Mrs Ashton luxuriating in her success. Their path lay a couple of hours north, while Sir Charles's agents chased the decoys to Dover. Mrs Ashton wore mourning and a thin gauze veil; the fashionable full mourning veil must be avoided, being so thick as to disable her – and besides, the dye gave her a skin rash and a cough. Maisie played a servant, with extra black ribbons. Mrs Bradshaw wore a matron's uniform and a cape, and her green glasses quite altered the shape of her face.

Maisie had been out of London once, a day trip to Margate. She had shed tears to part with her little family under the tender care of Mrs Colquhoun, but her eyes were long dry. The spirit of adventure gripped her, she had her nose to the window, soaking up suburban villas and then the countryside.

Hard years for country folk, the papers said. Not only cheap corn but now frozen meat from the Americas undercutting prices. Mrs Ashton knew the sordid depths of poverty, but she had no grand scheme to cure it.

Grennard. This cluster of smoking chimneys, this sprawl of sooty red brick thrown up without thought, old streets clamouring with wagons and drays. The town was a byword for the change of this vigorous and progressive century – a riverside town surviving the canals but swollen to great ugliness by the railway and the business it brought. With coughing smoke and crowded slums, it formed a hideous suburb of Purgatory.

The newspaper offices were at the heart of the town, where a pretty church, a market square, and a few streets of picturesque older buildings showed how it might once have been. The streets were clogged with modern traffic.

The editor expected them, a twinkle-eyed sceptic with vast mutton-chop whiskers.

'Mrs Leveret? Delighted, delighted. Come into my parlour. Hm, the girl should wait elsewhere. Delicate ears.'

Maisie rolled her eyes and claimed her position at the window with a book. Mrs Ashton found the parlour was too hot, but an ink-fingered boy brought a tray of tea.

The women sat, and the editor followed.

'Grace Overmorrow. Such wickedness, and such a drama,' he said. 'And exactly what brings your interest?'

'I heard whispers on the spirit plane,' Mrs Ashton said. 'They compel me. A restless, unavenged girl, I believe.'

The man smirked and smoothed his whiskers. Men were so predictable. He said, 'We have had experts in your arts come from London, saying they would find the murderer. They wandered the woods for days but never found anything of use. It made copy anyway. What do you need to know?'

His interest revealed the carnal. Without shame, she used her eyes, her words, the frequent placing of a hand on her ample breast to fuel his ardour. 'I am so grateful. Well, who was she? What did the investigation find? Why did it go astray?'

'Some of the details are distressing,' the man said, rather relishing it.

Mrs Ashton said, hand to breast, 'I am an Army widow. I have seen the troublesome side of life. Things in the dusty alleyways of the East that are not for delicate stomachs. And Mrs Vaughn has worked for the great healing temples of London. The angels who bind the wounds see the depths of fallen mankind.'

'Well,' said the man and began a well-rehearsed and detailed story. He licked his lips just a little too often.

Mrs Ashton's notes later read: *Kindly girl – bit simple – no enemies – family distraught. Body discovered cold in the woods – killed the day before. Hoofmarks on the track. Last seen in a village four miles away. Village horrified.*

'Yet they found no evidence of violation?'

'No, neither her clothes nor her person,' the editor said, pausing to sip tea. 'A vile murder but she was spared that. Her local suitors were easily discounted. The police arrested a villainous-looking peddler, then chased down an Irish tinker, then a commercial traveller from London. The facts proved inconvenient. An addled drunk claims he saw a well-dressed young man on horseback that dusk, riding west.'

As the bloodhound on the scent, 'What came of that?' Mrs Ashton said.

'A fortnight after the tragedy, he was entirely confused as to the day.'

It fitted. Sir Charles could have killed the lass and been in Grennard by sunset.

'And in the end, they got poor Stammering Will, a local lad and not strong in the head. Dead now he is, poor boy. He had terrible fits and didn't remember, and he had a locket the family identified as hers. He said that he had found it. The poor lad had been terrified twelve hours in a cell and by the end he didn't know if it was Thursday or Sunday. He put his X to a confession. No witnesses, no proof apart from the locket, while three farmers Will worked for refused to believe he would harm a fly and said so. The simple ones are often good with children and horses. Anyway, the magistrates sent him to the Assizes, and we guessed he would hang.'

'But he didn't,' Mrs Ashton said.

'Well, a bright young lawyer came from London, hired by the farmer who let him sleep in his barn. We all turned out to hear the case and this man of law... Well, I saw Dancing Ted Buxton in the boxing ring once, and this lawyer kept knocking the prosecution to the floor.

'First the defence made the police go through all their fumbling. He produced two great brain doctors from London who said Will's confession couldn't be relied on, then he brought two women in court with the same locket, and another who said she'd lost one like it. Gentle as an old friend, he got Pa Overmorrow to admit in tears that he couldn't be sure the locket they found was Grace's.

'All this time, Will stood quivering, feeling the rope round his neck. The prosecution was rattled by now, and the defence gave it everything.' The man declaimed from memory, '"This simple innocent stands at the gates of death and only you will decide if he passes through. No one saw him with the girl, no one saw him near the crime, no one has seen him do violence against any woman or child. This poor witless soul, more child than man, seized by force, bullied into signing a paper he couldn't read confessing to a crime he has no memory of committing..."

'The judge scowled at the prosecution and briskly laid bare their failings. The jury took twenty minutes to find the lad not guilty. Even Grace's family were relieved.'

'So, no one ever found the murderer?'

'No. A funny business. The farmer says he paid for the defence, but surely those fine London doctors and lawyers were more than his pocket could stand. The drunker I got him, the less I believed him. He's dead now. The trial was quite the event, people came from all round the county to watch and several of the quality from London.'

'An extraordinary story,' Mrs Ashton said, marshalling her thoughts. 'Have you summarised who came to the trial, persons of any note?'

'I have the list and you may copy it.'

'How best could we visit the spot? Hire a carriage, I guess?'

'Yes, then it's a brisk walk from the road. I would be pleased to take you.'

'Could we manage it today?'

'I'll do the same as I did last time.'

'Last time?' Braddie said, the first words she had uttered.

'Yes, another enquiring mind, two years ago. A little more, I think.'

'May I ask who?'

A big smirk. 'I will respect your privacy, Mrs Leveret, as you would expect. So, I will protect others.'

Mrs Ashton hesitated before using her power. She found him unattractive and too interested in her, and his zeal about the old case was unpleasant. She had no other option. She laid her hand on his.

'Of course,' she said, opening him. A late-middle-aged, determined, wealthy woman stood before the editor, and he had sworn secrecy about her visit. Mrs Ashton jolted with the shock. She had seen the woman's face in Lady Violet's mind and in newspaper reports: Lady Herncastle, Violet's beloved mother.

Her mind reeled. Lady Herncastle had been insistent, learning of every detail and yet said nothing of why. She read the list of prominent attendees at the trial with obvious frustration – maybe she was looking for a specific individual – and she brought out a glass to look at each sketch in the paper.

Lady Violet's mother had been looking for Grace's killer. Then she had died, little more than a month later, under Sir Charles's roof.

Not proof. But Sir Charles was a monster, and for a moment Mrs Ashton considered fleeing. Maybe even to America. But Lady Violet faced such deadly danger.

'Please, may we visit the scene of the crime?' she said. 'It will be invaluable to my research.'

The man consulted the clock. 'I'll plead with Cook for a hamper, and delay showing you the papers until this evening.'

Mrs Ashton expected Maisie to be bored and urchinly but found her in great good humour. Out of town, she drank air fresh with country smells – some advantage to air not tainted with soot. The sun sat lower in the sky when the trap reached the junction. Maisie asked a string of questions, which avoided the need for adult conversation. Fields were green, cattle and a few sheep grazed, spring blossom in the hedgerows and the trill of birds. Yet silence fell between those on the journey, this monstrous pilgrimage.

Mrs Ashton changed her shoes, took the man's arm, and they set off on the trail. The enormity of the crime hung over them. That and the man's modest anxiety that he might lose the way, or that the exercise might bring back his heartburn. She wondered how much the scene would have changed.

Through the woods, Maisie throwing out a question here and there. 'That, my dear, is a cuckoo! Surely you must have heard one when we went to the Heath? And, ah, *Mrs Vaughn* will know more of these flowers and their uses than I will.'

Then the slow realisation... Here was the spot. Spring not summer, decades later, but no mistaking the old oak up on the rise. The scene as Sir Charles remembered it fell clear in her mind. The cleft in the ground started narrow but fell away and widened – it gave a glimpse, a long view of the wooded hill. The memory showed higher up; they found the girl here, the papers said, but Mrs Ashton knew she died up there, with that view behind her.

The sceptical editor was testing her.

'The body lay here but she died elsewhere. Up and to the right, with her back to the vista.'

'By Jove,' the man said, impressed. 'That's my theory. I think the monster threw her poor corpse down, but then – perish the beast – he realised that she was still visible from the path. Came down to cover her with branches. Let me show you how I think it happened.' He bounded like some great dog now, eager on the scent.

For a few breaths Mrs Ashton thought she saw a country girl, somewhat like the sketch in the papers. Grace standing where she had died, a face she would never forget – in an eerie calm, not in the violent act of dying. The girl looked down at Mrs Ashton as if she knew her. Mrs Ashton shivered, and the girl was gone.

Mrs Ashton's poetic soul did not make her a fool. It must be her imagination in the tyrant's grip of this old crime, a pure fancy that summoned its victim.

Mrs Ashton climbed after the editor, picking up her skirts. In one silent gaze she had won an argument with dear Braddie: they had been right to come. But she sent a hopeful prayer for guidance spiralling to heaven, like a message tied to a kite. She had no clarity what to do. She must write to Lady Violet warning her. She dared not be specific – something about danger lurking. How far could she go without endangering her client?

Unless she revealed her secret, she had no proof. And revealing her power would bring many more dangers.

Chapter 12

A Decision and a Division

The St George Inn, Grennard, that evening

Maisie and her employers were eating supper in their room. A tired conversation limped along between the adults, while Maisie ate and listened. What had happened to poor Grace's family? Old Adam Overmorrow had died within the year, the editor said, and the widder and family had sailed to Canada, funded by a public subscription. The family were Chapel, and their minister had kept in touch for a couple of years. Then a new minister came, and the letters stopped.

Maisie found people interesting and the two odd birds more than most. Mrs A had been so shook up at the murder site, like a cat on a hot stove. She had known the fatal spot, which had to be trickery, not magic or speaking to spirits. The editor man got all excited, in a way his wife might not have liked. How had Mrs A known? But if her employer could raise spirits, why hadn't she raised Maisie's poor Ma for real?

Mrs Ashton looked thoughtful. 'We know that Sir Charles killed Grace and it seems likely he killed Lady

Violet's mother. Consider this. His elder brother died, and the baronetcy, the wealth, and the seat in Parliament all passed to Sir Charles. Were it not for those witnesses, I would wonder... Cain slayed Abel for less.'

'We can't prove any of it,' Maisie said. 'We gotta make him confess.' Maisie knew about torture, but to do it herself? Her guts churned their opposition.

'I cannot see how. Supposing we cannot prove it, we must get Lady Violet to safety.' Mrs A's frown flickered, a hint of a smile. 'Thank goodness she has her own money. Could Sir Charles stop her living with her righteous godfather, for example?'

How did the pair of fakers know Sir Charles killed the girl? And yet not have a witness or proof? *How* did they know that lady had visited?

'How did Lady Herncastle get here?' she asked. 'A posh lady would never travel alone.'

'Eat your greens,' Braddie said. Braddie liked fruit and vegetables undercooked and tough, like she was, and she was enthusiastic about making children eat them.

Mrs Ashton smiled. 'Another good question, dear child. Alas the editor, so fond of each detail of this horrid case, doesn't remember. I asked him most assiduously. Lady Herncastle made her own arrangements.'

Maisie frowned. 'A posh lady who gets unwell wouldn't travel without another woman. Probably a man too.'

'I would assume so. So, tomorrow we will seek out Captain Cairngorm, dear comrade of Lady Violet's far-off brother, and discuss how we may safely see her. And persuade her to find a safer refuge.'

Braddie scowled, as the Thames scowls in winter rain.

Immediately after breakfast, Braddie – silent and angry – drove Mrs Ashton and Maisie to seek Cairngorm's help. They found a pleasant, well-to-do home on the less-smoked edge of town, from which came the distinctive noise of a child attacking a piano one key at a time. Mrs Ashton sent in a card, 'regarding Lady Barrington-Stewart', which produced the man himself in only ten minutes. Young, weather-beaten, and upright, he walked briskly with a stick and a stiff leg. He greeted them with a slight twinkle and brought them into a masculine study. They sat, and Mrs Ashton declined refreshment, to Maisie's obvious irritation.

'Dear Captain, I am to remind you of the pergola, and the roses from Alice,' Mrs Ashton said.

'Aha.' He grinned. 'Pass, friend.'

'Lady Barrington-Stewart said that you would help us without question, with complete discretion, and that she would bear any expense.'

'I will indeed,' he said, more serious now. 'What do you require?'

'I need to see her at Corwood Manor and return, without my arrival in the area being known. I might need to leave expeditiously. I must avoid her husband knowing or obstructing us. He will doubtless be furious if he finds out.'

'Well, a dear friend from my youth speaks and so I must obey. As for Barrington-Stewart' – he looked stern as a general ordering a charge – 'I have no fear of his famous temper or worldly power.'

That was encouraging, but she needed to be sure.

'I should say, Mrs Ashton, I reserve my judgement as to your beliefs,' he said.

'I don't ask more.' Mrs Ashton edged closer, which surprised him. He went on.

'Know that once your client and my dear friend was everything to me. I was something to her – something fine, but not enough.'

An old school friend of her brother, indeed!

He looked away for a moment, then he smiled a little. 'I am blessed. My darling wife has made me the happiest man on earth. I have watched from afar these five years, as a dear friend, and Violet's marriage is not a happy one. Her letters the last year have alarmed me. A man should stand as a shield between his wife and misfortune, not blame her for it. And that man, I know, has raised his stick to unarmed man and gentle beast alike. She is too worthy to be tarred with his name. I say to you only what I have said to his face. I wish he had proved worthy of her.'

Still on first name terms! Mrs Ashton opened him to find the inner man and the outer as one. Yes, a strong affection, but wholly honourable. She chose her words accordingly.

'Sir Charles terrifies her, he has also abused us brutally, and there is help only we can provide her.'

'Is she in danger? Might she need to leave the house?' An efficient string of thoughts, questions, and options ran through his mind.

'I hope not, but a grim possibility.'

'How I wish the dear lady would flee north, to one of her sisters.' *A cold stony gospel, he mused. Could they keep Violet from her husband forever?* 'My heart's desire is that she sue for a separation. But she must prove cruelty and I believe the brute is too cunning to strike her.'

Could she talk Lady Violet into faking an injury?

Cairngorm regained his composure. 'As to your travel, too many prying eyes at Bellingley station. I am there regularly on my uncle's business, so unremarkable, but you may be watched for. Every third man in town is under his thumb. We will drive from the stop before, and use the King and Lion, a country place. The landlord is a fine old Tory who would not give Sir Charles so much as the time, even at sword-point.'

The briskness of his answer surprised her. Clearly, he had long-standing plans to reach Violet. He went on, 'I can get an unseen message to her. We won't hear tomorrow; we must allow for Sunday. So, God willing, Tuesday will be the day.'

'Will you take us to the house?'

His face was disappointment itself.

'I had to swear not to. Sir Charles is not one to have his wife's former suitor around and my face is known. Of course, just prove she is in danger, or let her command me, then I would go. Now, you must meet Mrs Cairngorm and the children.'

Mrs Ashton had a sudden thought. 'You must have known Lady Barrington-Stewart's mother. What did you think of her?'

'A kind-hearted woman, good works among the unfortunate and all that. Perhaps a little shocked by the changes in the world. But we need to learn.'

Her mother had been on the trail of murder. Surely, she had confided in someone? Mrs Ashton's disappointment at so little must have showed.

'Let me say this. Both of the dear lady's parents thought she could do better than me for a husband, in wealth and rank, and her mother told me so, with great firmness. Then she sighed, and said, "If in a year she asks for permission to marry you, I will do my best to put your case to my husband." A rare woman, I think.

The King and Lion was a fine old inn. The couple commanded Maisie to the attic room, so the women could have it out in the better bedroom. Braddie had been in a foul temper all day and she sprung her ultimatum.

'I'm not daft enough to stick my head in tha man's jaws. You sneak around the werewolf if you like. I'm not going.'

Mrs Ashton's face burned.

'What do you mean, you're not going?'

Braddie shook with emotion. 'You'll kill us all. Ride alone into that man's lair... Ald Nick, that murderer. Every soul in his pocket... owning all the land for miles around... just for you chasing tha fancy skirt and her gold. I bet ten shilling she'll ask us to tak her awa...' She wiped away an angry tear. 'He'll set tha law on us. Prison would kill me.'

Heavens, dear heart, how ridiculous. Braddie would rage, and cry, and threaten not to come, and in the end come round. She always did, and with such bad grace. 'We know Sir Charles is detained in London, dearest. We have Violet's latest message confirming it, so the sooner we go, the safer. We go disguised, as charitable ladies of Violet's acquaintance. We have transport of our own...'

Braddie thundered. 'You don't care about the danger, to you or me or the lass. All high and mighty, with your witch's power. I'd wish your gift gone to hell for five pounds of common sense.'

Such danger lay in discussing her gift in any public place. Is the window shut? How childish.

Mrs Ashton tried to touch her dear heart's cheek, to console her. Braddie pushed her hand away, tears flowing now.

'Dearest, we must never...'

'You use me,' Braddie said, and her hinny gasped. 'No servant, no mistress? You alwa' get your own way. Stretch our necks out on a butcher's block. You ignore my warnings. You laugh at me, scattering money to chase moonbeams.'

Oh, hurtful canards. Mrs Ashton's whole torso flushed hot with anger. No truth in any of this.

'Dearest, we decide all things together.' Braddie's eyes rolled, and she snorted. Change tack. 'Our delightful cottage will take money, my sweet one. Fine wishes will not be enough. We cannot save on skimmed milk. Violet could achieve our dreams with a single cheque.'

'You don't want that life, you never have. You just lead me on, time after time. I must stop pretending.'

'Who is pretending, dearest? Use sense, I can hardly take Maisie alone. We are such a team. I badly need your wise head.' Bad as this tantrum was, they had weathered worse. On a matter of this importance, Braddie would always follow.

'You don't care what I think. I followed you like Naomi, into foreign lands and the temples of wickedness, and maybe we did a little good. Certainly, a dung heap of trouble. But you are queen of yourself, you truly are.'

Mrs Ashton lost her last caution.

'I must say, dearest, this is an ungrateful and spiteful shaping of our time together. How we laboured together for both our benefit. When have I ever gone against your wishes?' Mrs Ashton put her hand up as Braddie drew a great breath, and she kept talking, louder and more forceful. 'I am speaking, dearest. How pleasant our life has been, and now you abandon me when I need you, at the point of success in securing our future. This is selfish, dearest, and unkind, and you are defeating what you claim to want, that blessed retirement, through childish jealousy. I feel one of my heads coming on.'

'You wave tha headaches around like a chorus-girl's fan,' Braddie said.

Mrs Ashton gasped. 'We will sleep on it, and tomorrow I pray some of us will be in better tempers. I will leave for Corwood Manor tomorrow exactly as planned. You can support me or abandon me, as you decide.'

'I'll take the girl back with tha Cairngorm. If you care about your promises and fine words, if a day of our eight years matters, you will come too. Send Violet the best argument you can to leave his house. Tha duty done.'

'What an absurdity, dearest.' Soothing Braddie might mean a good night's sleep. 'Let us seek wisdom in rest. Let me do your hands...'

Braddie grabbed the bottle. 'I'll do it mysen and sleep in the girl's room.'

Tuesday dawned delightful and fair. Mrs Ashton scarcely could taste her coffee at breakfast, taken in a discreet side room. Braddie stood as firm as that great rock on the moor, red-eyed and silent. Their possessions had been divided into different cases, and a scrupulous division of the cash. How would Braddie manage? She had no bank. What work could she get? Should she scribble a character for her dear heart, as for a servant?

'Dearest, do this just for me.'

'I won't go. You corrupted Maisie's mind with your poison and she's going with you. Her blood will be on your hands. How will her family manage?'

Mrs Ashton paused. But Maisie would be so useful, and they would be back at the inn by nightfall.

Maisie demolished prodigious quantities of bacon and toast. Braddie, in tears, tried one last plea for her to stay safe. 'Wealth and adventure,' the lass said. Braddie strode out, her stick rapping.

Cairngorm entered, flourishing a telegram.

'"Prime goods and delivery as described." A trusted London friend confirms that the wicked beast is in his London lair. Is Mrs Bradshaw ready?'

Mrs Ashton tried to swallow her eggs. Braddie and her cottage and her temper and her sullen drinking. Her foolish jealousies. It was Boulogne all over again. And Cardiff, and the first time they were in the Burning Bird. Honestly, Braddie was so difficult.

How untrue that Mrs Ashton's chivalry extended only to the young, wealthy, and beautiful. She listened assiduously to the wisdom of her dear heart, from time to time, and had on occasion been glad of it. Time for the unpalatable truth.

'Dear Captain, Mrs Bradshaw is declining to come.' Cairngorm's vast astonishment needed placating. The world turned upside down, a servant refusing an order. 'I should say, she has no family. Truly, she is my old companion as much as my servant, with no one else in the world, and I have indulged her too much. Might your man be spared to drive myself and the girl? Bradshaw says she will go back to Grennard, but that is bluster.'

Cairngorm took three breaths to answer. 'It's not for me to run your household. Yes, my man will do it for you. Tell him as little as possible, for his own sake.'

It was late morning, and to reach Lady Violet in good time, they would need to leave. The bitter strangeness of it, with anger and tears fighting in them both. Mrs Ashton and Braddie stood behind the carriage in the yard, speaking low so none might hear them. The bags, like the women, were divided. A pose, a posture, when success lay within their grasp.

'My darling, you are throwing everything away,' Mrs Ashton said. 'The lady is a golden bridge to our future. That vapid miss is nothing to me otherwise.'

Braddie glared, wiping her eyes. 'I wish you'd see sense. In your boots, you know I'm right. We walked a long road to get here, but each wrong turn was yours. Bitter herbs and gall, but true.'

'Be with me, dearest.'

'You leave me no choice.'

Don't risk affection in public. 'Wait here, dearest. I will be there not an hour longer than needed. It will make our swift reunion easier.' Mrs Ashton held optimism in all things, but would things ever be the same?

A long pause. 'I will stay here.' A useful concession.

Mrs Ashton knew she was right. She was no butcher or bailiff to be subjected to Braddie's granite will. Foolish, to feel her eyes water. She got into the carriage with Maisie, turned her head away, and only produced her handkerchief when out of Braddie's sight. Assured there was only one good route from the tavern to Corwood Manor, Mrs Ashton had the man wait for an hour at the junction while Maisie, in her best clothes, explored the meadows and asked questions. An hour later, still no Braddie, and they must not be late. The carriage set off again.

'I think I need a share in this endeavour,' Maisie said.

What astounding cheek! Offended and pleased in equal measure, she responded, 'My dear, your per diem is generous, and we pay Mrs Colquhoun more than generously, as well. Many of your fellows would have been cheaper. Do not overreach.'

'I am the best. And bringing a wicked murdering baronet to justice for long-forgotten crimes... I need a detective's pay, for danger money. And the lady can pay it.' Maisie was deadly serious.

Mrs Ashton mused. 'If there is a profit – *if* – then perhaps we can find some modest bonus.'

'I could go on strike.' Maisie grinned. The lass so reminded Mrs Ashton of herself at fourteen, ragged and thirsting for knowledge, knowing nothing would be easy.

'I would have to leave you by the road. We will discuss this when we have our profit.'

Birds sang, and Mrs Ashton looked forward to her encounter, the riches it would bring. But what did the future hold? A troublesome light shone, which she tried to ignore. Braddie's accusations held some truth. Was she as gentle and generous to Braddie as she told herself? Life without Braddie would be hard.

She checked her disguise. A sombre dress. The hat, a wig, and the glasses would need only acting and a little artifice.

She would prove Charles a brute, ensure Violet's safety, and enlist her aid to bring him to justice. And, richly rewarded, Braddie would admit her error.

CHAPTER 13
A Patroness Awaits

The grounds of Corwood Manor, later that day

They entered the grounds in good time. Mrs Ashton admired the curves and views, the park and woods designed by man and only finished off by God. Doubtless the original owners had moved whole villages out of sight. Braddie would lecture her on that injustice, or the enclosure of the commons, or the wealth from slavery, or maybe cheer on the courageous Zulus defending their homes against the British.

Corwood Manor was soon in view, its classical glory ruling the panorama with quiet authority. A wide Palladian front, extravagant in its use of a honey-coloured stone hewn far away, its columns glowing in the brief sunlight. The balustrade around the roof suggested a builder who liked to stand and view from the highest point. Sir Charles's father – his wealth from trade – had bought it from a bankrupt peer. Neither Charles nor his father had marred that pure vision with the later Gothic enthusiasm for pinnacles and buttresses.

This was Sir Charles's bone-scattered lair, prison tower of the woman she had come to save. She only needed proof of one murder to be rid of that man.

The lake lay north, behind the house, and to the right. A lake was as much an accessory to the aristocracy as a Japanese vase served a social climber. From the old print she had seen, the lake curved behind the house, adorned with two wooded islands. The old boating tragedy had been hidden from the house, though not the grounds.

A moment's chill in her poetic soul, but eagerness set her pulse racing. She smelled the prize. Mrs Ashton's cover – a philanthropist and her ward – required her to insist on the front door. Too long in the carriage. She needed to move.

Two servants in livery came to greet them and help her down. Grand steps rose to the first floor, the ground floor being sunk somewhat below the driveway. This plan ensured the service floor of the house had windows. There in the magnificent hallway, servants took their cloaks under the eye of ancient nobles – hunting trophies included a bear, an elk, a python, and a crocodile – and the gas lighting was of the most tasteful modern design. Sir Charles skimped nothing.

The footman walked them into a long room of magnificent paintings.

The servant announced the pseudonym. Lady Violet rose from her chair in a subdued dress of dark blue. Out of half-mourning. How did she look? Stylish, like one who had stepped from some fashion plate, or a painting. In appearance, more colour to her cheeks – real or artifice? – and a strange neutrality to her gaze. She met Mrs Ashton's stare and did not greet her.

Mrs Ashton's nerves bristled. This was staged. Something was wrong, out of place...

'My dear Mrs Ashton,' came a man's voice from behind her. 'Welcome to Corwood Manor.' Dear heaven, it was Sir Charles.

She whipped her head round and there he stood in the doorway, between her and escape. Triumphant and magnificent. Her body shook with the danger. Behind him she caught glimpses of two big women in matching grey – a species of uniform.

Rat in a trap! Towards the window, the footman. Along the room, another door in the long side. Through that came Willoughby, the faithful coachman. She wasted two breaths wondering if she could leap through a closed window in corset and heels. From the first floor, and what might she land on?

'I will be in the Chinese room, dearest,' Violet said, and turned.

This betrayal plunged a sword in her heart. She had checked every source. The papers, the telegram from London, Violet's letter. All elaborate lies. Could her power have misread honest Jack Cairngorm too?

Sir Charles walked into the room, charming and as powerful as a stalking tiger. The two women in grey followed. She had seen cheerier prison warders. Willoughby stood tall and disapproving at the other exit.

Sir Charles said, 'A sordid business. Mrs Ashton has been using my wife's name to get credit. Forged letters to stave off unpaid bills.'

'That is a lie,' Mrs Ashton said, with every ounce of conviction she could summon.

'Unfortunately, it is true,' Lady Violet said, cold and beautiful as a winter photograph. 'I have seen the letters. Please, it is too dreadful. It must be dealt with.'

How faint the hope that the servants might be turned. Mrs Ashton pleaded; only her golden tongue and her gift stood between her and destruction.

'This is slander. This man sent men to abuse me and my congregation, he had my apartments set on fire. He tried to ruin me. His dear wife is terrified of him.'

Her heart was pounding. They were outnumbered, and she could hardly run.

Sir Charles looked rueful, shrugged. 'Good heavens, she could be on the stage – an honest living at least. What a loss to the music hall.'

Violet paused at the door and looked back. 'My darling Charles, you swore.' A little too fast, a little too breathless... The first time she had showed any emotion. Sir Charles placed his hand on his heart.

'I am my wife's loyal subject in all things.'

Mrs Ashton fired her only shot. 'Sir Charles has sired a child on another woman. Lady Barrington-Stewart's life is in peril. An accident, a burglar... Sir Charles has killed twice before.'

Telling Sir Charles that she knew and threatening him with exposure. What else did she have?

Violet, without expression, turned her face and passed through the door. A China doll, a Judas in silk.

Mrs Ashton was at bay. She stared at her enemy, wishing she could call down flames on his head.

Maisie had been still and silent. Now she feinted towards the wall to their right, and one of the women tried to grab her. Maisie twisted, the two women lunged for her, and she turned. She ran, no rat followed by a pack of dogs raced faster, knocking over a vase of dried flowers and a small bust as she did to confound those following. Willoughby crouched to grab her; the man should have just shut the door. Maisie had her knife out and slashed at him, once, twice, to keep him away, not hurt him. He dropped to one knee, grunting, and she kicked him.

'Hellfire,' Willoughby said, and Maisie was out the door.

Mrs Ashton wondered if she might get past Sir Charles the way she had come. She turned and saw him crouched a little, ready to move. A boxer, an athlete, and not in corset and long skirt. Then a growl came from behind her, and an iron grip on her forearm. Unasked, her power read the woman: *malice and fury, plunging screaming women into freezing water – how the fancy ones hated that, the locked cells, those women scraping their flesh with their nails.* The woman got drunk on terror and humiliation. Ashton's gift betrayed her; immersed in the woman's mind, it froze her.

'I can't touch her,' Sir Charles said. 'She makes my skin crawl.'

The woman and the stone-eyed footman manhandled Mrs Ashton into a chair. Mrs Ashton looked away from the flushed face of her conqueror. At least the other woman in grey returned empty-handed. Maisie had got away for now. Yet this vast house thronged with servants to search for her. Braddie was right – her arrogance had put her and the lass in danger.

Willoughby rose and stared at her.

'Thank you,' Sir Charles said to him, warmly. 'That will be all.' The coachman limped out and the footman had slipped away. She now sat alone with Sir Charles and the two female brutes.

Sir Charles stood out of range of her kick.

'Oh, Mrs Ashton. We meet again. How few more times we will meet. What a choice lies before you. I could call the police, of course. I find my wife is a convincing actress when she puts her mind to it. Forgery is a serious crime.'

'She is terrified of you.' *She may turn. She may save me.* A foolish voice, grasping at straws.

Something odd passed across his face. Some warmth.

'My dear wife is a remarkable woman. I underestimated her. We have had the most tender reconciliation. But, to business.'

A pause, to enjoy it.

'These two delightful angels come from the county asylum, where I am a patron. The new warden is a man of science and reason. He says that those who see spirits fall into three categories: the frauds, the suggestable, and those with a disordered brain. We could be there after a pleasant ride. How he would enjoy having the famous Mrs Ashton under his tender care. The famous, the supernatural, and the unnatural in one patient. He will never believe you.'

There had been so many scandals. How easily the powerful might imprison a helpless woman. Surely the outcry would make the asylum more cautious?

Every sense in her was alive, alert for any clue as to what she could do. She prepared to read Sir Charles at a distance, even it would drain her. She gathered her strength. He kept talking, relishing it.

'You are in luck. Alone, I asked my wife what she wanted for our wedding anniversary. Ask the world, I said. And she asked for your life. Would you believe it?' He sighed, a little melodrama. 'In that moment of bliss, I swore it to her.'

Mrs Ashton's heart skipped a beat. Astonishing. Guilt, or desperation, or a trick...?

'She did not ask for your hag's life though. Or the urchin who has been following me, and a boy – her brother, I think. Bradshaw could be the forger. Imagine the police, the scandal, and the asylum. Confinement for her would be with the poorest of the poor unfortunates. Someone close to me has betrayed me and given you intimate details – things that you could not know. I am a foolish man, Mrs Ashton, to have told my wife I would not hurt you. But I did not promise to spare your hag.'

Oh, my dear heart, Braddie. You were right. Will I ever see you again?

Mrs Ashton could not waste time lingering on her mistake. She was on her own. Perhaps she could sell her captor her secret? Imagine his power if he had her, a slave to his ambition and his cruelty. Imagine each day wondering, will the cat use the mouse or bite it? Give this man the power, however limited, to read the minds of ministers and captains of industry, and how he could rise towards the pinnacle of power and wealth, sweeping his rivals away. In a few years, this murderer, this killer of women, might be the Queen's first minister.

To live, never knowing when she would outlive her usefulness and be killed.

Yet, Braddie a prisoner. Braddie subjected to every indignity. Mrs Ashton would crumble if her poor dear heart fell into his hands. Trembling, she knew she would do his vile bidding to keep Braddie alive. Words froze in her throat, for he might well get away with this. Surrender to him loomed.

He enjoyed watching her. 'So, I will do as I promised and then I am rid of you. This is what we will do, my dear Mrs Ashton. You will write a confession, and I will call a couple of sound men to witness it. You will say Spiritualism is a lie, that you are a fraud and a thief. That you defrauded Lady Westfall, and stole the Westmacott jewels, and hoaxed your other clients. Take particular care to explain how you deceived my wife and used her name to steal. I have studied you, Mrs Ashton, and you are the queen of liars. I expect detail, corroboration, and conviction. You will implicate Bradshaw fully in each crime. That witnessed, I will arrange for your arrest.'

He acted surprise, like a ham actor. 'Good heavens! By some stupid error, you cunning she-criminals will slip from my servants' hands! My men will take you to Liverpool, your passage paid to cross the stormy Atlantic. Papers under an assumed name for you and that hideous hag. Disappear, Mrs Ashton, like one of your party-trick ghosts. Disappear forever. The girl will go to the reformatory school in Grennard, where I am a patron. Discipline will be good for her.'

'How could I trust you?'

'Mrs Ashton, I don't care. My wife has bought your life, and today I am in a mood to please her. This is your choice: the asylum or my generous plan to get rid of you. I will offer a large reward, of course, to be sure that – should you ever return – some low sort will sell you out. I think you will choose to die in obscurity. I admire American vigour and common sense; maybe they will hang you, but I will not bet on it.'

Again, her guilt stabbed her in the chest. Dearest Braddie had been right about the risk. She had been right that Violet could not be relied on. Lust had not brought Mrs Ashton low, but hubris – a vast pride in her abilities.

Sir Charles studied her. As a cat viewed a tasty mouse, too tired to run.

'I will have Bradshaw shortly. If you wish to save that unnatural creature, your only hope is the confession. Trust me or not.'

She had nothing. Except, who knew, she might be able to talk her way out of the asylum. How could she warn Braddie? 'I need to think.'

Sir Charles smirked. 'I see you need a little time, perhaps. Ladies, escort Mrs Ashton to her quarters to think about it.'

Use her power on them to find a weakness. Use it on Sir Charles.

The women gripped her, both strong and used to force. She would be frog-marched to some hole in the ground. Dear Maisie, would she be captured too? She had brought the lass into danger, and what future did her brother and sister have without her?

She opened Sir Charles with a shudder. How he crowed, revelling in his power and triumphant at her humiliation. He would soon be rid of her. The strangest thing... Sir Charles fretted at the promise to his wife, like a tight collar, but truly, he planned to follow it. A small price to pay. Vile images flickered through his mind, gloating dreams of Mrs Ashton at the mercy of the rough women of the asylum. But mostly lust and triumph, and an extraordinary goodwill towards Violet. That reversal shocked her.

The women pulled her from the chair, without mercy.

'Wriggle and I'll break your fingers,' the sadist hissed.

She saw in his mind that Violet had sold her out. She had kissed Charles and promised to make no silly fuss about Esme and her baby. *She will still be as a sister to me, dearest. But more than anything, I want you to give me a child too. Please, my darling.* She had been truly eager these last days.

He was the Merry Monarch who bore his name, he was some conquering Caesar with his choice of the world, and he was irresistible Zeus descended from the heavens to take whichever woman he wanted.

Mrs Ashton fought the two warders younger and stronger than her, for pride, for time to think. One punched her in the stomach, driving the air from her body. Gasping, she struggled to shout her innocence before they gagged her with a stinking cloth. One tore the precious bee brooch from her dress. The other took her silver watch.

Laughing, Charles glanced at a clock and said, 'I think I will go and read to Mother. It calms her so. Don't fight the inevitable, Mrs Ashton. At dawn tomorrow, your written confession or I will finish you.'

Chapter 14

An Unexpected Ally

Corwood Manor, later

Maisie ran like a sparrow fleeing the hawk. A fortunate bird to find a key in a door, to lock it behind her. Rooms might be traps. She ran through those corridors, through maids dropping trays. One hard pull brought a suit of armour crashing down. She ran, her brain scrambling for a plan. Up might be the posh bedrooms, then above the servants' rooms and places, then the roof. Down would be servants and kitchens and cellars – and servants outside the house too. She needed wings. She should turn into a crow like in the fairytale or summon the flying chariot of the demon king Ravana.

A corner, a window, and she had reached the back of the maze. A plain staircase up and down, a corridor left and right, and a plain door ajar, with a key.

No good options, roll the dice, but she slipped through the door into a closet. Clean linen stacked to each side and its familiar smell from Mrs Colquhoun's. She locked the door behind her. Warm and dark, she went to the furthest corner. Like a trapped mouse, she made a ball of herself at the end, under the righthand shelf, and tried not to breathe.

The door rattled. 'Run and get Mrs Abernathy.' There would be a housekeeper, with a spare to every key at her waist. Then an argument, blaming each other. All she caught was the tone of it. It was a foolish place to hide. She would never see Pa or George or Tildy ever again. Horrible things would happen to Mrs Ashton and Mrs Bradshaw. They would put her away in the workhouse or even worse. Sir Charles killed people who got in his way...

Then another voice, a woman's voice, but she could not hear the words.

Then silence fell, except a gurgle of water in a pipe and a sighing like wind, not a person at all.

Time passed slowly, but perhaps five minutes or ten. Then there was a scratching on the door. A light tap followed when that produced no reply. A muffled 'Hello?'

Maisie unrolled herself and came closer. How quickly could she hide if the key turned?

A woman, a posh young one. 'I told them I saw you on the first-floor corridor. They won't have a clue – you could be anywhere by now. They will come back though.'

Silence. Maisie fingered the key. This could be a clever trap.

'Honestly. The door is locked and the key is missing. They'll be sure to come back. Charles will insist they search everywhere twice. Right now, the corridor is empty, and I can move you. Even that's a risk. Do you really want me to leave you?'

Of course they would search. What fools they were not to have left a guard. Whereas this woman might be a true coin, or at least a slower runner than Maisie, or posh, so she'd be frightened by the blade.

Maisie turned the key and opened the door, shiv ready. Right in front of her stood a young dark-haired lady, pale and poshly dressed. It took a moment to recognise her. Esme Shilling smiled, then looked alarmed at the knife.

'You won't need that. We must go to my bedroom and we'll need to look around corners first. What's your name?'

Was it stupid to give a name?

'Mine is Esme, so don't be frightened. I only want to ask you some questions about your friends. Or I could scream and bring the servants. I'd rather be friends though.'

Could she trust Esme, Sir Charles's fancy-piece, who was carrying his child? And the nobs using first names, as if they were close friends. It was to play friendly.

It was a strange winding trip through the house, with Esme going round corners first. She sent a maid off on an errand and invented a rat to divert a footman. After each lie, Esme sparkled and told Maisie, 'Oh, aren't I wicked?' But there they soon were, the bedroom door locked, sitting on a bed which looked warm and comfortable.

'If anyone comes, get into the wardrobe.' Maisie had an idea this was not life and death for the woman, but a bit of a game. If they were caught, only Maisie would be punished. There had been a lot of talk about Esme and Sir Charles and Lady Violet. A lot of adults dodging around. Circumlocution, Mrs Ashton called it. Maisie was neither a child nor a fool. If Esme and Violet had been washerwomen, they would have been pulling each other's hair out in the street by now. Mrs Bright had tipped fish guts over her sister before chapel.

'Now, my payment. How do you know Mrs Ashton?' Esme seemed friendly, but Maisie stayed as wary as a cornered tiger.

'I run and do things for her. Messages.' A harmless admission.

'And spy on people. Do you go to her meetings? Have you seen a ghost?'

'There ain't anything to see. The lights are on, and there is singing and stuff. No one sees anything. But Mrs Ashton sees people and hears them.' Or pretends to.

'Or says she does. Might she be inventing it?'

Maisie shrugged. 'People think she hears true things.'

'I lost my mother and father. Did she hear messages for you?'

That hurt. Maisie snapped, 'That's private.'

Esme looked sympathetic. 'How does your family take it, you running messages for a lady who speaks to ghosts?'

Maisie shrugged again. Change the subject. 'Are you and Lady Violet friends or enemies?'

Esme flushed and gave a gasp, which turned a little into a laugh. She turned her face away.

'What a question, dear Maisie. What have people been saying?'

'Nothing,' Maisie said.

'Dear Violet. She is a friend, a dear friend. I was weak and did my friend a deep wrong.' Esme turned to look at Maisie and touched Maisie's hand. 'She could have cast me away, but she forgave me. My truest friend. As close as a sister and as forgiving.'

Maisie sat stone-faced. Lady Violet had lied and handed Mrs Ashton over to Sir Charles.

Maisie had some idea of getting help, but Braddie had been left behind. It terrified her to be out in the country, which went empty in every direction forever. Everyone here worked for the Evil Baronet, and she didn't know anyone. In London, give her ten minutes to think of a story, and she could have rounded up a few angry workmen from the Burning Bird. But here, nothing.

'Are you worried about Mrs Ashton?' Esme said. 'I know Charles is angry with her. But Violet got him to swear not to harm her. I was there. Charles will send her to America. That's hardly a punishment. I am sure you could go too.'

Maisie's heart skipped, but she couldn't leave Pa and George and Tildy. She wanted to hear more, so said nothing. That vast adventure, America – Indians and buffalo and fancy streets with fancy hats.

'Dear child, here's the funny thing. Charles says he had the most extraordinary feeling when Mrs Ashton touched him. He told Violet and she told me. Violet is convinced Mrs Ashton has some unearthly power. You must be curious.'

Maisie could let a silence drag on as long as the other person wanted. They made the silence; they could fill it.

'Violet must speak to Mrs Ashton before her trip. That would be so helpful.'

Trip? Exile! 'Your friend snitched on her. If not for her, my boss wouldn't be here, in danger, and she wouldn't be in the clink.'

Again, Esme turned away. 'You don't understand, my dear. The world is a cruel place. We women must do what we can. My dear cousin and I will give Charles anything he wants to protect you both.'

'I'm Maisie,' she said, sticking out her hand. 'I need to get her free. Will you help me?'

'We'll see,' Esme said, shaking it. She laughed. 'You were the boy watching the house! A fine fellow you made.'

Maisie met the truth with silence.

'You were good. You know to act like a boy. You stood like a bold squire. Do you enjoy it? The freedom to swear and run and spit? I bet you had all the girls making eyes at you.'

Maisie said nothing. Dressed as a boy, she'd had both girls and boys – even men – be forward with her. Even when people's interest was useful, soppy stuff bored her. She skipped those bits in books.

Esme looked Maisie up and down. 'You bound your breasts then. They do so give you away otherwise. I will get you some other clothes. I have an old suit of my brother's somewhere.'

A disguise would do no harm. Playing a boy was exactly like playing a maid or a posh girl. Acting.

'How can we rescue Mrs Ashton?'

'I'll think of something. There's a storeroom with big iron bolts on the door – Charles puts poachers there. I bet she'll be there. I'll go and look in a bit. You'll have to stay here.'

Esme left, and Maisie stayed with her thoughts, the shiv close by. A swift search found little of interest, except some men's clothes among the rest – cut for Esme, too tall for Maisie – and a signed card of the famous music-hall star Nan Astley, dressed as a lord.

Braddie had known many sorrows, many bad twists of fate. This topped them all. The fury that drove her had burned down to ash, and now her stomach turned over with a sickening, cold fear.

She hung around the old coaching house, waiting for the horse and trap, today or perhaps tomorrow. Cairngorm had business in Bellingley and then might go back to Grennard for supper. Maybe she should stay here longer, in case.

Oh, better be proved wrong – she could swallow her pride and let her hinny gloat. Let Honoria be safe and rich, or safe anyway. Braddie knew what the world was, and she could not see a safe way through this.

Hinny, hinny, foolish hinny. Could they trust that fancy-piece Violet? Had her secret letters been read? Even if the hussy had a heart of gold, people might snoop. Even if Sir Charles was in London – with all the high-ups scheming and in-fighting he might well be – surely he would have left orders. A man who burned their rooms would be sure to have warned his servants.

Fancy Violet had walked into their life as pure trouble and not a thing had happened since to dissuade her.

Braddie wiped an angry tear. If she had a dozen dragoons under her command, she would go and do what was needed, but it was only her and her stick against a houseful of servants... Her hinny was so much better at that sort of thing. Besides – she must have hope – suppose all was well? They might miss each other.

Those eight years had been full of risks and disappointments. Her hinny was a flighty, selfish woman sometimes, and difficult to live with. Yet their life had opened an unbelievable door. Love was possible, love endured, even happiness might come to stay. Life might not be the meanest toil and loneliness. It became something extraordinary, for all its labours and contention. Without her hinny, Braddie looked at being alone, unloved and unlovable. Each flit ended friendships.

She ate a pie, thinking she could have made better, and read the paper. Professor Huxley, that great scientist, debunker of Church nonsense and campaigner for the education of the poor, might sink into the Spiritualist bog. A dozen eminent thinkers – spanning every opinion on bogles and banshees – had gathered at his home. Papers said his next monograph would shake up the world.

And here loped Cairngorm, making extraordinary speed with his damaged leg and breathing hard.

'Mrs Bradshaw, I need you in the carriage, *now.*' Brisk as an officer. 'Let me help with your luggage.'

Her heart in her mouth. 'What's wrong?'

'I had a telegram, a warning. "Regret former information incorrect. Goods arrived at county depot this weekend." Sir Charles is at Corwood Manor. The devil, what a cunning deception.'

She blinked, needing a second or two to take it in, then rose with a jab of pain. 'What can we do?'

'Our host will not betray us, but our location could be known. I will drive us elsewhere.'

A working woman had no time for the vapours. They flung the bags into the vehicle, and Cairngorm climbed into the driver's seat.

'Has Violet... I mean, Lady Barrington-Stewart lied?'

He looked grim. 'She must be under the most terrible duress. Sir Charles is capable of anything. He knows I might come.'

A great fear held her, her Honeybee in the hands of that man. And that lively London sparrow, Maisie. Sir Charles in his lair, that user and murderer of women.

'We must go to them,' Braddie said, quivering with fear at the thought.

'I must enlist a magistrate. Swear an affidavit, get a writ or something. Find a legal way to gain entrance to the property, even against the owner's opposition.' He clenched his fists. 'The monster. He has used Violet... the dear lady, I mean... as bait. And such a man on the Bench, and in Parliament. He must answer for this.'

CHAPTER 15
'In Durance Vile'

That day and after

Corwood Manor tops the rise. It has one long face towards the south, and the north faces down the slope towards the admirable lake.

The first floor holds grand rooms for dining and entertaining, reception and ballrooms – the chapel is worthy of note, as is a fine library – the second floor the family quarters, the third floor for staff.

The kennels, stables, and their staff are in two two-story buildings running north from the main building, one to the east, the other to the west. The courtyard therefore is surrounded on three sides by buildings, the fourth a two-story wall with the coach gate. The yard is level with the lowest floor of the main house.

The ground floor contains the 'machinery' of a great house – kitchens, stores, laundries, etc., which no guest will ever see. But no expense has been spared for the latest facilities.

Pomfret's Review

Mrs Ashton found herself in a storeroom with a stone floor and stone walls. They bolted the door from the outside, top and bottom. There were shelves, well-built and bolted to the wall. At the top of the wall, a narrow, barred window gave weak daylight and no sense of what was beyond.

Despair, and one of her headaches coming on.

The nurses had found the slim blade and the lockpicks concealed in her stays. They refused to return the brooch and watch. They had tied her wrists and ankles

then tied her to the chair. Mrs Ashton knew how to make someone believe your wrists were stronger tied than they were. Once alone, she made some progress on loosening those bonds, gritting her teeth against the pain and remembering fondly the plump little Indian lady acrobat who had taught her the tricks. Then the bolts crunched open, the door creaked open. She had never met her nemesis but recognised him at once. That straw-haired man in a suit of garish cut, that odious dentist's grin: Jabez Trephine. And with him another thug about a mile wide.

'Check everything,' Trephine said, chewing a spill and leaning on an inner wall. In two minutes, the thug found the loose rope on Mrs Ashton's wrists and the marks of her actions. She also realised that a stout chair sat beyond the room, with the sadist nurse-warder sitting and glaring at her. Horrid to have her suspicions confirmed; even a locked door was guarded.

'We should clap you in irons,' Trephine said, in that cheery way of his. 'Didn't think I would need to bring any. Lax of my esteemed employer not to be well supplied – rack, thumbscrews, and all. Hourly checks, my dear man. Can't trust those drunkards, those devil's nuns to do the job. Ah, dear Sunshine, bring Mrs Ashton a thunder bucket and the necessities. We're not monsters.'

The brutal thug left, and Trephine shut the door.

'The bonds on my feet are so fierce, I can barely feel them. It's torture.'

'Oh, Mrs Ashton, for all I know you are a contortionist, who could unknot your hands with your feet. I have instruction that once you cooperate, we can make this more pleasant. A blanket, perhaps. Sir Charles has a lovely Irish cook who has made a magnificent hotpot for the servants. The smell, Mrs Ashton! I could eat a bowlful right now. Be a good girl and write the confession.'

'Your employer is a wicked man and cannot be trusted. He'll slit my throat.'

Trephine's face changed, his swagger replaced by something softer. He pulled up a stool to sit.

'Mrs Ashton, before my compatriot returns, I am going to give you the best advice you have ever had. Grab your chance. Sir Charles is in a good mood, the best mood I've seen for years. His pretty wife has bought your freedom, and I am to make the arrangements. I know my esteemed employer – his mood can turn on a thruppence. Write him your confession now, this minute. Let him win, let him crow about it. Weep and tell him he has beaten you. Leave the country. I worry for the Kendrick girl, and the safety of your fierce old friend, the gargoyle.'

His words tormented her. Braddie, her dear heart, plunged into such danger from her folly. She and she alone had dragged Braddie and Maisie into this nightmare.

'No clever stories, Mrs Ashton? No defiance?'

'You have no morals at all.' That came out weaker than she expected.

'For all I know, his men have Mrs Bradshaw already and are bringing her here. Save the poor old dear her anxiety and avoid the dreadful power of my employer's anger. If I were you...' He shrugged. 'Write his blasted confession, flee and wait a few months, then repudiate it. You can spin a tale better than a dock-load of drunken sailors. Some of your weak-headed friends will believe you.'

Mrs Ashton sobbed. Because whether he meant to or not, Trephine had opened a crack of light. Braddie might still be free. There was the faintest smell of hope.

She tried to open him, but his thoughts were locked away. Some people were hard. The pain in her temples raged, savage.

'You burned our home,' she spat.

'Mrs Ashton, if I told you his first intention, you would thank me as a friend. I don't want your blood on my hands. And here is Sunshine with the bucket.'

A hard chair, but still Mrs Ashton dozed. The blanket and hotpot came as promised, and they let her relieve herself.

She had prayed from the depths and no answer came, no solace. She would have to decide. Every joint ached, and each time she nodded off, she jerked awake. Time passed strangely and a faint light came through the tiny grill window. The moon would be all but full. She was close to conceding, so close to giving up, so far from anyone who could help. Perhaps if she shouted, someone would come, she could confess, and they would offer her a bed.

What had woken her? A scratching at the door, a creak from a bolt, an odd wriggling noise.

'Who's there?' she said, not daring to shout. Friend or foe.

A rap on the door, then nothing. It might be a trap; it might be new torment. It might be someone oiling the bolts to open them without noise.

Agonising, slow, the bolts worked open. Mrs Ashton held so still, she could scarcely breathe by now.

Then the door opened. For a moment, a boy... but no. It was Maisie, with a shuttered lantern. She all but closed the door behind her, but wedged it, then un-shuttered the light. She wore a boy's suit of good tweed, her hair under a cap. And on her lip, a convincing dark moustache.

'Miss me?' she said, coming further into the room.

'The guards? Trephine?'

'The mad-nurses were drunk, then Esme gave them a bottle of plum brandy on top and now the pigs are dead till morning. Do you like Esme's suit? Champagne Charlie and Turncoat Violet are doing the beast.'

'A magnificent rescue. Untie me.' Even the hope of release made her joints creak.

Up close, she saw that the moustache was real hair. Maisie had a saw-bladed knife and began working on her hands. 'Never mind untie. We need to get out of here.'

'What's the plan? What time is it?'

'Half one. Devil's thunderbox, this is a tough one.' Maisie kept working as she spoke. 'I hope Trephine's not around. Esme said I should slip down after midnight. I went out to check the stables. There's a little trap and a friendly horse waiting for us. And by the door into the yard, voices and a lantern. Who a-wondered why the door was unlocked? Only that king of knaves Trephine and the housekeeper. Well, I ducked back and listened.'

'Go on. The rope feels no looser.' Any well-run house had a strict rule that it was locked up at night so the servants could go to bed. Trephine wandering around was dreadful news.

'Doing my best, Mrs A. Here it comes... Well, then she says, Jabez, if you're going to smoke one of the master's fumious cheroots, please do it outside. Very pally. And they went through the door, and a-chatted in the moonlight, him smoking and them talking too low to hear. Esme gave me this man's watch too. I had the horrors he'd come and check you and catch us.'

'So, Esme wants us to escape?'

'Her and the Violet Menace both, she says. They both want to talk to you about her dead ma. But they need you out of the way – they're frightened Charlie-is-my-Darling will change his mind and drown you. Good news, Mrs Bradshaw and Cairngorm scarpered, and Charles threw a bottle of his best champagne at the wall when he heard. Esme says write the confession and leave it behind.'

Mrs Ashton would not leave Sir Charles that weapon. They needed transport. The servants had her bag, her money. She couldn't hobble ten miles to the railway station in the dark. The trap sounded ideal. More time, more noise...

She was alert now, the pain prodding her to action. She rose and threw off the last of her bonds.

'Have you money?'

Maisie chuckled. 'Esme gave me two gold gleamers. A fortune. To the stables and out.'

Oh, her feet sang their complaints, but if she took her boots off, she would never get them back on. Her wrists were rubbed raw, and her back was killing her. An unfamiliar horse at night, but the way looked straightforward on the maps. 'Let us go to the stables.'

Mrs Ashton then remembered her precious golden brooch, feeling a painful stab. Reckless folly to look for it.

'And how are we supposed to contact Lady Violet?' Mrs Ashton said.

'Her lawyer.' Heavens, what dark maze awaited them. Mrs Ashton would not spend a minute longer in the monster's lair than she had to.

Glints from the lantern were the only light. Leaning on Maisie, Mrs Ashton limped her way past the slumped, snoring nurses on straw mattresses, through deserted storerooms and kitchens. She took sugar for the horse, knowing Maisie had already befriended the dogs. Ears out for any sound, and any unexpected light. Watched only by a one-eared prowling cat, they reached an external door. Maisie waited two minutes with her ear to it, before slipping the key in the lock. It turned easily, and the door opened with the slightest of creaks. Moonlight filled the yard with strangeness and shadow.

Maisie pulled Mrs Ashton's sleeve and pointed. Somewhere an owl called. They inched round the walls. The sides of the yard were two storeys high, topped with a balustrade. There could be people hiding up there, an open window might conceal a listener. A couple of warm lights burned at the top and the middle of the house – insomnia or some wasteful person who slept with a light on.

Then they crept into the calm, warm smell of the stables. A horse snickered and shifted.

They had spoken little.

'We need to let all the horses out,' Maisie said. 'Confuse the posse.'

'The horses won't want to go unless we frighten them.' Mrs Ashton lifted one foot to try to wriggle it, still weighing the options. 'Poor gentle servants of wicked people. I shall take one horse for the trap and lead another horse behind it. Dearest child, get those two lanterns.'

'I can ride a horse,' Maisie said, full of indignation. A couple of the horses were moving, uncertain.

'You've ridden a nag in daylight, led by a brewer's boy. We must lead the horses until we're out of sight of the house. It's a good road. With luck, if we are slow and careful, we can make the station.' Yet, Bellingley station was the most obvious place to go. Horses could be panicked by a waving branch at the best of times. Would the tavern-keeper hide them? Was Cairngorm to hand? 'Check the yard gate is open.'

No countrywoman, Mrs Ashton usually left stable matters to Braddie, but she found a sturdy brown beast, unfazed by an unfamiliar smell and voice, provided they had sugar. It went willingly to the two-wheeled trap. Alas the vehicle had the family crest on it, but they could ditch it outside the village. She knew broadly what to do. In danger, lit by a half-shuttered lantern which cast odd shadows, the house of her enemy pressed around her, as if silent wraiths listened to each clink and click. Yet, an error in the tackle might endanger their escape. It felt like forever, but from Maisie's watch it had been eighteen minutes.

The horses' names were proclaimed above each stall, and Maisie was looking for some horse Esme recommended. 'All set to flee the castle,' and she led the second beast out.

Fear strummed a note on Mrs Ashton's stretched-out nerves.

Holding the lantern shuttered in her other hand, she led the horse out, the wheels rumbling in the silence. Let drunken bluebloods and weary servants sleep. She would go along the shadowed wall of the yard. Maisie was already leading the spare horse through the gate.

Behind her, high up, a man's voice said, 'By God, what's that?' A little slurred.

Mrs Ashton's heart leaped. The horror! They'd been seen.

'The stables. Can you hear it?' the man said.

Mrs Ashton did not wait to see but set a quick pace to the gate. Maisie's horse whinnied – Maisie had to hang on to the reins.

'Hey, hey, thief!' A masculine bellow. And then a dull thud, a sickening noise reminding her of Braddie tenderising beef with a hammer.

Time slowed. Mrs Ashton needed to be at the gate and through it. She risked a glance back only to see something fall from the stable roof well behind her. A body. It cried out as it fell, a note of terror, and it hit the ground with a ghastly crunch. It reminded her of that time at the docks when a pig's carcass had fallen.

The horse shuddered, and she had to pull on the reins for control.

There'd been another sound, a thud in the courtyard. Had something fallen?

Her eyes darted to the stable-block roof. Yes, a dark shadow running back to the house. Maybe two, glimpsed from a poor angle. But at that moment, the thing on the ground gasped and she looked to it, astonished it had moved. It raised a hand a little, groaned. The person still lived. In fear and wanting to run, she chose. She went to their aid.

The body was twisted like a vindictive child's doll. It gasped as it moved. Mrs Ashton knelt by it, a big man, dark blood on his head. Her fears confirmed: the narrow beam of the lantern showed Sir Charles, wrenched with pain. Blood frothed from his mouth.

Sir Charles did not recognise her at first – a blow on the temple. From the legs, his back might be broken. His mouth full of blood suggested a pierced lung? Moving him might do serious harm. This far exceeded her knowledge of first aid.

Yes, she longed to flee. Yet his human need held her there.

He wore nightclothes with an outdoor coat, and unlaced boots.

He grabbed her arm and shrieked with pain. Without thinking, she opened him. The world filled with agony and rage – he knew he was dying. He wanted the world to burn.

'You!'

His desperation held her like iron. She had lost control of her gift. Each movement he made brought desperate pain, which she shared. He was slipping away, his courage fading. What could she do? Her enemy left the world in one long shout of agony and fear. The man had brought her nothing but anguish, yet she knelt beside him, holding him as he died. She prayed for him, as her human duty. She had been by many deathbeds and now she lost thought of herself. Never had she lived a death through her gift until now.

Time passed in a daze. Voices, a shout, a whistle blew. She rose, her hands bloodied, to see a couple of big mastiffs lurching towards her, barking like the hounds of hell. Behind them a bare-headed man with a coat thrown over a nightgown, calling the dogs by name. Horses whinnying from the noise. Another man at the door, and a window open.

Nothing seemed wholly real. In shock, Mrs Ashton stood motionless while the dogs stayed a few paces back, well trained. The closest man said, 'Hellfire, a woman. Don't move,' like she was a fool. He held up her lantern.

He gasped. 'It's the master!'

'It's that ghost lady,' said the second man. 'Shit my britches, she's killed him.'

She tried to speak. 'He fell. I didn't do anything. I only tried to see if I could help.'

'There's another one, out of the gate. Follow me!'

'Ring the bell!'

Maisie might get away – please, dear child, be careful – find Braddie, and seek help.

Minutes passed. More people came, and more were sent for. One of them threatened her with a fowling piece. A man wearing trousers over a nightshirt acted in charge, and he called, 'Send a boy to raise Doctor Culpe!' A light or two more had come on in the house.

'Who'll tell her ladyship?' the man in charge muttered into the air.

Mrs Ashton had shared much of the man's death, and it had consumed her. She could barely speak. Her hands were bloody, and she needed to wash them. Here, limping, came Maisie, still with that splendid moustache, on a face smeared with tears. Half-captive, half-helped by one of the stable-lads, and no sign of the horse.

It was only then she realised, Sir Charles could have fallen from the stable roof.

Chapter 16
An Honest Man

The coachman's cottage, the Corwood Estate. Wednesday, before dawn

Still dark in his warm bed. Someone was shaking him. Willoughby found mornings harder than he used to. Dolly was saying something... something that made no sense.

'The master's dead! Murdered.'

'Nonsense,' he said, eyes closed, 'you're a-dreaming.' His knee hurt, that little she-ruffian and her witch of a mistress.

'Mrs Ashton a-murdered him.'

Early for Dolly to be out of bed, and upset, and Dolly didn't get upset over nothing. He opened his eyes and sat up. Parts of him sent their creaking warnings. The young didn't realise... most things.

No time to dawdle. He lumbered from bed and learned that their Jem was going round the cottages telling people, and the House was like a kicked-over beehive.

'I'll go, they'll need us. Let's pray, Dolly.' They clasped hands. In few words aloud, he sought God's grace and guidance on that day's duty, asked for strength to do it, asked the master be judged fair and proper and given his rest, and called down blessings on the poor mistress – oh, the poor widowed girl – and the whole estate. They were true words, however humble, and he knew God would hear them.

'Those young ones have no backbone. I'll need to steady them.'

'I'll cut you some breakfast. And find the funeral bands.'

As he shaved, Willoughby remembered what the Good Lord had said: pray for your enemies. So, at the mirror, he offered up an honest prayer that the wicked woman be brought to swift penitence, to confess her crimes, to serve as witness to His Word, and return to Godly ways, if she knew what they were. Not for him to do justice, but for the police and God.

Dolly had fixed the mourning band on his sleeve. He took a lantern, but he could have walked that path blindfold. His knee still ached from the brat's kick.

What work there would be. No man of the family to take charge. Speaking no ill, the house steward and the land steward could quarrel like Tweedledum and Tweedledee. Even with an ordinary death like the old master or poor Lady Herncastle, to do it proper needed much attention. The hearse in good order but everything must shine. Black ribbons for the horses – Nocturne was now out to pasture, dear old girl, and Coal was that flighty. Who had a steady black they could borrow? The house dressed in mourning, his lads must look right. Clocks stopped, and mirrors covered in black. Yet, add to all this the wicked murder. Police wanting their carriages watched and horses fed and putting the estate in a rumpus, no doubt.

What an odd business yesterday – the young mistress asking him, her hand on his shoulder, to be there for Mrs Ashton's capture. That Trephine, slippery as an eel, nosing around in dark corners. And the mad-nurses, well... Mrs Ashton broke every Commandment, but as far as he knew, she was too crafty to be mad. He hadn't asked the mistress why, not his place, but the dear girl had said, 'I know of no more honest man. I want you there as a witness. That protects everyone.' Powerful rum.

Willoughby reached the courtyard gate, hiding the limp, slower than he used to be. All lanterns and men standing. The two stewards looked to be in charge.

Willoughby went to them. 'Sir, sir, a dreadful day. What needs to be done?'

The house steward spoke. 'We have covered Sir Charles's remains, but we must keep people out of the yard until the police come. As far as we can. A groom has gone to fetch them. Was there any reason for the little lady-trap to be ready last night?'

'No, sir.'

'That woman and her accomplice tried to steal it. They caught her red-handed over the body, now wailing her innocence. The mistress collapsed, so Doctor Culpe is up in her room. He commands affairs now.'

'The doctor?' That old soak, short, red, and fat, with those quivering hands and reeking breath. Him in charge?

Oh, the mistress would take the death very ill.

'Doctor Culpe is a trustee under Sir Charles's will and so, for now, master of this house, high or low. Willoughby, you'll need to steady your men. No one is to leave the estate, or deviate from their usual duties, without an excellent reason.'

'The men will know their duty, sir. Begging your pardon...'

'Speak.'

'A groom must run the mail to town at first light. Most days, Sir Charles has important letters, Parliamentary business. He was most particular, with the local mail shocking lax...'

'Of course. Make sure it is done. Would we had two of you, Willoughby.'

The side door was unlocked, so he went and checked on the horses and his men. Who was more skittish? 'Course, the master dying young by violence – everyone shaky as a colt in a thunderstorm, worried about the future, about their place.

It was Forty's turn to take the mail. Willoughby had a soft spot for the poor orphan lad. A steady worker, but he dithered, like a girl with one penny for the ribbon man.

'Should we still take the mail? Shouldn't we wait for the police?'

'Pull yourself together, man, and go.' No backbone.

'Do I have to take the parcels? It's only clothes for the poor sailors.'

Willoughby scowled. 'Men who served their country and now fallen on hard times. Yes, man, you do.'

Next, that Trephine came looking for him. All brass neck in a bright coat, and cocky with it. That dreadful morning, beneath the bravado, Willoughby saw Trephine mightily rattled.

'Dear Lady Barrington-Stewart has collapsed, and Miss Shilling too. Poor girl, such a shock.'

Oh, poor lasses. The mistress's curse of barrenness, how cruel, and old Lady Herncastle's death, and the unhappiness those misfortunes lay over the house. And the death brought back young Henry, an absolute joy of a lad, drowned dead, all those years ago. The grim duty to be one of six shouldering the mortal remains, to walk him up to the house. Sir Charles was just a boy, all but drowned himself, insisting he walk it too, sobbing with each step. Life is a vale of sorrows, but One walks with us through it all.

'They have Mrs Ashton and the girl,' Trephine went on.

Willoughby allowed himself to be fierce. 'A wicked, wicked day that woman a-schemed her way into her ladyship's life. I knew her a villain the day I met her.'

Trephine had no quip for that. 'It will be a while before Lady Barrington-Stewart can consider business.'

Willoughby knew a man edging round a difficult question. When the master needed to go on strange errands, he chose Willoughby, because Willoughby knew to keep his mouth shut. Trephine, that man of schemes and cheek, who sometimes met the master at night or in doubtful places. The mistress and her trustees should clean the house and send this man packing.

Maybe in this wicked age, a great man needed such a devious character. Maybe.

'Ask me what you want to ask me, sir.'

'About yesterday. Mrs Ashton's detention.'

Oh, that's why he was wriggling. Not for Willoughby to say what a stinking rum business it was. 'I'll do my duty, sir. When the police come, I'll answer any questions full and true, as if it were the Recording Angel asking.'

Trephine braved it out. 'Of course. We all will.'

Dolly would be worrying. The master had promised him and Dolly they'd keep use of the cottage long as they lived. Of course, you don't insult the master and ask him to write a promise down. The mistress, kind to a fault, would never turn them out. Patience. In good time, he would know for certain. The master always kept his word.

Then he had to settle a quarrel between two of the boys. Someone had smeared axle grease, a whole pot, on a long coach seat cushion. Each blamed the other. Dreadful stuff to clean off. With Ashton and her accomplice sneaking around, it would be summat malicious.

'The master dead, and the mistress sick. Be men. Shake hands, then both of you do it.'

Chapter 17

An Exercise Fad and a Golden Bee

Inside the manor

Mrs Ashton couldn't control the shaking. A small room with hard chairs, the door ajar. The blood on her clothes, her hands, cried out to her: murder, murder. Disgusting. She craved some spirits, for the shock.

Mrs Abernathy was Scottish even to her plaid dressing gown. She pulled on gloves. The middle-aged woman behind her glared, built like an ox.

'I am to search you,' the housekeeper said. 'If you cause any difficulty, Jane will help me restrain you.'

'I must wash, change...' Abernathy had brought a pile of clothing.

'Doctor Culpe wishes to sketch the bloodstains. His first duty is to the mistress of the house, so you are not to be washed and changed until then.' She muttered, 'Wickedness, wickedness...'

Mrs Abernathy searched her with care. Mrs Ashton accepted she would sit here bloody for a while.

'I didn't do it. He fell, I think from the roof. Like the Good Samaritan, I tried only to save him.'

The red, puffing doctor marched in, gave his name, and sketched the bloodstains.

'How is dear Lady Barrington-Stewart?' Mrs Ashton asked. Surely her patroness would stand up for her.

Culpe looked harrowed. 'I have the gravest concerns. Miss Shilling is a little better. The maid will come running if there is any deterioration.'

'I am innocent. Look how my hands are shaking.'

The doctor put two fingers to her throat, held her wrist. Brisk, and without regard to decorum. 'You'll live. Exactly what did you claim to do?'

'He was severely injured, I think his back... Bleeding from the mouth. I tried to see if he had bitten his tongue and find his pulse. What else could I do? I held his hand and prayed.'

The doctor looked at her, no, her clothes again. Added some more details.

'That will have to do. Let her wash and change. The clothes are to be locked up somewhere for the police. If tea is brought, she can have some. And a vessel to do anything necessary.'

Cold water to wash in and such coarse charity clothes, too large. The humiliation, to be clad like a prisoner, poor, a supplicant to the mighty. She had neither mirror nor her essentials to recraft her face, order her hair.

'I need to speak to Maisie. I am her guardian.' She touched the housekeeper's hand to open her. The death roared back, pain and fear, like she relived it. Sir Charles's venomous hatred filled the room. She gasped.

'None of your sinful tricks,' Mrs Abernathy said.

Dry-mouthed and seeped in misery, what would become of them? Braddie had been right – if her dear heart came, she might be dragged into this nightmare. Her angel should stay away. Yet there was no one in the world she wanted to see more. How she had belittled her dear heart and taken her for granted! Prison ahead, brutal silence, hard labour, solitary confinement, and grim food.

She had brought Maisie into peril; the lass might disappear into a grim reformatory. Who would look after her family? What danger she had summoned into her life? She prayed with desperation, her pride brought low, but nothing brought respite.

They left, taking the chair. The lock clicked, and she sat on the bed.

The housekeeper and Trephine, about in the house after midnight. Without them, Mrs Ashton and Maisie would have been well away.

Dear heart, I have failed you. I have brought you into danger, dearest, forgive me. Dear Lord, protect those I have damaged through my folly.

Chief Inspector Bullfinch arrived at Scotland Yard at his usual brisk hour to find a police two-seater ready to take him to King's Cross. The commissioner, Lieutenant Colonel Henderson, stood there looking harrowed. *By Jove, this is serious.*

'Dreadful news. Sir Charles Barrington-Stewart murdered, at his Belldownshire estate – the first MP murdered in seventy years. I'll ride with you to the station and tell you what little we know. The Home Secretary has told the local force to ask for our help. We need someone of your rank and experience there.'

Bullfinch's mind raced. *Sir Charles had denounced the Fenians!* Both sat, and the vehicle leapt into movement, the driver not hesitating to shout to clear a way. Henderson swore. 'With the Irish dynamite campaign and these damned strikes, we're spread damned thin. Lord knows if the local constabulary are any good. I'll send you some good men later today.'

'What do we know, sir?'

'Not much. They're holding the Ashton woman, the spirit-wrangler. Caught bloody-handed over the corpse.'

That twisted crook, caught for murder. Oh, may it be true!

Henderson went on, 'My first thoughts were political – the anarchists, or the Irish ruffians. You know of Ashton, of course.'

Oh, he knew her. Bullfinch tasted bile at her name. How she had humiliated him.

'A slippery crook, sir,' he growled. 'Third time our paths crossed, she was in the house when the Westmacott Emeralds disappeared. Maybe three years back? She took them, somehow, but we couldn't prove it.'

How had she done it? Those little smirking jibes.

'Has she revolutionary connections?' Henderson asked.

'Ashton craves the patronage of the well-to-do and wealthy. She professes no political views at all. Her servant – her accomplice – is a radical crank, but she's all hot air.'

Bullfinch mused a moment or two. 'If it's a political murder, we'll soon know. That's the point. The assassins will shout their wicked cause from every street corner.'

The commissioner looked grim. 'We'll have half the London press camped outside the manor by teatime. The coroner always burning to start the inquest. Questions in the House. Everyone will expect an arrest within five minutes. We must excel here, Bullfinch. Our reputation requires it.'

Every policeman knew the grim shadow over Scotland Yard. Four detectives had been convicted of gross corruption, bringing disgrace. They were breaking stones on Dartmoor. Bullfinch would have had such oath-breakers shot, and he'd volunteer for the firing squad.

The commissioner coughed. 'The Home Secretary made sure I knew, he and his think Lady Barrington-Stewart is delightful... she's been unwell... they're horrified she's now a tragic young widow. Your vigour and method produce results, Bullfinch. I'm confident there's no better man available. But if you tread on toes up there, important ears will hear of it. Let's be more the clever bird than the blundering beast, eh?'

That stupid jibe. He could kick the man.

On the train heading north, Bullfinch reflected, the high and mighty in shiny hats should let him get on with his job. As for the press, their job was to publish what helped the police and of course applaud their successes. Not to spin webs of speculation and hysteria, and bombard the public with the feeble advice of armchair detectives who couldn't find a trout in the milk. And local coroners and local police, Lord have mercy!

An MP had been murdered, and justice must be done. A wicked crime, perhaps the crime of the decade, and a chance for his talent to shine. And let it be Ashton.

Bellingley raised memories of his youth on rolling southern downs – red-brick, rural, pretty, even thatched cottages. The county detective was seasoned, brisk, and wiry, with an unapologetic handshake.

'Chief Inspector, your reputation proceeds you. We're glad to have you. The coroner took a colleague of mine straight to the manor, to secure the crime scene and so forth.'

'What's the coroner like?'

'Old naval surgeon, three years in the naval investigations branch, smart and thorough. May I offer you an observation?'

No dim amateur then. Bullfinch nodded.

'He is an intelligent man who listens carefully to *advice. Suggestions.* So long as we remember it's his investigation, so long as we never appear to *instruct* him...'

'Ha!'

'Handled well, you will find him admirable, an ally.'

A police four-wheeler stood ready to take them to the house, a silent sergeant in uniform following behind. Once they were moving, the man gave him a thorough briefing on the family. Prodded as to the character of the deceased, the county man said, 'A rising man, one I would have said for the history books. Yet many knew not to cross him.'

Bullfinch dared to hope the local fellows were up to their task. This could be the most important case of his career. He might even ask this steady chap to deal with the press, doubtless flocking to Bellingley even now.

They were met at the stable gate by two old men, one of martial stance in a naval coat – the coroner, the other a bleary-eyed drunk. Policemen waited for further orders.

Doctor Culpe assured him of the staff's cooperation. He advised that, 'Lady Barrington-Stewart remains most unwell – profound melancholia combined with the extraordinary shock. Her heart. She cannot be disturbed for the time being. I check in on her hourly.'

Blast. 'I must see her as soon as possible. Let's look at the scene,' Bullfinch said. The stable yard, where Sir Charles had fallen, and where Ashton and the girl had been captured. The body lay covered with a tarpaulin, and Bullfinch gestured for it to be uncovered.

Meeting the victim was uniquely solemn. A man who had the ear of the Home Secretary, now a bloody carcass. Bullfinch and the coroner took their time examining the remains, while an officer assisted a sketch artist to record the scene.

The coroner said. 'I'm told Sir Charles often walked on the stable roof, of an evening. Even after the house was locked up. There's a walkway. Bring us the weapon, man.' A constable brought something on a tin tray. A faded wooden Indian club, smeared with blood.

'The family's cast-offs used by the servants. No one spared from the exercise fad, Chief Inspector. Found over there.' The coroner gestured across from the covered corpse. 'There's a room where such things are stored, unlocked.'

Such clubs were used by everyone from schoolgirls to retired judges for exercise. Bullfinch inspected it and visualised the blow. The coroner continued.

'Fresh blood when found, and from the size and shape, little doubt this was the weapon. Culpe thinks the blow to the temple might have stunned the deceased, but he believes injuries from the fall killed him first. I agree. For what it's worth, Mrs Ashton said he was semi-conscious, and that's quite possible.'

'She's a crook, and a superb actress. Could a woman have done it?'

The coroner mused. 'Ashton's hands were bloody – she denies everything, says she was helping him as best she could. Medically what she says is plausible. A brutal crime but certainly a woman of reasonable resolution could have struck that blow, particularly if she was enraged or frightened.'

The man rubbed his hands together. 'Well, examine the scene, then we should move the body to the icehouse. I'll bring the jurors here tomorrow, to be sworn, and to see the body. Then the post-mortem. I cabled the great Dr Rutherford in London. He will come because I said I will ask his rival if he's unavailable.'

'Rutherford's a sound man.' Bullfinch hesitated a moment. The jury meant a circus, but it was the law.

'Ashton's all soft words and singing hymns, but she's the coolest customer I ever interrogated,' Bullfinch said. 'Did she strike him on the roof, then come down to check he was dead? Or did she try to finish him off on the ground?'

'There are stairs. She says she's never been on the roof. They found two tiny smears of blood on the balustrade. Sir Charles hated Spiritualists, but our friend the doctor says Mrs Ashton had a correspondence with his wife. Is there violence in Ashton's history?'

'Not her way. Her servant woman has cracked a skull or two, defending her mistress. Do we know where the accomplice is?'

'Bradshaw? Staying in the town, apparently. But there's a lass here. Maisie Kendrick.'

The county detective scribbled a note.

'One of their crew missing? We must get hold of her.'

And soon he heard a tangled tale from the local police of asylum nurses summoned by Sir Charles, but who claimed to know nothing, and forged notes of credit. And that slimy rogue, Jabez Trephine.

'We must keep that man out of everything,' Bullfinch said crisply.

'Anyway, could it have been an intruder?' said the coroner. 'The police did a close search of the roof. We should now search to find any signs of grapples or ladders outside. His Lordship's father feared thieves, so the drainpipes have patent deterrents and the outer-facing windows on the ground and first floor don't fully open.'

'The yard doors?'

'Found unlocked. The Kendrick girl had the key kept in the stables. Even if the Ashton woman did it, there might have been other accomplices.'

Oh, the relief of working with competent men – as much pleasure as a pint of plain and a good pipe. 'Very good. Vigour and method. That's what will give us the answers. Is access through the roof only via the stables?'

One of the policemen said, 'No, sir, there's a door from the roof into the main house.' He was known to smoke there, sometimes long after the house was locked up.

The coroner paused. 'Several minutes before the general alarm was raised... someone on the roof could have got some way into the house. Let me show you what our colleagues found on the roof and in the yard.'

In a small crate there were four cigar butts – expensive cigars – two from the roof and two in the yard. 'Sir Charles's personal supply.' A black wooden box found on the roof with the family crest in silver. The contents were a dead giveaway – the cunning pipe in two sections, trimmed with silver, a fancy spirit lamp, a knife, and a needle. Bullfinch picked up the pipe and sniffed the distinctive bowl.

'Smoking opium,' Bullfinch said. 'Filthy foreign habit. The pipe put away dirty.'

'Was the deceased known to use it?' the coroner asked. 'Rutherford will test the viscera, but that's a hit-and-miss affair. And they found this on the roof.' He produced and opened a handkerchief. A flash of gold.

It was a golden bee brooch, the pin bent. Was that a dab of dried blood? Mrs Ashton had worn one exactly like it, every time Bullfinch had seen her. That mocking interview when he realised that she had beaten him... Last night, she had been on the roof, the liar. She truly might have murdered someone.

This could be a glorious case, quickly resolved. His revenge was long denied but allowed to mature in the cask. He found himself grinning. In this feeble age, a woman murderer could sometimes escape the rope. But for killing an MP, a protégé of the Home Secretary, surely Ashton would hang? They might let him watch.

CHAPTER 18

'A Fine Day for a Hanging'

That morning

When dawn's rosy fingers touched the sky, Mrs Ashton remembered her mother. She often greeted fair weather with that macabre saying.

Another long wait, and Mrs Ashton suffered a servant's breakfast of bread, dripping, and leathery meat, served indecently late and sluiced down with tepid, over-milky tea. She dozed, and they woke her from half-sleep and told her some dreadful news. Chief Inspector Bullfinch had arrived to take charge of the case.

Her hands shook. She prided herself on courage – she had once faced down a mob, more than once a man with a gun, or a vicious dog – but Bullfinch was a tight knot of aggression and prejudice. Bullfinch had almost caught her with the emeralds. With sustained effort and a little luck, she had outwitted him, but he held notorious grudges.

She should seek a lawyer. They must let her send to London – her dear banker would know a man. Perhaps he would pay for it.

An hour later, they brought her to an astonishing library, a lifetime of leatherbound tomes with golden lettering. Bullfinch sat at the Georgian table with a constable to take notes and a local detective, who gave her the caution in the charming local accent. A common cloth covered some object in front of them. In her current state of nerves, it threatened her.

Dear Lord, bring me safely through this.

Bullfinch bristled at the mere sight of her. In his grating rumble of a voice, he said, 'Well, we meet again, Mrs Ashton. A bloody murder. Sir Charles was determined to expose you, and you wanted him dead.'

'Chief Inspector, I wish death on no man. He had sought to persecute me, openly and through associates. I know my Christian duty to pray for him and all lost souls. I was brought here under false pretences, held illegally, and threatened with the madhouse. I needed to escape.'

'You murdered him.'

'No, sir, I didn't kill him. I was in the yard, escaping my illegal detention. From the cry, I knew whoever fell from the roof would be badly injured. I sought to be the Good Samaritan. I went to try and help him, not knowing who it was. Even though it was that dreadful man... well, he was in need. Not that I could have saved him.'

Bullfinch smirked. He thought he had something. 'I put it to you that you were on the roof of the stables.'

'I wasn't on the roof. I haven't been on the roof, and I don't know how to get there. Dear Maisie will confirm that.' Mrs Ashton was sick to the stomach about the girl.

'We know you were on the roof,' Bullfinch said, permitting himself the first signs of a smile.

'I wasn't. I had no reason to be there. Am I supposed to have pushed him off the roof and at the same time been in the yard, taking the trap out...? Up or down, Chief Inspector? I am not some fairy godmother, blessed with wings. Or perhaps like some blessed saint of old – a miracle, the power to be in two places at once.'

'A fall may seal a man's fate without killing him instantly. Show her.'

The local detective took a handkerchief from his pocket and unfolded it. Something glinted, then a tear came to her eye. Her golden honeybee brooch – the precious symbol of Braddie's love, defiled by a speck of blood. *Lord, keep my dear heart safely away.* Mrs Ashton reached for her treasure, feeling more tears come, and the detective snatched it away.

She needed no stagecraft to show her contempt. 'It has been my constant complaint to the doctor and the housekeeper that those nurses stole that brooch from me – those drunken harpies, those slatterns. The pin is damaged. Examine my dress, you will see where they tore it. This is part of Sir Charles's absurd plot to have me imprisoned in an asylum. This is the most transparent attempt by someone to implicate me. And they took my watch too. It is French silver, a gift to an equerry from his Imperial Majesty, Napoleon the Third.' *Well, it might have been.*

'Have the nurses been searched?' the county detective said. 'If not, it will be done.'

Mrs Ashton needed them to understand. 'Sir Charles burned my house and property, and he sent men to harass my meetings. I desired above all else to *avoid* him. I certainly didn't kill him.'

That stuck a lance in the bull.

'You thought Sir Charles was plotting to destroy you? Ha! Every reason to kill him!'

'I demand to speak to Lady Barrington-Stewart,' Mrs Ashton said, as much to stall as to find out more. 'And to see Maisie. Her father will not forgive me if she is harmed.'

'You know Lady Barrington-Stewart is unwell.'

Something stirred in Mrs Ashton's mind. She sank into a gloomy mire of exhaustion and fear. The sound of that grisly blow before the fall. It might be the murder of the decade.

The thought alone brought another surge of Sir Charles's rage. filling her. It burned, like blinded herself staring at the sun. Mrs Ashton had to control her breathing so as not to panic. Nothing like this had happened to her before. Since before her womanhood, her gift had raised her from the mire. What did she have without it? And a familiar fierce headache began to beat its wings inside her head – not only tiredness, but the penalty for her gift. Jagged lights danced in her vision.

What a price to pay for kindness.

'I saw someone else on the roof,' she said, the pain showing in her voice. 'A figure in black, or two, moving away.'

'One or two? Men or women? Old or young?'

'I could not say.'

'You have no witness to support you. And to be honest, such a history of dishonesty, there is no reason to believe you. Show her the weapon.'

The constable took hold of the cloth on the table, and that action alone made her wince. Off came the cloth, revealing an Indian club, with dark, dry blood on it.

At the sight of it, fear swept in, an incoming tide. She gripped her eyes shut and tried not to scream.

Sir Charles's rage and pain in those last moments. The agony of the blow, the terror of the fall. Still conscious, still breathing, each breath a pain...

She could almost feel the stable yard, the night stars. Mrs Ashton shrieked. Someone had a hand on her shoulder – to hold her or reassure her she did not know. She faced madness, the loss of any grip on the world.

'The murderous witch killed me. I should have strangled her.'

Bullfinch's gruff voice. 'Spare us your dramatics. Justice is coming, Mrs Ashton. This crime requires punishment, and a full confession now will spare others.'

The county detective. 'I don't think she's faking. Get the doctor.'

Sir Charles's voice. *'I hope they hang you.'*

Braddie tossed and turned, long periods awake, terrified about her hinny's fate. And Maisie, the poor lass. They had promised her drunken father they would look after her. Exhausted, against her nature and practice, she did not wake until well after dawn. She came downstairs in that strange, rambling old house to find Cairngorm had left. An hour later, he came limping through the door. Braddie knew pain; he was hurting more than yesterday.

'What happened, sir?' Braddie said.

The man tried a jaunty smile. 'I decided to take a dawn ride and, like a fool, fell off the horse. My father always used to say at least one of the horse and the rider needs to have brains.' He winced. 'I have twisted it before.'

'I have summat for the pain.' Braddie had assembled her remedies and raided the kitchen to add to it.

'I dislike relying on the poppy, but today I need it. Well, the grim news. I took a detour, a minor errand, and the market is ablaze – Sir Charles is murdered, and they have arrested Mrs Ashton. I have no word of dear Violet, and I must hope that is a good sign.'

Braddie gave a great gulp. She walked life stone-faced, but this was too much. Good that the de'il was dead, he deserved worse, but oh, her foolish love! Tears came, and she used her sleeve.

The man put out his hand, held it awkward in the air, then gently put it on her shoulder. She brushed him off, not thinking about how he'd take it. His face showed genuine concern.

'You are a great friend to her, Mrs Bradshaw, a loyal friend and servant. We will go as soon as we can to the manor. I must ensure we will be admitted. Have you eaten? Let me make sure Cook gives you a sturdy breakfast.' He began to limp towards the kitchen. 'And I think your matron's dress might be useful camouflage.'

Time dragged. The horror of it. Braddie knitted and did mending, not knowing what else to do. Cairngorm sent boys running with notes. One was sent to the station, to the telegraph office there. A sober, lawyerly old man turned up and Cairngorm took him into a room of books, a friendly hand on the old man's arm. They were forty-five minutes. Braddie's hanky dripped with tears. She hated showing emotion in public. Cairngorm seemed affable, for a man, but still one of Them for all that.

Braddie even considered stealing a horse and trap, but of course they would send people after her. What would she do if her hinny went to prison? They would frame her for the murder for sure. Prison combined everything she feared – aching work, silence, abuse and control at the hands of men. How her hinny would hate the humiliation, dragged into the gutter. What help could she be, separated from her Honeybee by stone walls?

Perhaps They would come for her too. Her hinny had done many things They would disapprove of. In London, she rented her safety deposit box, and the key was kept safe. Better a box than have a crook-o'-law involved. But Braddie could not flee when her hinny needed her.

And the prospect of life without Honoria... no friends, no family, just an old woman working as she could while her body could stand it.

Often, like today, she wished her hinny had no power. What would their life have been without it?

She found herself gnawing her thumb again, a terrible habit, and here came Cairngorm at last. She could have bit his head off for the delay.

'I go armed with excuses, and we can go now. Cook has provided lunch.'

He drove the trap at brisk speed. Pleasant weather, and the route seemed easy enough to remember. The road was better kept than she had predicted, for rich families wanted no potholes on the way to town.

Braddie sat in a silent fury, mixed with moments of sheer terror. From time to time, a lark or a cluster of trees touched her heart. It was not the country she loved, only soft coddled southern rises not worthy of the name of 'hill', but any country beat the smoky hell of cities. And the strength of spring cheered her.

Cairngorm said little, occasionally pointing her to useful landmarks if she had to return without him.

'It is easy to take the turn to Gray's Quarry by mistake. Flooded now.' He coughed. 'I was not wholly honest with you, Mrs Bradshaw.'

What did you say to that?

'I rose before dawn and took a horse. My plan was to ride to Corwood Manor and confront Sir Charles single-handed. Too much of Robin Hood and King Arthur at bedtime, not enough sense. I did not know the horse, I drove that sensitive soul too hard, and she rightly threw me. Proof I needed to be careful and, I think, to remember your needs too.'

Reckless fool. 'I'm grateful, sir.'

'So now I am sworn in as a special constable and instructed in writing by the magistrate to assist the investigation. They won't bar us from the door. But if the police hold Mrs Ashton, our jolly beak will let them work.'

A leader of men, utterly fearless.

They came to a great gatehouse, the main house being well beyond it in parkland and not obvious. Between the open gates, a couple of men in country gear sat on rustic chairs. Their shotguns were broken and pointed away from others. But guns there were.

Cairngorm tipped his hat and drove the trap right up to the gate.

'Captain Cairngorm, formerly of the Belldownshire Regiment – huzzah for the Valiant Fourth! – and today as special constable sent to aid the investigation.' One of the men touched his hat. 'And this good lady comes to assist the afflicted and check after their welfare. Why the guns?'

A scowl. 'They journalists. This is private property. And Doctor Culpe has men with dogs walking round the house.' The men stepped aside and waved them through.

The road curved round, revealing in careful views through the trees the massive palace built on the backs of the poor for the comfort of the few. What a fine sanatorium it would make – healthy air, and a farm so the sick and the staff could eat good food. The castle which held her hinny and poor Maisie, that place where that wicked man had died. Dead and gone, food for worms, but he might still take them all to destruction with him.

'The errant brother Rupert will not get a shilling,' Cairngorm said. 'That sottish rogue, Barrington-Stewart Senior, insisted. Yet under the law of England, a debauched rake will become a baronet. Rum, isn't it?'

Robbers and thieves, stealing the land from the people and giving themselves gold hats and fancy names. Awa, awa with the lot of them.

Chapter 19

Reunion and Ruin

Later that day

Mrs Ashton knew Braddie from the scent and the tender touch on her cheek. She opened her eyes – alas, that strange little room with the truckle bed was not a nightmare. Braddie perched on the bed, and she could not hold back the tears. Braddie. Her dear heart, dear one, her soulmate, her Naomi. How strained she looked! Every year of her hard life showed. She sat by the truckle bed and took Mrs Ashton's hands.

Oh, my heart, be strong as I cannot. Am I going mad?

Doctor Culpe entered and took the chair, reading through a black bound tome. He glanced up from time to time.

'Do you need anything, mistress?' Braddie asked.

'I am so ill, the shock of seeing him die... The kind doctor gave me a draught, but my head is swimming.'

Mrs Ashton lived on her wits. She had drunk only a quarter of the drug and tipped the rest in the chamber pot. Still, it wearied her, made her vague and weepy. It also blunted that strange horror, that living waking nightmare, into weary fog.

'That de'il!' Braddie growled.

'Be careful, dear Braddie. He has gone to judgement and we must pray for him.'

Mrs Ashton flicked a look sideways; the doctor's attention lay elsewhere.

'My gift is gone,' she mouthed.

Braddie tightened her grip and looked horrified. Used wisely, the gift had got them out of many troubles. It had fed and clothed them.

The joining of hands gave her no way to wipe her eyes. 'Oh, my dear, I have been so wrong. You were so wise. To tell me...' Not for men's ears.

'We can talk later, Mistress.'

Mrs Ashton dared not ask what would become of them. And what could she say anyway, but her fears and doubts? As far as she knew, Lady Violet had stayed secluded in her quarters. She had betrayed them yet contrived their escape. Maybe she knew Charles could not be trusted. There was a missing power at the centre of this house.

Braddie talked of soothing oils and country teas made from herbs, remedies against shock and headaches.

The doctor had begun listening. Looking up, he said, 'Well, such things do no harm, and if they are familiar, they may do some good.'

A dislikable man, a little too inclined to attribute Mrs Ashton's illness to the weakness of her female body. How often men were governed by their stomachs and their masculine organ, and how often they moaned at pain any woman could bear with stoicism. However, being too ill for Bullfinch to bully her proved an advantage for now.

Braddie gave the briefest sketch of the situation in the house, choosing each word with care.

Such peril, with no obvious exit. 'Cairngorm will be a great assistance. How is dear Maisie?

'They won't let me see her,' Braddie growled. 'She has refused to say anything at all.'

'Oh, the dear girl. What a spirit she has. Her account is essential. They must know the details of our escape. Braddie, ask to let us send to London for a lawyer. Engage the good Captain in that endeavour. Surely my banker friend will assist. And get a note to the mistress of this house, widowed, that we need her assistance.'

Braddie's frown suggested a hailstorm of disapproval. 'Too ill to rise, they say. I'll ask tha Captain to ask it.'

How she had wronged her dear heart. She wanted privacy with Braddie, time to wash, and anoint, and seek the reconciliation of a good bed. Staying in large houses, they rarely got to share true intimacy. Watched as they were, under close suspicion, she might as well wish for the moon.

Memories of her encounters with Sir Charles flocked, whispering threats and malice. Would she have no peace? No gift and her wits disordered, what could she do? The asylum beckoned after all.

The police wanted to interrogate Mrs Ashton again, and Braddie had to leave. They refused to bring Mrs Ashton either a Bible or writing paper. Lunch was an indifferent sandwich. Hours later, she was visited by dear

Cairngorm. He looked far from the cheery soul she had left yesterday. Not least, he was in pain... a cloud over his sunny disposition.

'Dear Captain, how delightful to see you.'

Cairngorm gave a sad smile. 'A dreadful business, Mrs Ashton. I bring a proposal from the investigators. If you are an honest woman, I cannot see this is to your disadvantage. They wish you to walk the path you did last night.'

'Why?' For all her sea of troubles, feeling drained and ill, her curiosity still burned.

'My lips are sealed, alas.'

The housekeeper brought the bloodstained dress. Efforts had been made to remove the mark of Cain, but how distasteful to wear it damp. Mrs Ashton had little choice but to change into it. She did take the shawl she had snatched to cover her head at night.

Her hands began to shake. If the murder weapon had created such a violent effect, what would the murder scene do to her?

Cairngorm and the housekeeper helped her downstairs to meet a local detective. He explained that she was to walk into the yard from the same door as she had done last night, as if leading the horse and trap, and walk as she had done at a similar speed. At the correct point, she was to turn and go back to where Sir Charles had died.

The walk required her to pass through the approximate area where Sir Charles had fallen and then back to it. That thought alone made her shudder.

'The light is utterly different.'

'That doesn't matter.'

Well, get on with it. Concentrating on the job in hand, holding all her courage, she walked the path required to the stable door, parallel to the long wall. A cluster of people stood on the facing wall. As she passed the fatal spot, her whole body shuddered with the memory of the death. She guessed roughly where she had stopped, turned, and went back.

She remembered a blind Dutch girl, working for a master fence in Amsterdam. The man gave her goods to see if she could read from them with her hands – in particular, the girl knew whether they were loot from a recent murder. Mrs Ashton was a fraud and always assumed fraud, yet the girl had passed a cunning experiment entirely under Mrs Ashton's control. Three times in a long life she had found other people with powers not easily explained by science. Could she have acquired a new gift and lost the old?

Of course, turning allowed her time to inspect those watching. Bullfinch, another detective, and Cairngorm. All oddly impassive. The gentleman in the naval coat might be the coroner. The kennelman, a kennel boy of about ten, and one of the footmen.

Coming back, she braced herself for the sensation and yes, like Sir Charles himself raging there. How utterly bewildering.

Bullfinch came over with a curt demand: show roughly where the figures she alleged had been on the roof might have been. In the dark, the confusion... well, she did her best now.

She suddenly realised the kennel boy was who mattered. Cairngorm sat with difficulty and the kennelman too. The detectives asked questions and the boy answered. After no more than a few minutes, Bullfinch gave the child something – from the child's grin, a coin or sweet. The boy and the man – his father? – and the other servants dispersed.

Bullfinch lit a pipe, the other detective a cheroot, and the coroner joined them. They talked in low voices, walking off to ensure she could not hear.

Mrs Ashton's head spun. She had to sit. It was Cairngorm who came over, took her arm, and brought her to a bench, away from the murder spot.

Sir Charles is here watching. How absurd. It was tiredness and shock and the lingering confusion from opening someone as they died. She did not trust the drug she had taken.

Dear Lord, there Charles stood, where his body had lain. Dressed coat over nightclothes, as he had been last night, translucent. His face distorted by his rage, shouting, *'Murderous witch!'* Ridiculous. Sheer madness. Don't look.

Bullfinch and the other men returned.

The coroner introduced himself. 'Mrs Ashton, a few questions. A jury is being summoned, and whatever you say, you will have to repeat on oath before them.'

She steeled herself against Sir Charles, whose noise was fading. 'I am accustomed to telling the truth, sir.'

'Do you know that boy, or his father? Have you ever spoken to them? Or have you met any staff in the house before?'

'I don't know either of them. Apart from the coachman, Willoughby, I haven't knowingly met anyone else who works here. There were several men in the courtyard – if the kennelman was there, I don't recall it.'

'And Maisie?'

'You would have to ask her. She has never been north of London before.'

'Gentlemen?' the coroner said. Bullfinch gave a weighty sigh and said, 'I agree.'

The coroner said, 'The boy... quite an extraordinary little chap. He is in the habit of waking at night and going to sleep with the dogs. Last night he heard something in the yard, but frightened by the death, did not tell his father for some hours. A most precise and pedantic child.'

Bullfinch coughed. Get on with it.

'His account matched yours. We staged a reconstruction, and he recognised the person in boy's clothes was not your assistant. Now, he recognised not only your face, but also your gait and the sound of your boots.'

Cairngorm grinned. 'So, he heard the blow, and saw Sir Charles hit the ground, while Mrs Ashton was already in the yard. As she said. And he heard the club fall too.'

'That is his evidence,' Bullfinch said, ruminating.

'Did he see the roof?'

'He had no clear line of sight.'

'I am innocent,' Mrs Ashton said, feeling faint. Thank goodness she was seated.

Bullfinch drew a puff of his pipe. 'I remind you, in a common endeavour, all are guilty of the crime. You might be an accomplice to murder. I would also remind you of the forgery, and attempted theft of the horses and trap. Lady Barrington-Stewart may press charges. You are not going anywhere.'

'But surely neither Mrs Ashton nor the girl should be locked up,' Cairngorm said. 'I vouch they will not try to escape.'

'Neither of you, nor the Bradshaw woman, are to leave the manor,' Bullfinch said. 'One step outside, I will arrest you for obstructing the police.'

'Even to walk in the grounds? My head would benefit from some country air.'

He snorted. 'Absolutely not. You'll have to tell me, and I'll assign an officer to come with you, if one can be spared.'

'Two, Chief Inspector, or three of your toughest men. Two old women and a girl are terrifying criminals.'

She must be feeling better to bait the man and watch his moustache bristle, even his nose hair indignant. Her delusion of Sir Charles evaporated, thank goodness. Such nonsense.

'Don't think you have proved your innocence, madam.'

The house pressed down on her, a gloomy blanket. Charles might have murdered Violet's mother, Lady Herncastle, in this very house. And she could prove none of it. Even if she revealed her power – that she had seen the crimes in his mind – you couldn't offer that to a jury.

'Black clothes. You say these figures wore enveloping black,' said the local detective.

'I suppose we must look for them. Although a house this size has mourning cloth by the roll,' Bullfinch said.

Cairngorm said, 'I will bring Maisie, and I hope some tea. Now it is clear you are no murderer, I am happy to set out what the police have found. And I have many questions about your ordeal. What a vile business it is.'

'Yes, we must support the investigation. How is poor Lady Barrington-Stewart?'

'Oh, too ill to see an old friend on a social call,' Cairngorm said. How gallant he was. What shadow now lay over him? 'What a bad business, for her, for the county. We make these choices, and we never know how they will end.'

Someone brought Bullfinch a note. 'The warden of the asylum. Mrs Ashton, I will call for you when I need you.'

Braddie and Mrs Ashton found a point in the yard where they might avoid hostile ears.

'Dearest, we must help the police solve this crime,' Mrs Ashton said. 'That will throw off the pall of suspicion.'

'You've lost your cursed power. Maybe forever.' Braddie's courage was failing. Usually, she could face down a bull. Seeing Braddie so fearful strengthened the feeling of doom. Mrs Ashton sent upward a silent prayer for them both.

'Dear heart, I am not well. I see and hear Sir Charles in the yard; I felt him when they showed me the murder weapon.'

'Honeybee, sweetest.' Her dear heart shuddered. 'What a tribulation. Ald Nick himsel'.'

'My blood runs cold; my nerves are shot to pieces. We are three innocent women. Yet, I remember past times, my angel, how once suspicion is raised, it hangs over us for months. Friends turn cool to us, favours are declined, and purses shut. Those of any status fear loss of their own reputation. Remember the emeralds.'

Braddie darted her gaze in all directions, then mouth close to ear, 'You stole tha bloody emeralds, hinny. I warned you it meant trouble.'

'No need to be coarse, dear. Our friends who turned so cold didn't know we did.'

Braddie had brought her luggage, and Mrs Ashton changed attire, strengthening her morale. Twenty minutes later, a policeman brought her to the library. Braddie came, swinging her stick with a martial air. Two detectives, and in a comfortable chair, a doctor of the swell sort. An overdressed popinjay, he looked strained, but not as much as he should have.

Bullfinch, oddly, gestured that the women could sit. Mrs Ashton came ready to fight and would stand. The other detective sat too, with an amused look.

Mrs Ashton summoned her anger. Too many asylums hid monstrous crimes – women taken at night and locked up at the mere whim of men, for bearing a child out of wedlock, wishing to leave a brutal husband, or being unable to bear a woman's life of servitude. Her fight back began now.

'Your nurses, sir – trulls, drunks, thieves, brutes of the lowest kind – unworthy of the title of nurse. Blasphemers and liars sent to imprison me. Chief Inspector, I wish to file charges today of false imprisonment, and the theft of my brooch and my watch. Your staff, sir, reflect badly on you. I will complain to the Board of Regulation and to the General Medical Council.'

The warden was a smooth one. 'My dear lady. Sir Charles as Patron said that he needed two nurses and I agreed to take you for observation. He said a doctor's note would be forthcoming. But madam, I assure you, I confine no one without my own considered judgement.

For common decency, if the patient protests my diagnosis, I always call on another opinion. Such diligence protects the patient, but it also protects me. Let me show you the regulations, which I wrote, with their stern words to guard against false accusations and false imprisonment.'

She brushed the offered paper aside.

The detective showed Mrs Ashton a watch. She grabbed it and looked closely.

'It's mine,' she said.

The warden looked sorrowful. 'I directed the nurses to submit to a search,' he said. 'Theft and drunkenness. Their conduct has been abominable. Be assured, Mrs Ashton, when our discussion finishes, I will go and dismiss both on the spot, without a character.'

'You wicked son of damnation.' Braddie flourished her stick. 'You despoiler of women. I shall smite your grinning face.'

The man was suitably alarmed and looked at the police. Bullfinch snapped, 'None of that nonsense, woman. I don't have time.'

Mrs Ashton gave her dear heart a stern look. 'Justice will be done.'

Bullfinch waved Mrs Ashton away, as if his hand could make her disappear. He said to his local colleague, 'Obviously a matter for you, whether to take Mrs Ashton's complaint.'

The man dipped his pen. 'Tidier to do so, don't you think?'

'I want my bee brooch back,' Mrs Ashton repeated.

'That's evidence,' Bullfinch snapped.

Sir Charles had favoured that chair by the fire. That bookcase cunningly concealed another behind it, for the most expensive or disreputable books.

Anxiety twisted her gut. *'How dear Violet will be shocked if she sees them,'* Charles thought.

Mrs Ashton liked to look over the possessions in a great house in case she needed a little extra cash. She knew a couple of admirably crooked booksellers.

How did she know about the secret bookcase? Odd things leaked during an opening – once, a recipe for Dutch herring pie – but Sir Charles certainly hadn't been thinking about erotic pictures when he died.

No, she couldn't see him, but his brooding presence could not be denied.

'Can you hear me, you thieving fraud? What is this? Where am I? Where is my darling wife? What have you done with her?'

She swayed, heart pounding and balance shaking. Madness. Or was this some terrifying new reality she didn't understand?

CHAPTER 20
Telling 'Em Nuttin'

A small attic, Corwood Manor

The attic room door was locked, the skylight screwed shut. Maisie didn't believe in British justice – not for people like her. She didn't believe in St Nick Down the Chimbley neither. Cairngorm was all right, but more a copper than an ordinary person. So, she'd said nothing to the grumpy lawyer, to Bully Bullfinch, or to the country copper. They were trying to starve her, but a day without food held no fears for her. She hadn't eaten since a supper stolen at midnight from the kitchen.

The key turned in the door.

A red-eyed maid came in with a tray. Proper fodder, it looked like. A pie, with greens and potatoes. That cloudy glass was lemonade. At once, Maisie was raging hungry.

She thought she'd seen the lass before but could not remember where. Behind, a young copper hovered.

'My mistress wanted to make sure you were fed,' the maid said.

'How is your mistress?' asked the copper.

'Oh, my poor lady is like the life was drained out of her, sir. Her heart still fluttering like a bird at the window. The doctor doesn't know how long it will be. What terrible times, Lord protect us from such wickedness. Can I put this here...?'

The tray smelled gorgeous. Maisie and the maid eyed each other up for a moment or two.

'I better be getting back, in case my mistress needs me. Leave the tray outside and I'll get someone to call for it.'

Maisie's mind clicked, like a clock before it chimes. The maid reminded her of Forty Wilkins, the friendly groom. His sister Prudie was Lady Violet's maid. Maisie wanted to get out and pump Forty for information.

The old birds had taught her about the social ladder in a big house – what had Braddie said? *The mistress of the house hires and directs her own maid. A lady's maid acts very superior to the others.*

So, in normal times, not Prudie's job to run odd errands for Cook. Were Lady Violet and Esme checking up on her?

She devoured the rich pie. Licking the plate, Maisie thought the posh duo as tricksy as a barrel of snakes.

That ghastly murder brought back Ma, coughing up blood, then still. So still. Pa borrowing money they couldn't afford, so Ma wouldn't disappear nameless into a hole. A horrible choice – you can't eat a coffin or put it on cold kids' backs.

What a strange world for Her Mightyship now. For the high-up widders, they disappeared for the first couple of years, a choking great veil on, like a bag over the head. Imagine keeping a place this size, with a different servant for each type of fork, and having no one come to visit and nowhere to go. If you lost someone, you needed friends and family around to hear you wail. And ordinary people still had to make a living, however sad and over-darked they were. Pa had had to work, like she had.

She must write to Sal, to pass a message to Pa and George and Tildy. She missed them like someone had taken her heart out. Mrs Colquhoun would have a mighty sermon waiting, and she almost wanted it.

Who could have been on the roof, bashed the rich bastard on the noggin, and got away? Dacoits and punishers who'd got off the roof by ladder, silent like. But wouldn't they bring their own cunning weapons – cosh or garotte or knife, or blowpipes with exotic poisons? She'd heard the coppers say Sir C was whacked with an old exercise club from the stables. *An inside job!*

Kate Warne had never been arrested. Maisie would solve the murder, then Mrs Ashton would have to cut her in on the profits.

Then Cairngorm came.

'If you give a statement, I'll be there, then you can meet up with Mrs Ashton and Mrs Bradshaw. We've a witness who proved your dear employer didn't do it.'

'Told you!'

The main problem with that pie was that she now craved another one.

Mrs Ashton resolved that she would not be crushed by misfortune. No one was in the orangery, so they occupied a table. Delightfully warm, with apple, pear, and citrus trees, mostly for show. Spring flowers too.

When a servant frowned at them, Mrs Ashton ordered tea and cake, as if they were at a fashionable London café. He rolled his eyes and disappeared, probably not to return.

'So, the tattie-bogle speaks to you?' Braddie kept her voice low. 'Is he here now?'

'What am I to think, dearest? Perhaps such a connection at death filled my mind with ghastly thoughts. It might just pass. If I start to speak of these matters, I will end up at the asylum.'

Cairngorm entered. Oh, how resolute Maisie looked. What a remarkable lass. They embraced, Braddie hugged her too, while Cairngorm looked on. How drawn he looked, and how handsome.

The butler came and glared at Mrs Ashton.

Cairngorm rose and took his hand. 'Dear fellow. Your brother served nobly under my uncle. How is his poor wife? Now I am here to solve this dreadful crime. Could the marvellous Mrs O'Grady possibly arrange tea and some cake for four? Or I could come down, if you like.'

For Cairngorm, the butler thawed. 'My sister-in-law is better, sir, thanks for asking. How is your uncle? I am sure we will manage something for you and your' – the mouth tightened, and he struggled – 'guests.'

They sat, and Mrs Ashton produced paper and a mechanical pencil. Her enemies would blame her, so it was in their interests to see it solved. What doors might open if she found the solution?

'Where have the police got to?' Mrs Ashton said.

'Well, Bullfinch still thinks you are involved.' Cairngorm looked apologetic. 'He wants me to keep an eye on you. And I'll keep an eye on him. They're briefing the coroner. Nothing new on the body. On the notion it could be an outside job, we've all been searching, and no signs of grapples or ladders. I'm to manage the search for stuff hidden in the grounds... the woods and the lake... a wild goose chase.'

'The murderer might have been splattered with blood. Head wounds can generate a surprising amount.' Mrs Ashton made a mark. 'Clothes might be stained. No certainty, of course.'

'Hands long washed,' Braddie said.

Cairngorm nodded. 'The detectives are thoroughness itself. They will interview everyone in the building. The whole house will be searched, rich and poor, garret to stables, for unexpected laundry or unexpected clothes drying. Perhaps your mysterious dark clothing. The servants hate it, but between the police and their superiors, they don't have a choice.'

'Might a soiled item be burned?' Mrs Ashton said.

'Where, without smell?' Braddie said.

'The boilerman sleeps in the furnace room with his dog. The kitchen staff found the range as they expected, cold. This warm spring, the servants won't have fires on their floor – and anyway, burning two man-sized cloaks in a room fire? Even with time, it is hard to avoid evidence. And the grounds are being searched.'

'I would stick them up a chimbley not in use. Get them later,' Maisie said. 'Anyways, I want to walk from the roof. See how far a person could get before the bell rang.'

'Yes, littl'un,' Cairngorm said. 'They've already done that. Most of the house is in reach, for anyone fit. There's a nervy maid who reports someone wearing a foreign beard in the orchard yesterday – I hesitate to ask what a foreign beard might be – which Mrs Abernathy dismisses as imagination...'

'Get her to sketch it,' Mrs Ashton said. 'Which staff can we rule out?'

The Captain said, 'Well, the young'uns I suppose, and those too infirm to be fast movers. Not all staff live in the manor.'

Mrs Ashton raised an eyebrow. 'Anyone of interest?'

'The land steward and his family have a house. The gamekeepers and a few of the pensioned servants have cottages. Old Willoughby has one, the dear man. All at least a mile away. There are three lady pensioners in the Dower House, a mile and a half if you know the shortcut. Charles's mother, the Dowager Lady Barrington-Stewart, is too ill to live there. No obvious suspects.'

'Those not in the manor itself seem less likely,' Mrs Ashton said.

'Bullfinch insists we interview them, to see if any were wandering around at night,' Cairngorm said.

'And servants share rooms?'

'Of course. The higher ones have their own – the butler, the housekeeper. Some of the young staff might be three or four to a room. Most adults share as two. Mrs Abernathy found all doors between the men's and women's accommodation properly locked.'

'Could both men and women reach the roof?'

'So I am told.'

Maisie snorted. 'For most people that means two men, or two women, giving each other an alibi. Hardly copper-bottomed.'

Braddie frowned. 'Why was the doctor here?'

Cairngorm shrugged. 'And that man Trephine, of course. He snooped around me, after Charles and I had a disagreement in the street.'

Would Trephine kill his employer? Mrs Ashton wondered if the doctor knew of Esme's condition. Perhaps Charles might have wanted his diagnosis of madness, or for him to witness her confession.

'It is dizzying,' she said. 'The police search for physical clues, and by and large they will search things before we do. We can only follow. Dear Captain, we must meet regularly, and you will keep us briefed. I think we women must look to history, to character, and to motive. I pray Lady Violet soon recovers to meet us. I want all suspicion dispelled. And I am resolute to carry out the spiritual research I have long advocated. The beginnings of this murder lie in the deceased's wicked past.'

Cairngorm frowned. 'Mrs Ashton, I hardly think that's decent, spinning tables and the like. Her husband was no gentleman, but this house is in mourning.'

'Lady Violet wished me to do so. I am certain that Sir Charles's misdeeds found him out.' Was this some mystical kismet or karma, or the more mundane working out of earthly revenge?

Mrs Ashton had a room clearly not for persons of quality. But it did have a side room with a bed for Braddie. Exhausted, they each laid their heads down and snoozed.

It was dark when they woke, disturbed. A rap on the door – oh, to be found with her boots off. She swung her legs down and called, 'A moment!'

A male voice. 'Message from Lady Barrington-Stewart.'

Mrs Ashton threw propriety to the winds. 'Come!'

A footman entered, sullen, glanced at her stockinged feet, and sneered. Few staff hid their dislike of her.

'Lady Barrington-Stewart wonders if it would be possible to drop by her reading room shortly.' By now all the staff had black mourning bands on their arms or dresses, the senior staff in full mourning.

Mrs Ashton sat up. She called into the side room. 'Braddie, dear heart, can you help me with my boots?' Then, she asked the footman, 'How is her ladyship?'

'She's up and talking to the Chief Inspector. Such a burden on her.'

'Well, I am flattered to be so high in her estimation,' said Mrs Ashton, an odd mixture of pleased, fearful, and furious. The injury of her gift blinded her...

Now the man glared at Braddie's dress. No wonder. Mrs Ashton had demanded her mourning bands, but Braddie refused to wear mourning for Sir Charles.

'Let us go, then.'

On Braddie's arm, Mrs Ashton walked the length of the house to Lady Violet's reading room, a pleasant room across the corridor from her bedroom, sombrely lit as for an invalid. Bullfinch stood there, seething. The county inspector too, standing back by the unlit fire, a genial man who hid his thoughts rather well. Anyone who managed the belligerent Bullfinch deserved respect. A pleasant-faced maid sat sewing under the light. Prudie, she supposed.

'Her ladyship invited us to hear this discussion,' Bullfinch said.

Lady Violet sat in a deep chair and her cousin Esme on a stool beside her. Both wore black. Unveiled, how pale they were, with shadows under their eyes. Mrs Ashton wanted an excuse to get closer. Touch her and use her gift – and risk the consequences.

Lady Violet spoke, her eyes closing. 'Dear Mrs Ashton, it is good to see you. I barely know how I can keep going. Oh, you warned me, you spoke of darkness and difficulty. What tremendous power you have. Chief Inspector Bullfinch, this woman has a great gift. And she is my guest and must be treated as such.'

Where to start? Mrs Ashton began with the pieties. 'My condolences on your great loss, Lady Barrington-Stewart. Forgive my plainness. I have suffered greatly in this house. I was invited here under false pretences then threatened with gaol and the madhouse. I would like an explanation, please.'

Lady Violet opened her weary eyes. She looked sad and hurt.

'You are owed a thousand apologies. As I told the Chief Inspector, I loved my husband deeply. But we swear obedience to our husbands, do we not? To the world he showed a generous and liberal side, and sometimes he showed me great affection. But he had a darker side. He had almost a mania about you, irrational and unjust.'

'Why trap me? Why send the letter, my lady?'

Lady Violet gasped. 'I know my husband's power. He talked of hiring ruffians to seize you in the night – shameful – and if he did, how could I ward off his anger? Weak as I was to go along, surely it was better to bring you under my roof where I could protect you?' She pleaded, convincing. 'In this room, I made dear Charles swear on the family Gospel, with Esme as my witness, that you would not be harmed and that he would pay for you to leave the country. Exile was harsh, but alas, what else could ensure your safety?'

What Violet said made sense. Mrs Ashton had seen in her enemy's heart not only that it was true, but that her enemy had resolved to comply.

'He kept that oath most shoddily.'

'I wondered how long his patience would hold. Understand, Chief Inspector, Mrs Ashton is a woman of great character. She declined to swear a lie. That is why Esme and I had no choice but to give them the opportunity to escape. Thank goodness.'

Violet was not evading her responsibility. Bullfinch quivered like an over-stoked boiler.

'You helped these renegades escape, my lady?'

Lady Violet put a hand to her heart. 'Esme hid Maisie. I know my duty. Dear Charles's death fell like a bolt from heaven. Even now I feel I could lie down and sleep forever. Yes, common decency required that we contrive their escape. We suggested that she *borrow* my horse and trap. What crime was committed?'

'These women stand accused of forgery,' the local detective said.

Mrs Ashton had unfinished business with Lady Violet. Reining in her temper, she asked, 'Did you know he framed me, my lady?'

Lady Violet raised a delicate hand. 'Oh, a terrible thing. The sums owed will be paid and may that be the end of it. On the table, there. I told the police I have no memory of these letters purporting to be in my hand. Although, something about the loops of the long letters is not right. A curious thing... A pretty notepaper, is it not? With the pattern of violets. Now I think of it, this new paper came from the printers only a few days ago. Yet these letters dated weeks earlier are on my new paper, not my old. How mysterious.'

'I will check this,' Bullfinch said, bristling.

Mrs Ashton was gripped. She glanced at Braddie, whose face showed a grim fury.

'Do, Chief Inspector,' the widow said. 'They cannot be genuine.'

'How easily might your paper be obtained?'

'Oh, it was safe, locked in my bureau.'

'But did Sir Charles have a key?' Mrs Ashton pushed. Bullfinch scowled.

'Of course,' Lady Violet sighed.

'And you told me, once he showed you papers with his signature, which he said his brother had forged?'

'Yes. Although Rupert, who confessed many errors, denied that hotly.' She swallowed. 'My dear Mrs Ashton, are you accusing my husband of *forging* these letters, and faking Rupert's crime too? Oh, it is too dreadful. There must be a more pleasant explanation.' Lady Violet dabbed her eyes.

Bullfinch growled. 'A serious charge, my lady, against a Member of Parliament and a Justice of the Peace.'

'I don't know the truth,' Lady Violet said. 'But, in sorrow and on my mother's grave, these letters are not mine.'

Braddie snorted. One day that snort would get them into deep trouble.

Those beautiful eyes, red rimmed through crying. How pretty the young widow looked.

'Chief Inspector, this is all so difficult. Mrs Ashton had no need to lie. She never asked for money but three times I gave to her charitable work, and once to help her after that dreadful fire. The sums in this fraud involved are not large – if she had asked me for twice that sum, five times, to help the poor in their grief, I would have given it without question. You knew that Mrs Ashton, I am sure.'

Her eyes closed, she put a hand to them. 'In any case, it is quite impossible that such a gentle soul could carry out such a brutal crime.'

The timing of the murder troubled Mrs Ashton. 'Someone killed Sir Charles exactly when we were in the yard.'

Lady Violet said, 'I cannot explain it. All I know is that Sir Charles sometimes rose from our bed to walk at night. He used the walkways on the stable roof, or sometimes even the walkway on the main building. He liked to look out at his lands at night, and up at the stars. I did not wake when he left, and the first I knew...' She raised her handkerchief.

From Violet's voice, her gaze, her posture... She could see this scene painted by the fashionable painters of the day. *The faithful widow.* Nothing denied that Lady Violet spoke the truth.

Yet, there were mysteries. She vowed to use her gift to prove it, with whatever pain it brought. She took a step closer, and Esme rose like a guard dog seeking to block the way. Well, she would read one or other of them.

Lady Violet looked almost childlike.

Esme's hands touching and untouching each other. Mrs Ashton had cried out in front of witnesses that an unnamed woman carried Sir Charles's child. Mrs Ashton had resorted to blackmail several times, but she wouldn't use this unless she truly had to.

It would look odd and rude to touch either woman, yet already she could feel echoes of the murder, the dying man. She tried to open Violet...

...and found Sir Charles suddenly near her.

'Where is Violet, the dear girl? Where is Esme? I cannot see them.'

Mrs Ashton stumbled. The other policeman grabbed a chair, and she took it.

'I feel faint,' Mrs Ashton said, slumping into it.

'Prudie, get water,' said Violet.

The maid darted to grab a glass, the jug. 'Shall I get the doctor?' she said.

'Hellfire. You witch, you've weaselled your way into her room.'

The force of it. She closed her eyes. Surely, they could hear the voice. Sir Charles's voice, without a doubt, as angry as she had ever known – as angry as when she had opened him, and he had wanted to kill her.

'Ashton, you fraud, you poxed whore, you lying witch, you burning devil's quim... You murderer!'

Charles had died: there could be no doubt. And yet, here he was. She promised her flock that there was life after death. Unless gripped by insanity, her worst enemy had proved it true.

What could she do to fight his rage? The twenty-third Psalm came to mind; she would say it in her head.

The Lord is my shepherd; I shall not want. He maketh me to lie down in green pastures: He leadeth me beside the still waters. He restoreth my soul: He leadeth me in the paths of righteousness for His name's sake.

He could not win. Braddie held her shoulder, spun the gaping watchers a line. After a few minutes of shouting in her head, her guts churning, Charles said, *'Damn you to the lowest pit of hell,'* and was gone.

Chapter 21
Opponents Confer

Mrs Ashton's guest room

Mrs Abernathy took them to their guest rooms. She looked like she'd eaten a plate of toads. Mrs Ashton assumed the most benign expression, enjoying the reversal. Braddie and Maisie looked on, amused.

'Her ladyship wishes to know if this room is adequate for your needs. And to say that I will ensure you get anything you desire. Cook will send up dinner.'

'How lovely. I think we will be comfortable, thank you. When subject to these malign forces, it is helpful for my servant to sleep in this side room.'

The rooms to either side of their two were unoccupied. Mrs Ashton dared a pleasant thought. If Maisie agreed to sleep in the garret, she and Braddie might make good use of the privacy.

'Mrs Ashton, her ladyship says you may breakfast with the other guests. Mrs Bradshaw and the girl will eat with the servants.'

'You may tell your staff that I did not kill Sir Charles, and I intend to find out who did.'

The housekeeper's jaw clenched. 'You will not spread your nonsense among the servants. The girls are in enough of a state without banshees and ghouls. And Cook will box your ears. On this, the Kirk and the Bishop of Rome are united. Is that all?'

Mrs Abernathy swept out in plaid annoyance.

'We should get what we can, and get awa',' Braddie said.

'I want to show the world Charles's true nature. Prove his former crimes. And so long as the murder is unsolved, half the country will think it is me. Lady Violet's good opinion is not enough.'

A long silence.

Maisie said, 'Most of the house could have done it. You only need your roommate to stay asleep.'

Mrs Ashton said, 'The murderer may have needed to wash. There seems to be no one with an obvious motive. That's what we need to find.'

'Violet might have done it, or Esme,' Maisie said. 'Who could blame them?'

'Why then is Violet so keen for the crime to be solved?'

Should she explain her power to Maisie? She trusted the girl as much as anyone. But Maisie's demands would doubtless grow. Knowing might put both of them in danger,

Mrs Ashton had opened two minds. Sir Charles foresaw a bright future with his women and even gave Violet her impertinent wish. At a deep level, his flawed affection for his wife had been rekindled. And she had opened Violet before and knew her character.

'The spirits are wise; they see no violence in her heart.'

Braddie gave that uncouth noise, like a farmyard animal.

Mrs Ashton went on. 'What I do agree, dear girl, is that she may well be hiding something – about the crime, or something else.'

'She knows who did it?' Maisie said.

'I cannot discount that possibility.'

Two hours later, and they had a very partial list of staff compiled. They agreed to meet regularly to update each other.

A confident knock, and Braddie answered the door.

Trephine, uninvited and unwelcome, stood grinning, bearing a tray of bottles, and glasses.

'Awa' to kiss Ald Nick's flaming arse,' Braddie said. She did not let him in.

Mrs Ashton didn't smile.

'I hoped that Lady Violet would have had you whipped by the gamekeepers,' she said.

'I am her newest and most humble servant. I thought we might toast the new mistress of this house. Oh, she admires you, Mrs Ashton. You have fallen on your feet. Or we could toast the strange fate that makes us strong allies.'

'Mr Trephine, no spoon is long enough for me to dine with you.'

'One glass of Grennard's Best, the humble cornerstone of all this finery. Murder offends my soul, Mrs Ashton. I don't believe you did it, and as for me, I can assure you, it's a foolish man who murders his main source of income. Let us find who did.'

'And what of the burning of my house, and my reputation?'

'What advice did I give you last night, Mrs Ashton?'

Sign the confession and leave as soon as possible. She suspected it was good advice. Had he known there would be murder?

'One glass.' She waved him to a chair. Braddie found her stick and sat holding it.

'Let us clear the air,' he said. 'A friend of mine works for a wealthy gentleman who has great dislike of a lady. The gentleman is so angered he asks the friend – forgive my brutality – to cut off her nose.'

It took all her self-control not to gasp. Such a violation.

'The friend shudders to do that. What a terrible misjudgement. Many dislike the lady, but such a vicious attack, almost an attack on all women... There would be sympathy in unexpected quarters. Public collections. Rewards offered. Even her critics in the papers would demand the police show impartial vigour. The friend offers these views, and then says, "Why not burn her house? What a dramatic sign of your power. Spread rumours the lady is committing fraud. Raise that hare, and she will have no sympathy. Those who dislike the medium can hate her, their consciences unstirred."'

Braddie snapped. 'Brigand! Pirate!'

Mrs Ashton scowled. 'To be a cowardly monster is still to be a monster.'

Trephine looked wounded but unbowed. 'How carefully it must be done, so no person, no pet, suffers. The friend is a deep humanitarian, but hark... if he offers nothing, the gentleman of great means and greater temper knows men who would maim a dozen women. The gentleman agrees. The only flaw is that the lady had a landlord too stupid to pay the insurance.'

Mrs Ashton dared not try her gift.

'Someone could have died.'

'You, Mrs Ashton, are a marvel. Will you tell me how you do what you do? Much of it is clear enough. No one in the British Library is a more assiduous researcher. But there's something beyond. And we both know ghosts don't exist.'

'More things on heaven and earth, Mr Trephine.'

He opened a bottle, and Mrs Ashton handed him her water glass, not one of his. Maisie found another for herself.

The horrid man. 'Why did Lady Violet not expel you from her house, like some unpleasant insect?'

The grin, the gaze, slipped a little. 'There are a few areas of her husband's life where I have some temporary use. His niece, for example.'

Mrs Ashton hoped she hid her surprise. Trephine leaned forward. 'Black sheep Rupert sired a bastard girl on an actress and fled domestic bliss. Sir Charles made a generous arrangement with the woman – pleasant rooms, a servant, in due course, schooling. To see a penny, the woman must keep his brother away from the girl and the money. I told the esteemed lady of certain arrangements to continue this. She approved and I am to go to London to finalise it. The lady offers to be the girl's godmother. And since Sir Rupert landed in the country some weeks ago, she wants me to find him.'

'He's definitely in the country?'

'There's no doubt. I heard last night that Mrs Abernathy's nephew saw him in London. In one of those strange French goatish beards. The Imperial has outlasted the lecherous Emperor that spawned it. Sir Charles and Rupert fought as boys, with fists. They share their temper, if nothing else. I can see them brawling on the roof. There'll be some old servant who thinks Rupert was hard done by and let him in...'

'Or not.'

'Or not. Coincidence happens. Here's another. The heroic Captain Cairngorm is in the house of his first love, having suffered a mysterious new injury, and Sir Charles barely cold. The Captain truly earned his decoration for valour. The citation was, he got three men back to safety, then – wounded – went back for his native interpreter. He once berated my former employer in the street about his conduct as a husband. Once, there would have been pistols at dawn. I imagine a fierce meeting at night. Ten shillings says the Captain did not strike first, but he is a warrior born and he would defend himself, with whatever lay to hand.'

Braddie had said nothing. Now, 'He hurt himsel' riding, the man already dead.'

'He says. Or he rode to the manor the night before, a route he knew. Hid the horse in the woods, killed Sir Charles and was injured... I wouldn't like to get off the roof at night and in haste. For a seasoned Army man, simple to wait in the woods until first light.'

'He's a married man,' Mrs Ashton said. Cairngorm glowed with love for his wife.

'Sometimes the man outweighs the married. Or, let us be fair, the knight in shining armour may save the lady for chivalry, not *l'amore*. It's already talk in the servants' hall. Keep him in mind.'

'You could have done it,' Mrs Ashton said. 'Your employer had the power to crush you.'

'Oh, I don't fear that.'

Well-hidden, but something there, she was certain. Trephine would know things dangerous to Charles, and cynical and intelligent Charles would protect himself. She sipped the excellent beer, remembering times when she'd been glad to get anything half as good.

She turned the conversation. 'I will bear those imaginative possibilities in mind. I believe that as a youth, Sir Charles murdered a girl called Grace Overmorrow and I have strong suspicions that Lady Herncastle's overdose was no accident. I want the truth of those crimes.'

He frowned. 'A curious name. Was there a trial, and the man was freed? I don't remember. Lady Herncastle, well, that was a sad accident for a kind woman who harmed no one. I shun murder, Mrs Ashton, and my employer would not waste his breath proposing it to me.'

'You think him capable of planning a murder?'

Trephine finished his beer.

She risked opening him. Worse than a roaring wind of Sir Charles's anger, it failed entirely.

Trephine, the viper, made an excuse and left.

'As crooked as a shilling made of cheese,' Maisie said.

'I don't trust him. I think he is throwing sand in our eyes,' Mrs Ashton said.

Maisie had some plan to get into the library after everyone went to bed, to see if there was a secret bookcase. Mrs Ashton was not so foolish as to steal in a house full of policemen. But she could steal what no one knew existed. Once the girl had slipped away, Braddie unburdened herself.

'I canna believe murder, and real ghosts, and those high ladies plotting with that Trephine. We canna stay here! It's like a lamb rolling in the butcher's mint bush.'

'We cannot leave. We would be arrested, and the whole country would be looking for us. Let's sleep.'

She found safety of sorts in her dear heart's arms, a linen chest blocking the door. Noise carried, so they must be silent, and they could be interrupted at any time. Still, kisses and hands, unspoken consolations and apology, as well as they could under the circumstances. Sometimes lovemaking is a kiss of the whole body, a peace making, not a raging fire. Mrs Ashton held Braddie, her dear heart, who had been true in the face of the worst provocation.

Chapter 22
Hunted in Dreams

Corwood Manor, Thursday

Mrs Ashton had turbulent dreams. She was hunted through woods rich in foxgloves, strong hands drowning her in a clear lake, wandering a dark labyrinth, ears cocked for the monster she knew followed her scent. Through it all, Sir Charles raged and screamed for her death. Once she woke, Braddie was no longer in their bed, and she went to gaze on that troubled face in sleep, loose under a cap. She stroked a long grey lock and wondered.

Mrs Ashton had never valued dreams for some inner meaning, far less assumed they were prophesy. Would she ever be clear of Sir Charles?

She returned to a troubled bed.

Morning, and Braddie sat by her, her face wrought with emotion. Dear heart! Mrs Ashton clasped both hands in hers. The rules of her world had changed, but Braddie had not.

'Is he watching us?' Braddie said. 'Can you feel him? What's it like?'

What an awful thought, to have a spook spying on her, let alone that bully, that murderer of women.

'Not this moment, dearest. When I do, it is unmistakable – the difference between a cartoon of him and the man breathing. Intolerable if he can spy unknown. Let us hope not.'

'I canna believe it – all these years and a real spook.'

'Well, my love, we must do what we can. I had faith in an afterlife, without evidence. As we are alone, let me say how sorry I am. Things must be better between us. How right you were. I vow, I will listen to you more, about everything. I must heed your wise caution and chase no rainbows.' She sighed. 'I have had long hours to brood on my faults.'

'And your gift...'

'Pray it returns. But, if one spirit exists, surely many do? Poor Lady Herncastle might tell us her secrets. How did she suspect Sir Charles? What did she know? If I cannot read the living, I can try to read the dead.'

'He's past hanging.' Braddie looked around again. 'And if the old wives are right, spirits are out to lure us into danger, one way or another.'

A vigorous knock brought Maisie, with a jug of hot water.

'They had a man sleeping in the library... all the investigating papers are hidden somewhere. I swiped this from by Bullfinch's door.'

Maisie went ahead of Braddie down the stairs. She heard loud praying from the servants' hall, and hungry as she was, praying made a poor sauce. Braddie said servants would have been working since five or six and took a proper breakfast when the family were served.

The butler read a passage in Bible cant. Then he gave a stern but kindly talk on the need to support the grieving family.

'Duty is the ship we sail in. You may know that twice journalists tried to reach the house last night. The dogs were diligent in their duties. Our orders are clear: staff must raise the alarm if they see an intruder, and anyone who speaks to a journalist will be dismissed. Am I understood? Then, I must inform you that the jury will be arriving this morning, to be sworn and to perform their solemn duties. Twenty persons. We'll use the ballroom, and they will need to view certain places and things.'

The body, all broken! And soon to be carved up by the surgeons like a turkey.

'Now, Mrs O'Grady...'

An Irish voice rang out, a woman. 'Men, I need you to be serving the police in the long scullery, and lunch too. I am having no girls in there – we have no time for nonsense. Today will be difficult enough. I will not have any familiarity the other way, either. I'll tell the inspector on any man who is too fresh.'

The commotion suggested people were moving, sitting, and serving. Braddie strode into the room, Maisie following.

Mrs O'Grady commanded, lanky in a cook's apron, and the butler and the housekeeper they knew.

'I suggest you eat in my corner,' said the cook, trying her best to be pleasant. 'Room for two, all cosy. Someone show them.'

'Mrs Ashton's nasty little spy,' said someone. Oh, Forty, the nice groom. Today he looked haggard and in a foul temper. He raised his voice. 'No one talk to her. She sniffed around the stables in London, snooping and lying and asking questions.'

'Good morning to you too,' Maisie said, even though every eye was on her. Except for Prudie, who was passing things and looking down. Brothers could be embarrassing.

The corner, a doorless cubbyhole, allowed them to hear people talking between the long scullery and the louder voices in the servants' hall.

'...All the press camped in the gateway, wonder what the papers...'

'...Wicked foreigners... Opium fixings, they found it on the roof... with his crest on the box...'

'...You know about the Captain though! Fancy him, a married man...'

'...Does she speak to the dead, for real?'

'...Ask them two villains, they'll know...'

Mrs Abernathy came past, drawn and muttering something about hot water bottles.

'You must keep mourning cloth in store, a big house like this,' Braddie remarked.

'Of course,' the housekeeper said, surprised.

'Was any missing?'

Mrs Abernathy looked bemused. 'No. As I told the local inspector, we have half a roll *more* than we should. I am most particular, all orders are checked, and I cannot understand the mistake.'

'Very odd to be over,' Braddie agreed, exchanging a silent glance with Maisie.

Mrs Ashton decided on a black shawl, not full mourning dress. She arrived at breakfast to a delightful room, hung with fine paintings and hunting trophies. The papers set out on one table, tea and coffee and chafing dishes on another. The savoury smells brought her appetite back. *When did I last eat properly and at leisure?*

Doctor Culpe looked horrified at her arrival, the county detective quizzical, and the coroner gave a pleasant smile. The men would serve themselves, while a manservant waited in case something needed to be brought.

'Good morning,' said the coroner. 'They have kippers. Capital!'

'I'm not discussing the case in front of Mrs Ashton,' said the doctor.

In this house, the papers were presented folded so the news pages showed. The headlines in *The Times*, *The Magister*, and *The Orb* shouted *MURDER MURDER MURDER*. No MP had been murdered since a Prime Minister long ago, before Mrs Ashton was born.

'Good morning, gentlemen,' said Mrs Ashton. 'Not a kipper day for me, I think, but I smell bacon.'

'This is intolerable,' Doctor Culpe said.

Mrs Ashton smiled. 'I was invited to this house by Lady Barrington-Stewart, and she wishes me to continue my spiritual investigations.'

In limped Cairngorm, that young face care-worn but trying a smile. 'Gentlemen, Mrs Ashton. I hope you have recovered.'

'I would rather dine with a vagabond fortune-teller,' the doctor growled.

Mrs Ashton wasn't having it. 'My dear sir, many people in this house may have been on the roof and done the deed. None of them are denied breakfast.'

Culpe gasped. 'Outrageous!'

The young man gestured to the servant. 'If the coffee is strong and hot, I will trouble you for a cup. I can help myself to the vittles.' To his audience, he said, 'Mrs Ashton is unusual among us – she has an iron-clad independent witness in her favour.'

Cairngorm sat to one side of Mrs Ashton.

Culpe growled. 'A Spiritualist carnival...'

'I wonder what those stout fellows, the jury, will make of it all.' Cairngorm belonged to that oblivious breed, who viewed silence at the breakfast table as an opportunity, not a hint.

'Doctor Culpe,' asked the county inspector, 'when might Lady Barrington-Stewart be able to see us again?'

'I am most concerned about her health. Her pulse is erratic with shock.' He looked seedy and unwell, and he ate breakfast as if it cursed him.

Mrs Ashton needed to know if her power had returned. Bracing herself against the possibility of horror, she touched Cairngorm's arm.

A strange unease floated around her. Again, she could read nothing.

'What are your plans?' Cairngorm asked her.

'The mistress of this great house expressly asked me to seek her mother's spirit. I will start in her rooms, where the tragedy happened.'

Encouraged by last night, Mrs Ashton must prepare for a significant financial ask, weaving together what she could promise and a reminder of what she had suffered.

'A sad business,' the coroner said. Not unkindly, he added, 'Mrs Ashton, I see your two dozen questions buzzing. I said everything I had to say at the time.'

'How great a burden that death is to her.' Cairngorm had a brooding look, a darkness over him she'd not seen before. 'Mrs Ashton, do you want an impartial witness for your... activities?'

'It might be dangerous for the inexperienced,' Mrs Ashton said. 'Mrs Bradshaw and I will do it alone.'

Bullfinch strode in, recoiled at Mrs Ashton, and said, 'By the Eternal, must we suffer this torment? Good morning, gentlemen.'

Mrs Ashton sat unbowed. 'Good morning, Chief Inspector. I pray for your success.' He growled.

'We are still agreed on the sketching, I trust?' the county detective said to Bullfinch. He explained to the table, 'For the papers. The scene of the death, and the best detective in Scotland Yard on the case. We must throw them the odd bone.'

Bullfinch grunted, and Mrs Ashton addressed herself to the county detective. 'Are the press very difficult?'

'They must do their duty, we must do ours. There is a shanty town by the gate, six tents already.'

No time to waste. Mrs Ashton said, 'This country butter is excellent. Do you recall the Overmorrow case?'

The local man nodded. 'Indeed. An old county name I have not heard for a while.' He speared more kidneys on his fork. 'As a youth, I think that wicked case stirred me to my vocation. The worst of humanity, and a textbook in how not to conduct a proper investigation. A disgrace. I read the papers and came up with wild theories.'

'The well-dressed rider...'

'Oh, many such sightings, not followed up. Even now, we could find a rope for the killer.'

The coroner drank coffee. 'No crime that old is solved, in my experience. The exception is some deathbed confession.'

The detective raised his voice a notch or two. 'Who knows, twenty years, thirty years after the crime, they might still be hunted down. In Rome, the murderer would be flung from a cliff.'

An odd passion for the breakfast table, and a curious observation about the execution.

Bullfinch addressed Mrs Ashton, chewing dislike. 'Why do you believe Sir Charles murdered this girl in his youth?'

'If we discussed my methods, Chief Inspector, we would quarrel.'

'I once conducted a post-mortem at sea,' the coroner said. A fascinating tale followed, gruesome and utterly unsuited to the breakfast table, but Mrs Ashton enjoyed it.

Chapter 23

A Spiritualist Experiment and an Important Departure

A little later

Rose, Lady Herncastle, had used three rooms: the Arbour Room, a room for personal convenience, and a place for a nurse or servant. The suite was so named for the paintings and fittings to a woodland theme. Since her death, the room had been unchanged, and unused, yet kept as if Lady Herncastle would return to it.

Mrs Ashton and Braddie made their way to Lady Violet's rooms nearby, while Maisie was left, protesting, in the care of a young constable. Mrs Ashton did not want Maisie seeing her in turmoil. Prudie opened the door, and Mrs Ashton wanted to open her. She reached out a hand ... and her power still did not come. Like an important memory that wasn't there. How could she live without her gift?

Prudie looked at her oddly, as well she might.

Mrs Ashton tried not to show her alarm. Lady Violet in black sat by the window, and Prudie returned to her sewing.

'Dearest Mrs Ashton,' Violet said, with a weary smile. 'I hope that you have recovered. What was it?'

'Some malign spirit hangs over this place,' said Mrs Ashton. 'I am now better prepared should it try again. A hazard of the gift, my lady.'

Lady Violet looked out of the window. 'This place is filled with sadness now. Even the light on the trees is full of it.' She looked back. 'Mrs Ashton, at last, we shall seek my mother. We will know the truth.'

'I will do so, in her room. Against these forces, I will be cautious. Mrs Bradshaw and I will try alone.'

'Are you quite strong enough?' Lady Violet looked troubled. 'The malign spirit overcame you rapidly. Do you know what it was?'

'I am better prepared,' Mrs Ashton repeated. 'These are creatures of guile and cruelty. I would not place anyone inexperienced in danger, let alone one so tragically bereaved.'

Braddie looked worried, as well she might. It might be beneficial to have Lady Violet in the séance. Yet, without her gift, how well could Mrs Ashton take advantage?

Lady Violet reached for a handkerchief. 'I long to be in your circle, Mrs Ashton... but after this awful death, it is too soon. Yet I truly believe my mother watches over me, more than ever.'

Lady Violet held out her hand and Mrs Ashton clasped it, only for a moment. Again, she felt nothing. It was like walking blind.

'My trustees are arriving. I feel my responsibility very deeply. All those lives now in my care, the estate and the business must continue. Yet I cannot decide the simplest things. I pray for you.'

Thus, Mrs Ashton and Braddie entered the room alone. The décor was overdone, and the furniture untouched by modern fashions. The door shut, and right on cue Braddie said, 'Do you have to do this?'

Two chairs and a table between them. An idle finger swiped on the surface showed Mrs Ashton no slackness in the cleaning. She sat and encouraged Braddie to bring the other chair closer. 'Sweetheart, I am ready for Sir Charles. Dear Violet cannot see me out of control. I hope to find Lady Herncastle and assure our fortune. But whatever happens, I am prepared.'

'But *now*?' Are you strong enough, my lass? I've seen a sick ewe with more strength.'

Mrs Ashton's heart pounded, anticipating an attack, and her mouth was curiously dry.

She took out her travelling Bible, a Book of Common Prayer borrowed from the house library, and a few brief notes. Once she had conducted a faux exorcism with a defrocked Welsh priest. Last night she had scribbled down most of a Prayer of Deliverance – what she could remember. Surely intent mattered more than exactness? She scanned her writing and then took out a candle in a patent holder and the matches. A flame proved useful as a focus for devotions.

Mrs Ashton prepared for a crucial performance in front of an invisible, malign audience. Or perhaps, for her descent into madness. What a wonder. There could not be only one ghost in the whole world.

'Suppose I do reach Lady Violet's mother,' she said. 'Or, if that vision was a true one, speak to poor Grace.'

'Too late to hang the de'il,' Braddie said, clutching her hand.

'I need your strength, dear heart,' Mrs Ashton said, and she meant it in a dozen ways. She withdrew her hand, lit the candle on the table, then took Braddie's hand again. 'Let us start with the prayer of Jesus. Our Father...'

Braddie of course would not join in. Mrs Ashton found one of the marked places in the Gospel and set it down.

Then she sent her gift out into the world. To open the air.

Two breaths before the pain and anger came.

Sir Charles snarling and vicious. *'You, snooping around.'*

Mrs Ashton spoke aloud. 'Against Our Lord all malign spirits are without power. I command you in the name of He who cast out evil spirits, be quiet or be gone.'

'Whore, murderer, witch...' Next to her, then all around her, close and stifling. Anger without a body, but certainly with a focus – on her. He screamed as if his breath was endless, sometimes without words, sometimes with the filth of the gutter and the barracks.

Although he raged like a wind, the candle did not flutter. Braddie stared, resolute and horrified.

'I feel nothing,' Braddie said. 'Your pulse hammers like a machine loom...'

The full force of Sir Charles's anger hit her, and she closed her eyes, like a storm. He wanted to kill her. *'I will rip your skin off, I will eat your flesh, I will flog you with iron chains. You killed me, whoremonger, you foulness, you sewer.'* Incoherent memories – killing Grace, how once he had fantasised of strangling Braddie with a chain in front of her. Mrs Ashton floated in the sea of his hatred, but she lived, and he did not.

Using all her control, she spoke in a low even voice. 'I did not kill you, nor did I plan t-to.' The typhoon in her head did not shake the flame.

The Prayer of Deliverance stoked his anger. The Lord's Prayer, a Psalm or two, Jesus stilling the storm, the Our Father again. Passages she knew by heart, on which she could concentrate. Fear said, *Stop reciting, raise a hand against an imagined blow.* Fear said, *Run*. Instead, she opened her eyes and picked up the Bible.

'Braddie, sweetheart, I am going to read more scripture to him. I will probably need a little from that fine flask you carry, to soothe my throat. And there are peppermints in my bag.'

The abuse came as a gust of words, but behind that seeped the sewer of her enemy's mind. A little opening and it trickled out. She flushed at his vile imagination, but she could tell fantasy from memory. None of this had ever happened. Voice quivering, she tried to be stern.

'To read the entire book of Psalms takes at least five hours. You cannot be comfortable shouting like that. I pity dear Violet for being married to such a rapacious Bluebeard.'

'Even the devil can quote scripture!' he screamed, and she replied, 'I am not the devil here, Sir Charles.'

Battle was joined. Mrs Ashton found the familiar rhythms of her words soothing; she could focus on them like the liturgy, or the Latin chants in Catholic churches, worrying less about exact meaning than the atmosphere they brought. Braddie, behind her, squeezed her shoulder every so often, leaving her both hands free to hold the Bible and turn the page. She remembered why she didn't read every Psalm; some were most curious, even unpleasant.

Snippets for a piece in *The Spiritualist Review* began to form.

'Can you keep this up?' Braddie whispered.

'For hours and hours. God's work does not weary the righteous.' Act with courage, despite her fear.

That burning rage lessened in the face of her resistance. Perhaps ten exhausting minutes in all before Sir Charles stopped forcing his memories on her, then five minutes of abuse in Latin, Greek, and the cant of the sewers, then a blessed silence. He brooded, he surrounded her, she could feel him as if he sat on her, but no attack. The frustration and hostility felt mutual, to be honest.

'Oh, send the disgusting old beast away at least,' Sir Charles said.

Perhaps it was a trap. Or perhaps she had survived his best shot.

Mrs Ashton took on her most haughty air. 'Even Chief Inspector Bullfinch accepts I am innocent. I went to your aid, sir, as my Christian duty, and much thanks I have had for it.'

'I hope they hang you anyway.'

'You face the mysteries of God's judgement. Lady Violet is shocked and mourning, but she is now free and need not fear you.'

'Hellfire – you're worse than ever. A preachy thief with no sense of decorum. You will die, Mrs Ashton, one way or another. As soon as I can manage it.'

'But I know that my Redeemer liveth, Sir Charles. I believe His promises and in Him I trust. I walk into the dark expecting judgement but confident in His love. Whereas you are a murderer, an adulterer, a perjurer, and a scorner of God's law. Narrow the path and steep the mountain you must climb. Repent!'

Eerie, the spirit all around her, but it was Sir Charles's laugh.

'I do not tire. You will. I won't be bested by an unnatural sanctimonious fraud. Why did you sit by me as I died? Were you picking my pocket? Did you steal my ring?'

'I saw a man suffering. He was hurt, and beyond my humble aid. I prayed for him as he died. Love thine enemies, Sir Charles, and pray for those who persecute you.'

'A likely story.'

'How did Lady Herncastle die, Sir Charles? How did she know about your murder of poor Grace Overmorrow, the girl you strangled? Were you scared that she would expose you?'

Oh, that all-consuming rage. A single vulgar word and he was gone.

Mrs Ashton found that precious gift, laughter. 'Can you imagine! I can name half a dozen mediums who would clamour to assist.' Now she knew spirits existed. Were any of her rivals gifted? Precious few, she suspected.

'And not a trace of Lady Herncastle,' she said. 'What will we tell the inspector, or Lady Violet?'

'Now that is a conundrum. If only the vile Sir Charles remembered his

Weary, violated, her head was full of the man's disgusting visions, which her excellent memory would retain. Yet each clean breath without him brought more relief. She embraced Braddie and said, 'I've got rid of him, for now.'

How good that embrace felt.

'I felt how hard it was, hinny. You fought him off, my lioness.'

'Yes, dear heart, he can be fought.'

Mrs Ashton pushed aside the latest horror. 'There was no denial of my accusation. And against logic, he still thinks I killed him.'

'Just like the brute to testify against you.'

'We must find the murderer – if nothing else, it might divert his anger elsewhere.'

A fear hit her.

'You do believe me, sweetness? That I truly hear him, and feel him?'

Braddie hugged her, the strength in her arms a sign of the strength and constancy of her love. Her dear heart was better than any man she had ever known. Mrs Ashton must vow to be worthy.

'Well, you're mad, or right. If you're right, it's the world that's mad. You know I will choose my hinny over the world.'

'Dearest, I am blessed, blessed. I am not worthy.' Not more tears, but if she could not weep in Braddie's arms, where could she weep?

And she dwelt a little on her ridiculous fantasy, of some pleasant corner of the world where two women might share a life, or two men, with the world knowing what each meant to the other. A priest who might bless them. In Paradise, perhaps.

Chapter 24

A Tragedy Revisited.

The orangery, later

Maisie clutched the leather-bound scrapbook, wondering if she was right. The table in the orangery waited, and one of the gardeners working nearby frowned, abandoned his task, and left. The servants kept all grim and hostile, so getting them to talk important stuff was worse than pushing a full dray up a high hill. Grace Overmorrow was a long-ago tragedy that didn't concern them, and Lady Herncastle... she had been liked, and no one wanted outsiders sticking their noses in.

Here came Mrs Ashton, leaning a little on Braddie. They both looked around, finding no one spying, and sat.

Maisie asked a burning question. 'Did you raise the murdered lady?'

'No, dearest.' Mrs A was clearly dithering what more to say. 'Only the dreadful spirit of Sir Charles.'

Was this one of her games? 'Did he see his murderer? Did you see him broken? Was he in his gory nightshirt...?'

'Dearest child, I am drained by such an horrific experience. Beyond your chatter. Can you run and see if we might have tea, or something more sustaining?'

Maisie had seen Mrs Ashton so many times put on her show. She conversed with spirits, answered questions, and dodged like an acrobat past difficulties and mistakes. Twice she'd even driven away evil spirits, more exciting than a fist fight. Mrs Ashton entertained as much as a magician in the music hall.

This was different. Now her employer and Braddie were... rattled. Shaky, almost as bad as their house being burned. It must be the murder.

Maisie wasn't going to be sidelined any longer. She had something to share.

Maisie bowled a corker. 'No one saw Charles's brother fall in the lake, except him.'

Mrs Ashton frowned. 'Dear child, I read the accounts in both *The Times* and *The Chronicle*. There were sound witnesses.'

'Yeah, but I found the full accounts in the local paper. Here's a scrapbook I found in the guest study. Commemorating dead Henry, ever so sad. Although, it was all dandy for Charles, wasn't it?' She swept a hand. 'All this lolly – all Lord Muck's titles and honours – are because of the accident he survived.'

Both old birds twitched, like cats who hear mice. Maisie read aloud.

'Hearing a cry, two workers came quickly and viewed the horrific scene, the boat overturned and Charles struggling heroically to save his brother. By malign fate Henry, a strong swimmer, had struck his head falling on the gunwale. The younger boy, the weaker, could hardly hold the older. With good fortune, one of the gardeners was a vigorous swimmer and did not hesitate to remove his boots and dive into the water. Otherwise, a double tragedy could have blighted the family.'

Mrs Ashton leaped in. 'But that is not correct. Those papers said, I recall most specifically, that the staff witnessed the boat capsize and Henry being stunned.'

Maisie opened another place she had marked. 'Here's the inquest report in the local paper. Every word. Someone on the jury asked the gardener.'

She put on a man's voice. 'But Jones, neither you nor your companion saw the boat capsize yourself?' The gardener said, 'No, sir, that's what the young master said, the poor fellow.'

Then the coroner leaps in. 'Let us not labour this point, it is merely for the record. Members of the jury, you will remember the evidence of the police and the doctor. This is a simple matter. The specific wound on Henry's forehead was of a width and nature consistent with hitting the gunwale, exactly as Master Charles described.'

The gardener said, 'I just want to say, sir, I know boys. Them two were true brothers, such pals they were never apart.' And the judge says, 'Thank you, Jones, no one who heard Master Charles give his evidence could be in the slightest doubt of that. Our thanks for your time.'

'Show me everything,' Mrs A said, and the three of them worked through the reports.

Mrs Ashton massaged her temple. 'Remarkable. Another paper need only omit a few lines, and the mistake is explained. Brevity, or a fault in the telegraph. And the coroner's charge to the jury does not touch on it and commends Charles's struggles to save his brother. The reports in the national press seemed full, I had no reason to look for the local papers.'

Braddie brooded. 'Them, all their wealth and power, protecting their own.'

'Or, we love a strong story – the younger boy struggling to save his idol, and a simple mistake.' Mrs Ashton closed her eyes. 'I need a walk, fresh air and exercise. Let us go to the lake. Perhaps the victim can be raised.'

'Jones is still a gardener here,' Braddie said. 'The other, I don't know.'

How odd for that detail to have stayed in plain sight all these years. What a find Maisie was, to have uncovered this truth. And how often she would doubtless bring this up, when her remuneration was discussed.

Mrs Ashton admired nature but it was best tamed, with a solid path, and the air fresh-laden with the promise of summer. She viewed the warmer weather with approval. Flowers bursting into bloom and a veritable orchestra of birdsong. Being well away from enquiring ears would be no bad thing.

With suitable hats, Mrs Ashton, Braddie, and Maisie set off from the house only be halted within fifty yards by a policeman puffing up to them.

'You're not supposed to leave the house,' he said, breathing heavily. He was a ruddy man at that tipping point between merely being large and his constable's uniform bulging in unfortunate places.

'I'm not supposed to leave the *estate*, Constable.' Mrs Ashton adopted her most drawing room voice. 'I have been expressly asked by Lady Barrington-Stewart herself to investigate the local psychic phenomena. We need to tour the lake, for that exact purpose.'

The man said, 'Well, you might run off.'

Mrs Ashton delicately lifted her skirt to reveal one elegant boot. 'I hardly think I could outrun you in these, Constable. And I would leave my luggage.'

'Well, I'll have to follow you,' he said, to Braddie's eyeroll and Maisie's snort.

'Very well. There are dark forces afoot, and you must be ready to face them with courage. In many tales, the spirits of the drowned are particularly restless. At least the poor boy who drowned received a Christian burial. In the Tsar's Finnish dominions, it is said a ghostly swan haunts the waters between life and death...'

Mrs Ashton set off for the far side of the lake, confusing the bobbie with tales of screaming lake beasts and eerie water maidens drowning their male suitors. Maisie ran ahead, Braddie's awkward gait suggesting her joints were bad.

They stopped to consider clear lines of view. Mrs Ashton confirmed to her own complete satisfaction that the picturesque island, a veritable overgrown forest floating on the water, stood between this quadrant of the lake and the whole house. On the main shore, the woods came down to the lake further round on the opposing side. The drowning happened out of sight of the house but there were many angles from which someone in the grounds could have seen it – a reckless place to attempt murder. Yet Henry had died with no witness but Charles to the crucial events.

Ahead on the shore, an odd little construction – a roof held up by columns – shielded a statue below it. The solemn memorial looked as though a white stone bandstand had birthed a young one. It was a lovely spot.

Maisie ran ahead, and Braddie kept walking, eager to sit.

Had Sir Charles had killed his own brother for raw ambition? What a horrendous crime, at fourteen years of age...

Unmistakable, Charles was next to her. *'Who's that?'* Sir Charles said. His gloom seemed to cloud the sun. *'You witches and the ruffian girl, and... who is this? Come to gawp at this dreadful spot.'*

She spoke inside her head, trying to keep her lips still. *'This man is a policeman, from the county force, and a simpleton. Do you remember your murderer, Sir Charles? Whatever our differences, the murderer should be caught and punished.'*

The spirit shuddered. *'I do not remember. The night air, a little moon. Pain and the fall. If I do recall, I suppose I should tell you. No one else can hear me.'*

A silence, as one who has more to say. A dark, sullen mood but without aggression.

'I came here often, to think of my brother. To muse on Fate and Death and what might have been. Did you truly come to my aid? I remember your hand on mine.'

'I did. We forget the Good Samaritan was a foreigner, a stranger, unclean.'

Very gruff, the spirit said, *'If true, I suppose that was decent. Though, I am sure you had some angle.'*

'How sad that the golden boy of the house drowned.'

A long pause, and she felt his loss.

'I never went on this water again.' To her astonishment, she could see a shadowy figure, bowed and grieving.

'Were you frightened his ghost would catch you?'

Sir Charles gave a snort, a laugh without warmth. *'Oh, Mrs Ashton. Had his ghost come to me, I would have changed my tune about table-tappers. I would have been a better man.'*

The policeman stared at her. She seriously considered telling him she was talking to the murdered man, to see his reaction.

'There is a presence of death, Constable. Be quiet before you incite malign forces to act. Go and be seated.'

Mrs Ashton turned her back. Sir Charles was close by her shoulder, waiting, silent, gloomy. Sometimes it is best to wait for the person to speak.

'Do you wish you could change the past, Mrs Ashton?'

'We cannot, and we waste time wishing so. Therefore, one learns from it and looks to the future.'

He sighed. *'If only Henry had lived.'*

'You would cede your honours, the wealth, the seat in Parliament?'

'He had a generous spirit. The sun went out, those months after he died. I think of him often. In my life, my duties in Parliament, I strive to be as good a man as he. My good causes. Giving a rogue of a servant another chance.'

'How did he die?'

A long silence.

'He hit his head on the gunwale, the boat overturned, and he drowned. A dark day for the world. Do you believe, Mrs Ashton, that we are judged? Or is that a fairy story to help your dishonest schemes?'

At that moment, Mrs Ashton pondered. She did. *'I believe we face a judgement before a Judge who knows every sin, every good deed. None of us stands clean before the throne. But He is merciful too.'*

The spirit shivered. *'Last night, my old house master came to talk to me, much as he did at school. Most spirits shun me or talk so much of their own woes they hear nothing else. Others... you know, there are spirits that have forgotten how to talk. They are reduced to fear and hatred and confusion – fragmented memories of life. It's like the worst of a madhouse, as they pass through me, into me. These lost things have almost reverted to the animal. Is being eaten by your base desires what happens when a spirit turns away from their redemption?'*

Extraordinary, to learn from a murderer what lay beyond death.

'What instruction did your tutor give?'

'That it is up to me, whether to set my foot on the path. That it will be hard toil, for my sins are many, and he says that it is far easier to set things right alive. He will provide counsel and others will come.'

Where was this going?

'Since my death no living thing has responded to me. Except you. You are my only chance to reach Violet and Esme and to safeguard the child I longed for.'

Humbled, in need. And he could tell her so much.

'Who could come that would terrify you so?' she asked.

A ghostly breath. *'You ask me that, here? Where he died?'*

Time to be bold. *'What is the truth of his death?'*

But Charles was gone.

Mrs Ashton looked at the lake. In her long career as a fraud, had spirits surrounded her? She had often preached that all God's promises were true. How would she be judged?

Chapter 25

A Good Walk, Continued.

...

Mrs Ashton rejoined her friends. Braddie had got the policeman chatting. The police had found a grapple in the boathouse roof, padded so it could be used quietly at night. The real possibility of an external assassin had returned.

'Scotland Yard are worried some radical group has an accomplice. We must check everyone – where and when they were born, and baptised, and check their characters.'

'I see why they think that.'

The policeman grinned. 'Your Captain Cairngorm was in a state this morning. The lady told him that with all the wagging tongues, he shouldn't meet her without his wife present. To protect him and his family from gossip. He says he hadn't thought of that, and were people talking? We said, tongues wagging like church bells. You can hear them a mile off.'

'The poor man. Let us walk further and cross the lake at the bridge.'

Standing above the water, a change. Sir Charles returned, chilling her flesh. Was this her fear or his, terrified of the retribution to come?

She waved the others on.

Time to be direct. *'You killed your brother.'*

'He died and my rise came from it. Yet believe me, I would rather he had lived.'

What a weight that confession carried, what guilt and what depths of loss.

'When I was little, he carried me. Yes, there was jealousy – he would be the baronet and have the estate. Yet Henry defended me at school, not all younger brothers had that. Even then, not yet a man's height, he promised he would divide the business or support me to run for Parliament. He was not a saint. No man can see his brother a saint, but he... he was the better man. Kinder to poor Rupert too.'

Mrs Ashton waited, her back to those watching her. Warm sunlight, pleasant breeze and bird sound. Yet she was chilled by Sir Charles's sombre words from beyond.

'Have I been brought so low? Am I so desperate that I will talk to you?'

Mrs Ashton tried to draw him out. *'You must face what you did.'*

'Do you believe that we are tempted by some external force? The thing was so sudden. Such a cowardly crime, a thing to disgust a beggar. We were larking about, and he fell, striking his head on the gunwale. The boat rocked, and he went into the water, face down, not struggling. Looking back, a hundred times, I think could have held his head out of the water. Yelled for help. Saved him.'

He could not hide his horror.

'Before that moment, I had never dreamed of his death. Yet, there it was, the temptation. The kingdoms of the world... all my father's wealth and power... laid out before me. I knew even then I would be greater than the old fool could imagine. What man wants to have second place when first lies within his grasp?'

Dear Father in heaven! Mrs Ashton filled the wait with a silent prayer.

She summoned all her authority. *'Tell me.'*

'I waited, perhaps a minute, looking in every direction, and he floated but did not stir. Then he began to move, without strength, not to thrash as a man would normally. It came to mind to jump on the gunwale and overturn the boat. Still, no one watched. Swimming in boots was harder than I thought... I climbed on his back, to keep his head underwater.'

A silence fell, while birds cooed and trilled their love, and a gentle wind blew on the water of death.

'There was no careful plan, just an ugly thrashing of water. If he lived, my panic would explain it. His movements weakened and stopped. I think I began to shout – time is unclear. Men came shouting. I could hardly test his pulse. Could he be revived? Would he betray me as I had betrayed him? For my own protection, now I pretended to save him. I found myself struggling, coughing water. The men saved me.'

Mrs Ashton was without words.

'I killed my brother, my best friend, and won such praise for trying to rescue him. I thought long thereafter, I deserved hell. And here I am.'

That story and his sorrow brought her close to tears. Braddie had come back onto the bridge.

'Some old devil chattering to you?' she asked, her look kinder than her tone.

'Yes, Sir Charles's dreadful confession to Henry's murder. A sudden whim, he claims.'

The spirit spoke. *'Can she hear me? Or the girl? It seems not.'*

'No, Sir, Charles. Only me.'

'Why cannot I find Violet, or Esme?'

'I don't know.' For almost a minute, only a faint spiritual sense revealed him. Mrs Ashton pushed him. *'Who knew?'*

'No one. I was in terror for weeks, but they thought it shock and grief. Some discussion about the bruises, but nothing contradicting my story. My mother might have wondered – she may have guessed. I never quite confessed and she never pushed me. I put away my love for him, as I had ruined it. Between me and Rupert, I was at once the favourite as well as the heir. As for the dread, I learned not to dwell on it. Time dulled the pain, and now I am butchered like a pig and called to account. I cannot face Henry. What could I say?'

Mrs Ashton had faced a thousand people with difficult stories from the past. What she said was a lie but had golden truths in it. Now she had to advise, not knowing.

'Be truly penitent. Tell him that you loved him, and that you will seek his wise guidance as to what reparation is due and possible. How fortunate to have one who loved you as a guide.'

The spirit said, *'Nothing can undo it.'*

This dangerous hateful man, a braggart and a deceiver. Yet, a human being in pain. A source of great information. And, Braddie would warn her, a lure for her curiosity. A plan was emerging, not wholly selfish – perhaps they could aid each other.

Mrs Ashton wanted more from him. *'Temptation exists, wherever it comes from. There are other deaths I want to know about. Grace Overmorrow. Lady Herncastle.'*

He used a foul word, but without passion. She tasted his shame.

'Too much... forgive me.'

Doom surrounded her. She might face a terrible reckoning, in this world and the next. While a wicked part of her rejoiced at Sir Charles's fear and humiliation, he showed her how far she herself had fallen. No murder stained her soul, but when she died, would she too face the judgement of those countless people she had robbed and lied to?

Chapter 26

Counted, Counted, Weighed and Found Wanting

...

Drained by the horror of Charles's confession, Mrs Ashton needed to restore her balance.

The delightful chapel showed Georgian order and beauty, with fashionable Gothic trimmings kept to a minimum. Impeccably kept, she wondered how often it was used; in happier times the family had attended church locally.

More flowers each time she came, neatly presented wreaths and bouquets, often with white dominating. The Prime Minister, the Home Secretary, and the Leader of the Opposition had sent flowers. Some were humbler, gathered from gardens on the estate, and clustered to one side. As with worshippers, the lesser flowers must give their way to the greater.

Mrs Ashton closed her eyes, breathed deeply in and deeply out to calm her nerves. If judgement was coming, what should she do? If Charles could remember his murderer, how easy would it to be prove that case?

From curiosity, she looked at the great Bible on its stand. How she needed its wisdom and guidance. It was open of course and with a marker on what she assumed to be the relevant passage for today: the fifth chapter of Daniel when the great King Belshazzar is told, *Mene, mene, tekel, upharsin*.

Counted twice, weighed in the balance, and found wanting. A haughty man dies and his kingdom is conquered.

It struck her to the heart. She thought it might be providence sending her some deep message of repentance. How far she had fallen short. After five minutes of prayer, a different view hit her. Was not Sir Charles raised high but slain in his feast of wickedness? Consulting the lectionary, she found indeed that text wasn't the appointed reading. Who made that silent accusation among the tributes to the dead? The chapel doors were never locked, so it could have been almost anyone.

Maybe she was not Belshazzar but a lady Daniel, a prophet sent to proclaim that truth.

Maybe action would help her. Mrs Ashton went in search of the portrait of Rose, Lady Herncastle, to focus her on finding the spirit. She had seen it before, enigmatic, although revealing she had been a great beauty. What a woman, to have sought to track down an old murder by her son-in-law.

She strolled into the Chinese room, keeping a constant eye on the clock. The house was full of such dazzling rooms, of riches acquired from across the world, and often with instructive labels. Here a jade-handled sword, rescued from the brutal Anglo-French destruction of the irreplaceable Summer Palace, and there a silver-trimmed black chest from Hong Kong, once used for opium samples.

Mrs Ashton never viewed a wealthy home without making inventory. Theft was an unsophisticated crime, but it might come to that.

Two women worked in the room: one of the housemaids on her knees, cleaning under a lacquered cupboard, and Prudie adjusting a bowl of flowers on a small table, holding two errant blooms in her left hand.

At once, Mrs Ashton turned her curiosity to Violet's maid. Prudie worked in front of Mrs Ashton's target; the portrait over the table was of Violet's mother. Like all the paintings, it was draped with black for Sir Charles. Add a candle and it would be almost devotional. Hard to read what the portraitist had seen in her – not the imperious gaze of some of the female portraits. Dear, blunt Braddie had dismissed it as, 'She had the toothache but is too fancy to show it.' Mrs Ashton's research into Lady Herncastle had not shown the inner woman.

Prudie wiped her eye and then saw Mrs Ashton. At once her face became guarded.

'Such a shame. Was she a good mistress?' Mrs Ashton said.

The briefest hesitation, then, with warmth, 'Yes, she was a lovely lady, ma'am. Very kind and she taught me a lot.'

'Another sad death.'

'It was shocking,' Prudie said. 'She was fierce careful with her medicines, usually speaking. But she'd not been well. They say that made her careless.'

A subtle shift in tone. Might Prudie and 'they' differ on the matter? Would she say what she thought? A pleasant face, awaiting orders.

A lady's maid would not usually demean herself to do flowers in a public room, which was mere housework. 'So, you do her flowers? How lovely.'

'Oh, her ladyship likes me to check when she can't. I'm not saying the other girls do her bad, not at all, but Lady Herncastle deserves the best. Such a shame she went to the Lord early.'

Prudie tucked the floral scissors in an apron pocket, and the delinquent blossoms followed.

'Have you worked here long?' Mrs Ashton took a step closer.

'Since a girl, ma'am. The master's mother, the dowager, was kind enough to take me and my brother in. Some have long tongues, but I always found her generous. She's so frail in mind and body now, surely Our Lord must call her soon.'

Mrs Ashton probed. 'You were her lady's maid?'

'No, ma'am, but she began my training, and when Lady Herncastle came, I served her until Lady Barrington-Stewart needed a new maid. I'm blessed to have served such fine ladies. Well, I mustn't dawdle, her ladyship will want me.' And Prudie bobbed, turned, and marched away.

Mrs Ashton hesitated and was lost. Once she would have tried to open her, now she was blinded without her opening power. Everyone thought her strange and pushy as it was.

At the door, ready to dart away, Prudie turned and looked at Mrs Ashton.

'On the Gospel, can you truly speak to the dead, ma'am?'

'I assure you that I can.' It deserved unusual emphasis now that it was true.

Prudie smiled. 'Well, her ladyship thinks very highly of you. If you find Lady Herncastle, thank her from me.'

Leaving the room, Mrs Ashton felt Sir Charles appear at her side. At once she was on her guard. The presence, the voice, was as if alive. The image, though, was translucent, and she wondered if her eye saw or only her mind? He was now clad as she had first seen him.

'Mrs Ashton, I am pleased we can be civil. Shouting at you has lost any pleasure.'

'It has never been me that was uncivil.'

He nodded. *'How are Violet and Esme? How is my mother? I have the greatest difficulty finding people in this sea of fog, these walls of mist.'*

'And no one except me can hear you?'

He laughed, an odd feeling. *'Touche, Mrs Ashton. Mrs Abernathy's cat feels me – it hissed at me twice – a most objectionable creature who always loathed me and I bear the wounds. On balance, I would rather talk to you.'*

'I expect a fair exchange. Can you remember your assailant? We struggle to solve the crime.'

Charles paused. *'I remember no one else on the roof. Might the assailant have surprised me? My mother must be taking this badly. Maybe they haven't told her, her mind is weak these days. Could you... see her? Tell her?'*

Genuine feeling there. Even the monster Grendel loved his mother.

'I wouldn't be permitted. Perhaps she has not grasped that you have died. A cruel illness when the mind fails before the body.'

'Hopefully, she will go to a better fate. I need Violet and Esme safe. They are very precious to me. Who told you Esme is pregnant? Do they pose a threat to her, or the baby?'

Mrs Ashton would not reveal her power, and she must be careful not to share what she knew. '*Be assured, Violet, Esme, and your child are safe from me.*'

The goodwill faded. *'Damned familiar with my wife, Ashton. Who told you? I need to know who betrayed me. I will pay you, in information.'*

'I am not going to tell you.'

'Spare me your cant. Who in my circle was a traitor? Trephine? I could cook his goose in a moment! Have the doctors been gossiping, or perhaps my lawyer has been unwise... Understand my alarm if they have betrayed me – I rely on them utterly to protect those I love. Or did you steal the news somehow? Don't be afraid to confess some clever trick or theft, Mrs Ashton, I will not be angry. That option is safer to those I love and far more pleasant to me than betrayal.'

Ashton took her courage. She must present him with his crimes.

'Esme is safe from me. I know you killed Grace Overmorrow. I believe you killed Violet's mother. Confession will surely help you. Help me understand these crimes and so heal those who grieve.'

Sir Charles surrounded her, oppressive, bullying. *'The name, Mrs Ashton, the name!'*

'That is unpleasant, Sir Charles, cease immediately.'

She recited the Prayer of Deliverance – aloud, to be sure of it. For the first time, the spirit realm *quivered*. Sir Charles gave a boxer's grunt, and he was gone.

Chapter 27
Kitchen Talk

...

In Mrs O'Grady's dominion, Braddie found the cook needed safe hands, and as every cook does from time to time, she steamed like an exotic volcano.

'Feeding the house, and her ladyship and Miss Esme ill... she's taking nothing but soup now. And the police... coming in at all hours, and those at the inquest will expect something whenever they come back. One of my dish boys is sick – drunk, more likely – and half the girls feel they must go and cry, poor dears. One lost her father not two months back. Like a fool, I gave her the day off.'

Braddie knew grief, she knew people reacted in different ways. 'Can a plain Northern cook help?'

Mrs O'Grady looked at her, a gleam in her eye. 'None of your raising spirits here. Help prepare that, if you please.' She waved at a table of vegetables and a single harassed-looking girl, then looked at something steaming.

'It's the funeral got me,' she continued. 'It was to be next week, but the papers say half Parliament might come. If they choose All Saints, Bellingley, like the old master, they'll never fit them all in. And if there are hundreds, they're not all coming back here, surely?'

A practical woman flustered by a big problem.

'They'll let you know. Or hotels...'

'Hotel food, my eye. The master deserves better. Always considerate, he was. Once late home from the hunt, I made something up, and he had a rose sent down as a thank you. Her ladyship will go, even if they must carry her in. She's that unwell, I don't want to press her about the funeral luncheon.'

Mrs O'Grady slammed a lid. 'The police think it was those devilish Fenians! I said, have you read the master's speech on Ireland? He had those disloyal brigands dead right! No treachery in my kitchen, I told them.'

Braddie restrained herself from unleashing her scorn on England's monstrous rule and bent to her work. Mrs O'Grady chatted here and there. Sir Charles had a temper, but a sense of justice. 'When he said, "I'll decide tomorrow," or "I must speak to my wife," you'd know his temper had cooled. And he wasn't so high and mighty. He'd come and talk to the gardeners and grooms and kennelmen, and smoke over a beer or two. Animals and the weather and perhaps masculine topics when no women were around.'

'Men!' Braddie said.

The cook stood tall. 'Mr O'Grady never stood for vulgarity.'

When a quiet pause fell, Braddie tried to bring up the murdered lass, Grace. Such a terrible crime.

'I'm afraid young Maisie has a bloody imagination.'

'Oh, she's a ghoul, that one. Who'd want to talk about that wicked deed, with the whole house turned upside down, the master's death, and all? Getting the boys to tease the girls, not that they know anything about the case. I sent your little slum-girl packing. And the men don't like her, all that sneaking around in London.'

'The lass means no harm. Motherless, two younger children to help, and a drunken father.'

Mrs O'Grady reduced her frown a bit.

'Never known Forty like it. Short temper and saying things about her I don't believe. The master liked him, so the soft-hearted boy took it very hard.'

Then word came that they were taking the body to Bellingley in an hour.

'I can't see the master off in this apron. I'd better get my hat.'

The whole house assembled outside to watch the remains of Sir Charles leaving the estate. The sun was sinking now, and a warmth on the breeze.

Mrs Ashton and Braddie were among the last to arrive at the front of the house yet had a good place to watch the spectacle. The doctor, the stewards, and the detectives stood on the great stairs to the door, where one might expect the family. A clergyman in severe vestments. The staff flowed left and right, in a steady decrease in rank, through the house staff then the garden staff. A great cluster of farmers and their wives stood a little back. Everyone wore the signs of mourning. Meanwhile, the police were drawn up on the other side of the carriageway, as a guard of honour.

Mrs Ashton leaned on Braddie's arm and walked slowly. Bullfinch glared at them as if their mere existence, mere breathing, affronted him.

Violent change had reached this place of order, and the future was uncertain. More than one maid, more than one farmer's wife, held handkerchiefs to faces. To live in service was to live through the life of your masters – a hard life resting on their whims, and yet a life many sought as easier than others. Particularly in these terrible times for country folk.

The family were coming, from the other direction. The new mistress of the house, Lady Violet walked veiled on the arms of her two companions, Miss Shilling with her veil up, and Prudie Wilkins.

Maisie elsewhere, Cairngorm stood with stony face, towards the back.

The sound of horses, at a sombre pace. Faithful Willoughby drove the great funeral carriage of black with silver trim and four black horses. Sir Charles – a person, not a mere feeling – still existed. It still stunned Mrs Ashton that something she had assumed might hold some truth shocked her so much when proved. Deep waters.

The carriage halted, the police saluted, and every man took off his hat or cap, swiftly.

The priest read a prayer, then another. One of the trustees spoke, lengthy words that did not carry. Clearly, Lady Violet would not speak, slumping a little against her cousin and her maid.

Then Bullfinch spoke, a parade-ground voice that did carry.

'A life of duty, charity, and service has ended too soon. At this hour of sorrow, I promise you that England will not let this death go unpunished. The hounds of justice are eager and on the scent. Those responsible must know the hours and days of their freedom are limited. Let anyone who knows anything meet with me now, for anyone holding silence on this matter is guilty under the law. You know what punishment awaits on earth, let alone the thereafter.'

How much this country was governed by such theatre, how the chaos of the Continent was held at bay with order and tradition. Yet the world was changing fast. Something came upon her, a vision. The estate, the earth, and the sky were but a stage – like a child's puppet theatre made of card. A deeper, richer world lay in the dimness beyond.

In the blink of an eye, the girl she had glimpsed in the wood stood by her. Grace Overmorrow, gazing at the scene. An unlettered lass whose calm face was unreadable, like the face of a saint who knows all things and is beyond all suffering. She looked at Mrs Ashton with the hint of a wry smile, which could have meant anything. Mrs Ashton had casually dismissed that first sighting as her imagination. It had been a true vision, and so was this.

Mrs Ashton spoke in her head. *'Are you truly the murdered girl? What should I do?'*

A gentle touch on her brow.

Of course, the spirit spoke as the country folk did.

'What doth the Lord require of thee, but to do justly, and to love mercy, and to walk humbly with thy God?'

The Prophet Micah.

'Dear girl, I long to see justice done. I know Charles murdered you...'

But the spirit had gone.

Chapter 28

Conferences and Conclusions

That evening

Mrs Ashton found from a footman that Doctor Culpe was in the visitor's study. She had longed to get him alone. The doctor who attended Lady Herncastle in her last days, and on her death. If he now attended Esme, did he know of her condition?

Each time she came here, she thought how odd this prudish age approved of paintings of naked women frolicking, and sometimes of naked youths, if on some Classical or Biblical theme.

The study was rich with cigar smoke and Culpe sat in the best chair, before a modest fire, with a decanter on the small table beside him. Tired, and in disarray, that glass of spirits was certainly not his first.

He looked at her as if she was a septic wound, then turned back to his book.

Mrs Ashton swept up and sat in the chair opposite. 'Good evening, Doctor Culpe.'

He grunted and gulped his drink.

'Do you know if Lady Barrington-Stewart is well enough to testify?'

'At present, I recommend that she does not. Mrs Ashton, I am not in a mood for conversation. Please do be sure to shut the door fully when you depart.'

Mrs Ashton settled herself more firmly into the chair. 'I wonder if some kind soul could bring me a glass. Or ring for a servant?'

His face a silent growl, he indicated the glasses on the sideboard. A calculated slight.

'As you know, Lady Barrington-Stewart wants me to seek her mother's spirit, concerned as to the cause of her death.'

'Dear God, digging over a simple matter.' He reached for the decanter and slopped a greedy amount into his glass.

'Lady Herncastle took her medication with her journal open, so she could record it.'

He drank, irritated. How she longed for her power to return, to crack this witness open like a book. Then he said, curbing his anger, 'Lady Barrington-Stewart is a delightful woman, but she is not willing to accept that her mother might make a mistake. They were very close, so it is hardly an unforgivable folly.'

'She took laudanum for pain, your prescription for her digestive system which also contained opium, and, in addition, a commercial tonic.' Braverman's for Digestive Strength, a well-known brand.

He glared at her. 'I swore on oath, Mrs Ashton, that I had seen Lady Herncastle twice take more laudanum than I advised, and sometimes she used a larger spoon than the measure. I reminded my patient of my recommendations.

An excessive dose can produce confusion and might lead to her taking more. Of course, I ordered checks on the medications, in case there had been some error.'

She knew this. Now it struck her as odd. 'Why? Was there any reason to believe error in the drug was the issue? Had you cause to doubt her pharmacist?'

'No. Of course not, a fine fellow. Reliable. A simple precaution against gossip. Tongues always wag.'

The drunk avoided her gaze. Dislike? Lying? A hatred of women?

'Forgive me, another question.'

Culpe stood, the book from his lap falling, and marched to the door, glass in hand.

She tried to open him at a distance – a sharp jab of pain, and a dance of bright lights.

'My spirits will find the truth,' she said, eyes clamping shut.

'Your fakery be damned. I never tampered with anything.'

She had it, a brief opening.

Dear God, does she know?

His rage came from desperate fear. He'd seen a man hanged outside Grennard Prison, and something else, deep and frightening... a middle-aged woman. Nothing clear enough to be useful.

Not much, but at least an opening. Her old power was not wholly gone.

They ate supper in their rooms. Neither the servants, nor Bullfinch nor Doctor Culpe, were willing to eat with them. Mrs Ashton chose her battles.

Maisie sat silent and kicking one boot with another – missing her family, no doubt. Mrs Ashton grasped her hand. What an asset her apprentice was, her defiant little sparrow. 'We will triumph, Maisie. I promise.'

The girl sniffed. Then she said, 'The boot-boy says Forty is sent back to London tomorrow. He doesn't know why and Forty hates London. I could follow him.'

'If we had but two of you, how blessed I would be. I need you here. How important you are to our success.'

Braddie pinched Maisie's cheek, then looked to Mrs Ashton. 'You think Culpe killed Violet's mother?'

'I am not certain what the spirits showed. He is terrified by interrogation about her medicines. And given the potent flavour of opium... the easiest way is to add more to the laudanum itself.'

'Your spirits should simply tell us what happened,' Maisie said, with a sly dangerous look.

'Would that it was so simple. I did not accuse Culpe of tampering with the medications. Nevertheless, he denied it. Either he is lying...'

'...or he did something wrong, but not that,' Braddie said.

'Could Sir Charles have done it?' Maisie said.

'Lady Herncastle had a nurse, as his mother has now. Indeed, the two women's rooms are close. Sir Charles may have gone into her room, for certain.'

Braddie frowned. 'Wasn't he in London the week she died?'

This was a big obstacle. 'He had public engagements, or private ones mentioned in the press. My secretary friend dug out the references. Twice he spoke in Parliament. Even Sir Charles could not subvert the Parliamentary record.' Mrs Ashton sighed. 'I would love to interrogate this nurse, but she now has a position in Harrogate. It has taken me until now to find her address, so I have written to her. Lady Herncastle showed a decline that week, suggesting more than one additional dose. The drug could only enter the body through medicines, drinks, food, or perhaps an injection or an enema.'

'How thorough was the coroner examining the body?'

'He is said to be meticulous. An injection would have been obvious. So, for food and drink, an invalid often eats something different. Maybe one of the servants acted on Sir Charles's order?'

Braddie shook her head. 'Two years, hinny. Will anyone remember who served the lady? A whole week's meals?'

'No chance,' Maisie said.

Mrs Ashton tried to sum it up. 'The reports did not mention the police attending. I should try to speak to the coroner, who is now in Bellingley, of course.'

Maisie absented herself, muttering about letters to write.

Braddie grasped Mrs Ashton's hands.

Mrs Ashton gulped. 'Dear heart, I wish this ordeal, the inquest, was not tomorrow. I am not recovered.'

Braddie's loyalty and kindness. Her soft eyes.

'My hinny. I must come with you. Tomorrow will be hard, but we will get through it.'

'I imagine the hotel will be packed, the press eager to twist and misrepresent my presence. The coroner is very sharp. And, of course, any of the jurors may put questions to me. I confess, from the depths of my heart, we may have bitten off more than we can chew.' Be honest with your darling. 'To say "we" is inexact. I alone got us here, and all your caution was justified.'

'Complaining won't paddle us to the shore, hinny. We do as we can.'

'I feel it deeply. Old crimes somehow show us the truth about the new. But perhaps I am running down the wrong path. I think I should tell Lady Violet what we suspect – Grace's murder and her mother's death and Sir Charles's brother...'

'Make sense, Honeybee! You'll truly tell the widow you saw that murder in his head, that he confessed himself to drowning his brother? You've no proof but phantoms. And your power – three can keep a secret if one is dead. As for the mother dying, you've not even got her ghost.'

'I wish I could read our patroness. The very first glimmers of my power may be returning. But still Sir Charles is nearby... a devious soul. And although he has some conscience, I would not rest my life on it.'

Braddie looked even more solemn. 'Can he read your thoughts?'

'A ghastly possibility.'

Time to raise the other matter.

'Dearest, for our future. Now Bellingley would not serve. May we never live within a hundred miles of it. But we could seek some rural spot, not too far from a town or at least the railway to London. You, my country mouse, would have your garden and healthy air. I could have the hope of company, and perhaps clients. Stays in London would not be impossible.'

'There are other cities with rich dupes. I long for home, honest air, and uncorrupted souls.'

Mrs Ashton longed for comfort and lively conversation. She was offering her dear heart a great tribute.

'There is wickedness in the North, dearest, and dark deeds among your frowning moors. And, sweetheart, my new powers may mean I would be duping no one. I advance towards you in a spirit of compromise. I have heard you.'

Braddie gave her a wry look, then kissed her. Tired and overwrought, the fires of passion kindled. How she wanted her dearest, body heart and soul. She needed her caresses, those deft fingers doing their magic. Yielding to her dear heart's vigour, a girl in the hands of experience... Was the dresser in their room strong enough to lean on? One does not want one's amours heard. Once she had explained two broken plates as a poltergeist.

Scented oil at bath-time was more practical. Undoing Braddie's long, faded hair from its severe knot and brushing it, stroke by stroke. How thin it grew. She imagined taking the remnants from the brush and kissing them before discarding. Braddie should crop it, but she shunned any act that spoke of the male sex she despised. Braddie's health might fail before hers.

Chapter 29
Evidence and Condemnation

Friday

The Leader of the Opposition: I thank the Prime Minister for those eloquent words on this vicious and treacherous death, this tragedy in our national life, and the character and promise of the deceased. I will add a few meagre thoughts, if I may. On this occasion, party strife and differences of opinion must melt away. We need to recognise the unique horror of this crime, beyond any ordinary murder – it is an attack on this House, on Parliament itself, and the order of the society we stand for. Sir Charles sometimes turned his wit against this side of the House. A few of us felt that lash. But we recognise in him an energy and purpose, an iron core of principle, and a gift of oratory that would have taken him far. We recognise his striving for the dignity of women, his commitment to the welfare of the labouring classes, how in his business he sought to be a progressive and liberal employer, and the seeds of a great philanthropist. He brought much to this House in his vigour and compassion. And we name him a great friend of Ireland, the true and honest Ireland, whose best interests he sought and whose place in this Kingdom and this Great Empire, thank God, is eternal.

A member shouting: A bailiff and a brigand!

Many members: Shame! Shame! Shame!

Mr Parnell and others rise:

Mr Speaker: Order, order. I did not see the member who made that disgraceful remark. That was unworthy of this House and an insult to the nation, let alone how it will strike the grieving widow and family. I will not hesitate to punish any repetition. The Leader of the Opposition.

The Times

Maisie sat in the window seat with her breakfast in her hands. She needed to keep an eye out for Forty in the yard. Her one last chance to talk to him before he was back to London. Looking down on the yard in daylight gave her a funny turn, bringing back memories of that awful night.

All her questions and provoking had made her unwelcome.

She missed Ma so much, Ma who kept everything going. However bad things got, Ma brought comfort and optimism and a plan. Maisie missed her family. She was worried about them and full of misery. She thought often of her friends, teasing and being teased by Dongmei Li, and bossing her gang about. She'd never got a straight story from Mrs Ashton about how she'd offended Dongmei's rich uncle.

Mrs O'Grady had warmed a little when Maisie had shamelessly played up her Irish roots and explained her less than fair complexion by saying her mother was a-taken from the tinkers, to be reared by the house-living folk. But Maisie wanted solitude.

When the three of them talked about old Lady Herncastle, everyone assumed they were trying to pin the death on the staff making a mistake. No wonder everyone scowled at her.

Everyone who had someone die could give up, and everyone in the world knew someone who had died, but the people living needed you. The world would stop if people didn't wipe their eyes and get on with it.

Forty walked in the yard; she wiped her eyes, tucked her sandwich in her pinafore pocket, and went after him.

Forty had been avoiding her like she was the cholera. She ran, to be sure to catch him. He wore going-to-church clothes, he had a big bag, and another man hitched up a horse and trap. He rubbed his hands against his trousers, then fingered inside his collar.

He looked fury at her.

'Go back to your hole of lies,' Forty said, half turning his back to show his disdain. 'I was kind to you, and you wanted to snoop on the master and the mistress. Shame on you, lying to a fellow. Bearing false witness.'

Maisie wouldn't take the rejection of a turned back. She walked round the front of him. He threw his bag into the trap.

'You were a proper gent. The lady asked my mistress for help and that's what she's doing.'

His eyes were bloodshot. 'Even if the mistress lets you stay, that don't mean I need to talk to you. I don't hold with raising the dead.'

'Mrs Bradshaw knows a sovereign cure for itchy skin,' Maisie said, feeling a little pot of it in her pocket.

'None of her poison. Those witches can jump on their broomstick and fly to the moon.'

Maisie paused, trying to work out how to beguile him.

'Who do you think did it then?'

Forty snapped. 'Curse you. I'm sent back to that den of wickedness, stinking London, with all its scheming heathens and wicked seductions. Away from the stench of murder anyway. Murder's no game, it's a terrible sin.'

'So it is.' Another groom would drive, and he glared at her too. 'Spilling grease in the stable we had to clear up.'

'Didn't do nothing,' she protested, with half her mind.

Wait – "sent"? Who sent him and why?

No other servant had been sent away, that she knew. She should check that.

Had Forty done it? Had he bashed Sir Charles, and now lay tossing and turning at night, haunted by conscience and plagued by his wicked deeds? Maybe he had eaten something which made his rash worse? Sal couldn't eat oysters nor cockles either without going red all over.

Mrs Ashton enjoyed her eggs and skimmed the papers. News from Afghanistan, from the lands of the Zulus and the Boers, from the Raj and the Caribbean where selfless British troops were spreading civilisation and keeping order. The Prime Minister had swept the country in last year's election, with his impassioned attacks on the irresponsible and immoral foreign policy of his opponents. Mrs Ashton only followed foreign affairs lightly, so as not to sound ignorant. It seemed to her that the sending of troops, the use of gunboats, and the spreading of civilisation had hardly slowed since the great Liberal had once again formed a government.

The press speculated that Sir Charles's funeral would be delayed so it might be in Westminster Abbey. How much would the young widow have a say? Would she be well enough?

The Orb had returned its fiery gaze to Mrs Ashton. A prominent article had its own take on Sir Charles's murder:

> *The slaying of a Member of Parliament strikes at the very soul of the nation. None might accuse us of being silent or ungrateful for the excellent work of Scotland Yard on so many awful crimes. Yet all is not well in*

the Barrington-Stewart investigation, and it is our duty to shed light on the perplexities.

The notorious Spiritualist sham Mrs Ashton, the bloody-handed woman found with the corpse, and her lowly servants appear to roam freely in Corwood Manor. For our newer readers, Mrs Ashton is a purported medium, who has often left one city or another, followed by the ripe odour of scandal. She is much accustomed to preying on the widow and the orphan with her shadow-monger's arts. Jewels disappear, wills are changed, and the vulnerable are parted with coins or notes, depending on their station.

Chief Inspector Bullfinch is a thorough and vigorous detective, of whom we have spoken well in the past. Yet, it cannot be right that Mrs Ashton casts her shadow across this most urgent of cases. The ectoplasmic enthusiast seems free to work her charms on the unworldly, grieving, and wealthy widow, Lady Barrington-Stewart. How wise the late Sir Charles was to denounce such charlatans. Those of any class may, in their grief, be beguiled by an experienced fraudster.

What further mischief may she now do?

Recent events add little to assure us. We can reveal that Mrs Ashton recently returned to

London from Scotland, after two shadowy years of spirit-farming and ghost-wrangling under the assumed name of Mrs Leveret. Readers may wonder what honest woman sees the need to assume an alias. Our Scottish correspondent is in touch with a sad club of those despoiled by her actions – traders who have been told she was abroad, beyond the reach of bailiffs, and those who gave to her purported work. How much regret emanates from disappointed and disillusioned members of her Scottish meetings.

A knight rides to their aid, clad in sober black, not shining steel. In Edinburgh, the Procurator Fiscal is as stern, clear-eyed, and moral a man as we might hope. His busy office may grind slow, but on the matter of fraud, it grinds with certainty. This Scottish prosecutor has sent a man to London to finalise the case. Mrs Ashton's English creditors might do well run to the courts if they ever want to see a penny.

Mallards Bank has been a byword for well over a century for honesty and solidity. We cannot remain silent. Do its directors and depositors know that Mrs Ashton has an account with them? Are they content that a bank trusted by the most revered name in the land is used by a fraud as her

> *calling card? Worse still, the manager of the most prestigious branch offers that mistress of miasma his house to summon and clip her sheep.*
>
> *The dead man's blood cries out for British justice. Scotland Yard must satisfy a nation that these matters are driven to the highest standard. And a clock ticks, for bills due will be paid, one way or another.*

A punch to her gut. She pushed away the remains of breakfast and gulped another coffee without tasting it.

Her steadfast ally in the Procurator's Office, a true believer... Why had she not had warning? Of course, any Scottish creditors who had found her, she had paid. Eventually, all true claims would be settled.

She must pay her creditors before they went to court, but how? The stinging spite about Mallards. The letter from her dear banker friend said her middling meeting was riven with dissent – indeed, three of its prominent members had denounced her, and others were not replying to his entreaties. Bankruptcy was a moral judgement. Her better-off followers would not respond well to her hiding from her creditors.

Braddie would so scold her and be right. Now, long warned, Mrs Ashton grasped the folly of running up debts and hoping, like Mr Micawber, that something would turn up before disaster struck.

Court proceedings to get the monies due would see her harried like a fox chased by the hounds. Judges routinely sent to prison people who had merely lost their jobs or been ill. Everything from the size of her vintners' bills to the cost of her hats would be censured by the judge and published with well-faked horror in the papers. Even a voluntary arrangement meant public humiliation.

She might get a judge hostile to Spiritualism, and at that thought, her hands began to shake. As criminals had been locked in the pillory to be pelted with filth, the press and the courts sought to ridicule and punish.

She needed to fight this. She needed Lady Violet's support. She needed a lawyer and an accountant, and there were good arguments for getting those two herself, in London.

Chapter 30
Inquest and Inquisition

The day appointed

Mrs Ashton caught Bullfinch about to leave in a trim four-seater with his county colleague. A grim black police wagon waited, a giant tin coffin. Her stomach somersaulted. Surely, she would not be carried in such a vehicle, like a pickpocket or prostitute.

'Chief Inspector, I am not a criminal. Travelling in that thing will prejudice the press.'

He bristled. 'Mrs Ashton, I need to get you to and from the inquest. I fear you will suddenly remember you have left the gas on and slip to London, never to be seen again.'

'Surely there is some better conveyance?'

The scowl darkened. 'I am not a fairy godmother, Mrs Ashton, able to whisk up a carriage and four from vegetables and vermin. You will have a mob of press at the gate here, and in Bellingley. They're insatiable. Be grateful for our protection.'

Mrs Ashton had to be bold. 'I will need to go to London, on pressing business.'

'I read the papers,' Bullfinch said, with evident satisfaction. 'I prefer you where I can find you.'

She returned to the chapel to think. A maid bringing more flowers left, and alone, she read the Bible turned to the reading of the day. On cue, Sir Charles appeared. In her mind's eye she could now see him, as tall and bold as in life, yet sombre and less full of himself. In the afterlife did earthly wealth or power count? Perhaps everyone knew his sins.

'Is there news of Rupert? Has he contacted Violet?'

'Not to my knowledge. There may or may not have been a dark man with a French beard.'

'I have a bastard niece, Rupert's child. The woman is an actress, who very sensibly preferred my support to relying on my brother. A pretty little child, Trephine says, and of course, I did the right thing for her. Pity she was not a boy. Without an heir, I considered adopting her anyway.'

'Your wife has sent Trephine to continue the arrangement.'

He smiled, more felt than seen in her mind's eye. *'Good. I remember, down by the lake after Henry's funeral, I swore to Rupert that I would protect him. I treated him poorly. I should have given him one of the houses and let him ruin it or learn sense. The last trouble he was in, I relented. His creditors would have broken his bones.'*

Interesting. *'You disinherited him.'*

'It's a small, grudging sort of man to scorn his own brother on his death, Mrs Ashton. I repented of that, at least.'

'Might he have killed you?'

'Rupert is one for the pen, rather than the sword. Though I testify his right hook ranked with mine, and he had cause. How are Violet and Esme?'

'Still unwell. Overwhelmed by what has happened. There is talk of a great funeral service in London.'

'Your Bible says something of the rich man and the leper, does it not? The glory of the funeral says nothing of the destination. You will only hurt and shame the two of them if you tell the world about Esme. Her condition must be kept private, of course. Maybe I can assist you, but you must protect them.'

'I have no desire to harm them. I seek to solve the crime to lift its shadow from me. What do you remember?'

'I strive to remember that night. I wanted your confession, so I could see the back of you. Violet was eager for our bed. She had only two demands – that we maintain a pretence of decorum to the outside world and that she wanted a child by me.'

'Did you smoke opium?'

'No. Why? Violet disapproved. Dragon smoke recalls that old saying, a good servant and a poor master. I have seen men ruined by it.'

A pause, and he said, *'If only you had seen us. My marital happiness had returned. Will Violet and Esme stay in the house? Or go back to London?'*

What was he fishing for?

'They haven't shared their plans with me.'

'I must go. Can we part as allies?'

'I can only judge you by your actions.'

'My regards to Mrs Bradshaw.' He waited. *'She must have found the burning of your home difficult. I'm sorry.'*

Maisie still believed the old birds were surprised about Sir Charles haunting them, and Mrs Ashton was uncommonly worried about what she would do about it. Evil murdering lords coming back as ghosts should be all her manor. She hadn't mentioned her dead Cavalier spirit once, until Maisie had asked.

Anyway, she had to find Willoughby, without the excuse of being busy. The grey-haired coachman sat on a chair under a fine chestnut, smoking his pipe. There was a slice of a tree next to him, stool height. He had paused wrangling some brass and leather thing to do with horses.

'Hello, missy,' he said, looking at her like she was short weight.

'I'm sorry I kicked you so hard.'

He snorted.

'Mind if I sit here?' Maisie said, sitting there. Willoughby kept smoking and looking at the trees and grass, down to the lake. He had the look of a man about to pronounce on something.

A few puffs later, 'I don't believe it was the master who burned the women out of their home,' he said. 'Not like him at all. Your old biddies shouldn't say that.'

'Who did then?'

Willoughby gave a long, long pause, puffing away.

'Don't like to speak ill of any man, living or dead. But I think that Trephine is a smiling fox. I wouldn't trust him with an egg, let alone a chicken. Maybe the master trusted him too much.'

Maisie thought Trephine arranged the dirty work, but he wouldn't burn a sausage unless he'd been paid to. Strictly a foreman.

Willoughby turned his head to her. 'No one shoulda burned their home. But it's not right, young missy, raising the dead and the like. Telling people you work miracles, getting their hopes up. In God's mercy we will rise again, in new bodies of light. That's the only hope we have. What do your parents say about those meddling women?'

He likes the money and cries about the idea of Ma as a ghost.

'Ma's dead. Pa thinks Mrs A tries to help people.'

'That nosey pair. You're nosey too, aren't you?'

She could hardly deny it. 'I like to know what's going on.'

He took a couple more puffs, making up his mind. 'A little bird a-told me, more than one did, you were asking about Grace Overmorrow. What a sinful world that such things could happen to a sweet girl, only a year or two older than you. A terrible story to be digging up. She's long at peace now, and best we a-leave her be.'

'They never found the murderer. What a wicked man he must have been and how much he deserved to dance with Dame Rope.'

'If weak men fail to do justice, trust God knows. His justice is certain and mighty, although we may never see it.'

'Well, if we did know who the murderer is... or was...'

The colour in his cheeks strengthened, and he added more force to his words. 'It's not some ghost story to savour like a pie; it's a father's grief and a mother's despair. Old Adam Overmorrow died of it. A good man, with seven children and three more already buried. That cruel murder crushed him. After that lawyers' circus – a fool could see that simple lad never did it – Overmorrow lost his only hope, that the villain would be a-found and stopped from doing it again. Some other father's child taken from them.'

He looked at her. Oh no. He wanted to Save her.

'You're not too young to change. God and hard work saved many a working girl with a rocky start. Life is not easy, but those crooked women will lead you down a crooked path to destruction. Kneel with me now, and we can pray.'

Some suggestions just needed ignoring.

'Were the Overmorrows good people?' she asked.

'Godly and hard-working, true examples. When Pa Overmorrow died, his wife took the family to Canada. Away from nosey ghouls like you. A woman like that holds up the world, whatever life throws at her.'

Maisie knew most of this, but it sounded like... You could see in his face. 'Did you know them? The Overmorrows?'

His face leaned towards hers, louder, going red. 'All the bloodsuckers, wanting to a-slander poor Grace, leave her dead without her virtue, and a-preying on the family like wolves and always prattling on about it, like a brutality of crows. He's gone, she's gone, and Ma Overmorrow over the water and under the earth. She's gone to glory, and let's hope they all rests easier, God rest their souls.'

He hadn't denied it.

Of course, if Sir Charles had gone to that fateful Assizes, his family might have sent a big, steady servant to drive him and keep an eye on him. Keep him out of trouble. Willoughby had served the family since a boy.

'Were you at the trial?'

Willoughby's face flushed. 'There is no stopping you, is there? Best left alone. I'm a-asking you and now I'm a-telling you: let it be. Be told.' He tapped out his pipe and lumbered to his feet. 'Tell your mistress to stop prying or, God help me, I will. Some of us have work to do.'

'I hear you.' She liked the man. She wished she had a grandpa like him.

Maisie went to find the two queer birds. They were taking all gloomy about money and the inquest. She had a bomb to drop.

She gave her report with care, and the two of them paid close attention.

She ended with speculation. 'You told me you both went across the Atlantic, you didn't like it and came back. Well, Willoughby insisted the Overmorrows went, and I believe him.' She kept them waiting. 'Didn't say they'd stayed there.'

'By thunder, you think they came back?' Braddie said, wide-eyed.

'Not a hint of it in anything I have seen.' Mrs Ashton licked her pencil and scribbled something.

Maisie said, 'You wouldn't. That queer name, it would be like lighting a beacon. I'd change it, wouldn't you?'

Mrs Ashton had her hunting look. 'What specific evidence do you have?'

'What he didn't say. He said Ma Overmorrow went over the water and under the earth, but he didn't say where. Don't you normally say if someone dies in foreign places?'

'Sometimes not,' Braddie snapped. 'We don't have proof.'

'Someone paid for that afflicted lad's defence,' Mrs Ashton said. 'Maybe the same people helped them move back.'

'Maybe they have friends right in this house,' Maisie said. For certain, Willoughby would not have murdered Sir Charles or shielded anyone who did.

Mrs Ashton said what Maisie thought.

'If a member of that sad family lives on the estate, or in the town, that would be a remarkable coincidence. Even the babe in arms would be grown now.'

Maisie scratched her ear. 'They'll keep it secret. Particularly now. That's a motive a mile wide.'

CHAPTER 31
Telling the Truth

To the Bellingley Hotel

Mrs Ashton travelled with Braddie in the vile prisoners' wagon, claustrophobic and smelling of carbolic. It had been cheerier the time she rode in a hearse. The only view was out the small, barred window high on the back door. The impressive vista of the estate felt eternally stained by death.

Cairngorm would bring Maisie, who would give evidence after the others. Mrs Ashton had drilled Maisie in what would work with the jury, and how not to be drawn.

They rattled up to the estate gates and the wagon stopped. Men shouting, then a terrifying bang on the side, then another. 'Mrs Ashton, Mrs Ashton!'

Men jumped up to the window, a roar of aggressive and impertinent questions. One man hung on to the grill, trying to get a letter to them. Mrs Ashton shook, locked in and defenceless – but Braddie slammed the back door with her stick. 'Be awa with you, frightening my mistress. Awa', awa'!' Then she whacked at the fingers through the grill, and the man screeched and fell back.

'A hundred more to come!' she shouted, smiting the bars again.

Someone fired a shotgun. Mrs Ashton prayed into the air, and the police driver cracked his whip a dozen times, bellowing, 'I'll arrest every mother's son of you!' After a minute or two, the wagon rolled forward slowly, among journalists' shouts and complaints. Mrs Ashton took Braddie's hand, which shook worse than hers.

'Dear heart,' Mrs Ashton said, unable to say any more.

The Bellingley Hotel proved easier, four men with truncheons out guarding the way into the courtyard.

The inquest had heard the identification, and a description of the scene from those first on hand, including Doctor Culpe. The jury heard the great London doctor on post-mortem results regarding the injuries. Chemical analysis had been inconclusive on the presence of opium. Bullfinch and the county inspector had summarised the investigations so far. Now the kennel boy, his father, and Mrs Ashton.

Mrs Ashton sent a note, querying why she and Maisie were excluded from the room. The coroner's officer brought a response:

> *Mrs Ashton, this jury will deluge you with certain questions, to which the evidence of the boy and his father provides robust and useful answers. So, they will go first, to speed matters. I am surprised you do not see this.*

Against the coroner's whim, there was no appeal.

This would be a crowd not disposed to like her – and the press would take down every word.

Lady Violet had called the Bellingley Hotel the best in town. The officer led Mrs Ashton into the function room, to be met with the smell of sweat, strong drink, and tobacco. Every corner was filled with chairs and the modest gallery was packed. The coroner sat at a small table, and the jury of nineteen on benches to his left. Each witness testified from a small desk to his right, with the press taking the front seats on that side – claiming the ancient right to be close enough to hear. Mrs Ashton would have to project.

A murmur... How they hungered to see the *scandalous medium*. Mrs Ashton's heart pounded, but she cultivated a calm she did not feel. The jury's eyes bored into her, interest amounting to hunger, distaste, and in a couple of cases, a burning hostility. *Have they prejudged me?* She forced her hands to be steady and her face calm as she took the oath. She planned no untruths, but she did wonder what she might have to reveal.

'Thank you coming to see us, Mrs Ashton,' said the coroner. 'Before you came in, the jury foreman posed a question which I will answer in front of you. Mrs Ashton, you are to testify on oath, and you will tell us what you observed and heard, the reasons for your actions and so forth. Provided these are set out on those terms, I do not see that your spiritual beliefs are relevant. I will not have these proceedings diverted. If you bring spirits into it, then the jury will doubtless have some hard questions for you. I ask everyone to stick to what is relevant – how did Sir Charles Barrington-Stewart die?'

Mrs Ashton nodded.

'Please confirm to the jury that you hold oaths sacred and that you understand the penalties of perjury.'

What cheek! 'I do.'

'Your factual evidence will be invaluable. Please explain why you came to be at the manor.'

Kindly and courteous, he took her through it. There were gasps at each revelation – that Sir Charles had surprised her, that she had been imprisoned, that her brooch and watch had been taken, the forged letters. Pressure to sign a devil's pact. The press scribbled when she spoke, and their eyes bored into her when she was silent.

The man knew what questions to ask. She tried to fudge who had helped them escape, and he pressed her. So, she explained briefly that Esme Shilling had released Maisie so they might escape.

Jabs of the pain of that night returned as she described how Charles had met his death.

The coroner wrote quickly but still there was a minute between her finishing her description of the death and his pen halting. He looked up at her.

He named the kennel boy. 'On your oath, do you know this boy, or his father, or any member of his family?'

She answered, too long a length.

'Have you through any third party approached the family, or offered them any inducement or placed them under pressure?'

'No, on my oath as a Christian.'

He smiled and addressed the jury. 'Now, gentlemen of the jury, you are close to asking your questions. I hope we will be able to hear from Lady Barrington-Stewart and Miss Shilling as soon as possible, perhaps on Monday.'

The burly foreman of the jury rose, a frown like thunder. The weight of his role, hostility to her, or what?

'Did you do anything when His Lordship died to hasten his end?'

'No. I tried to aid him. I knew his bleeding at the mouth meant that he might be badly injured – possibly a punctured lung. I know moving a man with a back injury can worsen it. I could do little but comfort him and pray.'

'After all you claim he did, did you want to kill him?'

'I do not wish death on anyone. I abhor violence. I was astonished when he shouted and fell.' Don't ask the man how on earth he thought she might have hastened the end; it would just generate more aggressive questions.

'Do you think that His Lordship was a murderer?'

Sweet Jesus, what a question to answer. She had said that in front of the servants. They had been talking about the Overmorrow case too. It would be all round the house and some would have relatives in the village. Indeed, the police knew she thought that.

And she realised the difficulty the coroner had placed her in. That kindly twinkle hid a steel brain. He tapped his pen.

'Mrs Ashton, please answer. It is not a complicated question.'

'I have no direct evidence for my views. Nothing I could swear to.' Not and be believed, anyway.

'The question asks your opinion, Mrs Ashton. I invite you to give it or leave the jury to make whatever assumptions they wish by your silence.'

She dared to look up at the press, their glittering eyes and dashing pens. Bullfinch stared at her as if he wished her struck dead. Dare she say, here, now, what she suspected?

'If I had evidence, I would present it to the police and to this court, as my Christian duty requires. What I say is that I sought to help His Lordship, as a man in need. As he died, I prayed for him.'

Weak, she knew, but maybe the least-worst option. In desperation, she tried her power at a distance, to find the coroner's goal. It failed her, absolutely, although the pain of the failure made her wince. And if she could have demonstrated then and there her power to read minds... well, then she would be a mere specimen in a jar, a tool of powerful men. Her history as a medium would be exposed as fraud. Those who thought she spoke to the dead would turn against her, when they learned she simply lied.

She looked at the jury, rows of solid country men, property owners. Like Sir Charles or loath him, he embodied order. The foreman sat with arms crossed. Humanity in those faces, grim duty, hostility, confusion, but – in a couple of cases – they were as unreadable as a waxwork. Her heart pounded, and she tried to avoid biting her thumb.

Her ordeal ran on, but she did not stumble. Once a man called out 'Liar!', and the coroner rebuked the crowd.

'I will have no disturbance in this court.'

The jury did not challenge her statement that Sir Charles spoke. Both Culpe and the great doctor from London agreed that was possible.

The coroner thanked her, and at that point a tremor ran through her. It was over. They led Mrs Ashton back to where Braddie waited, standing. Those stairs led down to a kitchen entrance. Soon Maisie, without them, would be giving her evidence. All she could do was pray.

'It went as well as one might expect.'

Braddie frowned like a winter mountain. Here came the county detective and a rather common-looking fellow in a blue coat. His fighting-cock stance and fist of papers suggested, nay shouted, the vile profession of bailiff. Mrs Ashton considered running, but the policeman would block the way.

Mr Blue Coat at once stepped forward and thrust his papers into her hands, ignoring Braddie's growl. His breath stank.

'Mrs Ashton, I am an officer of the County Court, and you are duly served. You are hereby summoned this day four weeks hence to hear cases filed by seventeen persons seeking payment of your debts.'

The detective seemed oddly unenthusiastic.

The bailiff went on, 'His Honour is frightful busy, and always a ready man to rule in the debtor's absence. I warn you sincerely to attend, or to be proper represented.'

'Mrs Ashton is an important witness to the murder of a Member of Parliament,' said the county detective. 'Her debts, while important to those involved, hardly compare to affairs of state. You have done your duty, man, kindly leave us.'

'His Honour will thank you for the cooperation.' The man turned, and Braddie deftly placed her stick between his legs. He tumbled, Braddie wincing at the jolt.

The man swore, scrambled to his feet, puffing with indignation. 'That, madam, is an assault.'

'I didn't see it exactly,' the detective said.

The man left with an odour of self-righteousness.

Mrs Ashton had once seen crows gathering around a lamb caught in a fence. It struggled and they flapped off, but still they waited. Her enemies were circling her, ready to pounce.

The detective remarked, 'I am no friend of that profession, though an important cog in the wheel of justice.'

'That must place you at some disadvantage.'

'When you see them take your mother's dressing table, you see her tears... I had never slept on the floor before. A man may do the job with a little compassion, but these brutes mocked us.'

'A sad story.'

'Indeed, the old master of Corwood Manor, Sir Charles's father, ruined mine. And the wheel turns, and I must see justice for the son's murder. We must succeed, Mrs Ashton. This has shaken the county to the core.'

Mrs Ashton feared she had let her surprise show. She quickly changed the subject. 'Have we resolved the mysterious dark clothing?'

'If it ever existed. Well, we chased the charity clothes sent to London on the day of the murder. Four parcels, enough to hide a dozen cloaks. Our London colleagues visited the Mission to Seafarers on Tidemark Street, a most respectable and thorough organisation. Each parcel is opened with a senior woman supervising a junior. No question of theft or concealment. Each garment minutely checked and described in a book. Nothing damp, bloodstained, or indeed of a shape and colour to be your nebulous garment.'

'Commendable thoroughness. So, if bloody clothes there were, they have evaporated. Nothing further from the grapple?'

'The device looks to have been bought at the Great Imperial Stores, London, sometime in the last three years. We have men working through their postal orders, but so far nothing.'

'What will the coroner do then?'

'He must hear Lady Barrington-Stewart when she is ready. I wonder if Miss Shilling will truly be of interest, although the jury seem hell-bent on being thorough. But if I were a betting man, I think then adjourn. No point dragging those steady fellows of the jury to meet with nothing to tell them. Better adjourn and let the police do their job.'

Evening, and Bullfinch summoned Mrs Ashton to the library. He wrote who knows what reports his superiors demanded, and his face showed fury when he looked up. He had asked her to come. What a twisted case to solve, with the press constantly seeking some new angle. The county detective worked beside him, looking up and giving a polite nod, then returning to his own papers.

'The sooner I have this case solved, the sooner you can go,' Bullfinch said. 'Tell me everything you have learned since our last discussion, of any relevance to the case. I am in such a state of frustration, I will hear any credible theory.'

'I am happy to help. But I need to go to London, to manage my affairs. Now I have given my evidence, I need the coroner and the police to let me do so.'

'Ha! And disappear, no doubt? Why are you three pursuing this old murder, and the death of Lady Herncastle? Do you have any hard evidence of its relevance?'

Mrs Ashton considered telling the truth, but he would never accept ghosts.

'Nothing you or your colleagues would accept.'

Bullfinch issued a long groan. 'Do you or the girl know where Forty Wilkins is?'

That startled her. 'I don't have your wide organisation. He returned to London, or so I was told...'

'And disappeared that evening, with his valise. No one at the London house knows where he is. He never mentioned family or friends in town. Do something useful, ask your girl or the old woman if they know.'

'How remarkable.' How weary she was of bad news, of the dead man who haunted her, and what terrible confessions might come next.

'What is your interest in Forty?' she asked.

'He's disappeared, it is my job to be interested. He was the first servant to leave the estate at dawn, the day of the murder. He might have witnessed something or know something.'

The county inspector looked up. 'We have checked the bone fides of everyone in the house – I asked each of the servants for their birth and baptism details. Forty and his sister come from Stanning St Jude, in the north of the county. Anyway, the minister at their old chapel commended them and confirmed their birth details. I have the letter. The minister at Bellingley Tabernacle confirmed their baptisms as adults, as the Nonconformists do.

'Wilkins is walking out with a local girl in the village, but she says he has been moody and distracted. He all but dropped her and she fears he found another in London.'

'The man is all nerves,' Bullfinch said, fiddling with his pen. 'The weak sort to jump at shadows. It may be nothing. Yet did we miss something?'

'I hate to say it, but even an honest man can be fearful of the police,' Mrs Ashton said.

'Indeed,' Bullfinch said. 'We once chased a man three weeks to find he was frightened we'd uncover a conviction for poaching twenty years before. His employer thought it hilarious.'

Chapter 32
A Terrible Reckoning

That evening

A vexed hour in their rooms, as Mrs Ashton and Braddie struggled to list their debtors and what each might demand. What funds did they have in their London safety deposit box or elsewhere, and what could they raise as loans from their friends? A terrible thing to ask, under these circumstances.

They needed to be in London. Maisie had breezed through her account of her evidence and now was off following some project of her own.

A knock at their door. Braddie answered, and Prudie gave a little bob.

'Her ladyship wouldn't mind a word, Mrs Ashton.'

'I'm delighted she is better. Give me a minute or two to order myself.'

'Well, a little better,' Prudie said. 'I am that worried, she's so low.'

'Why is that?'

But the faithful servant didn't answer. 'And alone, if you don't mind, ma'am.'

Mrs Ashton wanted Braddie there, always. What choice did she have? She made her way up to find Lady Violet in bed, surrounded by piles of documents, and Esme Shilling in the chair. The lady, mistress of this house, thanked her for coming and waved her to sit. Prudie moved to serve tea.

Her host seemed lost in a revery. Mrs Ashton decided to begin. 'I am pleased to help, my lady.'

'I appreciate it. I am faced with difficulties all around. Yet, you are one constant I can trust. I do feel my mother's blessing upon me. Do you?'

'That is gratifying. I regret that I have not yet found her. Your husband's death has produced turmoil, like none I have experienced, and weakened me greatly.'

'Truly, I am sorry for what you have suffered. A great wave of scandal is coming. Your honest testimony may be disbelieved. The time must come when I am well enough to testify. I must decide between my love for my husband and the truth.'

Her patron was wavering. *Heavens, will she accuse me?* If she denied the accusations against Sir Charles... Surely, she couldn't change her statement to the police? Mrs Ashton had been in the room when Violet had demolished the case of forgery against her.

She tried a neutral question. 'What need you change?'

'I cannot be caught in a contradiction. I might decline to answer or be vague. Let other evidence stand.'

Mrs Ashton needed her wits about her, even this weary. 'The coroner... the jury... will be piercing in their questions. What is it that you wish to hide?'

'Oh, his criminal acts, I suppose. The police do not need my word to prove them. I have protected you, Mrs Ashton, do not worry. I can merely decline to answer, because a wife cannot be forced to testify against her husband.'

Poor naïve girl. 'But your husband is dead and cannot be convicted of a crime. Surely that ancient rule cannot apply. Why not tell the truth?'

'A great lady, who wishes to be my friend, has a wise mind on these things. She has the ear of men in power. She hopes to visit to guide me.'

How embarrassing Sir Charles's misdeeds must be to the government, with their rising star mired so quickly in this astonishing story. No difficulty guessing the great lady's name. Sir Charles's patron was the Home Secretary, whose wife Lady Bergamot was one of the great political hostesses of London. The lady proved so astute and effective in the Liberal cause that jealous Tories called her 'the best mind in the Cabinet'.

'Well, I do not claim to have a political brain,' Mrs Ashton said. 'Surely you must ask, what is the right thing to do?'

'We must ponder this, Mrs Ashton. I have a more pleasant task.' She picked up a bundle of papers, and Prudie moved to pass them over.

'My husband bought up every one of your debts he could find. I can only assume, to begin bankruptcy proceedings against you. I apologise. Please take these as a gift.'

Mrs Ashton breathed a little easier. One vindictive creditor who preferred revenge to their money could make full bankruptcy inevitable.

'I have only been able to meet the trustees for an hour before I was exhausted, and they spent a third of that warning me against you. I told them I hope to remain your patron and friend.'

'I am most grateful.' A bulging envelope with Lady Violet's handwriting among the others. A shaped thing, not paper. Curious.

'And your sisters,' Esme said, with twisted mouth.

'My dear sisters wish to visit, out of their deep love and affection, but I am disappointed in them. Their love is not so deep that they will stay under the same roof as you. A less kindly gospel than yours, or mine. I could hide you in the Dower House, but my mother brought me up to revere truth.'

Mrs Ashton didn't want crusading puritans here either.

Esme had the look of someone about to speak. Mrs Ashton encouraged her with a gesture.

'Mrs Ashton, you shared my unfortunate state when Charles deceived you.' Esme flushed. 'I don't blame you, under the circumstances.'

'I regret I did. I feared for my life.'

'How wicked it is, that when a woman falls, the woman bears the scandal and the man does not. I am so worried for my baby's future.'

'Esme is a true sister to me,' Violet said. 'My dear Mrs Ashton, I hope you will throw your protection over her too. I ask a priceless gift to us, your silence. We women must stick together.'

Was that all? An easy bargain to accept.

'Have no fear,' Mrs Ashton said. 'I did not name Esme. I have no reason to spread it further. My companions will follow my lead. The mad-nurses will not be believed, and I doubt Sir Charles left any record. Willoughby and the footman I cannot answer for.'

Violet relaxed. 'Dear Willoughby, we can trust him, the finest of men. What a friend you are, Mrs Ashton.' She sighed. 'I want to be away from this place, where two deaths haunt me. Charles must be decently laid to rest. The Cabinet want a monstrous circus of a funeral, I crave a smaller affair, and a national memorial in a few weeks. Let Charles rest with his father and his brother, in the vault prepared for him.'

'Where would you go? Your brother's estate?'

'Not in his absence. I crave our Derbyshire home, Dunnock House. Spring there comes weeks later than here; the hills and the air are refreshing. An austere beauty in the view. How happy we were, those first months of my marriage. The Charles I knew at Dunnock House would have made me happy forever. Indeed, I wept to see he had left it to me absolutely in the will. I am afraid we will worry the staff, so please do not discuss it. No one will lose their place.'

Mrs Ashton agonised, but surely, she needed to divulge her secret. She kept her eyes on her client.

'Lady Violet, a truly odd development. I have encountered the spirit of Sir Charles.'

Violet shot her a look, startled. Then thoughtful. 'How extraordinary.'

Mrs Ashton went on. 'I suppose, being so close to me in death, it is easy for him to remain.'

'I did wonder if he was the raging spirit behind your faints. How unpleasant, turning his great anger against you. Does he spy on you? It is too much to hope he is penitent...'

'I am strong in faith, and I can manage difficult spirits. He grows calmer.'

Some fuss to the side. Prudie was mopping Esme, who had spilled her tea. Mrs Ashton regretted not having Braddie's sharp eye and sceptical mind in the room. Focus on Violet.

Violet said, 'Well, do tell my husband that I forgive him, for his trespasses against me.' Something crossed that aristocratic face. 'Why, Mrs Ashton, you have the answer to the crime. Though the police will not accept him as a witness, he must know who struck that foul blow. When we know the solution, we can work to prove it!'

'He does not remember.'

Lady Violet sighed. 'How vexing. Many people might ask you to prove this marvellous development. Of course, I believe you. There is perfect trust between us.'

Mrs Ashton needed an example. 'He is worried about the secret bookcase in the library. He thinks some of the books are, indelicate, in nature. Not ones he would like you to see.'

'I must take your word for it. Sketch for me where it is. The library is never empty of course, the police. And does Charles watch me?'

'He says he cannot see you.'

Lady Violet rubbed her forehead. 'I am tired, and my migraine returns. Prudie, the tincture please. Mrs Ashton, forgive my rudeness, but we must wait until tomorrow.'

'I look forward to it.' Using her ordinary skill, Mrs Ashton had minutely watched Violet's reaction. Nothing belied her words. She had no choice but to put the question and use her power. She needed Braddie.

'My lady, is there any light, any clue, any theory that could help us solve the murder? Is there anything you have not told the police?'

Violet opened her eyes, and Mrs Ashton could drown in them.

'Why, good heavens, no. Nothing.' Innocence itself.

Mrs Ashton tried to open her. And it was if she had no power at all. Only the power of suspicion.

As soon as she left the room, she opened the envelope and found it contained a diamond brooch. The note said only, *This was my grandmother's, it is given to Mrs Ashton in thanks and the gift is witnessed.* The three signatures. A jewel, and with provenance. Another gift the trustees would not know about.

Saturday and Mrs Ashton, Braddie, and Maisie breakfasted together, an odd, thoughtful meal, served by one of the most disagreeable footmen. The papers were chewing over the plentiful inquest evidence detrimental to the character of the deceased. They did so in a cautious and longwinded manner, but more than one writer suggested that had he not died, Mrs Ashton could have made more lurid allegations.

Ironic that the same papers carried the news of a committee to raise funds for a statue for Sir Charles, in some prominent square. The fervent terms in which his virtues and promise were expounded might begin to ring hollow. As well as four worthy Liberals from politics and business, the committee included two titans of business whose politics she did not know, and three Conservatives: the Lord Lieutenant of the county, another peer, and Mrs Ashton's least favourite cleric, the Bishop of London. One might expect the Home Secretary to head it. Perhaps his wife had warned him to see what the inquest brought.

Mrs Ashton worked through her post – pestering questions from the press; friends she had not spoken to for years; signature hunters; long screeds demanding she repent, one accusing her of being a priestess of Dionysus, no less; offers of matrimony; a fierce eight-page denunciation from a prominent Spiritualist matron; two requests to find a lost will, six to find lost persons, and one to trace some buried treasure; and a remarkably sympathetic letter from a member of the Doctrine Committee of the Church of Scotland, seeking her advice for a parishioner troubled with a poltergeist. She began to sort the hateful into 'abusive', 'ignorant', and 'hostile but amusing'.

Some former clients wrote in support. Cheeriest of all, two people she knew – and one unknown – had sent her cheques. The unknown one was ten pounds, an excellent sum. But as cautious people did, they so endorsed their cheques that they could only be paid into her own bank account.

She feared the long official envelope and left it till last. This strict order, worded as a polite request, directed her to meet with the Procurator Fiscal's deputy at her earliest convenience.

Braddie had supped late and well with the cook, and it showed. She snorted. 'Read this!'

The London Panjandrum had revived the scandal of Mrs Ashton's marriage, calling her a knowing bigamist. Even *The Orb* hesitated to use that vicious lie. The Major had assured her his first wife was dead, and she had found the truth only after his death.

Her London safety deposit box held several of his letters, kept a little for sentiment, but much more to demonstrate that she had been lied to. What would her respectable friends in London think if that lie gained credibility? Mrs Ashton needed at least shreds of standing left.

Good that the police did not think her a murderess. But how damaging a place her failures and bad luck had reached.

Once breakfast had departed, they were alone. Gathering all her strength, Mrs Ashton said, 'We must try to draw these threads together. What intelligence did you find last night, dear heart?'

Braddie finished her coffee. 'After our third glass, I tried to see if any staff had lived overseas, and if she knew anything about the Overmorrow case. Mrs O'Grady changed the subject.'

Maisie said, as she had before, 'I'm worried about Forty. He hates London. I think Willoughby knows more than he is saying about the Overmorrows. And I think Willoughby took Charles to the trial – he worked on the estate, so I can't see why else he would have been there. And we still don't know how Lady Herncastle went hunting Grace's murderer.'

Mrs Ashton said, 'If the lady went by carriage, Forty might have driven her.'

'Or Willoughby or any of the grooms might,' Braddie said.

Braddie had ordered her thoughts around her hangover. 'Mrs O'Grady says Forty has been all nerves since the murder, but he was a nervy child too. And a few weeks back, he parted with his girl in the village. O'Grady is big friends with the housekeeper – she knows all the house staff. So, I asked about who Lady Herncastle took out, on errands and the like. I wish we'd kept the coffee pot.'

'Go on, dearest.'

'Well, Lady Herncastle had a fine nurse who went to Harrogate, and another not so good who went to Devon, so it might have been them. And Prudie worked for both the old mistress and Lady Herncastle.'

Mrs Ashton's instinct said something was emerging.

'So, you are saying Prudie might have been in attendance, however Violet's mother travelled. And Forty might have driven them.'

Braddie sighed. 'Or Willoughby and a nurse might have done it. Or a senior groom and another maid.'

'Braddie, dearest, always keen to keep our feet on the ground.'

'Women can drive a horse and cart,' Maisie said.

Mrs Ashton nodded. And not unusual, if a smaller vehicle.

'As the dear Major used to say, not a conjecture I would use to bridge a chasm. But possible. How is Prudie seen in this new dispensation?'

'There's trouble,' Maisie said. 'Quiet grumbling. One of the maids doesn't mind who she tells. Prudie acting like she owns the place.'

Braddie leaped in. 'Silly jealousy. What sort of fool thinks bringing a message from the mistress is the maid giving the order?'

'I think Violet knows more than she is saying,' Maisie said.

'I cannot deny it.'

Mrs Ashton was as close as she ever had been to revealing to Maisie her power. She chose caution.

When Mrs Ashton had opened Violet – it seemed so long ago she read a great gush of her terror about Charles – if the woman had even *suspected* that Charles had strangled a girl to death with his bare hands, never mind *murdered her mother*, that would have been at the centre of her fears.

The terrible reality. Lady Violet remained her strongest ally against humiliation and prison. Maybe one of the brother and sister went with Lady Herncastle to Grennard or received her confidences. Or not. A hypothesis, with no actual evidence. What a maze she was in.

Bullfinch entered Lady Violet's room, trying to be calm. The lady of the house lay in bed, eyes closed. Miss Shilling was absent, although the maid wiped Lady Violet's brow.

'Lady Barrington-Stewart, you wished to speak to me about Mrs Ashton?'

'I do. Dear Chief Inspector, she needs to go to London, and I am sure you will release her to do so. There is some difficulty with the Scottish authorities she is keen to resolve.'

'My lady, these matters are never that simple. During this investigation...'

'My head, Chief Inspector. May I plead with you to speak more quietly? The coroner has been so obliging. His note says he doubts he will need Mrs Ashton again, and she is too wise to ignore his summons were his needs to change. And with her other troubles, surely, she will not add to them.'

'On the contrary, my lady, I am concerned that Mrs Ashton will simply flee to the Continent. She has a long history of flitting, travelling in disguise and under an alias.'

'Why, Chief Inspector, she gave me her word! If she flees, she will be bankrupted, humiliated – however unjustly. She will face her creditors, I am sure.'

Mrs Ashton's word and a penny would buy a large bun.

Lady Violet opened her eyes. 'You know dear Lady Bergamot, the Home Secretary's wife. She is in the county and intends to visit on Sunday. She has always been so kind, and I think I must meet her. Of course, I hope that I am well enough to testify on Monday.'

Bullfinch gritted his teeth. 'Mrs Ashton has a record of disappearing, my lady. From England to Scotland, then back again.'

'She has been so badly advised, and one cannot expect a great spiritual gift to come with careful bookkeeping skills. I have suggested better people for that, and I believe she will pay every penny owed. How are you progressing with finding my husband's murderer? I tried to review our meetings and I am not sure what leads you are now pursuing. Perhaps you could summarise for me to understand. In writing – I have one of my headaches.'

Bullfinch knew a mountain of solid, thorough work had little to show for it. He feared the authorities might bring in the other star detective of Scotland Yard to stand on the work he had done and seize the reward of success.

'I would be happy to meet Lady Bergamot myself, my lady.'

Lady Violet said, 'That's so very kind.' Bullfinch realised the mistress of the house meant no. What steel behind that pretty face. She could praise or damn him behind closed doors. Many said to convince the Home Secretary's wife was to convince the man himself. Commissioner Henderson had specifically warned him.

'I want Mrs Ashton where I can see her.'

'Oh dear, how vexing. I must ask my dear friend, when she comes, what I should do.'

Bullfinch pondered the admirable Mrs Bullfinch, who after discussion usually bowed to his wishes with a simple, 'If you think it best, my dear.' Occasionally, by specific phrases, he knew she meant war. A long emotional war where she would simply wear him down. To avoid long and tiresome crying fits, on those occasions his policy was to negotiate a surrender, restoring marital bliss.

The mistress of Corwood Manor held the cards. 'I will see what can be done, my lady,' he said, holding his temper.

'Oh, Chief Inspector, you are the very best of men. I will be sure to tell Lady Bergamot my high opinion of you.'

'We understand Sir Rupert has returned to England. Have you heard from him?'

'Rupert is a fool and a wastrel. We haven't spoken for years, and no one told me that he has been seen in the county. Yet Charles provided for his child. Secretly, Charles paid his debts after his banishment, to keep him safe from his villainous creditors. Rupert wrote an emotional letter of thanks some months ago, which Charles kept from me. And I find, despite his harsh words, Charles left him a modest income in his will. I thought the brothers beyond reconciliation – how pleasing to be wrong. What a truly curious moment for Rupert to kill his brother, knowing of his kindness?'

Indeed.

'One last thing, Chief Inspector.'

'I am at your service.'

'When you have a moment, what is the news of the dreadful arson of Mrs Ashton's home? Please, be candid. Are you sure the men in charge are pursuing this horrible case with the exemplary vigour you show here? Should I mention this to my visitor?'

'I will write and ask for a progress report, my lady. And I shall warn them certain important persons are taking an interest.'

The high-up woman had got what she wanted. He'd never been beaten by someone with such beautiful eyes. She could act. If she was sick, he was a carnival goldfish.

Chapter 33
Accusing and Accuser

...

In her room, Mrs Ashton found her accounts as much a headache as her power. Staring at them summoned no extra funds, so she enjoyed a vase of humble garden flowers instead. Braddie had disappeared, muttering about 'finding supplies' – that could mean anything.

Sir Charles coughed.

'Mrs Ashton, I hear that you are leaving.'

'Fascinating. Hear from whom, may I ask?'

He frowned. *'Never mind. Will I have the choice to remain here? I followed you to Bellingley before... but I can find little on the mortal realm without you being there. I cannot find my mortal remains anymore.'*

'I simply can't say.'

Being rid of Charles would be an affliction gone. Except, a genuine spirit, and one with invaluable information.

He seemed dejected.

She prodded him. *'Your murder continues to perplex us all.'*

He tried to probe her mind, which she resisted.

'Sir Charles, a lady is entitled to her privacy.'

'My apologies. You are right. We must be patient with each other.'

What a contrite and mournful spirit. Mrs Ashton burned to learn more but prepared herself for a storm. Charles might remember more about the murder.

'Forty Wilkins went to London and disappeared. I believe that Lady Violet knows more than she is saying.' She stiffened herself against any prying.

He was bewildered, at first.

'Why? Forty is a good fellow, salt of the earth. I took a beer with him now and again. He liked my cigars.'

Sir Charles's memories fluttered. A soft spring night on the stable roof... he remembered Violet's scent... a girlish laugh. Which night had that been? He missed her. Husband and wife reconciled.

Could he read her? She raised a wall against his prying and at once he did the same.

'I believe you murdered Grace Overmorrow.'

He withdrew a little. The pause lasted perhaps a minute.

'That's an extraordinary accusation. I was a mere youth, not out of school. Why would you think that?'

'You were tall and strong as a lad. I have my powers. After all, Sir Charles, you called me a fraud, and here we are.'

He laughed, a colourless laugh.

'Oh, Mrs Ashton. I confess only a morbid interest in the case. It was more intriguing as the police bungled, and that poor fool was nearly hanged. I even had a scrapbook for other gruesome murders. My mother had it burned in front of me by the gardener. I can see myself doing the same for my own son.'

Her face flushed hot. *'I know for a fact you killed her. For what, pleasure in her suffering? Pride, because she denied you? The thrill of it? Then you went to watch the trial. What a gutless, coward's crime. Rising from the Parliamentary benches to speak when you deserved to hang.'*

'As you will, Mrs Ashton, I am sure.'

'You have confessed to one murder. Only confession can begin your redemption. I think you murdered Lady Herncastle because she knew. Something took her to the local paper's editor, for proof you were at the trial.'

'Oh, she was a nosy old besom.'

He considered attacking her. How did she know? A gathering of his energies, she supposed. A focus of his presence. She had no exact vocabulary. She prepared herself.

He did not act. As cold as a frozen lake. *'Good day, Mrs Ashton, and my best wishes to Mrs Bradshaw. What patience that poor old woman must have. I feel a deep sympathy for her.'*

He was gone.

Saturday evening. Maisie sat out of everyone's way in the window seat, full of gloom. Cairngorm would drive them to the station tomorrow – only three trains on a Sunday. He'd disappeared after Violet told him they couldn't meet, and she wondered about him. Maisie ached for her family and her friends in her gang. Adventures grew wearing unless you kept making progress.

Suppose Mrs Ashton couldn't get out of her trouble. Maisie was no fool, she would scarper rather than go to jug. That meant being a sewing girl for long days and looking after the little ones. She didn't suppose a girl not fourteen could start her own detective agency, not without cash.

The three had a plan to investigate Prudie and Forty's background. Braddie would try the cook and she would try Willoughby again – although he'd been so discouraging last time. She needed a good angle. Mrs Ashton stayed vague about her intentions.

Maisie would wear her boy's suit tomorrow, and the servants wouldn't approve of that at all.

She had a plan. She wasn't terribly comfortable with it, but you had to play these things by ear. It took a while to find Willoughby, with one servant after another shrugging or telling her a lie about where he was.

He strode away from the house, towards his cottage, and she put her head down to run. For an old 'un his hearing was good, and he turned before she reached him.

'You,' he said, but not as cross as last time.

'I wanted to say goodbye. And we're worried about Forty. He was nice to me in London.'

'A good lad but easily led. London's the City of Destruction, a-full of corruption. I know the mistress has sent men to find him.' He gave a stern smile, ever so slightly. 'Little Miss is being nosey.'

'Will you pray with me?' He blinked and she ploughed on. 'I feel ever so low, and Mrs Ashton is all for praying and reading the Bible, but it doesn't work for me.'

'She's hardly a Godly woman. But even the hanged thief repented.'

'And we could pray for Forty too. And my Pa to stay off the drink and find a good woman to marry, and George's cough to get better. My Grandma and Ma died of bad lungs.'

He smiled, proper this time. 'And may I pray for you to get honest work away from those two?'

'Yes, do.'

Willoughby held out his hands, and she took them and closed her eyes. His strong, worn hands. How she wished sometimes to have an adult she could truly rely on. The words didn't mean much, but she'd kicked him, and made him angry, and he still wanted to use Bible magic to help her.

Odd, he ended the prayer, 'And Lord, a-keep Forty safe, from whatever has afflicted him, and a-keep him from the wicked temptations of the evil city, that Babylon.' In the end he called for light to fall, as it did on the Apostle on the road. 'Use this child for your work, Lord, show her your grace and mercy.'

She said the amen, and realised her eyes were wet.

He found her a coachman's rag and she took it, even though hers was cleaner.

'You think Forty's ill?' she said.

'Something ails him. Swigging Colston's Purge by the cup.'

That'd scour you out. He must be bunged up down there something awful.

He looked at her, not unkindly now. 'You could start by confessing about the grease on the coach seat.'

'I would, I would. But it wasn't me or Mrs Ashton. And it's too thick to spill – you'd have to warm it up or spread it like butter.'

'Hmm. Words are cheap, actions speak louder.'

'Was it a cushion for the trap Forty wanted to use to run the mail to town?'

'Yes, but he had another. Mind your own business.'

Maisie threw her arms around him. 'Thank you. I will try to be good. And find Forty and keep him safe.' She kissed his whiskers, reminding her of Pa. Willoughby smelt of tobacco and beer and horses, and good country sweat.

Was Forty the murderer? Could he have struck the blow? Pa said a desperate man could do anything.

Nervy and ratty, sleeping bad, his bowels shut. Opium did that to you, among other things. Forty was one of Charles's commoner pals. Might Charles and Forty have smoked it together? You could drown your sorrows in laudanum cheaper than beer. Smoking poppy worked all at once, they said, strange floating dreams and bizarre terrors, slipping into a world of phantoms

Forty had driven off with the mail. Who wanted to grease the seat?Odd names Chapel folk had. Prudence and Fortitude.

Chapter 34
Leaving the Manor

...

Mrs Ashton, Braddie, and Maisie waited at the side of the house with their baggage. Cairngorm would drive them out via the eastern gate, where the press did not cluster. Around Mrs Ashton, her enemies gathered – crows, vultures, wolves – and the hostility of the press raged. Beneath this open danger, the deep murky waters of the crime. She had no more than glimpses of the truth. Violet held protection and condemnation in her hands, but a note regretted she was too ill to see her.

At last, she wore the golden bee brooch, its pin a temporary repair. The nurses had pleaded guilty and had been given a year in jail. Mrs Ashton felt an awkward tremor of compassion.

She took Braddie's arm, unclear who was supporting whom. Maisie kept close, their voices low.

'So, how did Forty hide the clothes?'

'In the seat cushion. None of them had time to go hide it in the trap that night. They must have greased the other seat before. The cushion buttons up, so easy enough to change the padding. Fold the bloody garments neatly. Then, at the quarry, add a brick, and throw the whole thing in the water.'

'There are a thousand places he could have hidden it,' Braddie growled.

'The deepest water and the trickiest place to search, only a five-minute walk from the road... He sat on the evidence. I'm sure I got to the bottom of it.'

Good to see Maisie smile again.

'Then he rides back with no cushion? Painful and obvious.'

'He had another hidden somewhere.'

Great strength was not needed to strike the fatal blow. Forty could have done it. This theory suggested premeditation. Had he accomplices?

Cairngorm drove a neat four-seater, and saluted them, whip to forehead.

'A good morning to you.' That cheery face clouded over. 'What dark deeds happened here. A cursed place now, I wonder if dear Violet will abandon it.'

They set off, at vigorous pace.

'This is a difficult business. I wonder what Violet will say at the inquest. There's a rumour of some shady business about Charles and Argentina. And another story that they've found some Fenian connection.'

Mrs Ashton replied, 'I hadn't heard that. When the press run out of things to write, they can fall prey to nonsense.' Or deliberate misinformation.

'What a bad man, worse than I imagined. I suppose Violet will defend him. Do you believe him a murderer?'

Sidestep that. 'I need hard proof, one way or another. May we stop by Gray's Quarry? Will we have time?'

'Only if we are brief. If you miss this train, it is a wait until supper.'

Shortly after, the three of them stood on the rim of the quarry, trees sprouting from cliffs, dark water. A little further round, the cushion might have been hurled into the water. What an effort would be needed to search for it. And if Forty had been in haste, he might have left it somewhere else.

Someone, two people, watching her from... wherever Charles came from. Wary and silent. Certainly not familiar to her. She tried, *'I mean you no harm,'* and they scampered away. Well, she had seen two ghosts at the manor, so there must be more.

Mrs Ashton took Cairngorm to one side and asked what troubled him.

'The whole miserable story, I suppose. And dear Violet was right, people were gossiping. My Persephone - Mrs Cairngorm - is the sun and the moon to me, and she doesn't deserve vicious tongues, too cowardly to speak to my face.'

He sighed. 'In confidence, I am so troubled. Don't be shocked – could Violet know who the murderer is? I think, I hope, that she would dislike lying to my face. Maybe that is why she decided to exclude me.'

'Dear Jack, if I may be so familiar. I suspect that you are right. I am convinced she is hiding something.'

The railway station had several men hanging around the entrance. One she had seen before in a county police uniform, though now only his boots spoke of the police. Three or perhaps four men she had seen at the inquest, at the press table. She did not want to be followed to London.

Another was a railwayman, and her observant eye showed an eccentric one. A winter coat pulled tight around his throat, ignoring the pleasant warmth, and an old-fashioned hat. He had a lantern raised, on this brilliant day, so bright indeed she could see through him. The spirit stared at her, hostile but not afraid.

Cairngorm looked awry at her. 'What is the plan?'

She flipped down her veil, and from now, each movement became slow, like an invalid.

'Ride past the entrance, to that fine oak.'

She hoped those watching would not notice them.

Twenty minutes before the express. Cairngorm gallantly unloaded their modest luggage on the ground.

'Maisie, get through unnoticed and buy our tickets.'

Maisie, spotting a group with an elderly woman, a man, and a girl, ran to help with their luggage. Thus appearing part of a family group, she passed the gate unspotted.

Braddie hailed a porter and asked for an invalid chair, while Mrs Ashton feigned fatigue, sitting on a low wall with her back to the press.

Braddie got the porter to bring the bags and bent low to Mrs Ashton's face as she passed the gate... concealing them both. A roll of the dice will sometimes work.

In a private carriage, Mrs Ashton set out the tasks ahead.

'We must meet our advisers. Sell or pawn or borrow what we can to buy time. Dear Maisie, I must give you an advance, and you must see your family. I will convene what is left of my middling meeting and try to reassure them. I can have no certainty that they will assist us. Certainly, our dear friends the banker and his wife wish to help, but they face such hostility from the bank...'

Bankruptcy had an ugly little sister, the arrangement with your creditors. Almost as humiliating, and one malicious creditor could derail it.

'And my partnership,' Maisie said, chin determined. 'Helping when you quarrelled, and helping you escape, and all the full detecting. I think a third is fair.'

Oh heavens, the thieving urchin!

'In no endeavour does an apprentice get the same as the master. You took no financial risk, and we fed you and your family. If I go to prison, Maisie dearest, you will get a precise share of nothing. Your per diem is generous.'

'I took every other risk. Didn't sign up for being chased by a murderer and arrested. And it's not my fault you spent money you didn't have. I'm not going to run around for you, get my gang together, and then not get paid, because your fancy hat shops needed it.'

'The labourer is worthy of her hire,' Braddie said. Heavens, outnumbered, and Mrs Ashton could hardly flee the argument.

'I often wondered how you did the ghosts,' Maisie said, very direct in her gaze, and Mrs Ashton suddenly feared the lass's ambition. 'You're so bothered with Charles, either you've gone bonkers or he's really there. And you stopped mentioning the Cavalier. But mostly it is something else – I know you never summoned Ma – and the world would love to know how you do it.' And she shut her mouth.

Did she know? Well, how does one handle that? Even at fourteen, had she been quite that fierce? Mrs Ashton found herself at a loss for words.

'A tenth of the profit, or the daily, whichever is larger,' Braddie said.

'No, the profit after the daily is paid. I'll accept Braddie's word on what the profit is,' Maisie countered. 'And if we have a deal – I don't squeal on partners.'

Mrs Ashton needed her Maisie. She admired how the girl had judged her blackmail and stood up for her worth. She extended her hand. 'I will pay your per diem, dear girl, and in time, at least a tenth of any profit we might scrape together. We are arguing over chickens which have yet to hatch. Have I not been generous to you and your dear family in the past?'

Maisie grinned, took her hand, and shook. Braddie offered hers and she took that too. 'Well, partners, what next?'

'We must find Forty – though a man can disappear as well in London as in the most intractable jungle. His drinking haunts around the house. Did he have friends in London? Where did he attend Divine Service? And Trephine is in London, doing who knows what dark deeds.'

'And his opium habit,' Braddie said.

'He need only claim an injury and buy laudanum at any pharmacy.'

Braddie growled. 'We have a mere four weeks before the bankruptcy hearing.'

'Dearest, money will take much of our time. But for all we know, Forty is in danger.'

'People will expect paying for a search,' Maisie said, and Mrs Ashton looked weary.

As the train rolled through rows of houses, as the great sprawling city engulfed her, the sounds of the material world faded. Around her she heard whispering, like the endless sea, or a vast forest in the wind.

The noise was neither waves nor branches, but voices. The nameless dead of two millennia greeted her, in a faraway chorus of need and regret. London was haunted, and her world had changed utterly. For good or evil, had their journey separated them from Charles?

Even on the Sabbath, the cavernous station filled with smoke and hurrying figures, all noise and confusion: three Indians, formally dressed for business, but wearing turbans; a woman with an enormous wolfhound – surely it would need a ticket as it would take the space of a man; a ragged child playing a massive concertina, with a one-armed father collecting coins – so pallid and gaunt, the tune so eerie, Mrs Ashton thought for one second they were spirits.

And, for a few breaths, a bare-headed woman walked a stately pace, red-haired and with a staff, her cloak of green leaves clasped with gold. There, and not there.

Silence fell in the cab. Beyond the bustle of London's streets hummed the distant crowd, Mrs Ashton's new audience. She tried to ignore faint voices calling her, wailing, soliciting her. Earthly matters would not wait.

The banks were shut, of course. She would go tomorrow and take what she could. Lady Violet had written a recommendation, but maybe the banker or the secretary would be safer choices. She would sell Violet's diamond brooch and her silver watch. She must also remember the passports – not essential for travel abroad but often helpful with difficult local officials. And she sent a message to Mr Oliphant, whose size, calm, and reputation could be a patent cure for stupidity.

Then Mrs Ashton's gang convened at the happy house of her two theatrical friends, who she could trust absolutely. The sister of one had married the other, an affectionate arrangement between three friends, and protecting them all.

Their parrots Eleanor and Sarah were thriving. As soon as Mrs Ashton entered the parlour, both bobbed up and down, and greeted them with squawks and calls. The two women paid them the attention they deserved. Eleanor paused as if for effect and squawked, *'Tighter than a bishop's ring!'*

This house full of personality, crowded with posters and magician's tricks, photographs of theatrical casts in costume and elegant Classical statues of young men untroubled by clothing.

A conference between the three, Mrs Ashton their general. She consulted her notebook.

Easy to lose a man in the biggest city in the world. And if he wanted to flee, trains and boats in every direction. How much money did he have? A plan of action emerged.

That evening, at last, a double bed to themselves and a stout door, so Braddie and her hinny could bathe and dry and dress and meet each other's needs.

How they wanted to make love. Yet in that comfortable bed, Braddie opened her heart.

'Will we get away it? Tha wolves, tha jackals. All our follies at our necks at once.'

She gathered Braddie's head to her breast and held her. '*Our* follies is rather kind of you, dearest. Had I followed your advice, it would have been a poorer life, with more hard work and less adventure, and less catastrophe too. But as rich in what matters, which is you.'

'We should flee... abroad, I suppose.' What despair in that for Braddie. 'Exile, at my age. I don't trust Violet and I don't trust Them.'

'Maybe even Sir Charles can help us. Let us at least see what we can do tomorrow.'

She kissed Braddie's worn, thin hair, and Braddie put her hand to her hinny's breast. Together again. Physical love flowed deep and strong, as long delayed – a warm river of pleasure given and received, and a promise of better times between the two women. They were united against a hostile world. Nothing was yet so bad that attaining the physical peak could not make it a little better.

Mrs Ashton woke in the night to see Sir Charles watching her, the longest gap between visitations so far.

'Sir Charles, this is not the action of a gentleman!'

His expression bemused her, not smiling but not furious.

'Mrs Ashton, apologies. I was not wishing to spy. It took a time to find you, but I had no desire to intrude on your private time.'

And he was gone. Most nights, drunk or sober, Mrs Ashton prayed before bedtime. She wondered, as before, if her childhood habit truly kept the dead at bay. How far could she trust her murdered enemy, or would that be another rash decision? And he was not bound to Corwood Manor.

Few people in Thameswake wore togs as posh as Esme's suit. The theatrical types had ever such a good time finding Maisie second-hand boy's gear. Her wig and moustache were fair-to-brown, as light as she could carry off with her complexion. She then mussed up her clothes a little, to be less obvious.

How the city stank of privies and the factories when you returned to it. When you could see it, the horizon was brown with smoke. Harsh air and rancid shit. How different from the earth and wet smell of the country. Maisie needed a bed tonight, she didn't love longish hair under the wig. She moved with caution, knowing that she might be watched. Good job she'd been smart approaching Jonah Court; a man waited that she had seen before. A man she believed worked for Jabez Trephine.

Sal would know what was going on, but there would be too many eyes in the Burning Bird. Bound to be full, the do-gooders had forced pubs to close early on Sunday evenings. Pa thought it positively unnatural to deny a man his pint.

Maisie went to look for Sal's eldest, a man grown who worked in the brewery. He had his own rooms with his girl. The air near the factory here smelt of sweet biscuit and burned grain, even strong enough to cover the stink of river and privies. She found him smoking and musing on the river.

An eyebrow up at her male attire.

'Best keep low, young... feller. That Trephine is around, and his sailor friend has been in the Bird. Offering hard cash. He's in league with Hanging Jacob's men looking for a groom called Forty Wilkins. And he wants to know if anyone sees you and the two old birds, for good money.'

Maisie's heart sank lower than her boots, down to the mammoths and the dinosaur bones. In much of the docklands, Hanging Jacob's writ was more feared and obeyed than the blue terrors.

Sal's son saw. 'Oh, Jacob's clear, goods as little damaged as possible. The blue terrors are after Forty too.'

Few people in Jonah Court cared for the police but the coppers were still a big problem.

'Well, I'm not going to get my people tied up in that. How's my pa? The kids?'

'Your pa's sober, by some miracle. The kids are fine. They miss you and the stories.'

'I'll figure some ruse to meet them, safe like.'

She liked and trusted him.

'Can Sal get them some pies or something? And here's some towards the rent.' She slipped him a few coins. She'd need the rest.

She missed Pa, and tired, sober Pa was better than wild, drunk Pa any day. Maisie wanted her Ma, just once more, to tell her it would be all right. How tough not to see Pa and Georgie and Tildy, and she sniffed away another tear. Maybe even Kate Warne allowed herself a tear when a case went bad.

Maisie would find a friend to stay with, and a bed, and so spoiled by staying in rich people's houses, she might even buy herself a bath. She was important enough they paid a man to watch her home. That counted for something.

She liked Forty but he might be the murderer. Maisie had her own network, fuelled by Mrs Ashton's promises of silver. The children of the street – the errand boys and newspaper sellers, the vilet girls and the young roughs –

dozens of eyes and ears like some ancient monster. Her people could find out what was going on.

And she needed to follow up Forty's opium habit. She must talk to Dongmei Li. Some preferred to smoke the drug. Dens were not pubs, just the back room of a shop or a boarding house whose sailors indulged and where others could join them. Mrs Makepeace would walk into the worst places of the slums in the name of her Jesus. The Mission had leaflets about God and more practical stuff in strange, beautiful Chinese writing, and Hindi for the Lascars too; the doctor Makepeace helped the poor for free. Preaching temperance, and against war and music halls and all sorts.

Dongmei's uncle was a big fish. He landed in London not some poor sailor but a merchant, with letters of introduction from a bishop, a rajah, and a dozen princes of trade across the Empire. How had Mrs Ashton so aggrieved him?

Thugs looking for her and looking for Forty. She'd need all her book cunning and her docks cunning too.

Chapter 35
The Next Week

...

An advertisement appeared in various periodicals that week, including three eminent Scottish dailies.

All creditors of Mrs Honoria Ashton née Leveret are invited to attend the address below or write as soon as possible to resolve financial concerns with her advisers. They will be seen individually between 10 and 4 this week or otherwise as mutually agreed. The intention is to meet all sums due in full, according to an agreed schedule.

Sir Charles hovered, like the smell of kippers, clearly waiting for her to be alone. So, she left Braddie in the kitchens, chatting to the theatrical lady of the house and that lady's own sweetheart. In her room, she sat on the bed, noting the ewer on the table, a vaguely Moorish design.

She called out to the spirit plane. *'Now would be convenient.'*

Charles came, guarded in his manner.

'May I be of service?'

'I will not help you unless you answer my questions.'

'I have no option but to do so. I still cannot find Violet or her companions. I need you for information, to be my eyes and ears and hands among the living. We suffer for our crimes after death. Undoing the wrong is harder. We should have been warned. There are friends of mine... I need to warn them.'

She would be the firm tutor. *'What do you think the prophets and saints taught?'*

'I see that now. I thought religion useful to manage the lower orders, not true.'

'The truth about the murders, Sir Charles, or leave me in peace.'

She glimpsed his face, no bluster.

'I killed Henry in a moment of greed and envy; I still barely believe it. The girl was different. It was arrogance and pride and fury. An act of monumental stupidity.'

'You confess to killing Grace Overmorrow?'

'What a petty thing to have done. She opened her legs to every ploughboy, yet she refused me – just because she could. Well, I could not take that, me heir to great estates and likely my father's seat in Parliament and her some straw-chewing nobody. I killed her in a red fury, and I gloried in the pleasure of it. More than I got from hunting or the shoot.'

Self-disgust certainly, some sort of remorse. She must guard against him reading her.

'I deserved the terror that followed. I thought every bush watched me and every man would see my guilt written on

my face. But with my father I had long learned how to lie, and to please my mother I could do the same. I got away with killing my brother and I got away with this.'

'They arrested an innocent lad. Stammering Will.'

'Well, I did not believe in God, but I knew I would never sleep again if that half-wit died. So, I cajoled my mother, and she got my father to pay for the lawyer. Willoughby took me, though I used the name of a friend. I watched the lawyer save that boy from the gallows – a great man now, and when they try to hang you, Mrs Ashton, I recommend him. He is worth the money. I hope that burst of conscience about the lad will count a little in my favour.'

'You destroyed her father. You brought the family poverty and suffering.'

'I see why the Church of Rome promotes confession. Yes, one murder had many victims. From kindness my mother helped the family leave the country, never to be heard of again.'

'Nowhere near payment for your crime.'

A ghostly shrug. *'I agree. I knew I was reckless. Every minim of intelligence said not to do it again. Yet I craved the sensation, the danger. Hunting, boxing, wrestling, and shooting. Even culling a horse or a dog. But I was the wolf who had tasted human flesh. I designed plans to kill those who would not be missed.'*

He paused. *'It's a very modest claim to virtue, but I did not kill for pleasure again. I fought the hunger, Mrs Ashton, the endless craving. Even now I linger on those fantasies. But I swear, I never took a woman against her will, I laughed off whores who declined me, I campaigned with vigour to protect girls and women from brutes...'*

He went on, as if half to himself. *'I know weakness. My father drowned in alcohol... and my foolish brother in whores and liquor and gambling... Perhaps the craving to kill is most like gambling or opium. With gaming, a roll of the dice, you are gripped by two great gods – Fear and Glee – each as intoxicating and ruinous as the other. I will not weary you with the struggle against that dark joy... How easy to stab some drunkard in a London alley. But I beat it, Mrs Ashton. I spared you. I intended you to live.'*

This might be important. *'Why did you smoke opium?'*

'How swift and strong the smoke can be... Flying with dragons, they call it. Fine champagne, not the beer of laudanum. The smoke brings a surge of pleasure, dreams tinged with all the power and poetry you can imagine. The Poppy Goddess is a subtle mistress, but she would rule me if I let her. And to see drugged men enslaved in apathy and squalor.'

'You smoked it with Forty Wilkins?'

A guess, but he said nothing, several seconds of it. Yes.

'Did you take it the night you died?'

'I do not remember. It is unlikely. Violet disapproved so, and I wanted to please her. And... I had a warning of its power.'

'You still remember nothing.'

'Nothing will clear my mind. Why your obsession with the Overmorrows? That old crime cannot be connected to my murder, surely. And the family went abroad.'

At once, he pushed to open her mind, threw great force against her. She gasped, concentrated, strengthening her power. He might become ungovernable.

'Surely, they did not return to England? Mrs Ashton, I have answered your curiosity. I have tried to help you. I can pay... in information if nothing else.'

She must divert his attention. She might have to dismiss him.

Never forget what this man could do. He resumed his push into her mind, as if prying her skull open. The first stab of a migraine. Colder and more clinical than his raging attacks, a specific attempt to pull something from her head.

'Why can I not see Violet? Surely, if my wife knows who did it... We reconciled. Why are you so concerned about that peasant family? I did what I could for them. Tell me!'

The words of the prayer would not come right in her head, let alone speaking. She squawked what should have been a scream for help... her hands up in futile defence. The china ewer of water. She kicked at the little table. Once, twice, the third time turned it over, and the pretty thing broke, a gush onto the carpet. It sounded loud, but would it be heard downstairs in the kitchen?

She tried to rise, to scream with full breath, to kick the door. But her mind held firm. If he got into her head, he might never leave.

Half standing, she managed the Prayer of Deliverance aloud. Sir Charles was gone, leaving only his anger on the air.

Braddie burst in – dear heart, her sweetness – and took her into her strong arms.

'That radgie de'il,' Braddie said.

'I beat him, dearest, I beat him.' She quivered and her head throbbed. But she had won, and she would be better prepared if he did that again.

A few of her middling meeting came at this short notice. They met in another house, the banker forbidden to associate publicly with her, yet he was here with his wife. Their faces fearful, the conversation stilted, as tea was served.

She heard spirits scurrying like mice. Would they swamp her? Would she be able to open her supporters to give good readings? Perhaps she should just preach, with more certainty, and address their needs without fraud... Would that be enough?

'Mrs Ashton... help me...'

'...the will... It was in the teapot...'

'My papist sister...'

'I did not do it...'

'What king...? What king?'

'My aunt...'

This spirit came with purpose. A solemn young man, resolute, his face familiar from her banker friend's mind. His lost son, who she had often counterfeited through fraud.

She staggered, with relief, then took in the vast sorrow at his disdain for her, this lying mortal. He wanted to have it out with her.

She closed her eyes, and called to her congregation – without preparation, without prayer, without the ritual and order they so wanted. Their cups undrained, and the servants hovering to clear.

'My friends, a spirit is near and will be heard. Please be still.'

'Mrs Ashton, you are a fraud and a deceiver. You took advantage of my parents in their despair.'

She shook at his displeasure. How just his anger.

'I confess it. I will seek to do better.'

'You lied to my mother and father, for your own profit. Your hats from the finest shops and your good wines. You put ridiculous words in my mouth.'

'I will atone. I will repay. Some of it I used to feed and clothe the poor, as Our Lord commanded. But yes, I am a liar, a thief, and a hypocrite. I confess and I seek to do better...'

In her mind's eye, he glared at her. Then his face relaxed a little.

'You steal and lie. Yet, you walked with my father in his grief. You took time with him, more than you need for your schemes. Where you gave honest counsel, it was well considered, and it proved healthy. You worked hard for your money – you turned his mind to life and simple pleasures, you urged him to serve others. His despair could have dragged my mother to perdition, but you gave her hope. And it was noticed – you did this for others, poor and broken, who could offer you no gold but their gratitude. Whose coins you returned.'

Weakly she responded, *'It pleases me when I can help.'*

'My parents believe in you. Do not take advantage of them again, for I am watching.'

She opened her eyes, the banker and his wife staring.

The wife spoke. 'Our dear John. As in life, there beside you. He smiled at us.'

Mrs Ashton's mouth dropped. She swallowed. But her wits did not fail her.

'Praise God,' she said. 'Let us gather our thoughts. Perhaps the servants could tidy the room, and we could begin with prayer.'

What did Sir Charles's title mean now?

'Today let us remember, Our Lord trusted fishermen and shepherds as His disciples before He preached to kings and the wealthy.'

The fire of inspiration descended. Mrs Ashton preached like a prophet of old. She spoke of her follies and those appetites she indulged, a rich apology for her weakness. She preached of life and its purpose, often told, and the mysteries of the thereafter. What a rich sermon she wove from the son's message. The ghost himself waited somewhere near the ceiling, listening and watching. A dozen unrelated voices clamoured for attention, but she needed to focus. Among her words, she sowed seeds, an apology that sometimes she went beyond the exact words of the spirits, that she covered for when they did not come. Pride, laxity in paying creditors, vanity.

A tremendous success. These few disciples were with her again, more fervent than ever. The plant had been strongly pruned, but the roots were healthy. Their purses gaped open, but she would not betray them. From today, every penny would be accounted for. Not because she was watched, but because they deserved it.

And soon, she would insist that servants could stay, or she would not preach.

Chapter 36
Astonishing and Astonished

Wednesday

Barrington-Stewart Inquest – Astonishing Testimony

Lady Barrington-Stewart's testimony was taken at the latter part of Tuesday. What a figure the young widow made in her mourning clothes, so shy and vulnerable, yet of striking nobility and beauty. Her faithful servant held her arm to assist her. The jury foreman rose when she entered the room, as did his fellows, out of respect. An expectant silence fell, almost reverent in its totality.

...

On her husband's use of opium, the extraordinary issue of the forged letters, on the presence of the asylum nurses, and her complicity in the plot to free Mrs Ashton, Lady Barrington-Stewart proved a reluctant witness who needed to be pressed by the coroner to answer. She asserted that she could not be forced to testify against her husband, but the coroner mildly corrected that error. 'Sir Charles is not on trial.'

And thus, some of Mrs Ashton's most curious testimony was echoed – such as Sir Charles being accused of using forged letters against the medium.

The coroner said, 'Do you believe that your husband forged those letters, or knew them to be forged?'

'I have no knowledge of where they came from.'

'Do you believe that your husband, a Justice of the Peace, knowingly proceeded with an imprisonment on a fraudulent basis?'

'I told him I did not recollect the letters and he should not rely on them. As I told the police, they must have been written later than the dates they bore. They made no sense. If Mrs Ashton needed money, why this ruse? She could have merely asked me for money, which she never did.'

Uproar in the court.

...

The Times

Every paper gave Violet's testimony extraordinary space. Three papers of Liberal sympathy ran commentary expressing their grief that poor, barren, bereaved Lady Barrington-Stewart, who they praised to the skies, had been ill for so long. Melancholia and now the most appalling grief. None openly said Violet was deranged or hysterical, but Mrs Ashton suspected that there would be many who whispered it, in men's clubs and wherever women of society gathered for tea.

The swift appearance of these articles suggested that powerful men – and a certain political wife – had moved to limit the damage.

After the success of her meeting, Mrs Ashton stood ready to face Sir Charles. Sometimes at the edge of her perception, he would only speak if she was alone. In her new lodgings, she called him for a scolding. Charles so subdued and sorrowful, she had no other word but defeated. You can be too angry to enjoy victory.

'I will not tolerate being attacked. My thoughts are private, and any further intrusion will end all cooperation.'

Some dread filled him. *'No apology is big enough. I can only say being murdered does put one out of sorts. My temper was unforgivable. You are, at present, my only chance to affect the earthly world, and I have been abominable to you. I cannot bring anything but an apology, and willingness to answer your questions. And I will aid you as I can – I cannot write letters or hand you gold. But I will share what I know.*

I know secrets you may use to raise money or perhaps deflect the authorities.'

'I will not be bullied,' Mrs Ashton said. *'What is on your mind?'*

'I am so plagued by a damnable fear, I cannot rest. Might my wife be complicit? Please be honest.'

Mrs Ashton had thought endlessly what she knew and what to say. Why not try the truth. *'I must confess I am unclear. Help me, Forty Wilkins is still missing. With his habit... where might he have gone? He might be in danger.'*

'London is a city of holes to hide in. We did visit the renowned den named by Dickens. But surely the police will have looked there? And you said Trephine is fronting a reward. Easy money to hand over a drugged man.'

'Where else might Forty have gone?'

'Forty and his sister were orphans, a good deed of my mother, without other relations. I think he had a girl outside Bellingley. Be assured, if I have an idea, I will tell you.'

'They came from Stanning St Jude.' Saying it, she thought how calm and thorough the county detective was. He would have chased this up.

'If you say so. We owned the living there, so my mother felt obliged to take a token interest in the place. I didn't.'

'I know how you poisoned Lady Herncastle.'

A colder note. *'Oh, do go on.'*

'The digestive tablets. I think they would not be difficult to counterfeit, adding more opium. The more the dear lady took, the more likely she would overdose. The laudanum might have been stronger than stated.'

Charles adopted an indifferent tone. *'The doctor had the medicines tested.'*

'Doctor Culpe assured me in precise terms, that he did not "tamper" with her medication. Such precision reveals a truth. You did or got someone else to. I guess that at your orders he swapped them at the deathbed for authentic products, so the authorities would find nothing. And I suspect his evidence that he had seen Lady Herncastle take double doses in the past was a lie.'

Charles stayed silent for a long while, not responding to her pressure to answer.

'You are a remarkable woman, Mrs Ashton. Let us talk of how I can assist you.'

'You killed your wife's mother. I know it.'

'Mrs Ashton, let us not quarrel. I can help you now or in three weeks – closer to your bankruptcy hearing. So much less time to be ready for the Procurator Fiscal. I truly want you free, even with your scolding. I need your company. And poor Mrs Bradshaw. Which do you prefer?'

With great distaste – the man had killed three times but at least regretted two – she settled to the task. Her deductions must approach the truth.

Sir Charles recommended a respected journalist on *The Magister*, that respectable Conservative journal. *'Privately he is convinced of the afterlife.'*

He shared several disreputable facts about figures in business, the church, and politics. Some were common gossip but not proven, the proof of others was in his private papers, which of course meant they were in Lady Violet's hands. Some of the targets could probably bluff it out. And a couple were guilty of crimes society abhorred but which she thought hurt no one. She had once blackmailed two men for their forbidden love in Edinburgh, after which her conscience gave her no peace.

The most useful treasure was a story that could hang that grinning rascal Trephine.

'He brought me to my senses, against harming you physically. I am glad he did.'

Mrs Ashton felt the pieces combine. Charles's mother sent the Overmorrows abroad. Charles's mother brought Forty and Prudie from the north of the county, orphans with no family. Fortitude and Prudence, what fine chapel names! Chapel, like the Overmorrows. Their ages were right for Isaac and Rebecca, the two youngest Overmorrow children mentioned in the papers. Yet, their minister in Stanning St Jude had vouched for their birth.

Imagine, Grace's brother and sister working at Corwood Manor. Prudie the diligent staff officer to Lady Violet and Forty a trusted groom. But this was pure supposition.

Mrs Ashton had a keen eye for family resemblance. Prudie and Forty looked alike. Nothing in their face shouted that they were related to Grace but nothing asserted they could not be. In her youth, Mrs Ashton had more closely resembled her aunt's children than her own sister.

Mrs Ashton took paper and, with some distaste, wrote a rather fawning letter to the old newspaper editor in Grennard.

Mrs Ashton had so many messages. The man's card said he was a lawyer, at a firm of ancient address and great repute. His note said only, *To resolve your difficulties, may we meet without your advisers present?* She met him at her lawyer's offices, keen to keep her current address secret. Braddie stood ferocious to one side, and Mr Oliphant was entertaining the clerks downstairs with tales of the ring.

This silvery man was too smooth, too considered. To dress that plainly and still suggest wealth took skill.

'Mrs Ashton, a pleasure.'

He refused tea and Braddie served Mrs Ashton a cup, with ginger and honey for her throat. Mrs Ashton loved talking but how she much she had used her voice, her weapon, these last days.

'I will come to the point and be brief. My client is willing to settle your creditors and the associated costs. Upon your agreement, I will review the papers and you will have a cheque within twenty-four hours.'

'Well, that would be enormously welcome. Who is your client, and on what conditions?'

'My client wishes to remain confidential. You are looking for a lost person of modest rank. Have you found them?'

'What is your client's motivation?' By normal means, this man was impossible to read. At least three spirits hovered, clattering like crows.

'A humanitarian – he wishes to secure the man's welfare.'

'And keep him from the police?'

'Well, Mrs Ashton, maybe you do too. My client's first concern is the man's welfare.'

He? She rather thought a young and beautiful woman lay behind this. The woman she had taken for a doe-eyed innocent. Braddie had been right.

She decided to give him a smooth, marble-hard silence. After at least fifteen seconds, she gestured, inviting him to speak.

'The man will be well looked after. We will pay twice the sum you owe.'

'Alas, I do not have the man.'

'Then help find him, but for my client.'

'Your client may wish him harm. I cannot honourably assist you.'

'Three times what you owe.'

A promise of gold to enter an unknown room, perhaps a trap. Mrs Ashton decided to try to read him. 'Surely I need to know his name, to judge his motives.' She touched his knee, as for emphasis. Blessed relief, she opened him, to some ghostly chatter. With caution, she could still use her old power.

By thunder, this is a queer case. This strange spirit woman. Who got old Sanderson involved?

Dimly, an older lawyer – bald, distinguished, a scar on the cheek – but reading from a written brief. Oh, ingenious to use a go-between.

Her visitor no more knew his true client than Mrs Ashton did. Only his admiration for the other lawyer's spotless reputation had swayed him to take the case.

Her headache announced its arrival, lights before the eyes. She sat back. How high would the man go? And how high would she value the price of a man? Perhaps a murderer, perhaps a sick man to be pitied. Perhaps both.

The lawyer regarded her with studied neutrality.

'My client is absolutely committed to this man's safety.'

'I believe your client could pay ten times what I owe, which I shall share with the needy. I will need to meet them first.'

The lawyer gave a studied look of shock. 'I thought three times generous for a woman one step off Carey Street. Your terms are absurd, Mrs Ashton, but of course, I will put that to my client, at once.'

'Thank you. I have truly promising lines of enquiry.'

'Good afternoon, Mrs Ashton. A pleasure.' He rose, tipped his hat, and Braddie showed him out.

'Another cup of that tea, my dearest.' She briskly explained what she had read. 'The client is keen not to be known.'

Braddie poured tea for two, added a thimble of brandy to hers, and sat in the visitor's chair.

'That wily miss, Violet,' she said.

'I assume so, until proven otherwise. Maybe I should meet this Sanderson. My gift is so erratic now. From Corwood Manor, does Violet seek Forty for his safety, or for his silence, ensuring no one else can find him? My gut says both, but my gut is a tiresome beast, given to fancies.'

Forty was the key, perhaps brother to the murdered girl. Yet the three groups of searchers tripped over each other. Either the police or Trephine were far ahead of them in questioning pubs and eating places Forty used; they had started earlier and were far better resourced. Mrs Ashton reached the minister of the chapel Forty sometimes visited, only to hear Trephine and a police officer arguing as they entered. The minister seemed worried but hadn't seen the groom for months. She slipped away through a side entrance.

She worried that Maisie would fall into the hands of dockland ruffians. Without a good lead, they could spend weeks more achieving nothing.

The note came by messenger: *My client sends his sincere apologies, but through pressure of business he cannot see Mrs Ashton until the end of next month. However, ten times the cost can be paid today if you wish.*

'Violet is too smart, she won't be exposed,' Braddie snarled. 'We'll just find him ourselves.'

In this dangerous maze, she needed to be firm. Who lay behind this and what were the consequences? She could not send the groom to his death.

Mrs Ashton sought Sir Charles, who had been elusive. He came in a wretched mood.

'I have spoken to three gloomy spirits who dispute my future – a Christian who lost his faith on death and now believes all is without purpose, a Hindu who says I will be born again, as some peasant or animal, without any choice where I go, and a Jew who says that the judgement passed on me at death must stand. Which is right?'

'I will talk this evening, if you wish.' The energy required to counsel a penitent murderer. She explained about the lawyer behind her visitor.

Sir Charles seemed thoughtful. *'There is more than one highly regarded Sanderson in London law. Half a dozen if you count the pups.'*

'An elderly gentleman, with a curious scar high on his cheek – rather as one sees sometimes on Prussian nobles.'

'Aha! Sir Danvers Sanderson, a German affair of honour in his wild youth. A man of great probity. Not a man we ever used but certainly acceptable to Violet's cautious advisers.'

He paused, judging something. *'I am fascinated you described him thus. Surely the first lawyer did not describe his client's face. Mrs Ashton, I do believe that you read mortal minds. Impossible, but so much would be explained.'*

Oh, by heaven! She had slipped up. He was an intelligent man.

She summoned a laugh. *'Certainly not.'*

He laughed too, almost boyish. *'My theory was right. Oh, my dear, dear Mrs Ashton. Suppose you had simply told me that. You could have named your salary. You and Mrs Bradshaw would have worn silk and eaten from silver the rest of your life.'*

Again, she thought how dangerous her power would be in mighty hands. She parried. *'And you might guess I would see Grace's death in your mind... or some other crime. I would now be buried in the woods.'*

The villain was shocked, and then she felt his remorse. *'Indeed. Dear Lord, I was a terrible man.'*

Charles turned his efforts to helping resolve her financial and legal problems. He had an unscrupulous idea how she could obtain a painting of his being cleaned in London, before the executors realised where it was. She enjoyed working with his sharp, ruthless energy. Yet, as to finding Forty, he produced only the most banal of suggestions.

The murderer felt lonely. He needed someone to talk to, and Mrs Ashton felt the full strength of his charm, now he chose to use it. At least this would not cause Braddie to be jealous. Mrs Ashton couldn't forget the depths of his crimes.

Chapter 37
Finding the Lost Sheep

Some days later

Maisie and the two old birds met over hot chocolate, to which Mrs Ashton and Braddie added a generous slug of spirits and Maisie a stingy one. She drank alcohol, of course, but she didn't trust the stuff an inch. Being drunk was dangerous and stupid.

'Weeks now, and no word of the man. My contact in Grennard informs me that Ma Overmorrow was a Wilkins on her grandmother's side. But he also took pains to point out it is a common name in the county. His butcher, his sub-editor, and an alderman share the same. Dear girl, have you anything at all?'

Maisie got the bad news over with. 'Can't find nothing, not even a rumour. Biggest city in the world. You could lose a dozen grooms and not notice. A couple of times, Hanging Jacob's men approached Pa, caps off and very civil. He told 'em nothing because he's worried sick what I am up to – half the docks know I'm not telling my folks where I am. The only good news is Trephine and the coppers surely haven't found Forty because they're everywhere looking. Posters and advertisements.'

'Forty could be anywhere.' Braddie brooded. 'All he needs is one or two people to feed him and keep their mouths shut.' Bless her, like the parrots, Braddie circled back to the same points.

Mrs Ashton sighed. 'We cannot search every dosshouse, every hospital, or question every dispensary and druggist...'

'Trephine must know something.'

Mrs Ashton drank her hot chocolate.

Maisie knew this would be unpopular. 'I'll kip here tonight. Maybe I'll go talk to Dongmei again. Perhaps her uncle can help.'

Braddie put down her cup.

Mrs Ashton looked vexed. 'Dongmei is a lovely girl. I was foolish and I offended her uncle. His overseas connections open many doors.'

Maisie knew that. Mr Li had a posh house on the river, and a white wife. 'Dongmei says Uncle never forgets a slight. But word is Hanging Jacob is ever so careful around him. I will talk to Dongmei, we'll look round the smokeries and maybe get her uncle to help.'

'At least a new route to pursue. Be careful, dear girl. I could not live with myself if you came to harm.'

Maisie dug up the newspaper which had so annoyed her.

> *The East End of London, in the shadow of great commerce and lapped by the timeless river, has become a sore on the city: a swamp of vice and degradation. In dark streets and hidden corners, each of the Commandments is broken. At worst, in our new East, the heathen Lascar, the Chinaman, the dregs of Ireland and the Caribbean form a degenerate stew. While mere English debauchery abounds, the Oriental vice of opium smoking is encouraged, doubtless to entrap and ruin English women. To enter such a devil's den seeking an exotic heaven is to find a smoky hell, in which fools succumb to entrancing demons of smoke. In California, vigorous laws have been passed for the suppression of the habit in public, for our clear-eyed cousins see the danger. Parliament sleeps, breathing fumes of indolence and cowardice.*
>
> *The Orb*

Paper for the jakes! Lying nonsense! Among London's tribes, the Chinese were tiny. She'd walked those streets, the same middle-to-wide streets, crosscut with a hundred little alleys and backways. The difference showed as a scattering of Chinese names on shops and the elegant Chinese language, the Chinese Freemason Society, and the dress of some of the people.

Most Chinese were sailors – and yes, a few Chinese men married local wives. Sal said briskly, 'Better a sober

Chinaman who works than a drunk Cockney.' The papers hated the Muslim Lascars too – poorly dressed for winter and paid less than the white sailors - and the papers always snarled about the Irish.

Maisie was no fan of opium. To lie stupid drunk among strangers was dangerous, and the poppy was the same. Places where it was used were hot, smoky, and smelled. Easy to be clean and lecture others when you have plenty of clothes, and someone else washes your stuff and dries it. The high-ups were such hypocrites. The Empire had fought two wars with the Chinese to sell them more opium and give them all the habit. Now they complained when a few Chinese used it on their doorstep.

Mrs Colquhoun had come from Ireland as a babe in arms, and her children said London was their home. Why shouldn't Dongmei say the same?

In boy clothes, Maisie headed to the Thameswake Mission. Its presiding spirits were the Makepeaces, a couple of posh do-gooders. Mrs M wore no jewellery, not even a wedding ring. Their servants called them by their first names, and sometimes Mrs M cooked like a poor person, and everyone ate at their table. The man Makepeace was a doctor and ran free clinics, and the lady bossed other posh people into providing clothes and food and firewood, and helping people get jobs. Mrs Makepeace thought that Spiritualists were fools or crooks, and suspected Mrs A as the latter. Maisie, however, was a prime candidate to be Helped and then Saved.

She walked there, resigning herself to at least one lecture. It was in the neighbourhood, a few streets from the first Chinese shops.

Light rain, and she huddled in her thick man's coat. The Mission was a new brick church, and two houses knocked into one. Signs offered welcome in Hindi, Chinese, and Church English.

Rain didn't mean an absence of watchers. Several poor souls huddled under rags. Get inside and be out of it.

Boots splashing, she got across the road and through the door.

Dongmei was in some complicated discussion with two elderly coves in Chinese. It got quite animated.

Maisie waited; you had to be good at that as a detective. Mrs Ashton said that Mrs Makepeace's odd little church let women preach, how wonderful! Hmm. They all sat in silence until someone felt like talking. Maisie wondered about Mrs Makepeace staying quiet for anything – it didn't seem like her.

Dongmei came over. She wore trousers, and Maisie realised she had suddenly got even prettier. Raven-haired and eyes of night, and a sweet mouth, even when she was being rude about people. Boys and girls her age were interested in all that soppy stuff. At least two boys in her gang made cow eyes at her; Maisie found them entirely resistible.

'Boy Maisie. And your golden locks suit you,' Dongmei teased. On the other hand, her puckish humour did not preclude a soppier motive.

Dongmei is a cully, a pal. Keep your mind on the case.

'Protection,' Maisie said. 'So, poor Forty... I wonder if your uncle has heard anything.'

'He won't forget Mrs Ashton. He expects people to try and weasel money from him, but he won't be taken for a fool.'

'Oh, she knows she made a mistake. She's ready to kowtow and apologise. She can grovel mightily when she has to. What has he heard?'

Dongmei frowned. 'Of course, he told the police he will assist them. But here, tell the blue terrors something at breakfast and Jacob will know by lunchtime.'

They sat, heads together for privacy.

Dongmei said, 'What makes you think Forty Wilkins came here craving the smoke?'

'It's a guess. We're told he's been to at least one den. We have to follow up everything.'

Dongmei smiled. 'Why would my uncle know anything?'

'Because he likes to know what goes on.'

'I feel a trip to leaflet the dens and the shops. And I'll get Sirdar to come with us.'

The lad nicknamed Sirdar was tall for a Lascar and had impressive moustaches. He looked fierce but Maisie thought she'd eaten meat pies tougher than he was.

Rain faded to a threat. The first den was only the back room of a humble shop, packed with everything from dry fish to curious red papers. An old woman greeted Dongmei in Chinese, and they spoke to and fro in it.

The back room – too hot, dimly lit, and the air thick with a distinctive smoke both sweet and fetid. Six bunks had been crammed in, where people lay unstirring with long pipes between their lips. Little lamps burned, to heat the bowl of the pipe; opium is not burned but inhaled as vapour. Rags were stuffed around the edges of a boarded-up window to keep the precious smoke in.

The men were all colours, and one woman hid her face when they came in. Sirdar used Hindi when other tongues failed. Again, crazy to dope yourself among strangers in an unknown place. Forty could have been robbed a week ago, weighted down, and thrown in the Thames. She hoped not.

A boarding house run by Lascars, only two smoking. Then another house had four men playing the Chinese game with tiles, while on stacked wooden bunks behind them, people slept with pipes between their lips. One coughed fit to wake the dead.

They were wasting their time. The rain hardened. The three came to where an alley joined the street on either side. Out of the alley came Trephine under a fancy umbrella, and his big sailor punisher, hood up.

Her heart hammered, but she kept her face still. Turn and run back, probably easiest.

She heard hobnails behind her.

'Maisie Kendrick,' Trephine said with that big fake grin.

She looked behind. Two big brutes of sailors, gold glinting at their ears, standing arms to their sides, ready. They growled something, she didn't catch what, and one had a knife out. Sirdar looked terrified. She'd always thought he might be useless in a real fight. Time to give herself a scolding later.

Breathe. Her shiv was at hand and she was ready to run. The wet stones might be slippery.

'These two fellows work for a well-known gentleman of the docks,' Trephine gloated.

'My uncle is the honourable merchant Mr Li,' Dongmei said, 'and he will be angry if his favourite niece is accosted. And the well-known gentleman knows that.'

'Miss Li, no accosting necessary. I wouldn't dream of stopping his niece and do please give your uncle my warm and most respectful regards. We're only looking for a poor lost soul, and Maisie can help us.'

'She is under his protection.'

'And I'm the Kaiser,' Trephine said. 'He's no friend of her boss.'

Outnumbered and surrounded. Running might work.

'Come with me, Maisie,' Trephine said. 'You're an admirable girl, and you'll be perfectly safe. I think I'll take you to Mrs Trephine for a feed, perhaps some respectable clothes, where we can talk about working for me. Sadly, Mrs Ashton will be in jug before long.'

She wouldn't trust him as far as she could spit.

Dongmei flourished a police whistle.

Trephine said, 'Don't bother those fine fellows. I drank with them last night, and they can be obligingly tardy. Miss Li, please be on your way, and take the Shaking Jimmy with you.'

Sirdar was as useless as a ham trombone. Maisie hoped what Mrs Ashton had told her would work. 'Shame about old Gunderson,' she said. 'Fell in the river but took his boots off first.'

Trephine, so cool and collected, twitched a few hairs of his eyebrow. A small hand gesture to the men behind her. She couldn't look round: she needed to lock her gaze on his.

'Very sad,' Trephine said. 'The sawbones said he had a weak heart.'

Maisie wriggled the hook. 'Mrs Ashton gets to speak to Sir Charles now. He says he asked you to scare Gunderson, for treachery in business, but very particular not to kill someone so useful. He got so furious you botched it, he threw a decanter of port at you' – oh, Trephine twitched at that – 'and threatened to flog you with his stick. If I disappear, Mrs Ashton will tell the blue terrors.'

Trephine gave a great impression of his patronising smile. 'You've been listening to too much drunken gossip in the Burning Bird.'

Maisie locked her gaze on his, tried to still her thundering heart. One last card to play. 'The Greek is ever so worried, said he told you not to. Back in London for business, it's on his conscience, and he's keen to turn Queen's evidence. Funny chap, more rings than the king of the travelling folk.'

Again, that twitch. 'I enjoy a good bluff. If Mrs Ashton talks to my late lamented employer, then I am Father Christmas.'

Time to improvise and hope. 'You know Bullfinch, and how he hates you. Him and Mrs Ashton had tea yesterday, with cake baked by Mrs Bullfinch, ever so pleasant. He doesn't know about the Greek.' A pause. 'Yet. If I disappear, who will Mrs Ashton suspect? Ever so fond of me, she is.'

'She's watched.'

'You lost her leaving London, didn't you?' Go big or go home. 'You didn't know she was at Scotland Yard. If Bullfinch can't have my employer in pokey, he'll settle for hanging you. The Greek will talk.'

Lying was a survival skill, and Maisie intended to survive.

Trephine swallowed. Dongmei took Maisie's hand, turned, and walked through the two sailors. Her friend raised her hand and said with force, 'My uncle will not forget an insult!' and they stepped out of her way. Sirdar suddenly found his courage and followed them.

Dongmei held Maisie's hand all the way back to the Mission. Maisie liked it, they must make a touching couple, although it confused her that she liked it so much.

'My pulse is wild,' Dongmei said, guiding Maisie's fingers to feel it. 'People will gossip, me out with a handsome boy.' Lummy!

Maisie knew at once two things.

First, that if she took Dongmei somewhere private and kissed her, like in a swoony book, Dongmei wouldn't make any sort of fuss – though Maisie didn't feel a need right now. Dongmei was a good cully and sometime in the last few months, something had happened. To Dongmei, or to Maisie herself? Something had been added between them. Suppose Dongmei asked, or kissed her first? You were supposed to know, weren't you? This smoochy stuff. And, Maisie didn't want to upset her.

Finding Forty was urgent. Figuring swoony stuff would have to wait.

Second, what Dongmei could do is warm up her uncle to give Mrs A her hearing.

Chapter 38

A Summons to the East

A day or two later

Summoned by a note of stern formality, Mrs Ashton and Braddie took a hansom to Mr Li's place of business in the docks. A fine old house turned into an office, on a street humming with industry. Inside, it combined modern efficiency – gas lights – and fashionable touches, with silk hangings, various idols, and a painting of Jesus walking on the water drawn in the elegant Chinese style.

Mrs Ashton quivered with nerves. Braddie looked the place over with a sceptical eye. Mrs Ashton sent in her card. 'With an abject apology and a plea for help.' A pleasant young man with good English offered them a comfortable chair and tea. Mr Li's son was handsome. Mrs Ashton thought, as a lover of all beauty, how every race and mix could stir her admiration. She felt nerves in her stomach, and the longer they sat, the worse it got. The sense of disquiet, of being watched, grew.

'Dear heart, do try to bow, or at least look penitent. I misplayed my hand very badly a few years ago.' She sipped the scented green Chinese tea and thought it rather refreshing. On the spirit plane, things scuttled just out of her sight, and growls and mutterings nagged her.

Sir Charles urgent at her ear. *'There are some very odd things here. Hard to even see what they are or were, and they're not very friendly. I find myself hungry, an appetite I cannot serve here. A roasted ham sandwich with mustard and a pint of porter. Mrs O'Grady's steak-and-kidney pie. A duck shot on the estate...'*

'Kindly keep those thoughts to yourself. Years ago, I tried to reach Mr Li's dead business partner, and he swiftly saw through me.'

'You mean, your fraud was inadequate.' But Sir Charles was more distracted than being unpleasant.

The pleasant man returned and said if Mrs Ashton could wait an hour; she would be seen today.

'That would be wonderful, thank you.'

Mrs Ashton felt a growing spirit crowd staring at her, a strong feeling that people were discussing her behind her back. Were these the simple dead or something stranger? The air tightened with uncertainty and danger. She set her jaw and resolved to be strong.

Seventy minutes later, they were shown into Mr Li's office, and the sense of foreboding increased. He did not rise or move his head a hair's breadth. She gave a bow, in the eastern style, and made it as humble as she could. A single chair sat before the desk, and another some way back. Braddie dipped her head briefly.

Li wore elegant English dress. He was small, white-haired, in his sixties, and he had a poker face. The women sat.

His English was exact. 'Mrs Ashton contrite? An eighth wonder of the modern world, to rank with electricity.'

'I owe you a great apology, sir. When my spiritual power failed, I resorted to subterfuge, and you rightfully exposed it. Everything you said was fair – I accept that I was disrespectful to you and to the dead.'

'The true disrespect was to lecture me on something I knew. My people have our own tradition of ghosts, good and bad, and our own mediums who speak with them.'

'I feel a great presence here, and I still have much to learn.'

'Tell me what you desire so much that you would apologise.'

Mrs Ashton briskly set out the importance of Forty, and what she knew of his London movements. 'I believe the groom may be in danger and he holds the key to the case. Unknown people offered me a substantial sum to stop looking.'

'To what end do you, a private citizen, seek this man?'

'To see that he is safe. To see what he knows. When I know the truth, I will know what conscience calls me to do.'

'The Chinese in London are few. But I accept that the docks are not a bad place to hide. A conundrum faces anyone who, by chance, knows where the man is.' Li took a pencil and a delicate knife to sharpen it. 'One searcher comes smiling, but he is allied to a gentleman of the docks, a leader of violent and despicable persons with too much interest in these streets. He can speak quietly but the cosh, chloroform, and the river lie behind him.'

'A thuggish gang led by a murderer.'

'Yet one must do business. The gentleman of the docks is a fact of life and things could be worse. A wise man avoids conflict. Which is more dangerous for the intelligent man, Mrs Ashton? The crafty lion who fears and respects him, or a dozen jackals too stupid to be cautious?'

Mr Li was a deeper mystery than she knew. She tried to make sense of this strange spiritual presence. Mr Li's rise among London merchants, despite his colour, might have some hidden dimension.

He tested the pencil point. 'The constabulary. How we admire the fine servants of order, and who would set out to vex them? But they might not treat the man well. And there is idle talk that some of the police in these districts are bought – surely not many - so he might still fall into disreputable hands. Perhaps this poor man is sick and needs to recover. Decisions could then be made. A murderer, or a frightened witness? Two very different things.'

Li knew where Forty was. What game was he playing?

'His wellbeing is important to me and my friends,' she said.

'Words, Mrs Ashton.'

Powers swirled around her, ominous and menacing. Ravenous creatures out of sight but utterly there, so hungry that so her own stomach complained. Bold, vigorous Sir Charles dissolved into nerves.

'Mrs Ashton, I feel outnumbered. I don't know that I can help you.'

'Why would a hypothetical gentleman, known to be a humane and honest businessman, tell a discredited medium anything at all?' Li asked.

'I am poor, I cannot offer you wealth, you have no regard for my powers...'

'You do me an injustice. I have watched your career with interest. You have some skill, beyond the tricks of the music hall.'

He placed his hand on a stack of newspapers. 'Macao, Hong Kong, Shanghai, Bombay, Aden. Ports from which I gather news. A rise in superstitious events, curious sightings as we have seen in England. I am a good Christian, and I welcome the advances of science, but I also know that my ancestors were not wholly deluded. Difficult powers are moving, and our traditional practices to avert them remain wise precautions.'

Should she tell him what she knew? Every nerve jangled at the thought. Try to read him with sinister forces around her which might be goaded by her power? Or place her life in his hands?

'I do speak to the spirits, but I also exaggerate and guess,' she said. 'As I did with you – a terrible, shameful error.'

'I accept your honest apology. One day – it might be tomorrow, or five years hence – I will ask you to repay the debt that involves. Promise that and promise that you will not betray the man's location without my agreement. Do this, and you can see the man today, before he leaves these crowded streets. Tonight is too late.'

He had an honest reputation, for all the slurs she had heard about him. His philanthropy was quiet and generous. And with these forces around him... There was far more to Li than she had ever guessed.

'Come, Mrs Ashton, it should not need saying that I am a loyal and law-abiding subject of Her Majesty. And like you, I have a particular dislike of murder.'

He rose and offered his hand. Braddie gave a minute shrug, so Mrs Ashton shook it. Then Li raised a hand, as if in command. Around her on the spirit plane, the sinister figures retreated, but did not go. The docklands attracted scavengers – birds, and animals, humans, and, it seemed, other things too.

'An ally found him two days ago, trying to buy a proper pipe. The poor man needs country air. There he can be nursed to health.'

He rang a bell, and his son appeared. The son, Mrs Ashton and Braddie, and Mr Li left in that order.

It turned out there was a door into the adjacent house. Up steep servant stairs, to a servant bedroom big enough for two. It smelt of sweat and disinfectant. On the bed was Forty Wilkins, unshaven, eyes shut, moaning a little, his hands rubbing. 'More pipe, more pipe.'

'We are friends. Your host will take you somewhere safe, somewhere quiet,' Mrs Ashton said.

'More soap... the blood.'

His hands were bleeding, bandaged from being rubbed raw.

'You need to leave off rubbing this.'

'Got to get it off.'

Mr Li spoke from behind her. 'The drug demands its victim resume the habit, like it were a living thing, like a spirit possessing him and attacking him with physical and mental distress. The doctor in Hampstead is willing to try traditional medicines from my homeland, which can ease the inevitable struggle.'

'Blood... The master's after me... Second cousin to the devil. I see my place in the lake of fire...'

'Wilkins, help is coming,' Mrs Ashton said.

He gripped her arm with a wretched hand, too tight. 'I see the master all blood.'

'You killed him.'

He struggled a little. 'Prudie said I was too weak. He comes in the night, all broken.'

Mrs Ashton dared not open him – the unknown spirits around her, and to open a disturbed mind shook her own sanity. She had tried to read a fever patient once and hallucinated for days.

'I know you are Isaac Overmorrow,' she said. Pure bluff, she had no proof.

His fear poured off him. 'No, not that name, never that name, never Isaac. Fortitude.'

So, there it was, and Prudence was once Rebecca Overmorrow.

Something had protected Violet, Esme, and Prudie from Mrs Ashton's power to read minds. Something consciously hindered her. No, *someone* on the spirit plane.

Pieces fell into place. Violet knew who had killed Charles, and she had sought to protect the Overmorrows from the beginning. She would pay any price to keep this poor man hidden from the police. Violet can lie.

She may have been on the roof. Could she have struck the blow?

The only certainty was that Mrs Ashton had underestimated her client, time after time.

Chapter 39
A Scotsman Seeks Judgement

A week or more later

> *Sir Rupert Barrington-Stewart has been interviewed in Cloisterham. It is clear the renegade brother of Sir Charles has a credible alibi, staying with his godfather at the time of the murder. Far from being disinherited, we understand that he receives a modest income under Sir Charles's will, conditional on him sticking to some honest trade. As much leave a leopard your estate, on condition that it change its spots.*
>
> *The Orb*

Mrs Ashton found using her powers in London attracted spirits – with meandering tales of woe, heart-rending pleas to right early wrongs, or merely wanting an update on the state of the nation. Those weeks were a series of exhausting meetings, with her advisers, with creditors, with the Scottish investigation, then back to her advisers. She blustered, she wheedled, she promised, and where she could, she paid. While she did obtain Sir Charles's picture from the cleaners, the sharp dealer queried the provenance, and she had to settle for a wickedly low price.

Forty suffered torments, and she could not make any decisions until he could be involved. Raving, Mrs Ashton would be taking advantage; Lucid, he was terrified and said nothing. Something, someone, protected him from Mrs Ashton's power to open – his dead sister Grace, or Violet's murdered mother? – and Mr Li had a smiling and determined assistant guarding him.

Mrs Ashton soon realised the Procurator Fiscal's man in London, his second in command, took the stage as her greatest danger. He sat incorruptible, diligent, intelligent, and beyond any English influence, every pronouncement like a hanging judge. His senior in rank would accept his recommendation.

By tremendous efforts, testing every friendship to its limit, and thanks to Sir Charles, she had the money. She could cover her creditors' bills and costs, settle the ludicrous lawsuits, and begin to assuage her guilt where she had caused hardship. Every loan she took now would have to be paid within months. Was it enough?

In their lawyer's office, Braddie was silenced, although she was also under threat. Mrs Ashton's heart pounded so hard she might be sick. The Procurator Fiscal's man had a face like a righteous axe. He could have preached from a Calvinist pulpit – dour, determined, and hostile. As well expect mercy from Arthur's Seat.

His correspondence had threatened charging her under the Witchcraft Act as a fraud. She had been one. The awful truth, she suspected, was that if ruin came, it was what she deserved. *Kismet.*

The man preached like the dominie who has the errant sinner in his rooms... *Get on with it.*

Finally, despite all reasoning, her lawyer's assistance, her careful diversions, he reached his point, which she had guessed from his first words.

'Which is why I will recommend to the Procurator Fiscal that we charge you.'

She opened him, the third time now, and what a self-righteous scourge he was. A man who tore claims of spirits from the newspapers so the aunt he lived with would not read them.

'I regret that. I intend to make full restitution where I have been at fault, and given time, no one need be out of pocket. I think the Procurator Fiscal should consider my offer sufficient.'

'Your client does not appear to have heard me,' the man said to her lawyer.

'Well, if you charge me, I will come to court. But you might not like what I do.'

'Why?' he snapped.

'If I prove I truly raised the spirits, I must be acquitted. So, I will demonstrate my powers in court. I will be acquitted, and then I can use that finding of truth elsewhere.'

He ground his teeth. 'We'll have no fools' circus in the court. Not that any Scottish jury could be fooled.'

If only she could manifest Sir Charles as visible. She knew no rhyme or reason as to when spirits were seen, nor could she make it happen.

'I will show my powers and any jury on earth will be convinced. May we speak alone?'

'We may not.'

Her senior lawyer coughed. 'Mrs Ashton, perhaps we might confer on our next steps?' They had a plan to defend her by conventional means.

She had seen the Procurator's weakness in his heart, but to use it was risky.

She could not get him alone: she must risk a note. She kept talking, scribbling a note as she spoke. 'To speak to the dead is to learn shocking truths, many *secrets*, many *scandals*. I believe my business and credibility will be greatly increased by a trial which ends in an acquittal, with great revelations to the press. Shameful things men of rank need to hide.' Take the hint, man. 'Please do charge me if you want days of ridicule in the papers.'

His gaze grew even more hostile, his mouth even more clenched. She passed the man her note – he unfolded it in fury, glanced at it, and twitched.

It read, *If Miss Annabelle does not learn her lesson, she must stand in the corner. I have spoken to her governess, and I know where the wardrobe is. I have both photographs and sworn witnesses.*

He went so pale that she worried for his health. A few breaths, and he recovered. 'A minor point.' He put the letter in his pocket and added, 'We do need to consider the dignity of the court. Shall we perhaps meet again towards the end of the day?'

'Yes, dignity is so important,' Mrs Ashton said. He would be cabling Edinburgh, but at great expense, she had sent Scottish friends to collect the evidence of his pastime. The beautifully made outsized dresses and shoes, the dolls, the schoolbooks, and the careful embroidery sampler.

She thought it was a rather sweet failing, not really anyone's business. In his cold, grim world of duty, lacking children, pets, or any other excuse to play, only as Miss Annabelle could he find gentleness and contentment. And the 'governess' doubtless found it excellent employment, well paid, without needing to sleep with him or to use the tawse on him.

He looked at her, and she read a curious admiration.

Chapter 40
Bullfinch's Report

Some days later

To the Commissioner, the Metropolitan Police

Dear Lt-Colonel Henderson,

Further to the enquiries surrounding FORTITUDE WILKINS, I am pleased to confirm that I apprehended him this morning in Hampstead. Here is my report.

You will recall Lady Barrington-Stewart's urgent concerns about his welfare and that Jabez Trephine had been hunting him, allied to criminal elements.

Bullfinch thought, *It all stinks like last week's fish, to be honest. Nothing with Trephine involved ever comes to any good.* Dare he write his suspicions that the young widow wanted the servant safe, but not in the hands of the police? Anyway, Trephine had gone fishing in Scotland, a likely tale.

> *Information received took us to the Hampstead Sanatorium, whose superintendent was treating Wilkins for an opium habit – a professional interest of his – and dipsomania. He claimed that he did not know his patient was the man wanted for questioning, which I don't believe. He stressed that the man's recovery is fragile – as is common in severe cases, the man suffers from poor sleep, bizarre hallucinations, digestive disorders, and periods of confusion. His hands were bleeding from neurotic, excessive use of strong soaps and cleansers, and they were dressed with emollients. I was told he was deluded and sees his hands stained with blood.*

'He does a Lady Macbeth,' the sawbones had said. 'Neurotic behaviour, washing off the blood. Did you see Ellen Terry in the role? Extraordinary.'

Bullfinch understood the allusion, even if he had no time for high falutin' theatricals. He preferred to let off steam at the music hall... He returned to the report.

> *Wilkins was clearly alarmed – a highly nervous young man, with rapid eye movements and much shifting on his bed.*

> *His hands were wrapped in bandages and Wilkins confirmed the origins of his wounded skin.*
>
> *I conducted a brief interview, which only heightened my suspicions. Wilkins often resorted to claims that his memory was failing. He quivered in fear of sinister enemies, but he gave no indication who they were.*
>
> *I insisted that Wilkins be examined by a police surgeon and questioned further. I expect the Superintendent to file a complaint.*

He reflected, jaw rigid with feeling, on his entrance to the sanatorium. The well-to-do lady escorted a girl out of the door as they entered. The girl was dressed as a nursing assistant. Only later he had realised, like lightning from a clear sky, that he had been fooled. The Kendrick girl had eluded him.

Bullfinch double-checked his notes. His copper's nose led him to follow Mrs Ashton's preposterous claim.

> *Under sustained questioning, Wilkins stayed silent as to any previous name. It is now unclear who the Wilkins siblings truly are, the new minister at their old chapel wholly relying on his predecessor's letter and the local register being notoriously poorly kept.*

He must write up the county detective for a commendation, a stout persistent fellow.

> *As you know, the idea is afoot that Sir Charles killed Grace Overmorrow. I have no evidence to prove that, but Wilkins needs only believe it to be true and we have a possible motive for murder. Wilkins has not the will to manage his opium use, which has led, in other cases, to extreme actions. I will report further as information becomes available. Lady Barrington-Stewart's maid, Prudence, is likewise now a suspect.*
>
> *His alibi is his roommate Perks, who we will arrest.*
>
> *I have the honour to remain, Sir...*

He signed it, blotted it, and sealed it in an envelope. An officer would run it over. How odd that Mrs Ashton appeared to have unpicked a lot of the mystery.

What an intricate web had been woven, so many years ago. The old minister writing that he had seen original birth certificates for the Wilkins siblings which now seemed unlikely.

It was time for one of his favourite manoeuvres. Let Perks think Wilkins had implicated him, in return for lighter treatment. Tell Wilkins that he would have neither opium nor alcohol until he talked, and that Perks had sold him out. One or other would crack soon enough.

Then he would know the truth about Lady Violet Barrington-Stewart and her cousin.

Chapter 41

The Commissioner's Office, Scotland Yard

Three days later, evening

Gaslight made the commissioner's office glow. Henderson looked tired – they all did – and sat in the leather armchair. He waved Bullfinch to a wooden chair, but Bullfinch preferred to stand for any confrontation. The detective tried not to show that he was a prize-fighter, raring for a title match. It might be the last fight of his career.

Bullfinch handed his guvnor the report.

Henderson read it, muttering, at one point gasping, and a couple of times looking up at Bullfinch as if to say, 'Really?'

Forty Wilkins's confession, signed two hours ago, fell like a thunderstroke.

> *My sister Prudence and I were christened Overmorrow. Before we were old enough to know, our sister Grace was murdered by a beast in human form, the innocent lamb taken by a monstrous wolf. The kindness of the*

old mistress had allowed us to come back to England under a new name. Our mother had spoken sometimes of Grace, but we learned not to talk about it. Prudence grew up wanting her murder solved and the man brought to earthly justice. A couple of times Prudence told me Grace might still receive her due. That surprised me but she would not say more, even when old Lady Herncastle died so sudden. Around three months before the new master was murdered, Prudence brought it up again. When at our dead sister's grave, she made me swear an oath to keep it secret. Things were terrible between the master and the mistress, and she hoped at some point to get the mistress's assistance.

I was hurt after a fall and using laudanum. I was encouraged to smoke opium by Sir Charles, who supplied it from time to time, saying I might find it more pleasant. He was an occasional user, saying he found it delightful, but he intended to remain its master. How well I rue not following his example. A few times I took it with him when he was in a mood to indulge in male company. We mostly talked horses and dogs. I had found him a fair and generous employer, although he had a fearsome temper with slackers.

To my astonishment, ten days before the murder my sister reminded me of my oath and said that the master had murdered our sister and that hard vengeance was coming. 'You are too soft,' she said. 'The women will be as Yael and Judith, hands of the Lord doing justice to wicked men. All we need you to do is help us dispose of some things.'

Usually, me or Perks took the post and messages of a morning unless someone higher needed to go. Since Sir Charles had become so high and mighty in Parliament, we went each day, in any weather the horses could stand.

I found my pulse racing like I was ill. I have never been in trouble before with the law or anything. But she said he had killed Grace and maybe his own brother and Lady Herncastle and maybe other women too, and he might kill again. It was Divine Justice, and if I said a word she would hang, because a Member of Parliament would be protected and ordinary people would stand no chance. I was in such a muddle and gorged on my weaknesses to quiet my mind. The plan would be that the women would drug him – make him take the smoke or leave signs he had – and drop him headfirst from the stable roof. The master sometimes wandered at night when the mood took him. Indeed, we had smoked together up there. It would be impossible to prove that it wasn't an accident.

I dreamed of the noose every night and I could not hear Sir Charles speak without jumping.

The day before the murder my sister was furious that she was not to lay hands on the man. 'My mistress is keen to protect me. Anyway, I have made three sets of dark robes for the Kindly Ones and you will need to hide them if they get blood on them.' I asked why and she said, 'If that brute struggles, we may have to stun him, as you do a pig. If we drop him headfirst, it won't show.'

I did not understand the Kindly Ones. Prudie said they were from the pagan Greek stories before Christ, of fearsome she-devils who did justice to any man who killed their own kin.

That day of all the fuss with the spirit lady, they killed him. I spread grease on the trap cushion and hid the spare so I had an excuse to bring another. That evening, I made sure Perks was asleep and at the appointed time I went to the linen closet nearest the door to the stable roof with a shuttered light. Prudence never told me they were going to free Mrs Ashton and the girl. I felt that I waited there a year listening to my heart. Then a rap at the door. Our family uses four taps for OVERMORROW.

Prudence held a bundle and stepped in. Her

eyes were so bright and her breathing fast. 'It did not go smooth as we hoped, but it was a righteous deed. He fought the drug, the beast, but they stunned the pig and threw him off the roof.' I took it and the bundle unwrapped. I had blood on my hands, his blood. I wiped them on the clean parts of the robes and Prudie had left a damp towel there for she thinks of everything. We folded everything damp inward to get them into the long cushion cover. I was so anxious to be back to my room nearby, and she to her own bed. We looked to see if there was any blood on us or the floor, while she said, 'I hope they are stoking the fires of down below hot enough.'

Prudie took some things of the mistress's things to explain being in the closet and checked the way was clear. I went and was barely in bed when the bell began. I shake to think of how risky that night was. People were roused quicker than we thought, and my heart stutters every time I think how we might have been seen.

I hear the master's voice when I see the blood. Abel's blood cried out for justice against Cain. Sir Charles comes to me broken, as the corpse was, and said I did it and I must hang.

I could not stop my heart pounding, I nearly fainted when the bell went. If anyone had challenged me, I would never have kept my nerve. I let Perks spend ages rousing me and then I dressed. When everyone knew about the murder, and we all realised most of us could have done it, I made out we could be each other's alibis and he fell for it.

I got to the stables early to replace the cushion and asked Willoughby if I should take the post, knowing he would say yes.

I did not see what happened on the roof, but if my sister had struck the blow, she would have been righteous and proud of the crime and she would have said so.

We agreed to throw the cushion weighted with bricks into Gray's Quarry. Today I drew a map as best I could that shows where it went under, the deepest place I could throw it.

Now I have betrayed my oath to my sister, and I know in my dreams my dead master will still come after me. He is damned but our vengeance has damned me.

Signed, Fortitude Wilkins

The confession was witnessed by the police surgeon and Forty's doctor, both stating that in their opinion Wilkins understood what he signed.

Henderson stared at Bullfinch, who stared back. The high-ups would not like this Sir Charles a murderer, and his wife implicated in *his* murder! Well, the dice had been thrown. Bullfinch would not back down.

Henderson found something to say. 'The man is ruled by his weakness. He admits to delusions.'

'Yes, but he is precise about detail, for the crimes. There was something about the grease in one of the other groom's evidence. Of course, physical evidence will help. I will get authority tomorrow to use dredgers aided by divers and even pump out the quarry if required. I have found the local force most helpful. My recommendation now is that I interview Lady Barrington-Stewart, Miss Shilling, and the maid as soon as possible under caution. They are in Derbyshire.'

'Wait. We need to think this through.' Henderson checked his fob watch. 'The House is not sitting today. I will send a messenger to the Home Secretary – if not there, his club or his home. Who else has seen this?'

Bullfinch stared at him, hoping the force of his glare would feel like a slap. Bullfinch thought, oddly, of that Egyptian obelisk by the Thames. He must be as solid and immobile before his superior.

'It would be wise to warn the Home Secretary of developments,' he said, as if that was what Henderson meant. 'But not until we have ensured the three women... Well, we don't want them deciding to take a holiday abroad, for their health.'

'We can't put this to a jury. The man is seeing things.'

'I had two doctors, one with a particular interest in opium, talk to him. It is clear what is fact and what is nonsense. We need not believe that Sir Charles is rattling his chains at the man. Wilkins says his wife wore her mourning gloves, with her monogram. Her gloves stained with blood! The dullest jury will understand that.'

'I mean, sterling work. This might be invaluable,' Henderson said. 'But let's not tell the press right now.'

Bullfinch had thought better of his superior.

'Sir, there are four detectives breaking rocks on Dartmoor. The good name of Scotland Yard is dragged in the dirt by their corruption. We must pursue the case wherever it takes us. If we stand for anything, it is that we do impartial justice to all. Be you ever so high, the law is above you.'

The English cut a king's head off and sent another into exile for that principle.

'Bullfinch, I commend you. But I ask again, who has seen it?'

'Well, sir, I thought it my duty to inform the coroner, by sending my most trusted officer. That ancient office of the Crown orders the investigation, not us mere police. I am sure he will wait a few days before reconvening the jury if we give him cause – he is not an unreasonable man.'

As well ask the sun not to rise, as stop the coroner for Belldownshire from his duty. At least, he hoped so. You never knew who was bought or weak.

Henderson's face fell. 'But no one else knows...'

'Well, several doctors know – strong opinions they have on right and wrong. And Mrs Ashton – she had one of her people with Wilkins at the sanatorium. She always said that the Overmorrow murder lay behind it. Who knows what she might say? And I am due a pint with a few of the more reasonable pressmen at the Beggar's Pulpit about now... I can send word it will not be today.'

To call that awful woman in aid, but she might be useful.

'Mrs Ashton? Aren't the Scots going to prosecute her?'

Bullfinch felt something rather odd, something he would deny for years to come. Mrs Ashton's bloody-mindedness mirrored his own. For cynical reasons, she had still strived to see justice done.

'I think they might have bitten off more than they can chew. Short of a troop of Marines, I don't think anyone can stop that woman.'

Steady man, no need to praise her.

You could not predict juries, or judges for that matter. But Bullfinch intended to push this case to its conclusion.

His superior put a hand to Bullfinch's shoulder. 'Don't meet the press. Let me show this to the Home Secretary. Give us time.'

'To do what, sir?'

'Let our political masters be ready. I will say a storm is coming, and like the wrath of God, it cannot be stopped. But we will be praised for the warning. Yes, the coroner should see the confession at once but be asked to wait a little. We must act.'

His boss wanted to protect Scotland Yard but not shield the guilty. Bullfinch could accept that with a clear conscience.

'I need to question Lady Barrington-Stewart and the others and we should drain the quarry.' Bullfinch said, refusing to seek permission.

The Commissioner had made his mind up. 'Proceed, discreetly. Be ready to warn the ports. By heaven, it would help if she fled, it looks so guilty.'

Chapter 42
From the Scrapbook

Various

Our Pictorial Correspondent has sent these extraordinary sketches of the operation in Gray's Quarry, under the watchful eye of Chief Inspector Bullfinch. These behemoths of the current age, the steam pumps used to speed the drainage of this artificial pool, steam and clank like dragons. The divers, we fancy, resemble the knights of old armoured for their task.

BULLFINCH TO DERBYSHIRE: ARRESTS EXPECTED

The inquest into the death of Sir Charles Barrington-Stewart reconvenes today to hear a confession, and our sources are confident it will produce an astounding verdict. Chief Inspector Bullfinch left for Derbyshire last night on official business relating to the murder. That fair county includes a house owned by the deceased, now a quiet retreat for his wife. Evidence was found yesterday in Gray's Quarry, a flooded pit outside Bellingley, and we can assure our readers they must stand by for astonishing developments, revealing a murderous conspiracy.

The Times

LADY BARRINGTON-STEWART SURRENDERS FOR ARREST

Lady Barrington-Stewart, Miss Esme Shilling, and their maid Prudence Wilkins offered themselves for arrest in Liverpool yesterday. The women were believed to have left for the Continent a week before.

Lady Barrington-Stewart is understood to have said, 'I urged my companions to flee, but they refused. All three of us have confidence in British justice. We are innocent of any crime.'

Local police sources said an escape plan had a very high chance of success. A private steamer owned by the lady but under a foreign flag had departed some days before, headed for South America via the Azores. It is hard to avoid the conclusion that Lady Barrington-Stewart, having evaded the police, could have safely fled to a foreign land, from which extradition would be impossible. For whatever reason, she chose not to do so.

Has the committee to erect a statue to the late Sir Charles met recently? The word is revelations to come make the proposed appeal far from appealing.

The London Panjandrum

CHAPTER 43
A Trial and a Verdict

London, several weeks later

Summer bloomed hot, and the smell in the poorer districts ripened to a ferocious presence. Another Fenian dynamite outrage, and a diplomatic row between France and Russia, and Dervishes did terrible things in sandy deserts.

But nothing would drive the trial from the papers. Violet, Esme, and Prudence were charged with murder, and Forty would be a witness for the prosecution. The story grew endless. It was sensational. Lady Violet had hired the defender of Stammering Will, now one of the greatest lawyers of the age. That fearsome prosecutor, the Attorney General, acted for the Crown, flanked by two other great names. The press covered it like some prize fight between the two great lawyers.

The trial plied novelty upon scandal. At their arraignment, the three women pleaded not guilty, and withheld their defence as entitled to do. Their lawyer argued for their right to bail. 'Lady Barrington-Stewart could have fled the country but as a woman of moral character, she chose not to do so.' In effect the judge ordered house arrest in London, and the extraordinary bail was the deed to the Corwood Estate. London society was scandalised and speculated wildly as to what more was to come.

Most assumed self-defence would be their shield, whether it was true or not. Or would they blame another? Forty's confession, read to the inquest jury, was damning, and secured the verdict of unlawful killing.

Lady Violet knew exactly what she was doing, and sparing the government's blushes would not bc high on her agenda. Sensational, almost salacious articles about Sir Charles appeared – *The Pall Mall Gazette* seemed especially fertile ground – and their accusations were spread by those who approved or denounced them alike.

From pulpits to a meeting of international anarchists, Sir Charles's temper, his other women, and his crimes were discussed, condemned, or argued away.

There could be no better show in London, or the world. The three women wore mourning, and Lady Violet stumbled as she entered the dock, more pale and more beautiful than ever. Her lawyer asked if the women might be seated after entering their pleas. 'Miss Shilling's condition is known to the court, but I must report that Lady Barrington-Stewart is also pregnant. She too carries Sir Charles's child.'

A great gasp from the court. The judge looked about to explode but nodded. The women answered the charges. Lady Violet's voice rang out clear, 'Not guilty'; Esme was as firm, and Prudie was every inch the faithful servant. She stood until directed to sit.

The prosecutor set out the case and damning it sounded. Had not Forty Wilkins confessed?

The defence rose and stated, in tones no less dramatic than the end of the world, 'Sir Charles was held in high regard in the land and we will show beyond any doubt that his reputation was undeserved. We will show that he was a murderer, a killer of women, a violator of women, a Cain to his Godly brother's Abel, and a debauched rake dedicated to the most abhorrent and unnatural vice. My clients plead not guilty, on the ancient, righteous, and lawful grounds of self-defence. For on that roof, that night, only Lady Barrington-Stewart stood between her husband and the violation of her maid Prudence Wilkins, a virtuous woman as untouched then and now as God made her. Sir Charles wanted to despoil that maiden, and he left his poor suffering wife no choice. This frail woman versus a vigorous brute, a man who had killed and killed and killed, and escaped justice through cunning, corruption, and rank. She seized a clumsy weapon somehow to hand and she alone struck the fatal blow. My client does not admit this as shameful – she proclaims it to the world. A weak and feeble woman, she showed the "heart and stomach of a king, and a king of England too". She acted at the risk of her own life to prevent a hideous and degrading crime and, doubtless to follow, the death of both the victim and the witness.'

Many times in the days ahead, the phrase would be used, 'Sir Charles is not on trial.' In vain, because the defence made it so, as much as if his corpse had been dragged from its coffin and hung in chains like days of old. Mrs Ashton wondered at the absurdity of British law, that every witness was sworn on the Bible, but the defendant's address remained unsworn. A lot was true. Charles had been a forger, a perjurer, an arsonist, a perverter of British justice...

The judge fought to keep the case on track. The defence wanted to introduce the contents of Sir Charles's library in evidence. 'The jury must see and hear his personal choice of reading.'

The prosecution protested relevance. The defence argued that the jury must be allowed to judge for themselves. 'Why is the prosecution so worried by the jury hearing the mere titles of these volumes – words and pictures of such depravity they cry out to heaven – held in a store to which only Charles held the keys?'

Every day brought new revelations, new drama.

Doctor Culpe, wiping his brow, testified about Lady Herncastle.

'Did you, at Sir Charles's express order, tamper with evidence after the death?'

'I did, to my shame and disgust. I broke my oath. I replaced the medicines Lady Herncastle had been using with fresh supplies.'

'To what end?'

'He did not tell me.'

'As an intelligent man, what purpose do you think he had?'

He swallowed. 'Only one possible purpose. He had tampered with the medicines and needed me to remove the evidence. To mislead the inquest and have the death ruled an accident.'

Uproar in court.

'And did he tell you to commit perjury?'

'He did. I lied on oath that Lady Herncastle was prone to error in her medication.'

But the greatest drama of all was Charles's wife. The moment Lady Violet said, without fear, words which led the news the next day: 'I struck the blow, I alone, in fear of my life. I knew he would force himself on Prudence, and if she fought, I feared that he would kill her. What else was I to do? I had hoped to stun him but he fell.'

Sir Charles needed Mrs Ashton's patient ear and moral support, as his earthly reputation was shredded.

'I like my women happy. The pleasure is greater and the risks far less. I swear, Mrs Ashton, killing that poor girl taught me not to trust my darker side. I should have burned my father's books.'

Mrs Ashton would read the accounts to him, and as time passed, he ran out of rage and grew more hurt, and more thoughtful.

'She is fighting for her life, like a tiger. What a woman. How I misjudged her. I hope the jury buy this ridiculous story.'

'Sir Charles!'

'Esme's child is mine. Violet's is probably mine – and anyway the law will say it is mine. Those children are doomed to a wretched life if the jury finds against their mothers. Let them all live.'

Mrs Ashton prepared for her testimony as if her own life depended on it. The Old Bailey hummed with disgruntled spirits, including a wicked old judge condemned to stay there for his disregard for natural justice. His fate was endlessly to whisper warnings that were not heard. Her theatrical nature could not be but excited when she entered the witness box. A fear that kept her sharp. She took the oath without hesitation, before the living and the dead.

With a few questions from the prosecution, his aim was clear. He wanted her seen as a reliable witness – or at least one whose testimony chimed with others – and to confirm there were 'at least two people' on the roof. She could not say that for certain.

Likewise, the famous defender handled her gently. 'Mrs Ashton, on one point only I must ask – you seem unsure whether there was one figure or two on the roof. You were under strain, it was nighttime, your imprisonment, and then a bloody death. I put it to you there was one, and one only. The second person cowered out of your sight.'

'I cannot be certain.'

'Yes, you have always said you were not certain, from your first evidence to the police until today. The jury will note well that Mrs Ashton, even under pressure from my learned friend, does not contradict Lady Barrington-Stewart's account.'

Mrs Ashton had ceased to be the story. She avoided the court thereafter.

The Attorney General fought hard against the narrative, deploying facts and common sense. 'Gentleman of the jury, this crime was coolly planned and coolly executed. The weapon on the roof – why? Were those dark clothes for *charades*, truly? The hiding of the evidence and the lying to the police – why?' The judge often stepped in to curb the wilder excesses, such as refusing a string of witnesses to Sir Charles's alleged sexual habits. The three he had to allow were scandalous.

Forty Wilkins's confession should have been damning. The press spoke of him fidgeting with gloved hands. The defence's opening approach destroyed his firmness. 'Do you agree that you have a desperate and uncontrolled craving for opium?'

Forty stammered, and the famous lawyer then said, 'The police give you opium, do they not? I cannot hear you. They do? How much each day?' To a stammered answer, the lawyer pounced. 'Do you suffer from delusions? For example, that everyday items are soaked in blood?'

A confident man could have weathered this. Forty botched his answer, and the defence was ruthless. 'So, you sneaked these dressing-up clothes to the quarry, believing they were soaked in blood? You have other proof, do you? Or deluded, did you bloody them yourself?'

It was painful. Finally, the defence said, 'And did the police offer you treatment, and a much lighter sentence, in return for your dubious testimony?'

Forty muttered, 'Yes.' English jurors never quite trusted such a man.

'Even though your testimony might have been pure delusion – nightmares produced by the drug you crave. Testimony your sister denies on the Gospel. No further questions, m'lud.'

Then came the extraordinary summing up speech for the defence. 'Dressed in darkness, Lady Barrington-Stewart stands before you and before God, in the light of truth – a faithful wife betrayed, a pure woman abused and defiled, a Christian dragged into the sewer of Sir Charles's barbarous depravity. Gentlemen of the jury, what country is this? Not some pagan shore ruled by lawless brutes little better than animals, but England, that most precious jewel in God's crown. This Lady stands in the dock, English Womanhood herself, who in that fleeting moment acted to defend her honour, her betrayed cousin, and above all, to protect the honour of her maiden servant. Gentlemen, has England come to this? Do you say what was done to the women that monster killed and violated is just in God's eyes? What would you demand if it were done to your wives, your daughters? Gentlemen of the jury, any decent man among you will burn in righteous anger, wishing to be on that roof that fateful night, to stand between this lady and a brutal man's uncontrollable passion. If you were truly a man, you would have struck him down yourself. Before God, you must say that a frail and virtuous woman has a right to defend herself. Before God, it is your duty to shout the truth and to find her innocent – likewise, those others Sir Charles abused. If you do not, the laws of God and men mean nothing, and England is lost.'

The Kindly Ones sat in a large room, awaiting the verdict. They looked drawn but composed. Prudie was reading from the Bible. A guard stood in the door, stone-faced, listening.

Mrs Ashton walked in, carrying three posies of flowers. She did not know what else to bring.

Lady Violet, serene, rose and kissed her on the cheek. A pregnant woman was usually spared the rope... but this was an extraordinary crime. 'My dear Mrs Ashton.' Prudie tucked a piece of paper into the Bible and closed it before meeting Mrs Ashton's gaze. Esme looked, to be honest, a little absent. Perhaps she had required some medication for her nerves.

Lady Violet spoke to the guard. 'Dear Cobble, Mrs Ashton is like our confessor. Could you give us a few minutes' privacy?'

The guard flicked on a smile and left them. Oh, that weak milk-and-water creature Mrs Ashton had once seen was gone. How Lady Violet had turned and fought.

'Thank you for seeking justice for my sister,' Prudie said, and it was her normal countrywoman's voice, that rural burr. 'And for dear old Lady Herncastle too. Whatever the men decide, we did God's work and we are headed for glory.'

Mrs Ashton would burst with curiosity. 'Prudence, may I ask? I shall tell no one. How long did you know?'

The maid quoted, '"Though the mills of God grind slowly; Yet they grind exceeding small." I had patience, for the Lord was with me. It was only as an adult I understood some things I learned as a child. Long I laboured, suspecting that devil, as the Lord gave me one by one the signs I needed. I followed His light, as did His people of old, willing to do my duty.'

'Dear Prudie, may I suggest we do not burden Mrs Ashton,' Violet said. Goodness, she saw Prudie as her equal. 'A few threads. Perhaps. That dear woman, Charles's mother, found his vile scrapbook of murders and ordered the head gardener to burn it in front of him. Willoughby once let slip he had taken Charles to the trial. Then, after her stroke, she hinted to Prudie it was Charles who had persuaded her to hire Stammering Will a lawyer.'

The maid had not finished. 'Even if we hang, God's work has been done. Sir Charles is even now waiting in the lake of brimstone, and if unjust men murder us, it is three further charges against him. I hope the devils have iron prongs three yards long and they spit-roast him like a piglet, mouth to tail.'

'Dearest girl,' said Violet. 'Prudie is rather Old Testament in her desire for justice. But she has borne his crimes the longest and bless her.'

In the Bible, Judith cut a man's head off with his own sword. Yael hammered a tent peg into a man's skull. Violet had been Delilah, sleeping with her enemy to betray him.

Mrs Ashton could never resist a bit of drama. 'Oh, Sir Charles is following the trial with interest. I have the doubtful pleasure of managing his rage and hearing his confessions. I happen to believe that his rocky path may be towards redemption. He has certainly said often he wishes you acquitted, so his children may live.'

Lady Violet blinked, then smiled. 'Mrs Ashton, you are remarkable. It is when you are most unbelievable that it is wisest to believe you. Charles was a fool to believe that Esme would choose him, or any man, over me. Dear heart.' She touched Esme's shoulder. 'She told me of his offer, as soon as she could.'

Esme blushed, and at once Mrs Ashton understood how Esme felt about Violet. She had no idea if it was reciprocated. Esme said, 'He said if Violet were to die... a man may marry again. Well, a child could guess his meaning. Then Violet agreed with Charles that we would hide in Derbyshire and pretend my child was Violet's. A legitimate heir. A good plan but, Violet told me, it did not need Charles alive to work.'

Mrs Ashton found a delicate way to assuage her vulgar curiosity. 'And after all this time, Lady Violet, you are blessed...'

Lady Violet looked serene. 'I tried to do my duty as a wife. Sir Charles did his that week, several times, and providence brought new life and hope from it. I am blessed at last. And if they hang me, they will wait until it is born.'

The law would rule such a child legitimate, and it would inherit.

'Doctor Culpe colluded in the murder of your mother.'

'He confessed it to me,' Violet said. 'He was willing to pay the price. He showed me a bottle of laudanum and said at my pleasure, he would drink it in front of me – or jump from the highest roof. I had prayed long on this, and I spared him, for Charles coerced him, and what good would his death do? His confession ended his medical career overnight and the poor woman he shares his bed with needs him. And if I am acquitted, I suppose it might be convenient to have a trustee so deeply in my debt.'

The tipstaff came back with the guard. 'Jury coming back, my lady.'

Lady Violet touched Mrs Ashton on the arm. 'Guilty, they will hang me under his cursed name. Innocent, I will go by my mother's, and *honi soit qui mal y pense*.'

Prudie looked over at the other two. 'Flowers is frivolous, taking the jury for granted,' she said. It wasn't for discussion.

'Our Captain has spoken.' Violet took Esme's bouquet, gave both to Cobble, and said, 'For your wife.'

Prudie gave hers back to Mrs Ashton with a smile. 'Thank my sister.'

Cobble said to Mrs Ashton, 'They're sitting on each other's laps up there. You need to go outside.'

Mrs Ashton found Braddie, and they made their way out. So many questions still unanswered.

The Old Bailey stood stern behind them, a crowd big enough to block the road. The sun beat down on a horse-drawn carriage decked with violet ribbons. A black police wagon would take the three women if condemned. Police stood in ranks ready for trouble.

The announcement of a verdict must be close, very close. Around her the spirits waited too.

Here came Jack Cairngorm, forcing his way through the crowds.

Mrs Ashton gave the posy to Braddie, and Maisie in her Sunday frock looked almost innocent, and behind them, several members of the press wanting Mrs Ashton's comment. Across the way, Trephine tipped his hat, as cocky as ever, as if his last tense confrontation with Maisie had been nothing. What a lithe serpent to escape his doom.

Sir Charles was at her side.

'Not guilty! The foreman smiled at Violet when he stood, and that told everyone. That poor fool Forty will go to jail for telling the truth. That's not justice.'

A muted cry from inside the building, people burst from its doors. 'Not Guilty! Not Guilty!' Cheering began, and booing. Huzzahs and 'Shame!' and worse things. Someone threw a bottle, and a man with a sandwich-board began to bellow about the woman from Revelation, the great whore of Babylon, steeped in every wickedness. A docker pushed towards him, turned him round, and floored him with a punch.

Time to walk away. She knew the signs of a riot.

Charles in her head. *'Violet won because she was titled, rich, beautiful, and a brilliant actress. If Prudie had killed me in my sleep – which I own would have been entirely justified – she would have been hanged. Or thirty years sewing uniforms, at least.'*

Then, shy as a schoolboy offering a little posy... *'I want to write to Violet. To make amends. To talk about my children. Will you do that for me, Mrs Ashton?'*

'Have you forgiven her?'

'It's not absurd... I see that I might. Death gives me a new start. I forgive young Cairngorm for his impertinence. Much of my dislike was envy. She must have good men around the children. They will need godparents.'

'Sir Charles, are you suggesting... him?'

'Maybe. I need to shed the titles of this world. Perhaps return to the pure name my brother gave me in happier times.'

They were unhitching the horses from the cart. Brawny men, some women too... some in fine skirts and some with worker's aprons on... They were going to pull Lady Violet into the history books. Who had organised that show of bravura, of hubris?

Braddie would not embrace her hinny in public, although both wished to. But Mrs Ashton took her arm, feigning a little weakness, and they walked away from the crowd. The rap of Braddie's stick warned men to clear a way. Oh, her faithful Braddie was the earth and she a fickle moon.

'That Violet is a one,' her dear heart growled. 'All that money and notoriety, and innocent under the law.'

'Dearest, rest assured, I will have nothing to do with her in future. We will live humbly, and my living will be entirely honest. London grows wearing, and we will need a break somewhere less... spirit-infested. That little place in Kent, by the river.'

'Ald Nick deserved it. But was true justice done, hinny?'

Mrs Ashton liked the old Irish witticism. 'Like the old man of Tralee, I would not start from here. It is never right to take a life, for the victim may have work still to do in this world. Yet, if they had not killed Charles, how safe were they? Might more innocents have died? I think the papers and the politicians, the priests and the scholars, will debate the rights and wrongs long after we are dead.'

Braddie's scowl would pluck a chicken. 'Men claim women cry violation without cause. What a wicked thing it is to give them an example.'

'I can only agree. Dear heart, let us turn to happier thoughts. And dearest, if ever I seem too sure of myself, taking us into danger... do feel free to whisper the words "Corwood Manor" to me. It will be a warning.'

Chapter 44
Coda

Their theatrical friends' parlour, November

> *Asked about the rise in Spiritualist phenomena and whether the government had a view as to what threat it posed, the Prime Minister replied with his ponderous wit. 'I think of the poor burdened taxpayer. With every clergyman and scientist so keen to offer me their opinion for free, and at generous length, we have no need of a Minister for Phantoms, a Department for Vapour, some Bureau of Absurdity, to leech off the revenue.'*
>
> *The Times*

Mrs Ashton sat, every bone weary, her vigour vanished. Their visit to a dreary, foggy London was supposed to be two weeks but had stretched to four. She had conducted nine séances, and a dozen personal meetings and demonstrations, and two packed public meetings in an elegant West End theatre. This had left the papers near hysterical, and her exhausted, prostrate in bed for two days.

In addition, her spirit companion was being tiresome. *'Dearest Mrs Ashton, if my wife can be acquitted for self-defence, I plead the same right regarding Lady Herncastle.'*

She had an invitation to go to Edinburgh, all expenses paid. An opportunity to turn a bitter enemy with good connections into a devoted admirer should not be turned down. The *little girl* who deserved schooling wrote so nicely about her wishes, and her devastation if Mrs Ashton did not come.

Braddie's temper brewed, like some great Northern storm. She knitted like an act of war.

'I want to be in Kent. I don't trust the workmen,' she growled.

The cottage needed improvements if they were to winter there. Everyone told them the phenomenal cold last year had been very hard, the Kent roads snowed solid for weeks. Elegant company, interesting company, even different company – well, that was a long ride away.

'It will be good to get back,' Mrs Ashton admitted. 'Away from the crowds, of the living and the dead. Even the spirits there are gentle. I feel no need to paint in the city – but the riverbank and the woods beyond are wonderfully pretty.'

One can only sketch a scene so often though. There would be few passing visitors now. Vigorous country air was a tonic – although it also smelled of damp mud and agricultural pursuits.

'A few weeks' rest is what the doctor would order,' she finished, laying a tender hand on Braddie's. Dear heart, faithful, her north star.

'We're not staying in London this winter,' Braddie said. Oh, holed up for months without diversion.

'We could visit our friends, surely. A week here and there. If we stay with them, no expense. And dearest, if we are to live within our means, which I earnestly desire, I must keep up my meetings. A single patron, however generous, has its dangers.'

'You've bought a blasted library,' Braddie said. How like her to return to this morning's dispute. Mrs Ashton frowned at the vulgarity.

'For research, for the book.' For long winter evenings when they had exhausted conversation. The delightful village schoolmistress was a ball of fire – they could talk to her for an afternoon at a time – but the vicar was an utter dullard, and the local squire exuded disapproval.

'I will never go through all that again.'

'Absolutely, dearest, we are as one. Live modestly, save, and strive towards regular income.'

She must prepare. She had let it be known via friends that this afternoon's meeting in the East End would be spectacular. That the audacious Mrs Ashton would perform an impudent miracle. The press had responded like starving wolves shown a steak. Her publisher let it be known that Mrs Ashton's mysterious book was a confessional. They had not revealed whose confession it would be. She would leak it to her enemies, so the publicity would be extraordinary. Hopefully a bishop would preach against it and some MP seek to ban it. There was no better method of promotion.

Meanwhile, in the back room of the Phoenix pub, Maisie helped Tildy into her new frock. They were all dressing in new-to-them Sunday best, for Mrs Ashton was in London, holding a new meeting at the Great Eastern Music Hall. Maisie's family, and the old gang from the poor meeting, were honoured guests.

Sal always fussing over Pa, who wore new Sunday clothes like they were a suit of armour, always tugging here and rubbing there. Sal put a rose in his lapel, and Pa did something quite close to his old smile. Nothing official yet. Maisie and Sal had an understanding; they had shaken hands, and she felt less alone. Sal said, 'If he disgraces himself, if he goes on the drink again, I'll kick his arse from here to the Old Bailey.' Maisie had said, 'And I'll kick it all the way back.'

George sat admiring his new book with his name written in it. Tildy had one too.

She must visit Forty again. He'd confessed and been given a year's hard labour, which all the papers suddenly decided was an affront to British justice. The high-ups only pretended they were tough; Forty went straight to the prison infirmary, and after a week back to Hampstead. He was in the Sanatorium on licence, working in the garden, caring for the horses, and able to walk on the Heath without a murmur from the press. Maisie tried to go every couple of weeks. He was beating his demons one day at a time, and the last couple of times, he'd smiled to see her. His girl had visited.

The Kindly Ones lived in Derbyshire, quietly preparing. A shocker, Violet's magic pregnancy was real. And Willoughby had given his notice – given up his job, his future, and his family home – because he could no longer work for those three schemers. Maisie thought it was gloriously moral, and impressively stupid. Violet had wept, pleaded, and tried to bribe him with the cottage. Her country grandpa had declined. Cairngorm got his rich uncle to give Willoughby a job.

Bullfinch had got a commendation. The Home Secretary found another apprentice, also notably young and handsome. The Irish were demanding their own Parliament, which Braddie said was the least the English should do after pillaging the place for a thousand years. Someone had blown up the Tsar.

It was a great excursion. Such a fine crowd outside the hall, every ticket sold, but not everyone in yet, and people touting them at five times the price. Every sort of beggar and chancer, preachers and the press and people selling pies and a dog doing tricks.

As honoured guests they got to go past the queue, into the swells' dining room where the food was. Posters explained that the hall hire had been given free and the ticket price went to Mrs Ashton's charity committee. A pop-eyed peer obsessed with spirit photos, some money cove from the City, and the Dean of Southwark Cathedral, all to keep Mrs Ashton honest. It was ever so funny, Mrs A said the Dean had mostly agreed to annoy the Bishop of London.

'Oh, if Ma could have seen this!' Maisie whispered to Pa, and he wiped an eye with his spare hand and said,

'Oh, she'd be proud of you, Nubbin. Solving that dreadful murder.'

This was a happy day and detectives didn't cry.

The queer old birds greeted their guests. 'Dearest child,' Mrs Ashton said. She had worked her art on her face, but it was hard to disguise how tired she looked. 'How lovely to see you, and your family.'

She wore a robe of blue scattered with stars, all like a sorceress, and a small, matching hat, star-clad too.

'Been busy, Mrs A?' Maisie said. Sceptics had tried to disrupt her fancy demonstration in the West End, and she had humiliated them with the voices she summoned.

'Private meetings and other things. Good to be with the common folk, those who were with us before we were famous.'

Braddie looked towards the table of food with distaste. 'I think we deserve better at that price.'

'Well, what rabbits from the hat can we expect today?' Sal said.

Mrs Ashton smiled. 'I will offer the Good News. And a warning, easier to right the wrongs we have done whilst alive. Who will join us when the time is right, to testify from beyond the grave? That's in the hands of the spirits. The papers think I will stage an impertinent miracle, more outrageous than anything done before. I have no idea why they think that.'

Some famous scientist called Huxley had written a proper article jointly with the dead Charles Darwin – the fact the live one now believed in ghosts was apparently much more news than what the essay said – and there'd been a giant serpent spotted in Loch Ness.

They all took their seats, every seat full and some of the tables put away as they wouldn't be serving. The warm smell of too many people, in layers like archaeology.

A Spiritualist choir sang, with a Spiritualist orchestra. Maisie liked the rousing songs best, the music that made her think of Ma.

Mrs Ashton made her entrance, followed by Braddie, and the hubbub dropped away into a solemn hush. She raised her hands, and the meeting became hers, expectant, waiting for her to speak. The eerie calm before a storm.

'Dearest friends... for Jesus calls us to be His friends... Hear the Good News. He is the faithful judge, He who keeps his sacred word, and the breaker of all chains. All His promises are true. No one is beyond His message of repentance and new life. Every sheep may be saved.'

And Maisie for one moment saw Sir Charles beside Mrs Ashton on the stage, back as straight as a soldier. He met her gaze with a wry smile – he gestured at Mrs Ashton and rolled his eyes without obvious malice, as you might for an irritating aunt. *What is she like?* Then he was gone. It was a few seconds, but it was almost real.

What was going on?

No! Mrs Ashton wouldn't! She couldn't! Not conjure up the murderer in front of all these people – those seats full of press – to get him to confess his sins. What a brass neck!

It was never boring with the two queer birds.

Acknowledgements

It seems every book I write is a long sea voyage, of storms and being becalmed. I owe many people thanks, for factual aid and for moral support and apologies for those not named through my ineptitude. All misjudgements are mine, totally.

For feedback on full drafts Deborah, Caroline, Lucy, Sarah, Sophie, Fred, Peter, Eris Young, Anne Perry, Alex Cochran.

Dr Helen Rutherford and Barbara Copperthwaite (inquests); Kathryn Wheeler, Sarah Lawton Coombs, and Lisa Shapter (horses).

The Savvy Writers leaped in with comparison titles or helping any other bizarre requests, a healthy functioning community of online goodwill. The Empowered Author ditto. The All Good Bookshop Writers still totally rock. I love everyone in Team Weird and thanks to Eliza Chan for her thoughtful insights and Dan Pinchbeck for cover sense.

Chele Cooke provided self-publication handholding of the highest standard. Matt at Inkspiral Design did the cover; Kate Nascimento the copy-edit; Kerry Barrett kindly proofed it. Chris Brosnahan gave blurb advice and much more. ALLi is a life saver for self-publishing authors.

When I started this book working in the pandemic, my adult children had three lovely grandparents, and now they have none. Everything I wrote stood the test of those deaths and the grieving for three people I loved. Peter, Joyce, and Jenny - may their memory be a blessing.

An author's historical note

This is a work of historical fiction, a work of the imagination. I have been keen to express the flavour and mores of the early 1880s, and where I talk about bustles or two-storey buses or the law on married women's property, I set out to be accurate. Indeed a book set in 1889 would be slightly different from one in 1881. However, Mrs Ashton's world does not unfold exactly like ours, and sometimes I've taken licence.

The UK has seen many waves of people come here with differing stories.

Much old writing about the Chinese in London is distorted by an exaggeration of scale. The 1881 census found less than 250 Chinese people in London, mostly sailors waiting for a new berth. To compare, there were maybe 10,000 Black residents of London and certainly thousands of 'Lascars' – mostly Indians, often Muslims, essential sailors for British ships but treated abominably.

As for Maisie, my own mother's grandfather married an Indian woman when on duty in the Raj. We have a picture but not even her name.

I struggled with forms of address, an alien way of thinking for me. I took some liberties with Lady Catherine Howard's ferocious 1885 *Etiquette*. Lady Violet should be addressed as Lady Barrington-Stewart almost everywhere, but fortunately Mrs Ashton does not think of her as such.

Other books by Stephen Cox

I remember telling myself stories as a kid. I started on novels in 2012, and I'm now a full-time writer in ordinary London. I worked for various organisations you've heard of. Making things up can be a great way to tell the truth.

Our Child of the Stars

This is the year of Woodstock and the moon landings; war is raging in Vietnam and the superpowers are threatening each other with annihilation.

Then the Meteor crashes into Amber Grove, devastating the small New England town – and changing their lives for ever. Molly, a nurse, caught up in the thick of the disaster, is given care of a desperately ill patient rescued from the wreckage: a sick boy with a remarkable appearance, an orphan who needs a mother.

Sympathetic characterisation and fine storytelling - *Guardian*

I dare anyone not to fall in love with the Meyers family... I could gush about this book forever -*Angie (bookseller)*

A powerful combination of warm-hearted hope and steely-eyed realism... heartfelt, richly imaginative and gripping - *SciFiNow*

Part ET, part Wonder, part Snow Child, it has the same combination of science fiction and heart-tugging tenderness that Stephen King does so well - *Grazia*

Our Child of Two Worlds

The Earth faces devastation from space, will Cory's people come in time? And if they do, will the Myers family be separated forever?

Riveting, compelling, and emotionally charged: a page turner I loved – *Annarella, book blogger*

Help me and other authors free

A great many marvellous books are published every year. Few get as much visibility as they deserve. You can help authors of books you love without spending much time or money.

I always like to hear from people who liked my work.

If you like a book, tell your friends, suggest it to your book group, or maybe your local library.

If you use social media, people like personal recommendations.

You can use review sites like Amazon, Goodreads, Storify etc. Reviews help individual buyers and make books more findable online. You don't have to write an English essay. A couple of paragraphs is good.

My books make perfect presents!

You can sign up for my occasional free newsletter with special offers, updates on my work, and bookish talk. www.stephencox.co.uk

Copyright © Stephen Cox 2025

All rights reserved. The moral right of Stephen Cox to be identified as the author of this work has been asserted in accordance with the Copyright, Designs and Patents Act 1988.

No part of this publication may be reproduced, distributed, or transmitted in any form or by any means, including photocopying, recording, or other electronic or mechanical methods, without my prior written permission or a specific non-commercial exception under law.

None of this book was made with generative Artificial Intelligence. Neither the text nor the cover may be used to train a Large Language Model / genAI to generate text or images without the written permission of the author in advance. The author asserts all rights to prevent this under all national and international laws.

The story, all names, characters, and incidents portrayed in this work are fictitious or used fictitiously. No identification with actual persons (living or deceased), places, buildings, and products is intended or should be inferred. It's not the real world, folks.